I0737651

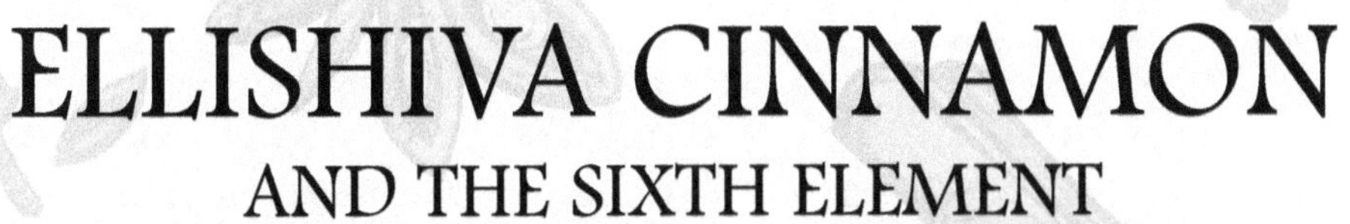

ELLISHIVA CINNAMON

AND THE SIXTH ELEMENT

ELLISHIVA CINNAMON
AND THE SIXTH ELEMENT

BY

NIRMALA NARINE

ILLUSTRATIONS BY SABRINA E. SULLIVAN

VANADALA

Printed in the United States of America

VANADALA

244 Fifth Avenue Suite N266
New York, New York 10001

www.ellishivacinnamon.com

   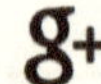

Publisher's Cataloging-in-Publication data

Narine, Nirmala.
    Ellishiva Cinnamon and the Sixth Element / by Nirmala Narine ; illustrations by Sabrina E. Sullivan.
    pages cm
    ISBN: 978-0-9962071-2-6 (Paperback)
    Summary : Ellishiva Cinnamon journeys through prehistoric New York City and learns to use magic to sustain Earth's ecosystem and defeat evil.

[1. Nature -- Fiction. 2. Magic -- Fiction. 3. Animals --Fiction. 4. Manhattan (New York, N.Y.) --Fiction. 5. Ecofiction, American. 6. Fantasy Fiction. 7. Science fiction. 8. Alternative histories (Fiction).] I. Ellishiva Cinnamon and the 6th Element. II. Sullivan, Sabrina E. II. Title.

PZ7.N1621 El 2016
[Fic] --dc23   2015904904

FOR ALL OF EARTH'S CHILDREN AND YOUR CHILDREN'S CHILDREN.
TAKE CARE OF OUR PLANET AND IT WILL TAKE CARE OF YOU.

CONTENTS

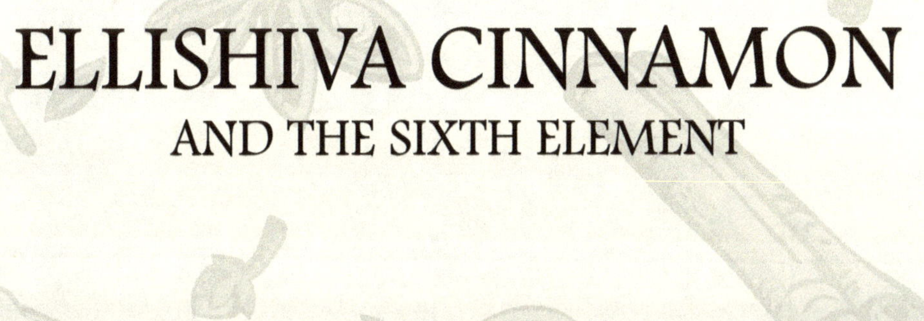

ELLISHIVA CINNAMON
AND THE SIXTH ELEMENT

CHAPTER ONE
THE LOCUST TREE

On a hazy summer afternoon long ago, in a not-so-different world, a girl as tender as a young green fern ran as fast as her legs could carry her through a dense forest. Her bare feet stomped and crumbled the copper leaves scattered below her. On the first joint of her second toe, a golden ring carved in the shape of a lotus flower gleamed in the dappled afternoon light.

Low dogwood branches laden with creamy flowers lashed her cinnabar locks—parted in the middle over her round face and amber eyes—as she sprinted beneath them. A brown sling-bag stuffed with schoolbooks bounced on her back and, attached to it, the J-shaped hook of a Puluma stick bobbed over her head. She wore a maroon singlet, on the back of which, stitched in white letters, were the words:

Ellishiva Cinnamon
01 Mannahatta Maples

Ellishiva's chest fell and rose. In her veins she could feel her blood pumping, rushing away from her heart and gushing into her ears, beating like a war drum.

"We're lost!" she yelled, vaulting over a spice-wood shrub and stumbling through another shaft of afternoon sunlight. She had begun this adventure with a tickle of excitement beneath the soles of her feet. Now, however, her voice trembled, and her insides churned like clouds in a thunderstorm. Even the shadows between the leaves seemed to be peering at her with hidden, beady eyes—like an enemy from one of her human history books.

A tiny shudder trickled down her spine, and Ellishiva ran faster. She nearly fell into a bramble-choked, bubbling stream instead of leaping over it. Her eyes were on the green ceiling of trees.

"Sam—where are you?" she cried, frantically searching the canopy above her. "I—I can't see you . . ."

There was no reply.

A murmur of dread spread through Ellishiva's body.

Then, "Stop worrying, Elli," came the distant, happy voice of a girl. "There's nothing to be afraid of. We're getting so close."

Somewhere high above her, an object flitted swiftly through the branches like a hummingbird.

"Sam, we're in serious trouble," Ellishiva warned the flittering thing gravely. "We've been gone a long time. The forest will be dark soon. Rajah must be looking for me." In her chest, her lungs tightened at the thought of the search her worried guardian must be holding in her honor . . . and of the punishment he would no doubt see fit to reward her with.

She stumbled to a halt.

Above her, however, the hummingbird-like creature showed no sign of slowing down. Ellishiva let out a frustrated huff. It had already been a long day, and there was still no hint of their destination in sight. She reflected, not for the first time, that following Samara into things half-blindly was not always the best idea—especially since it was almost impossible to get her friend to stop and think once she'd started something.

An idea flickered through her mind, and she seized it. Cupping her hands around her mouth, she called breathlessly, "Had . . . had enough running at the . . . Puluma ball court." She braced her hands on her slightly bent knees—only partly for effect—and dropped her voice so that it sounded low and, she hoped, pitiful. "Please fly . . . fly down, Sam. At least help me carry my stick. Too much stuff to . . . run with . . ."

Above her, the flitter in the branches slowed, and came back.

"Elli, is this a real plea or just a trick to get me to lighten your load so you can outrun me?" Samara's suspicious voice floated down to her, trailing in and out of range among the treetops. "Wish I was allowed to play Puluma using my wings. Maybe then I'd be able to beat you just once," she added, grumbling under her breath.

Annoyance prickled under Ellishiva's skin. Only Samara could whine about Puluma matches at a time like this—with the nameless, beady-eyed *something* watching them from the shadows.

Another shiver dripped down Ellishiva's backbone. Even though she had stopped running, her heartbeat picked up its pace. Somewhere above her, Samara was still—*still*—floating around out of sight.

Ellishiva lost her patience.

"Where are you?" she demanded shrilly, standing up straight and planting her palms on her midriff. Her cheeks were still flushed from the sprint, and fine beads of sweat gathered on her nose and over her crimson upper lip. She yanked her hair back, coiling it into a loose bun that exposed the many faint brown circles tattooed around her ears, neck, and shoulders. She glared up into the thick forest canopy. "How can you be so . . . so . . . ," Ellishiva wracked her brain for the right word, but it wouldn't come to her. "We've never been this far away from home!" she shouted instead. Her hand shook slightly as she unfastened her Puluma stick and laid it on the ground. In her stomach, the thunderclouds were still churning, growing larger by the second. "I wish this day had never happened," she snapped at the sky. "I shouldn't have followed you—shouldn't have followed you . . ."

She choked on her tightening throat and stopped, pressing her lips together. Unsteadily, she wiped the sweat from her forehead with the back of her hand.

A moment later, a sudden shaft of sunlight flashed, and a fairy of about her height appeared, floating in the air before her. She was perhaps as pretty as Ellishiva herself, but her face lacked any trace of seriousness. Her iridescent wings whirred like a hummingbird's, shining even brighter than her halter top of scarlet silk and her matching shorts. Even now, she looked ready to flit up and away into the treetops again at any moment.

Ellishiva fixed her with a stony look.

The fair legs and bare feet landed softly, reluctantly, on the ground.

"It's going to be dark soon," scolded Ellishiva, her gaze darting into the shadows around them anxiously. "Don't you have any idea what they'll do to us if we're not home by sunset? I don't want my face on a poster, pinned up on tree trunks."

"Oh, just take one of your yoga breaths, Elli. You worry too much," dismissed Samara. Her lips twitched into an impish smile. "You're just nervous because we've never gone this far before, that's all. Anyway, only dofauns go missing, not Va'nature like you. And besides," she added temptingly, taking in Ellishiva's sweat-drenched form from head to foot, "when we get to the Muheekantuck River, we can have a nice cool swim."

Ellishiva scowled at her, but to no effect. Samara continued to radiate careless optimism. Her blond cornrow braids glistened like corn silk in the sun, as did the black velvet drawstring pouch—her noli— hanging at her hip.

"Sam, this is not funny," Ellishiva snapped. "You don't understand how much trouble we're in. I've changed my mind. Let's go home." She began fiddling with the buckle on her sling-bag, trying to get it loose so that it would stop digging into her shoulder before they set off again. "I've been running all afternoon, following you to *nowhere.*

You said you knew the route," she added accusingly.

A faint rustle stirred among the bushes nearby. In Ellishiva's stomach, the thunderclouds tossed again. She swallowed hard.

"You're so dramatic. Don't you want to help me get a wand?" pouted Samara, reaching over to help Ellishiva with the buckle. "Anyway, you should *want* to get out of here. You're the one being kept in Mannahatta—in this *prison*—while the dofauns get to go wherever they want, planting *your* saplings, doing *your* work." Samara's thin fairy fingers got the buckle loose at last, and she tossed the sling-bag on the ground, triumphant. "Don't tell me you're not a bit curious to see the human world, Elli," she gushed, sweeping her arms out wide above her head as if to catch the sky.

"Right. I'm the dramatic one," muttered Ellishiva under her breath. She rolled her sore shoulder, and her gaze flitted away into the shadows of the trees again. She ran the tip of her tongue over her dry lips. "The human world. Right. Yes, Sam, I can see it now," she snorted, her voice dripping with as much sarcasm as she could muster. "Hello, I'm Ellishiva Cinnamon. I'm a Va'nature. We give life to every sapling in your world to keep you from starving to death, so I *know* you couldn't *possibly* wish me any harm." She crossed her arms over her chest and pinned the fairy in front of her with another withering look. "Is that what we'll say if the humans catch us in their world, Sam? You think they're just going to pat us on the head and send us on our way again? You've seen the headlines of *The Mannahatta Times*."

Samara did not reply. She seemed, Ellishiva realized with surprise, to be giving this some thought.

For a minute they stood at a standstill, a strained silence hanging between them like a thick fog. There was no pushing her friend to make up her mind about something, Ellishiva knew. But the dangerous feeling in the pit of her stomach did not care about Samara's stubborn streak. With every passing second, it grew stronger, and stronger still, until she could almost feel it on her skin—like a monster's wet breath on the back of her neck.

When the goose bumps became too prickly to bear, Ellishiva took a deep breath and cleared her throat. "Sam," she began gently, practically, "we're going around in circles. And there's something else. Something isn't right. I can feel it." She cast another furtive glance at the shadows around them. "Please, let's just . . . let's just go home to Banyan Tree."

It was, unfortunately, the wrong thing to say.

"So *now*," Samara pronounced, glaring at Ellishiva with narrowed eyes, "*now* you don't even want to help me get a wand anymore." She slapped her open palm to her forehead in a show of frustrated disappointment, turning the skin pink.

Ellishiva winced, but didn't take her eyes off the shifting shadows around them when she spoke again. "Listen Sam, whether you believe me or not that something is . . . is wrong about this forest, we still have rules to follow. We're sneaking around behind the elders' backs. I haven't even changed out of my uniform." Ellishiva picked up her Puluma stick and automatically began to nervously rewrap the fine bark strings on its handle, which had come loose. "Besides," she protested, "do you really think I would be here if I didn't want to help you get a wand?"

Samara gave a sullen roll of her eyes, and kicked a pebble. "No," she grumbled finally.

But Ellishiva was on a roll now. "Anyway," she plowed on, "Sam, even if we do gather the *illegal* olivine rocks from the shores of the river and mold them into a wand, what then? How are we supposed to fill it with a fairy's spice dust? The Rojorine, Sam—how are we supposed to get *that*?" She paused and bit off a piece of the bark string, spitting it out on the ground at their feet. "I bet you didn't think about that part, did you? What good is a wand without Rojorine in it? Are you going to *pretend* to use magic?" Ellishiva's eyes drifted back to the shifting shadows around them, and her voice dropped to a mutter. "You just don't think ahead, do you?"

"I do, too," Samara pouted. She knelt by Ellishiva's sling-bag and began rummaging through its contents, a hobby of hers that Ellishiva had long ago given up trying to put a stop to. "At least . . . at least I would *look* like a complete fairy again, carrying a wand. Even if it didn't work. Not *everyone* knows it was taken away from me."

A silence broken only by the muffled sounds of Samara's rummaging billowed up between them. Ellishiva shifted on her feet and clenched her jaw, feeling more like hunted prey every moment. But grabbing Samara and dragging her home against her will was impossible. The hot-headed fairy would escape in no time. And then she'd probably fly backward into the clutches of . . . of whatever it was.

Finally, Ellishiva took a risk. "I have an idea!" she suggested, with forced optimism. "We can ask Jipsin Smilodon—you know, that dofaun that sells strange things—on his next visit to Bear Market. He must have all sorts of rare ingredients and useful information. Maybe he even has some olivine rocks that we can mold into a wand for you. We'll forge a note and you can say they're for a school project. Then we can pour Bluzure spice dust into the wand-core, instead of Rojorine. I'll help you gather enough at the Foxfire Harvest. It's bound to work." She gave what she hoped was a convincing nod.

It didn't work.

"What? My custom-made wand will *not* have Bluzure spice dust in it!" Samara protested, lifting her nose from the sling-bag with an indignant sniff. "It's . . . it's like . . . so domesticated. I am a fairy! And they can keep my old wand for as long as they want," she went on grimly, "because this one is going to be better than all of theirs—even Queen Neive's. *This* wand is going to contain green spice dust." She paused to admire her neatly trimmed nails, and her eyes glinted smugly. "*This* wand is going to contain Khlorus."

There was a beat of silence.

Then, "Are you joking?" Ellishiva blurted. A humorless laugh escaped her throat in spite of herself. She knotted the loose ends of the bark strings tightly near the hook of the Puluma handle—no easy task, with her eyes still fixed nervously on the shadows. "You're referring to the same Khlorus spice dust that only comes from Amma, the Supreme Va'nature, I suppose?" she almost snorted. She bent to retie the stick to her sling-bag, and then thought better of it as the shadows rustled again. "Come on, let's—" she began, gripping the handle tightly.

"I read that Amma's entire body is made of Khlorus," Samara gushed excitedly, standing on the straps of the fallen sling-bag. "It's like, she *is* her own container! Like she can harvest her own powers!"

Ellishiva tightened her grip on her Puluma stick, and clenched her jaw. Sam, as usual, didn't notice.

"You know, I overheard Rajah once," the hapless fairy babbled on, "saying that Khlorus is what protects us—what separates us from the human world. It's invisible. Amma can go through the worlds faster than you can blink—like that!" She snapped her fingers.

"Sam," Ellishiva growled. Her skin was starting to feel like a microscopic honeycomb from all the prickling.

"Well," said Samara thoughtfully, still wrapped up in her own world. "There must be *some* way to get Khlorus. Rajah keeps a supply inside his olivine orb—you know, on the crown of his staff."

She turned a shining, mischievous, and all-too-familiar look on Ellishiva.

"I don't steal," Ellishiva snapped, jumping as a twig snapped in the distance. "*Especially* not from Rajah. What good is a Va'nature prefect without that orb, Sam? And anyway, his staff is controlled by mantras." She stopped, and forced herself to take a deep breath. It gusted over her parched tongue, reminding her of how thirsty she was. "We'll get Bluzure spice dust for your wand. It's easily harvested and voice-controlled. You won't need to learn any complicated mantras. Now let's *go*," she said, pounding the end of the Puluma stick into the ground like a stake.

"Fine, fine," muttered Samara. She muttered other things, too—things that sounded like, "Some friend you are," and, "Bluzure spice dust . . . ha!" But, since she picked up the sling-bag and started walking back the way they had come, Ellishiva was content to let her mutter whatever she liked.

Five minutes passed. Then ten. Ellishiva's dry tongue began to feel like a desert wasteland. She could almost taste the sand. "Got your water bottle on you?" she asked the grumpy fairy finally. "I left mine at the ball court."

"No. But there's a locust tree over there. I like their water. It's sweeter than the other trees. Get a lot. We'll need it for the walk back." Samara was still muttering, but at least she was responding to questions, Ellishiva thought. The fairy's small button nose flared as she hiked the sling-bag higher up on her shoulder. "There has to be a way to lighten this load," she grumbled.

Ellishiva didn't reply. She was looking at the locust tree. For a moment, the shadows shifting around it seemed more sinister than the others. But no, she thought. She was lightheaded. She was seeing things. The tree wasn't far off. Nevertheless . . .

Lifting her singlet to her sweaty face, Ellishiva plucked up her courage. Then she shoved past the doubts churning in her stomach, and made a dash for it.

It took only seconds to shimmy up the alligator-hide-like trunk. Ellishiva plucked a handful of pinnates—each with eight oval leaflets hanging from its stem—from a low branch. In one more light bound she was on the ground again, striding quickly back toward Sam.

Ellishiva focused on the leaflets, her lips moving in a silent mantra as she walked. The marks on her palms glowed a soft green and, as always, the leaves began to swell. She lifted one above her upturned face and squeezed it, letting the water stream between her lips.

A bitter, rotting taste filled her mouth.

Ellishiva stumbled in her step, coughing and spitting out the few drops left on her tongue. She wiped her mouth and touched her throat, feeling her entire face wrinkle like a dried mango.

Not once in all her life had the water from a locust tree been bitter.

The thunderclouds in Ellishiva's stomach came roaring back in full force. Pressing her lips together again, she marched the rest of the way back to Samara. "Taste this," she demanded, thrusting one of the pinnates at the kneeling fairy. "The water is . . . ," she cast about for the right word, "salty. Slimy. *Briny.*"

But Samara was digging through the sling-bag again. And this time she was scrutinizing things. "Elli! I should have known," she griped. "Why are you carrying these human books? We were supposed to travel *light.*" She plucked one of the offending books out of the bag and waved it in the air accusingly.

"I—" began Ellishiva, swallowing hard. Something felt stuck in her throat. "There aren't *that* many of them," she protested weakly.

"It's summer, Elli. Forest Academy is closed," Samara explained slowly, and not for the first time. "*Freedom* from books." She frowned at the one in her hand, *Conquerors of the Great Seas, Volume V: The Quest for New Spice Routes.* "Another one on ships, Elli?" Samara gave a long-suffering sigh. "When were you going to read it? Between chukkers? No wonder you don't have your water bottle. Your bag is filled with stupid books!" She shoved the book back into the bag, exchanging it for a tiny rose-colored clamshell filled with lip balm. Shaking her head in weary disappointment, she rubbed some onto her lips, and then smacked them together.

"That's the fifth edition," said Ellishiva distractedly. There was still something stuck in her throat, and her stomach was beginning to churn with more than just thunderclouds. She tossed the remaining pinnates as far away from them as she could. "Headmistress Ulima let me borrow it. You should read it at our jungle sleepover tonight. If we ever get home," she grumbled, trying for a pointed look.

Samara bit her glossy lower lip for a moment. Then, "Oh, come on, Elli. Let's go back and get the olivine rocks for my wand, *please?* We're so *close!*" she pleaded. "I'll keep carrying your sling-bag, even with all the books in it. We can make it to the river's edge and still be home before dark—"

"*No*, Sam!" snapped Ellishiva. "We are not going to the river." She pressed a hand to her throat, swallowing hard for the umpteenth time. "Look, I—I'm having this weird feeling," she began.

But the fairy's attention was already elsewhere. "Wow! Look!" breathed Samara, her eyes widening as she pointed to something above Ellishiva's head. "That's amazing. Just totally itutu! What's happening to the locust tree?"

Ellishiva turned, and the dull pain in her stomach morphed into a cramp. "Sam," she answered in a strained voice. "That's not itutu."

The green leaves of the locust tree were changing. Like dark snakeskin slithering in the shadow of a rock, they shimmered on their branches, sprouting beaks, claws, and wings. In moments the entire tree had darkened, its limbs hidden under swarms and swarms of iridescent black ravens. Their dark, beady eyes glittered piercingly down at Ellishiva, and she clutched her twisting stomach, frozen with fear.

Slowly, the creatures began to lift off of the branches. For one heart-stopping second she thought they would swoop down on her and Samara, burying them alive under a plague of black wings, but the ravens did not descend. Instead, they rose higher, and higher still. They wheeled in the air, calling and turning, rising from the locust tree by the thousands as they twisted ever upward. Ellishiva watched them, barely breathing, until the final feathers of the vast black tornado had vanished into the sky.

Then she looked at the tree.

It, too, had changed. A rash of oozing black burls had erupted across its sturdy trunk. Long tendrils of molding brown moss dangled from its spiny limbs. A rotten stench like the bad water from the leaves wafted over to them, and Ellishiva felt her stomach turn again.

On the ground where she had tossed them, the discarded pinnates warped into dead ravens, and crumbled into the earth.

"Okay, maybe it's not itutu," squeaked Samara, grabbing Ellishiva's arm. "What does it mean, Elli?"

"I don't know, Sam. I've never seen a raven in our world before. None of the dofauns are ravens," muttered Ellishiva. She was trying hard to think, but the blood was pounding so loudly in her ears that she couldn't hear the thoughts. She shook her head and grabbed the sling-bag off the ground. "Let's just get out of here. Hurry."

"Are you sure you don't know what they are? Doesn't it say anything about them in your books?" asked Samara, snatching up Ellishiva's Puluma stick and falling into step beside her.

"No, there's nothing about ravens in my books. They're not endangered or extinct, so Amma doesn't give them refuge in our world," Ellishiva managed, pressing her palm against the knot in her throat again.

"There's nothing about them anywhere?" Samara pressed, shooting a nervous glance over her shoulder.

Ellishiva glanced behind them, too, but there was nothing there. She took a shaky breath, and made herself think. "Rajah has tons of books in his study," she offered at last. "Some are about non-dofauns. There's an author—Verro or Varro or something—who writes about them. We're not allowed to read them, though. He says they talk about evil things, and we have no business with that. Come on," she grabbed hold of Samara's elbow and dragged her faster through the forest.

A minute later, the rotting locust tree disappeared from sight.

"Well," said Samara. Her face was already beginning to brighten up again, and the mischievous spark was back in her eyes. "We could sneak—"

"We need to figure out what this means," interrupted Ellishiva bluntly. Her voice was shaking. "How did ravens get into our protected colony?"

"Well," huffed Samara, "if you'd *listen* to me when I was talking to you . . ." She crossed her thin arms over her chest, nearly stabbing Ellishiva with the end of the Puluma stick.

"I always listen to every word you say, Sam," Ellishiva muttered, peering over her shoulder at the spot where they'd left the locust tree in the distance.

The tip of the Puluma stick struck the ground like a gavel. "Oh, come on, Elli. At least hear me out," insisted Samara.

But Ellishiva was caught up in her own thoughts. "Slimy brown moss and burls bursting like sores on its limbs . . ." She shuddered and rubbed her forearms.

Samara made no reply. A deep scowl crossed her face, and she pressed her thin lips into an even thinner line.

They hurried on in silence for a moment, only the dry leaves below whispering in low, crackling rustles under their feet. Ellishiva glanced around. Nothing looked familiar. "Are we on the right path?" she mumbled, almost to herself. Still, Samara said nothing.

Then, in the distance behind them, twigs began to snap.

Ellishiva jerked her head around, staring into the empty forest. "Did you hear that?" she whispered. A chill shivered through her blood, raising bumps on her forearms.

Samara shrugged her shoulders, but even she looked nervous as she muttered, "I bet it's just that annoying brother of yours, Hektor. He's probably trying to scare us again. We're on the right path," she insisted. Then, as if she needed to prove it to herself, her small feet lifted off the ground.

Ellishiva caught her by the ankle. "I don't think so, Sam!" she hissed through gritted teeth. The thunderclouds in her stomach felt as though they were ripping her insides to shreds. She leaned her whole weight backward, dragging the fairy back down to earth.

"Let go, Elli. I want to see where we are," Samara said. But the scowl was still on her face.

"No you don't. Wait—" Samara twisted out of Ellishiva's grip and fluttered away. Her shimmering wings vanished into the high canopy again, leaving only a faint glimmer behind.

Ellishiva's stomach turned. She sprinted after Samara.

"Oh, come on, Sam. Don't be upset. I'm listening to you!" Ellishiva called as loudly as she dared. "You saw what happened back there. How can you even think of making a wand now?"

No reply came.

Frustration began to mingle with the fear in Ellishiva's stomach. "It's not my fault you lost it in the first place, is it?" she half-shouted at the treetops angrily. "Honestly, Sam, I don't know what you were thinking, breaking into Queen Neive's chambers, let alone trying to steal her journals!"

Silence reigned from the canopy. Ellishiva bit down on her tongue to keep from trying again. She knew all of Samara's tricks, and the quickest way to deal with this one was to ignore it.

But the snapping twigs and darkening shadows refused to go away, and, in the silence, guilt bloomed in Ellishiva to keep the fear company. The thought of Rajah's face when he found out that she had ventured beyond the protected colony—to collect illegal olivine, no less—was almost unbearable.

Even worse, however, was the nagging feeling that she'd some-how awoken the locust tree by touching it. An image of swarms of ravens loose in their colony—digging their sharp claws and beaks into her friends and neighbors, wreaking havoc everywhere— flashed through her mind.

But I didn't do anything, she told herself as another wave of shame and guilt rolled through.

. . . Did I?

A sudden cry overhead jolted her out of her thoughts, and she looked up, heart pounding, to find a white-faced Samara landing gracelessly on the ground beside her. Before Ellishiva could ask what had happened, a flock of unseen birds erupted in flight through the crowns of the trees above, making them both jump. Frozen with dread, they stared into the canopy.

First one by one, then in droves, tiny green leaves began to fall around them. It was only when they drifted down to eye-level that Ellishiva could see that their edges were blackened and crumbling away, like a sandcastle in the wind.

The leaves were decaying in midair.

She looked at Sam, who was staring back at her with huge, round eyes. Ellishiva's own tongue felt numb in her mouth. At last she managed to force a word out of it: "*Run!*"

They ran.

Back over the bramble-choked stream, under the low-hanging branches of the dogwoods, through the endless, scratchy spice-wood shrubs, Ellishiva flew at a dead sprint. Whether any of them were the same ones they'd passed before, she couldn't guess. The only thing that mattered was to keep running.

And running, she realized with a sinking heart, was growing harder by the step.

The thing stuck in her throat swelled again, making it hard to breathe. Worse, her body felt heavier with every passing second. Samara noticed this and took the sling-bag from her shoulder without a word and without stopping, but even that relief was short-lived. Her insides burned as though she'd swallowed a fireball.

And all the while, the twigs kept *snap-snap-snapping* behind them.

"If that's Hektor . . . rooting around for . . . acorns again," Samara gasped as she ran, "I'm . . . going to . . . kill him."

But Ellishiva had been trailed by her brother enough times to know that the thing behind them wasn't him. Every ominous, horrible headline that *The Mannahatta Times* had been running lately was tumbling through her head. "*Wisps of Strange Black Clouds Thought to Be Seeping into Colony . . . Heart Ripped out of Ice Fairy by Unknown Monster . . .*"

Unknown monster . . .

Behind them, the snapping twigs grew louder.

"Sam," Ellishiva gasped with an effort. "Fly up. Look for home . . . the crown of . . . Banyan Tree."

Samara shook her head and gripped the sling-bag tighter. "Not . . . leaving you down here by . . . yourself," she panted.

"I'll follow your voice and . . . your wings," insisted Ellishiva. "We need . . . help . . . someone must be . . . must be . . . ," she trailed off, wheezing for breath.

Samara glanced at her doubtfully. "Are you sure?" she asked.

"Yes!" Ellishiva blurted. "It's our only . . . chance." She clamped a hand over her stomach as another cramp struck.

Next to her, Samara hesitated another moment. Then she gave a curt nod, and seconds later she was only a glimmer again, darting high above the branches.

Alone on the forest floor, the dark shadows of the wood seemed to close around Ellishiva. Even the air grew suddenly thicker—humid and suffocating.

Somewhere behind her, a slow creaking of branches pierced the silence.

The blood shot to Ellishiva's ears, beating like a human war drum. She forced her sluggish limbs to run faster, fixing her burning eyes on the glimmer of Samara's wings high above her. But before long, even that speck of pale light began to flicker in and out of sight. Ellishiva opened her mouth, but the thing in her throat was now so large that she could barely breathe, let alone call out.

At last, with a dim, final wink, the wings vanished altogether.

Ellishiva swallowed hard to keep calm, but her throat was tight and parched. To make things worse, a vile stench was beginning to flood through the woods. It smelled, she thought, sucking in shorter and shorter breaths, of smoke, stagnant water, charred flesh, and burnt animal hair.

Her stomach turned again.

Somewhere in the unseen shadows, she heard the slow, screeching splitting of tree trunks. She stumbled. Fresh needles of fear scurried up the back of her neck, like a thousand poisonous spider feet. On her skin, the tattooed brown circles struck up a faint, throbbing glow. She glanced over her shoulder.

A tall, dark shadow was creeping toward her.

It flowed from trunk to trunk, far too large to be any kind of animal. Before she turned away, it passed through a last, dying ray of late afternoon light, and Ellishiva glimpsed what it was. She gasped and tripped over another bush.

It can't be . . .

But in the next moment the locust tree itself was looming up in front of her, and she slammed to a halt in her tracks, speechless and staring. The hideous tree's roots twisted and writhed like so many black snakes above ground, as though it had slithered all the way here. And the rest of it was writhing, too. Brown-green moss dangled from its huge limbs as they creaked and stretched downward, reaching toward Ellishiva like a thousand bony witch fingers hungry for their prize.

Forcing some life back into her heavy limbs, Ellishiva bolted back the way she had come.

She could hear the locust tree slithering along behind her, pushing aside the other trees in its path as though they were no more than weeds. From somewhere high above, the cries of thousands of ravens came shrieking back.

The tip of a long, spiny tree limb grazed Ellishiva's shoulder blades.

Sam, she wanted to scream. *Help!* But the narrow straw that had become her throat wouldn't let her. She wished desperately that she, too, could fly.

And then, so quickly that she barely felt it happen, four ropes of slimy, brownish moss snapped tight around her legs like whips.

Ellishiva fell, landing hard in a patch of sharp brambles. The side of her head cracked against the forest floor, and what little air had been left in her lungs escaped in a single *whoosh*.

Somewhere above her, the wild calls of the ravens grew louder and more savage. Ellishiva felt more moss coiling around her wrists, her waist—even her neck. The same vile stench of smoke and burnt flesh invaded her nostrils. She struggled to stand, but the moss gripped her tighter, dragging her feet out from under her again and again.

Then something wet and cold as a winter wind inched its way over her midriff, and a sharp pain cut into her right side.

Ellishiva tried in vain to scream as a venomous spasm spread from the wound through the rest of her, throbbing like a mouthful of infected teeth. She managed to kick free of her bindings, but in the next moment fresh ropes of moss were cuffing her ankles tightly together again. She shut her eyes and felt herself being dragged, feet-first, up into the air—felt the blood collecting in her head as she dangled helplessly in the void.

Then, upside down, she forced her heavy eyelids open again.

The towering black expanse of the locust tree stretched away from her in two directions, as though it tied the sky to the earth. Ellishiva barely had time to feel the size of a matchstick, however, before her eyes fell on something else.

Through a gaping split in the tree's ravaged trunk, something was moving. It pulsed madly in captivity, suspended and shining in the dark. Ellishiva stared.

It was a wet, silver heart.

Ellishiva's eyes nearly fell out of their sockets. She had read about these. There was only one kind of being in the world that had a silver heart.

"F—fairy . . . ," she mumbled through swollen lips, so quietly that she barely heard the word herself.

Above her, on the locust's trunk, long scars began to burst open, like lipless, twisted mouths. Sticky black ooze dripped from the gaps, followed by another whirlwind of ravens that fluttered upward, screeching, to join their brethren at the crown of the tree.

Ellishiva jerked and tried again to call out, but her heavy tongue choked her.

Then, from the dark, came a woman's voice. It spoke in the endangered language of Pali, and its tones touched Ellishiva's ears with pain and poison. She whimpered, and a shiver danced down her spine.

"Feel my suffering," hissed the horrible voice. *"The Sixth Element is upon you. With the last quarter moon comes destruction to your world."*

A high-pitched keening filled the air as, somewhere, a girl began to scream. Dizzy and half-blinded by the blood throbbing in her head, Ellishiva glanced frantically around for the source of the sound, but the forest was dark and empty. Then, quite suddenly, the coils of moss around her ankles loosened.

She fell.

The blood in her brain numbed everything, and she was barely aware of hitting the pile of decomposing gray leaves. She only knew that, when her head cleared enough for her to think again, her eyes and ears opened to a deathly silence.

She was alive.

Ellishiva lay perfectly still for several seconds. Then, from somewhere nearby, a thin, sharp sound—like a whip slicing through the air—disturbed the muffled quiet of the woods. With a huge effort, Ellishiva opened her eyes and pushed herself up onto her elbows. Then she froze, staring.

Hanging before her was a jagged rip in the air. Its edge listed faintly in the deadened breeze, almost like a tent flap. A bright green glow traced its outline in the dimness, and bright, tiny motes, no bigger than specks of dust, drifted through the opening like magic.

"Khlorus," Ellishiva breathed. She had never seen it before, outside of Rajah's staff. It was beautiful. Amma's own spice dust . . .

The dust that protected her world.

Another sharp *whoosh* sounded nearby, and Ellishiva craned her neck around. Several yards away, the locust tree's sharp branches were singing through the air, fresh gashes of bright green Khlorus appearing in their wake.

Suddenly, Ellishiva knew—with a dead certainty that made her stomach cramp again—that she hadn't been spared for long. Her heartbeat thundered back into her ears. Clutching the stinging wound on her waist, she moved, slower than a banana slug, off of the pile of leaves.

The locust tree heard her anyway.

It spun around on its snakelike roots—the long strings of slimy moss on its branches flying outward in all directions—and lunged for her. Ellishiva barely had time to stumble to her feet, let alone run. There was only one place to go.

Gritting her teeth, she summoned every scrap of courage she had, and dove through the Khlorus-lined gash hanging in the air beside her.

There was a blinding flash of green, and a tingle passed over Ellishiva's skin. But solid ground was still beneath her, and she clambered to her feet again and staggered forward, hands outstretched and groping, eyes blinking madly as she struggled to regain her sight.

It was her other senses that returned first, however. Her ears caught the drumming of a bird's beak on wood, and the buzzing of a handful of bumblebees. Her cheek felt the flutter of a lacewing moth's wings as it brushed past. When the blurred world at last came into focus again, the woods were brighter, filled once more with late afternoon sunlight. Patches of blue and yellow flowers bloomed among the underbrush. Ellishiva glanced over her shoulder.

The locust tree was gone.

She stumbled to a stop, bracing herself against the trunk of a tree with one hand. The heaviness was lifting from her tired limbs, and the thing in her throat had disappeared, but the wound in her side stung as sharply as ever. Ellishiva gritted her teeth against the pain and brought her nose closer to the tree's bark. The smell was familiar, comforting. She tilted her chin back, and looked up.

"What a tall white pine," she murmured to herself.

As if in agreement, the leaves at the top of the tree rustled gently in a stray breeze. Ellishiva turned her head to rest her cheek against its trunk. A few inches in front of her nose, a tender young vine was twining its way upward.

Without too much thought, Ellishiva reached out and touched it with her fingers, focusing the way she did when she grew saplings. The palm of her hand glowed softly, and the vine stretched, growing taller.

Then, before her eyes, tiny, exotic purple flowers began to bloom along its length.

A frown of confusion creased Ellishiva's forehead. "Impossible," she murmured. "Your species of ivy doesn't even bloom flowers. Unless—" she stopped.

Not far off, footsteps were crunching through the brush.

Ellishiva dropped down among the bushes at the foot of the pine, gritting her teeth against the new flash of pain in her side. Not even daring to breathe, she peered through the leaves in the direction of the sound. There was a voice mingling with the footsteps now, talking to itself. It grew louder as it came closer, until at last Ellishiva was able to make out the shapes of the words.

"*Kwihëluta! Kwihëluta!*"

"Lenape language," she whispered in disbelief. "I'm in the human world of Mannahatta."

The blood drained out of her face, turning her cheeks a paler shade of green. She craned her neck up at the massive pine tree again. "You should hide yourself, or someone will make you into a ship's mast," she warned quietly.

The voice was dangerously close now. Ellishiva crouched lower, pressing her back against the pine's trunk so hard that it ached. She wanted to bury her face between her knees. She wanted to cry.

"Stay calm," she breathed. "Think. When I got trapped with the garbage in one of the pitcher plants, what did Rajah say to me? *Think*," she scolded herself, struggling not to twitch nervously—noisily—in the bushes. "'When you face fear, change your ways.' Change your ways . . . When faced with fear, change your ways."

But it was no use. The wound in her side burned as if it were on fire, and her courage had already been drained to the last drop. With shaking fingers, Ellishiva touched a cluster of leaves in front of her, willing them to grow thicker.

A few sparks of bright green shimmered briefly, like spice dust, from the lines of her palm.

Ellishiva stared at her hand for a moment. *That* had never happened before.

Then the sudden snapping of twigs, almost in her ear now, yanked her back into the danger of the present moment. She froze like stone and peered anxiously through the leaves of the bushes. Across the small clearing, something pushed free of the curtain of trees. Ellishiva felt her eyes go wide.

"A human," she whispered.

For a moment, all that had just happened vanished. Ellishiva's eyes fixed themselves, fascinated, on the man before her. Disheveled long black hair fell thickly about his oval face, which was painted in designs of red across the eyes. He wore a breechcloth of bearskin, and in his hand he carried a spear of polished elm that stood a head taller than he was himself.

Ellishiva's insatiable curiosity took all this in. Then her eyes fell on something else.

Slung over the man's shoulders was the carcass of a calf so young that its antlers had not yet begun to bud. The animal's large black eyes were open wide, frozen in an abyss of fear. Her last tears had crusted hard at the corners of her eyelids, like pearl droplets.

"A baby eastern elk of Kanata," Ellishiva breathed, leaning forward slightly in the bushes. Then she remembered where she was, and froze again.

But too late.

The human halted in his tracks, and slowly looked around. Then he gripped his spear grimly in his hand, and walked straight toward the white pine.

When he was only a few feet away from Ellishiva, he stopped. He knelt, studying the forest floor with sharp eyes. Then he cocked his head, and sniffed the air. "*Mahchikwi kèku le, shëkw ntamama Kahàsëna Hàki,*" he mumbled, looking at the flower bushes.

Ellishiva forgot how to breathe.

Then more calls in the Lenape tongue sounded faintly from beyond the clearing, and the human paused. He tilted his head, listening.

Then he stood and walked away from Ellishiva. The frozen eyes of the baby elk seemed to watch her as he went. "Poor thing," she mumbled, drawing in a shaky breath. "One day, your kind will become a dofaun in our world. We'll keep you safe."

Ellishiva had no sooner mustered the will to stand up again than a chorus of terrible, wailing screams erupted nearby.

She fell to the ground once more, pulse pounding. The shrieks echoed through the forest. For a moment she was baffled that anything in such a tranquil place could scare people so much.

Then the faint, grating *caw* of a thousand ravens trickled into the clearing.

The wound in Ellishiva's side burned anew. "It's after the humans," she muttered, fear fluttering back into her chest like a swarm of black butterflies. Just out of sight, the shouts and screams grew louder. Bones crunched and cracked. Then all was silent.

It would come for her next.

Peeling herself away from the white pine, Ellishiva sprinted back through the underbrush in the direction from which she had come. But she'd had her eyes closed when she first arrived, and even after she'd crossed some distance, the Khlorus doorway had still not reappeared.

She kept running.

Under her bare feet, the forest floor grew wet. She splashed through a puddle, spitting out the water that flew into her mouth. Salt marshes.

A way back.

There had to be one—had to be. It was the only thought in Ellishiva's head as she dashed through patches of tall reed grass, setting off a frenzy of quacking ducks that had been feasting on their dinner of small, silvery fish. Overhead, numerous white and gray seagulls wheeled and cried their displeasure. *Caw-caw, caw-caw!*

And then the caws didn't belong to the seagulls anymore.

A poisonous dread settled in the pit of Ellishiva's stomach as she felt her limbs grow heavy, felt the thing in her throat reappear and swell again. The gash in her side seared like a burning poker. But she was close to the river; she could smell it. If a way back existed anywhere, it would be there.

Ellishiva set her jaw against the pain, and pushed herself to run faster.

She heard something sweeping through the forest behind her, breaking tree limbs, splitting thick bark that had stood the test of years. The wild calls of the ravens resonated louder in the woods.

And then, just as she was about to despair, a flash of bright green caught her eye, glowing between the trunks nearest the bank of the river. Out of breath and shaking, Ellishiva lunged toward it.

A coil of strong, brown moss lashed her ankles together, and she fell to the ground with a *thud*. Then, before she could so much as push herself to her knees, another moss-rope wound around her wrists, and a third closed around her waist, dragging her away from the bright green gash of hope.

Ellishiva fought with every ounce of her strength to twist free of the moss's grip, but it was no use—the brown cords only tightened their steely hold on her flesh. Fear boiled over in her heart. An image of the baby elk flashed through her mind, its dead eyes staring . . .

When faced with fear, change your ways.

Ellishiva stopped struggling. She gazed at the black locust, pulling her closer now to its infected trunk—off the ground and into the air again. Through the gaping cracks in its twisted bark she could see the silver heart of the ice fairy beating a frantic, rapid tattoo, like a trapped animal in a cage. Like Ellishiva's heart itself.

And then a thought struck her, a simple thought—so simple that it couldn't possibly work. Every day, for as long as she could remember, Ellishiva had been bringing saplings to life in the Arboretum at home, much like she had made the vine grow and bloom on the white pine only a few minutes ago. She looked at the rotting black trunk of the locust tree, looming ever closer, and licked her lips. After all, she told herself desperately, it *was* a tree.

She grabbed the coil of moss around her waist and, with so much purpose that her palms glowed brighter than she had ever seen them glow before, willed it to soften, to loosen.

The brown vines squirmed for a moment, twitching like snakes without heads. Then, one by one, they recoiled from her waist, her knees, her wrists.

Ellishiva gripped the string of moss that had been holding her wrists and slid to the ground. Her feet touched down with a *thud*, and the gash in her side gave a sharp throb. Ten feet away, the shining green slit of Khlorus dust rippled gently in an unseen breeze.

She lunged for it.

Above her, the tree let out an eerie, echoing screech, like hundreds of wounded ravens, cursing her. Ellishiva ignored it. She did not look back as she dove through the blazing rip. She did not see the fresh tendrils of brown moss snaking after her again.

She did not even see her own body glow a sudden, bright green, sealing the doorway to the human world behind her.

THE LONG JOURNEY HOME

Ellishiva did not know how long she lay alone in the dark before the kind and familiar voice found her.

"Ellishiva. Ellishiva—" it rumbled deeply. "Get up, child."

A modest glow of hope flickered to life inside her. She heard the chirp of crickets, and knew without having to look that the day was ending. In her mind, the memory of what had happened in the forest lay heavily on her thoughts, as though her brain were being smothered with a big brush.

"Ellishiva."

She turned her head toward the voice. The heaviness and the thing in her throat were gone now, but the wound in her side stung worse than ever, and there was a growing stiffness in her bones that hadn't been there before. With a huge effort, she opened her eyes.

Above her stood a towering white bear—a dofaun. His fur glistened like new snow on a winter morning. He frowned.

"Get up, Ellishiva!" Atticus insisted again, a little less patiently this time. "Rajah would be displeased to know that I found you this far away from home."

"Att—" was all Ellishiva could muster.

A shadow of worry crossed the bear's brow, and he shifted on his large feet. On his broad reed belt, a carefully bundled bunch of roots and leaves rustled faintly, brushing a pouch hanging alongside his three-quarter-length burlap trousers. All the dofauns carried these pouches. Inside, Ellishiva knew, was a small, transparent olivine jar with Bluzure spice dust in it.

There was a flash of wings, and suddenly someone was vaulting over the bear's shoulder to land in the grass beside her.

"Elli, I'm so sorry! What happened?" Samara shouted frantically, almost in her ear. "Hektor! Over here—hurry!"

Ellishiva's eyes were wide open now, and her lips were parched. She felt as though something had stolen every ounce of her strength, and Samara's hollering wasn't helping her headache.

A moment later, the fairy wasn't the only one hollering.

"Elli. Elli!" gasped her brother, casting aside his slingshot and his Puluma stick as he dropped to the ground beside her in a flash of orange uniform. Hektor Cumin's handsome green face bent over her, locks of unruly red-brown hair falling into his amber eyes. Tiny marks peppered the skin of his neck like the seeds of the cumin spice. Ellishiva noticed a trail of acorns spilling from the bulging pockets of his shorts. Of course.

"She can't speak, Hektor! Someone attacked her," wailed Samara. "I don't know what happened! We were just following the path and—and suddenly I didn't hear her behind me anymore. I lost her . . ."

Ellishiva wished she could clap her hands over her ears to dim the fairy's piercing voice, but her arms wouldn't move. Her whole body, for that matter, felt as though it had been invaded by a paralyzing fungus—the very ones she herself often practiced removing from plants. The memory of the locust tree's slimy brown ropes of moss slithered through her mind, and she shuddered.

What had it done to her?

"Attack! Nonsense, fairy child," dismissed Atticus firmly. "She fainted from the heat and hit her head."

"But Atticus, she's not saying anything!" screeched Samara.

Hektor reached down and took Ellishiva's soft, limp hand in his own grimy one. "Say something, Elli," he murmured pleadingly.

"Give her some air!" snapped Atticus. "You know what happened—you should never have wandered off the path. Come now, we must hurry home to Banyan Tree."

Pushing through a clump of brambles, the huge bear bent and picked up Ellishiva, lifting her gently onto his broad shoulder. A shock of pain wracked her limp body, radiating from the wound on her right side. Her nostrils flared and she squeezed her eyes shut, trying to sink as far as she could into the dofaun's thick coat. It didn't help much.

Atticus set off.

Samara fluttered up and perched next to Ellishiva on the bear's massive shoulder, as though she were afraid Ellishiva would vanish before her eyes again. Behind them, Hektor quickly collected his things and dashed after them, grabbing a handful of fur and scrambling up onto the dofaun's other shoulder. Atticus seemed not to notice.

Ellishiva's thoughts were a tangled mess in her pounding head. Within them, she could still hear the locust tree's rasping voice hissing at her, warning her. *With the last quarter moon comes destruction to your world.*

The Sixth Element is upon you.

Ellishiva's tongue felt as paralyzed as the rest of her. It took every ounce of willpower she had to force it to budge. "Locust . . . tree," she managed faintly. "Fairy's . . . heart. Humans . . ." She stopped, exhausted.

Next to her, Samara's eyes went wide. "Elli, you think those ravens chased you into the human world?" she asked breathlessly.

"You're crazy, Sam," interrupted Hektor. "Aren't you listening to Atticus? She fell down running after a flying fairy—*you*! You were trying to drag her to the river again, weren't you?" he added accusingly.

"Shut up!" Samara snapped at him. "We weren't going anywhere. I was just training her to run faster. How do you think she learned to slam you flat on your backside at every Puluma match the way she does?"

"Stop lying again," growled Hektor. "And don't tell *me* to shut up."

Some arguments would never change, Ellishiva thought, wishing she could tell them both to drop it already. The gash in her side throbbed again. She could feel it leaking, and wondered why Atticus wasn't picking up on the scent.

"*Look* at her, Hektor!" Samara was shouting. "She can't even speak properly! Someone *attacked* her!"

"Give it a rest, Sam," Hektor replied, rolling his eyes.

"Silence, both of you!" commanded Atticus finally. "Fairy child, perhaps your memory fails you, but we are living in a protected world. Nothing can *attack* us here. Amma, Supreme Va'nature of Nicobar, protects us all." Ellishiva pictured his eyes glowing with love and pride. "We cannot just scamper off to the river's edge simply because we feel like it. It's forbidden," he reminded her gravely.

Hektor smirked at Samara, who ignored him. "Then how come you go there, Atticus?" she asked innocently, pretending to examine her painted fingernails for dust.

"Because we're elders," answered Atticus. "We know what we're doing."

"Well," rejoined Samara grimly, "I certainly am not an elder. But I assure you, someone attacked Elli in these woods just now."

"She tripped in some brambles," Atticus insisted, and Ellishiva could hear the growl under the words. "This island is full of basalt rocks and hills."

"*Which*," chimed in Hektor smugly, taking a quick inventory of the acorns in his pockets, "is what 'Mannahatta' means in the Lenape language."

"Correct, Hektor," Atticus commended him proudly. "Anyone could lose her footing around these hilly parts."

Pain shot from Ellishiva's midriff to the tips of her fingers. She struggled to speak again, but this time it was no use; her tongue had become a lump of stone in her mouth. She closed her tired eyes and her mind drifted, floating like butter on milk. She saw again the wet, silver heart, beating frantically in the black, cage-like trunk of the living locust tree. But how could that be?

Feel my suffering, it had hissed at her in the old language, in Pali. *Feel my suffering.*

Around her, the argument was far from over.

"The forest will be dark soon," Atticus was saying. "No place for you, my fairy. I will get you safe passage back to Central Pond." He let out a loud sigh that sounded more like a snort, putting a brief dent in the chorus of evening crickets. "I know Mr. Guo is somewhere around here," he muttered.

"I saw him earlier," piped up Hektor, inspecting his acorns closely, as though they were precious stones. "He had Baron Puck on board."

"Baron Puck," huffed Samara petulantly. "I don't like that elf. He's scary looking."

"Like you," Hektor mumbled under his breath, keeping his eyes on his acorns.

Samara shot him a poisonous glare. When she spoke, however, it was to the dofaun. "Atticus, why should I need '*safe passage*' in a protected world?" she pointed out triumphantly. "Didn't you just say that nothing can harm us on this island?"

The bear shook his great head in frustration. "Because I said so, child!" he growled. "Don't you know it's rude to question your elders? And you wonder why you are grounded so often. Queen Neive did a good thing, confiscating your wand," he added pointedly.

Ellishiva winced, though whether it was from pain or guilt she couldn't say.

Next to her, Samara's blue eyes grew wide and round. "Great!" she huffed bitterly, crossing her thin arms over her chest. "The whole colony knows about it. Now I can't even be seen with one." She scowled.

A fresh pang stabbed at Ellishiva's side. The wetness under her singlet was spreading. She wondered again why Atticus, whose sense of smell was usually so extraordinary, hadn't sensed it yet.

On the bear's other shoulder, Hektor opened his mouth (probably to fire another insult at Samara, Ellishiva thought wearily), but before anything could come out of it they were suddenly interrupted by the sweet, low melody of a lute.

Ellishiva's eyelids were drooping dangerously, but she forced them open again, and looked up. From the treetops high above, a flying vāhmana was descending. It looked, she mused, like a square chariot from her human books. Its four battered sides were the color of hardened lava, and the faded canopy above it flapped in the breeze. As it approached the ground, Ellishiva glimpsed the bright blue writing scrawled on the worn boards:

Cheeky Canteen
{Now serving Taftnook and Lilly Pilly Fizz}
Mr. Guo & Daughter, Proprietors
#59 Cathay Alley
Bear Market, Mannahatta Colony

Mr. Guo, a stocky elf with skin the color of wheat and long, ice-gray hair, was standing behind the last of the vāhmana's three benches, leaning over a lone table cluttered with objects. The only other passenger in the craft was tucked in the corner with a charcoal-colored cape over his head, his face buried in *The Mannahatta Times*. Even from where she lay sprawled over Atticus's shoulder, Ellishiva could make out the dramatic sketch on the paper's front page: distraught fairies standing or kneeling on a chunk of melting ice, all of them clustered around the corpse of one of their own, who was lying prone on the glacier with a hole in her chest. Above it, the headline blared black and bold: *"Ice Fairy Found Dead—Heart Missing."*

In her mind's eye, Ellishiva saw the silver heart of the locust tree, beating fast and wild. Her stomach turned. Still, the rock-tongue in her mouth refused to let her speak.

When it was about a foot above the forest floor, the vāhmana stopped, hovering unsteadily in midair.

"Good day, Mr. Guo," rumbled Atticus to its driver. "How was the harvest at the river today?"

The silver-haired elf sighed and tapped the olivine orb sitting on the table beside him. It was nearly empty. "Not so well, Atticus. The vāhmana had some trouble getting back into our colony again, from the outside world. Strange. Very strange indeed." He cleared his throat. "Can we barter? I need a few more grains of Bluzure to get home, it seems." He picked the orb up off the table and held it upside down, giving it a hopeless shake. "There'll be a good meal in it for you at the canteen," he offered.

"That sounds like a fair trade," agreed Atticus. His shoulder shifted under Ellishiva as he reached for the pouch at his belt—the one with the olivine jar of Bluzure spice dust in it. "Hello, Baron Puck. Good day to you, sir," he continued politely to Mr. Guo's passenger.

But the baron did not stir, keeping his face buried in the paper. Atticus cleared his throat.

In front of them, the vāhmana gave another precarious wobble. "Quicker the better, if you don't mind, Atticus," prompted Mr. Guo. Then, "Make fast!" he commanded, and the few remaining grains of dust inside the orb flickered faintly. The vāhmana gave another slight wobble, then went still. The handrails that were supposed to fold down, however, only gave a loud creak, and stuck in place. Mr. Guo shook his head at them reproachfully.

On Atticus's other shoulder, Hektor studied the vāhmana with longing. He'd always wanted to drive one, Ellishiva knew, but it would be years still before he got the chance. The wound in her side gave another throb of pain. Beside her, Samara reached down to brush the hair away from her face, and Ellishiva tried to motion to her midriff with her eyes. But the fairy's narrow gaze was fixed on Baron Puck.

Atticus was handing his olivine jar over to Mr. Guo. "Here we go. Just in time, I see," he said.

The elf tugged the cork stopper out of the jar. He turned the olivine orb upside down, and opened it. Then he carefully tipped the jar over the orb's opening, and tapped it with one pointy finger. Ellishiva watched as the shimmering grains of Bluzure spice dust spilled neatly into the orb. That done, Mr. Guo gave a curt nod and snapped the orb shut.

"Make fast!" he ordered again. The replenished dust in the orb swirled, and this time the vāhmana jerked instantly to a complete halt. With a loud creak, the three stubborn, worn steps unfolded from the vehicle's side and touched down at the white bear's feet, their hand-rails of thick rough vines unfurling all the way to the ground along with them.

Relieved, Mr. Guo put the stopper back in Atticus's olivine jar and handed it back to the dofaun—which was also when he finally noticed the limp body draped over the huge bear's shoulder.

"Why, what has happened to Ellishiva?" he asked, his silver eye-brows rising in concern. He took a step closer, and squinted up at her. "Are you well, child? Atticus, is she well?"

Ellishiva tried again to speak, but it was useless.

"Do not concern yourself, Mr. Guo," dismissed Atticus. "Ellishiva had a fall. She will be just fine. But if you could accompany the fairy child here safely back to Central Pond, I would be most grateful. That is, if you are finished with your seaweed harvest, of course."

The wound in her side leaked again, and Ellishiva wished Atticus would stop making small talk and just take her home already. *Why doesn't he smell it?* she wondered again, miserably.

"I would be honored, my friend," said Mr. Guo. His eyes strayed to the softening colors of the sky. "The sun will soon retire, and so must I. The harvest is done for the day. I should like to visit Fairy Alcove, in any case. They could do with some cheering up." He sighed and reached for Samara's hand. "Come, fairy child. I will take you safely home."

"Oh, no," Samara said bluntly, tugging her hand away. "I mean, I'm sorry, Mr. Guo," she amended, more politely this time, "but I'm not going home tonight. We—we're having a jungle sleepover at Elli's."

From her place tucked against his neck, Ellishiva felt a rumble of disapproval roll through Atticus. "Such things are not for you to decide on a whim, fairy child."

"Rajah and Queen Neive have already approved," interrupted Samara, her nose wrinkling as she took in the lengths of greenish-black seaweed strewn across the back of the battered vāhmana. Then she lifted her nose a fraction of an inch and added imperiously, "Oh! And Mr. Guo, would you kindly remind Asia that she, too, is invited?"

On Atticus's other shoulder, Hektor rolled his eyes and shook his head.

There was a rustle from the corner of the vāhmana, and Ellishiva looked over to find Baron Puck lowering his newspaper. Limp, silvery-pale hair brushed the tops of his shoulders, framing his angular face. For a moment, his shrewd, watery blue eyes fixed themselves coldly on Samara. Then, just as quickly, he disappeared behind *The Times* again.

Strange, mused Ellishiva somewhere in the back of her head, which was feeling dizzier by the moment. *Strange, for him to be in the forest.*

"I shall inform Asia," Mr. Guo was saying, though the words sounded ill-tempered on his tongue. He boarded the vāhmana again, resuming his post by the table. "Atticus, my friend, you certainly have your hands full," he commented with a pointed look at Samara. "A very good evening to you, and many thanks for bartering. Stop by anytime for your meal."

"Indeed," rumbled Atticus, giving Samara a disapproving glance.

Mr. Guo patted his olivine orb affectionately. "Bear Market!" he commanded. The Bluzure spice dust swirled, and the creaking steps folded themselves up again. Then the vāhmana turned northward, rising high into the air. Before it disappeared among the branches, Ellishiva heard the elf say, "Play on!" and the sweet melody he had arrived with struck itself up again, its notes lingering even after the vāhmana had faded from sight.

"Why would Baron Puck be reading *The Mannahatta Times*? He's the one who publishes it," muttered Samara as Atticus lumbered off again. Ellishiva had been wondering that herself. Before she could make head or tail of it, however, a sudden spasm of pain shot through her body from the wound in her side. Her nostrils flared, and a thin whimper escaped her throat.

Samara looked down. "Atticus," she said uneasily, a hint of panic creeping back into her voice, "why are Elli's lips turning purple?"

"She must have eaten some huckleberries," reasoned Atticus, sounding sullen.

"We didn't eat any huckleberries!" Samara snapped at him.

Hektor's eyes were on Ellishiva. "I don't think so, Atticus," he said, his forehead creasing in concern. "I've never seen her like this. Do you smell that?" He sniffed the air.

"She will be fine," Atticus growled. "And Rajah will make her even better. Cease this pointless fretting, both of you. We're almost home."

"But what about the smell?" insisted Hektor. "It's different. Bitter. I've never smelled it before." He searched Ellishiva's face. She blinked her eyes rapidly at him. The frown on his forehead grew deeper.

Make him run, Ellishiva pleaded silently. *Tell him to run.* But Hektor could no more read her mind than Atticus could.

Another crippling jolt of pain swept through her body, so strong now that if she could have screamed, it would have shaken the leaves down from the highest treetops. As it was, only another faint whimper seeped out of her parched lips. "Rajah," she whispered longingly, desperately.

"Yes, yes," tutted Atticus. "We are nearly there. Look, Banyan Tree is in sight."

Ellishiva looked. In the distance, Banyan Tree sparkled like a maharaja's crown, its vast branches brightly lit by thousands of firefly dofauns. All around it, the thin clouds of evening were washed in shades of red and purple. The outermost corners of the colony, to the east, west, north, and south, were marked by four majestic sugar maple trees, in the crowns of which clusters of fireflies gathered together, forming living lampposts. Atticus was approaching the eastern one—the entrance by Cathay Alley.

Ellishiva gazed at it as long as she could. But the last ounce of energy she possessed had slipped out of her along with the whisper of Rajah's name. She shut her eyes, letting the lids drop slowly closed against the purple sky.

A moment later, she felt Hektor's hand touch her shoulder. "Wake up, Elli. We're almost home."

But Ellishiva couldn't look at him. She couldn't even try.

Two small, delicate hands seized her arm and shook it. "She is not waking up, Atticus," said Samara's voice, and now it was filled with fear. "Something's wrong."

"Come now, Ellishiva. Wake up, child. We are almost home," rumbled Atticus. Ellishiva lay motionless, feeling the vibration of his words rolling through her. Then a large, wet nose was snuffling gently at her back.

For a few seconds, everyone else seemed to grow as still as she was.

Then, "Make haste, Hektor. Move her to my back, and hold tightly to my fur." For the first time, there was real urgency in the dofaun's voice. Ellishiva could have cried with relief.

"Are you going to run, Atticus?" asked Hektor.

"Indeed. You were right, child. I should have smelled it before, but I scratched my nose on a linodye branch this morning." Another low rumble hummed through the fur beneath her. "Blood," the bear growled darkly.

Blood, Ellishiva's mind echoed dully.

Atticus was still speaking. "Samara," he barked gruffly. "Secure those Puluma sticks to my belt. Hurry, child."

There was a rustle as Samara obeyed the order. More pain radiated through Ellishiva as Hektor pulled her onto Atticus's back. She could feel the great dofaun slowly lowering his body to rest on all four paws.

"Oh, no!" Samara shrilled almost in her ear. "Look! Hektor, oh there's so much of it. Oh no, oh no, oh no—"

"Compose yourself, child," snapped Atticus, but his own voice sounded strained.

Ellishiva felt her head being pulled, tightly but gently, to Hektor's chest, the way their little sister, Amborella, sometimes cradled her doll. The warm, nutty fragrance of cumin spice enveloped her, and for a moment the throb in her side seemed to dull.

"Hold on tight to my fur," commanded Atticus bluntly. Then the muscles rippled beneath his thick coat, and Ellishiva heard the sharp crunch of brambles as he bounded forward. Hektor's body arched over hers like a shield. Close by, the whirr of Samara's wings hummed behind them as she kept up with Atticus.

Fresh stabs of pain shot through Ellishiva's body with every leap the great bear took, but she was glad—so glad—that he was running anyway. Her heavy eyelids fluttered with his jolting movements and, through the crook of Hektor's arm, she glimpsed things as they flew past: the easternmost sugar-maple lamppost; a labyrinth of twisted alleyways; fine dust falling like mist from the mud walls and thatched roofs as the huge dofaun thundered by them; firefly families flickering or going dark at the tops of the lampposts where they lived; red lanterns swaying from the patio of her favorite outdoor eatery, Cheeky Canteen. A wave of rich smells from the bistro's pots of simmering, spicy broths filled her nostrils for a moment as Atticus charged through the maze of tables, upturning benches and knocking over rows of slotted wooden drying racks. The long brown acorn noodles and curly dark strips of green seaweed that had been hanging from the latter rained onto the unsuspecting heads of a black-haired elf girl and a round-faced, honey-brown boy, who had been sweeping up.

"Sorry, Asia. Sorry, Bairon. Emergency! It's Elli," Ellishiva heard Samara call out frantically to their classmates. But if Asia and Bairon shouted anything back, it was drowned out by the loud rumble of Atticus's voice.

"Hold tight, children," he ordered grimly. "We're taking a shortcut. Aurochs Alley."

Samara gasped. "The black market? But Atticus, we're covered in blood—" The rest of her sentence was cut short as Atticus turned sharply and launched himself high into the air, over the pointed top of a tall picket fence covered in vines. Ellishiva's weight slammed into Hektor as they landed, and a dizzying spell of pain raked her limbs again.

Then they were sprinting through Aurochs Alley.

Ellishiva had never been there before, and her first, flickering thought was that the place had a nasty, uncanny silence about it. A young black bull with braided bark bands knotted around one of his horns—a friend of theirs from school—strode from the shadows, blocking their path, but Atticus roared at him and, nostrils flaring, the creature moved.

"Geb, not a good time to barter for bands. See you later," Samara hissed quietly at him behind them, but Ellishiva seemed to be the only one who heard. The fairy didn't seem surprised to see one of their schoolmates wandering around the black market, she thought groggily.

Shadowy faces were flickering past, and a hush fell over the low chatter and whispered bartering as Atticus sprang by the vendors, galloping through smoky, narrow alleyways filled with tatty carts and crates. A group of gray dire wolves swung their heads around at the scent of blood, their yellow eyes gleaming. Ellishiva shuddered.

"Hurry, Atticus!" cried Hektor in a tense voice above her. She could feel his muscles straining to keep both of them on the bear's back. It had always been exhilarating to ride on Atticus before, Ellishiva thought miserably. This day, it was terrifying.

Finally, a gleam of light came into view through the tiny chinks in another vine-covered fence. Atticus made a second huge leap, and all at once the dank alleyways were gone, replaced by sprawling patches of grass and quaint gardens.

They had reached Banyan Tree.

Overhead, countless layers of massive branches stretched away endlessly, blotting out the sky. Vāhmanas of every size and color flew about, dropping off passengers by windows on the grand limbs. Some maneuvered gracefully around the hanging nests of wasps and birds.

Even through the blurred snatches of her fading vision, Ellishiva thought that she had never beheld a more beautiful sight in all her life.

Moments later, Atticus skidded to a halt in front of a colossal aerial root. Hundreds of them stretched gracefully from the tree's huge branches to the ground, and all of them were filled with vāhmanas that took Banyan Tree's inhabitants up and down the length of its massive trunk. But this one was different than the others.

The door opened before anyone had a chance to knock on it. An elf with fair, short hair stood before them—Dorian, the head supervisor of the colony and keeper of all the vāhmanas, including the most important one of all.

"We must hurry, Dorian," said Atticus breathlessly, without preamble.

"Goodness, Atticus. I heard you coming," replied Dorian. Without wasting time on questions, he ushered them into the hollow aerial root and onto the deck of a vāhmana much like the ones floating freely outside, but this one served a more specific purpose. "Rajah Valerius Allspice! Make haste!" commanded Dorian to the vehicle's olivine orb. Ellishiva's half-closed eyes caught the glow of light as the Bluzure spice dust rose and twirled.

The vāhmana shot up through the root.

In seconds they had arrived at a hollow limb at the very top of the banyan. Atticus sprang off the vāhmana without even a grunt of farewell to Dorian, and Ellishiva glimpsed the large, irregular round windows rushing by in a blur as they flew through the empty hallway.

Finally, Atticus came to an abrupt halt before a set of double doors marked with the number forty-six. A huge iron knocker in the form of a woman's clasped hands was bolted to the surface of the left one. Ellishiva noticed a symbol carved into their smooth faces: a five-sided pattern of interconnecting grooves, etched deep into the wood. She knew that symbol. She had watched Rajah carve it herself. And, suddenly, she found she could hear the words he had spoken to her while he worked, whispering in her mind.

The lost, weary souls who see this mark will know they have returned home.

Home, Ellishiva thought as her eyes dropped closed completely. *Home . . .*

She felt Atticus shifting as if to kick open the doors, but before he could do so, there was a sharp creak and a bang as they opened by themselves. Ellishiva heard the distinct shatter of teacups from somewhere in the room beyond them. And then a green glow was pulsing beyond her shut eyelids.

Mustering more effort than she ever had in her life, Ellishiva cracked them open.

She was staring at the Khlorus-filled olivine orb at the top of a staff. And, just above it, the face of a tall person was frowning down at her. A silver beard lined his chin, and the white hair parted in the middle above his forehead flowed to his broad shoulders. On his neck was a burn scar from another time that had withered into ridges and wrinkles. His amber eyes glinted with intensity as they took her in.

Rajah, Ellishiva thought weakly.

Then her eyes closed a final time, and she thought no more.

A THOUSAND SUNS

"**B**ring her to the Hall of Nature Healing."

Ellishiva's eyelids fluttered, beckoned back to life by the sound of Rajah's voice. She felt as though years might have passed since the last time she'd closed them, but the gnarled walls of the familiar hallway rushing past told her that it had been only minutes.

"Found her . . . forest. She's fallen. Some sort of stump must have . . . punctured her side," Atticus explained, breathless and faltering, above her. Ellishiva was keenly aware of her own small body sagging in his forepaws like a tiny wet hammock. The great bear's glistening black nose twitched, making the inner tunnels of his nostrils shimmer a dark red.

A deluge of haunting echoes from the forest flooded Ellishiva's head, and a fresh stab of pain—made worse by frustration and weariness— shot through her body again, singeing even the tips of her fingers. She darted her stinging eyes about hopelessly, pleadingly, toward Rajah.

But although her guardian's grave gaze met Atticus's, Samara's, and Hektor's in turn without flinching, it never once settled on Ellishiva herself.

"We will get a better look in the Hall," he said, quickly leading the way around the sharp bend in the long, L-shaped hallway. The hem of his embroidered tunic grazed the floor as he swept on in front of them. Ellishiva wondered if anyone else could hear the tension humming underneath the composed tones of his voice.

A moment later, ruffled, galumphing footsteps caught up to them. "Elli? Is that Ellishiva?"

Ellishiva swallowed, but her throat was as dry as sandpaper. Overhead, Atticus's eyes went wide, and she felt him hustle faster after Rajah, but it was no use.

"What has happened!" shrilled the piercing voice of Lady Malinia, her caretaker and the keeper of the warren where she lived with Hektor and their little sister, Amborella. An instant later Ellishiva felt herself being smothered by a flurry of well-meaning feathers. Lady Malinia was a plump dofaun, a Burmese pigeon with a stout black beak and round rosy cheeks framed by teal and copper plumage. When Atticus at length managed to pull Ellishiva free of the panicked prodding, she could see that her caretaker was dressed in a flowing, pearl-colored tunic with an embroidered apron tied about the waist. Her feathered fingers held a delicate teacup with a faint fissure in its handle. As she puffed and clucked along beside them, she craned her neck, and her coral-pink eyes narrowed in on the blood staining Atticus's coat, and then on its source.

The teacup fell from her shaky hand and shattered into pieces on the floor.

Ellishiva tried again to swallow. Lady Malinia treasured her teacups.

The gray feathers fell back a few steps, and Ellishiva could hear the faint *thump*, *thump* of Lady Malinia slapping her chest several times, as if to resuscitate her heartbeat.

"What has happened!" she cried shrilly between sniffles. "Samara, where did you lead her to? Hektor, you are the oldest. You're supposed to take care of her. Look at all this *blood*—oh! You children are going to give me heart failure!"

"She'll be fine now," Ellishiva heard Samara murmur uncertainly.

The sniffles ceased. "Not a *word* from you!" Lady Malinia bellowed piercingly.

Samara and Hektor fell utterly silent. Lady Malinia called to Rajah over Atticus's head. "Oh, Valerius. Is she breathing?"

Ahead of them, Rajah did not reply. At last, Atticus cleared his throat and rumbled quietly, "Yes, she is alive—breathing."

Alive? thought Ellishiva, bewildered. Her thoughts flashed back to the human in the woods. Had she become the bloody elk she'd seen tossed over the man's shoulders?

"Oh, you Va'natures!" squawked Lady Malinia. Ellishiva could almost see her shaking her feathered finger at Hektor. "I told you children not to wander off into the forest, but no—not one of you listens to me! I am your caretaker. You must have wax packed in your ears to be so hard of hearing. And you, fairy child! Queen Neive shall know of this, mark my words! I simply—I do not—oh! I shall deal with you later!"

If it was possible, Ellishiva heard Samara and Hektor's trailing footsteps grow even more miserable than before.

Suddenly, up ahead, a pair of huge double doors was looming above them. Ellishiva had passed more than a few hours staring at their towering panels over the years, though she had rarely crossed their threshold. Perhaps twenty-five feet high, their dark, massive surfaces were crisscrossed with hundreds of bright, narrow streams of colorful spice water that never ceased their twinkling flow. And, for all the time she had spent gazing at the water's winding trails, she had never once seen a drop fall from the surface of the ancient wood.

They had not been standing there a moment before the living mosaic swung slowly, effortlessly, open onto the Hall of Nature Healing.

Beyond, the rounded room was huge and dim. Ellishiva saw two serious-looking dofaun fireflies, each only a bit larger than a house cat, float down into view. Midnight black, with four upper limbs and two lower ones, they hovered in their crisp white tunics, as still as pond water on a windless night. Only their perked red antennae and glistening, glossy yellow eyes gave away their concern and curiosity. As another dull wave of pain hummed through her body, Ellishiva reflected vaguely that she knew them. They were Gustav and Onuris: keepers of the Hall of Nature Healing.

"Gustav, I'm afraid we have a new patient," Rajah murmured to the elder firefly without preamble. Ellishiva let her exhausted eyelids drop closed for a moment. Not two seconds later, she felt a gentle touch on her forehead.

"She is burning up," assessed Gustav, his voice as soft as new-picked cotton. "Onuris, let us have some light."

Ellishiva forced her eyes open again in time to see the younger firefly's abdomen brighten with silver light, shedding a warm glow over the room around them.

The Hall of Nature Healing was even higher than its doors were tall. A single, vast window facing the east filled a wide piece of the wall from floor to ceiling. Endless curved shelves lined the remainder of the roughly circular interior, rising nearly up to the ceiling themselves. Every inch of their sturdy planks seemed to be packed with tools and oddities. To the right, numberless jars glinted dully from their perches, some opaque and sealed with beeswax or resin, and others fashioned of transparent glass, their roots, leaves, seeds, barks, stems, and flowers clearly visible within them. On the uppermost levels sat an array of peculiar-looking olivine jars, some tall, others squat, and still others boasting marks and colors that had been etched onto their rounded bellies. Opposite the jars, to Ellishiva's left, was a wall filled with ancient books, their cloth covers and paper pages so old that the scent of them filled the room like timeless incense. Next to the books sat the desks of the fireflies, their surfaces almost hidden under piles of rolled papyrus, brimming bottles of ink, and long bamboo styluses.

And, in the very center of the Hall, lay the Neem Table.

The Neem Table was one of the most fascinating things that Ellishiva had ever seen, heard of, or even read about. Large enough for

Atticus himself to lie on comfortably, it was fashioned from the trunk of a single massive and ancient neem tree. Its edges were covered in thick, brown bark as wrinkled as dried dates. Thousands of life rings shone brightly on its smooth amber surface in Onuris's silver light.

It was used for only one purpose.

Atticus laid Ellishiva on the table as gently as he could, though it hurt her anyway. No sooner had her skin touched the table's surface, however, than a cornucopia of small plants sprouted before her eyes.

Forgetting the pain for the briefest of instants, Ellishiva watched them grow. Small vines emerged, their stems decorated with tiny leaves of curious shapes and colors. Then one of the stalks grew thicker. Roots pushed out beneath the leaves, and a small tree sprouted, budded, and finally blossomed with pale yellow flowers. Most incredible of all though, Ellishiva knew, was that each plant, flower, or seed that grew from the table had a unique medicinal purpose.

"My fairy child!"

Ellishiva darted her gaze sideways at the sound of the sharp voice and saw Samara's wings freeze in mid-beat. The fairy's eyes went wide. "Oh no. Queen Neive," she mumbled clumsily, as though her tongue had turned to lumps of stone in her mouth.

Ellishiva watched as a figure followed the voice into the Hall, fluttering in through the open east window that she had been flying past—no doubt heading home to Fairy Alcove after a recent meeting with Rajah, who met with her and Mr. Belanos for tea in his study quite often. The queen of the fairies had all of Samara's beauty, but there was a wisdom about her sharp eyes that her student clearly lacked. Her heavy blond hair was drawn into a bun at the nape of her neck. The hem of her long, flowing silver robe dusted the floor that her feet hovered above, and a red-tipped olivine wand was tucked into the belt encircling her slim waist.

In seconds, her shrewd gaze had taken in everything.

"Do my eyes deceive me?" hissed the queen, furious. Her feet touched down on the floor at the foot of the Neem Table, and her eyes pinned Samara with a scalding glare. "What has happened here? There is *blood*!"

"You can deal with Samara later," Rajah interrupted quietly. "We need you now. Please, lend us a hand, Neive."

Queen Neive pressed her lips into a thin line, and gave a curt nod. A moment later, Ellishiva felt gentle fingers on her midriff. Carefully, the queen and Lady Malinia lifted her Puluma singlet, revealing the line of deep emerald green running up the center of her body. It stopped just below her collarbone and, from there, spread out in a tracery of delicate lines over her skin, like the veins of a leaf.

Mustering all her effort, Ellishiva strained her eyes downward as far as she could without moving her head, and quickly regretted it. A wide, ragged gash was carved into her skin, stretching from her right hip all the way to the bottom of her ribcage. Blood was everywhere—dark and bright, both dry and fresh.

Feeling suddenly dizzy, Ellishiva let her eyes roll back to stare at the ceiling again. She was almost glad that her body wasn't working properly; nothing else could have stopped her from being sick all over the beautiful Neem Table.

"Turn her," instructed Rajah on her left, his grave eyes focused on the wound. "Please, more light, Onuris."

Above them, the young firefly closed his eyes, and his silver light glowed with new intensity.

Then the gentle fingers were on Ellishiva's midriff again, pushing her carefully onto her left side. Spasms of new pain wracked her limbs, and her eyes watered. She could feel rivulets of blood striping the tattooed curves of her muscles, trickling down over her spine and her belly button. Breathless, she darted another look at Rajah.

His face was as hard as stone as he examined the wound more closely, but his eyes were filled with apprehension. Flaring his nostrils, he braced his staff on the Neem Table. Then he reached over and lifted one of Ellishiva's eyelids as high as it would go, revealing a darkening redness underneath. His face grew harder still. "Gustav," he said at last, looking up at the hovering dofaun, "prepare a Serafi poultice."

The firefly nodded and flitted away. A few seconds later, the clinking of jars made its way into Ellishiva's ears as Gustav rummaged up and down the right-hand wall, gathering elixirs and other ingredients from the shelves.

Ellishiva strove to catch Rajah's eye, wishing desperately that she could tell him everything that had happened in the forest, and in the human world. But her guardian's gaze was intent on studying the curious plants on the Neem Table.

"Valerius, this gash is most unusual," muttered Queen Neive, and once again Ellishiva felt soft fingertips on the skin of her midriff. "Have you ever seen such a thing before?"

Leaving off his examination of the plants, Rajah leaned in closer to Ellishiva's wound again. He sniffed the air above it and his nostrils flared, as though filled with a disagreeable stench. Carefully, he touched the blood around the wound and brought it to his nose. He closed his eyes. "Yes, Neive," he said heavily. "Quite unusual indeed."

On the other side of the table, Lady Malinia was shifting restlessly from foot to foot. "Oh, Valerius. Does it . . . does it remind you of—" she began nervously, haltingly.

All around her, Ellishiva saw the elders exchange a grim look.

Remind him of what? she wondered.

Rajah turned to Hektor and Samara, who looked just as lost as Ellishiva felt. "Hektor and my dear fairy child," he said firmly, "be so kind as to fetch Mr. Belanos. I left him in my study."

"We both left the study, Valerius," Queen Neive spoke up, her eyes likewise on the children, specifically Samara. "He's wandering about the Arboretum. You will find him near the waterfall. Hurry up!"

Samara and Hektor hurried from the Hall.

"Atticus," Rajah went on, turning to the great white bear. "We need

Banog. This morning he offered to transport some saplings from the Arboretum for us. He must be off the coast of Yarrabah Colony by now. When you find him, do not let him fly. Have the prefect there send you back, and make haste."

Atticus nodded silently. Rajah returned the nod, raised his staff, and uttered a mantra:

"Vahati cavati!"

Green light bloomed from the orb at the crown of his staff. Then, like the bright gashes that the Sixth Element had carved in the forest, a living cloud of Khlorus spice dust gusted from its container. It twirled around Atticus and, just like that, he was gone.

Only Rajah, Lady Malinia, and Queen Neive remained, along with the fireflies and their patient.

Banog. Fending off another little wave of pain, Ellishiva mused that, as an eagle, Banog might know something about ravens. If only she could regain the ability to ask him . . .

There was a mismatched clinking as Gustav the firefly returned with several amber-colored bottles and dried roots. Rajah nodded his thanks. "Now, Gustav, if you could please fetch me the spice dust."

The dofaun was off before Rajah had finished the sentence, already combing through the large olivine jars on the upper shelves. Rajah turned to Onuris. "Ellishiva's jar is in my study, but no, I don't need hers for this. Please tell Mr. Belanos to bring me the jar with the Silverdine spice dust we were viewing earlier."

The glow in the Hall dimmed for a moment as Onuris rushed off and Gustav, taking up the torch, illuminated his own abdomen with the silver, bioluminescent light.

Ellishiva was puzzled. Rajah never kept her spice jar in his study. And Silverdine? Was he going to record her? Now? With someone else's jar? She struggled to keep her heavy eyelids open, but it was getting harder and harder to think. Faint, needle-sharp red prickles were beginning to flicker across her vision.

Next to her, Rajah took up his staff once more, touched its green orb to the table, and whispered a mantra.

The ancient wood glowed. A pod on one of the peculiar plants to Ellishiva's left opened, revealing round green seeds. Before anyone could touch them, however, the tiny kernels turned brown and fell to the table like stone beads.

Lady Malinia shuddered and let out a ruffled breath of air, then began to dab the sweat beading on Ellishiva's face with the hem of her apron, stroking her head and pushing her hair aside.

Ellishiva wished she would stop. The tiny red pricks behind her eyes were spreading. In seconds it had become unbearable, as though fire ants were swarming through her body, stinging her from the inside out. If she could have screamed, she thought, it would have shattered the huge east-facing window of the Hall of Nature Healing. And then something even odder happened.

She fell away.

It was like watching one of her own dreams unfold. She was inside her physical self, she knew, and yet she also seemed to be watching the still figure on the Neem Table from a great distance. What very little control she had had over herself evaporated like steam from a summer puddle.

Something strange had taken over her body, and it no longer belonged to her.

Her heavy eyelids closed. She felt her chest heave with several deep breaths. She saw the world turn wholly red behind her eyes.

Then she opened them.

It was easy—effortless, even. She stretched them wide and felt them sparkle with a great rush of life. For the first time since the forest, the pain was gone. And, at last, Rajah was looking directly at her. Yet somehow this brought her no comfort, and no relief. Rather, she studied him back coldly, as though she hadn't seen him for eons.

"She is possessed, Valerius," gasped Queen Neive in a whisper. "Under some great spell."

Ellishiva's eyes roamed the Hall of Nature Healing without her control, as though they had never seen it before. Lady Malinia made a strangled sound in her throat and pulled her feathered hands away, as if Ellishiva's body had suddenly become a hot poker. So much the better.

She could not move her limbs, she found—vexing, but no matter. There was one power yet within her reach. Her parched lips parted.

"*Ahaṃ āgacchati pitu. Asmi chaṭṭha dhātu. Carima disā canda. Ahaṃ āgacchati pitu. Ahaṃ āgacchati pitu . . .*"

Rajah leaned closer to her. Lady Malinia gave a frightened sob, as if she had been stung. "Since when can this child speak in the Pali tongue!" She slapped one feathery hand to her bosom. "That language is endangered! It has not been spoken since—oh Valerius, since—"

"Compose yourself, Malinia," chided Rajah shortly, his eyes still fixed intently on Ellishiva's.

"What is this Sixth Element? The last quarter moon?" demanded Lady Malinia, undaunted, between frantic sobs. "What do these words *mean*, Valerius? Destruction to *whom*?"

Ellishiva was barely aware of their exchange. The hot prickling was returning. Gradually at first, then with full force, it surged back and then faded, replaced by a violent, bone-shaking roar, as though gallons of blood were all rushing back into her head at the same time.

When it finally ended, the dream was over, and the pain returned tenfold.

Her eyes fluttered open weakly. Everything that had just happened was fuzzy in her head, as though it had been painted over with a thick coat of sea mist. Lady Malinia was sobbing. Rajah was no longer looking at her, but his face was a shade greener than before, just as Queen Neive's was a shade redder.

Ellishiva's stomach turned. She felt her breath catch and, of their own accord, sick heaving sounds began to rise in her throat.

Rajah threw a glance at Lady Malinia, who only shook her head at him in horror, then clutched her apron to her beak. Her plump, feathered body trembled with fear.

"Compose yourself, Malinia. It is nothing," said Rajah. But he didn't sound convinced.

In Ellishiva's throat, the heaving sounds grew harsher and louder. Lady Malinia began to stroke Ellishiva's face with her apron again, hesitantly at first. Then, throwing caution to the wind, she bent and showered her forehead with gentle pecks, like kisses. "Valerius, the child is in pain! Can you not do something?" she snapped.

Rajah did not respond. He seemed lost in thought or concentration, his fingers gathering up the fallen red seeds, then plucking furiously at the array of other petals, flowers, and leaves growing on the Neem Table. Using a mortar and pestle that Gustav had brought down with the bottles earlier, he began to crush them into a poultice, a soft paste. Gustav himself had returned and was close at hand, adding dried roots, honey, and turmeric to the mixture as needed.

"My poor, poor spice children," cried Lady Malinia half to herself, her voice trembling. Her sniffles grew into sobs again. "We must not relive another Madagascar Massacre, Valerius. We *must* not! My poor heart is weak. It cannot take such sorrow anymore," she blubbered, pressing her damp apron to her eyes.

"There, there, dear Malinia," soothed Rajah, but there was a note of tension underneath his words, and he pounded the poultice harder. "The past is the past. Let it be."

Through the relentless heaving in her chest, Ellishiva fought to understand what they were talking about. *Madagascar Massacre?* She wracked her brain, but it was no use. She knew that she had never read about a Madagascar Massacre in any of her books.

The fairy queen, who had not said a word for several minutes, now touched her olivine wand to the Neem Table's surface until the tip glowed bright red. Then she lifted it gingerly, and waved a fine drizzle of pure water over Ellishiva's wound. The blood only hissed and fizzed for a few seconds, sending up tiny tendrils of smoke, until the last wisp faded away without a trace, as if it had never been.

Another spasm of pain rolled through Ellishiva, and the heaving in her chest grew still more violent. She felt something wet at the corners of her mouth, but whether it was foam or vomit she had no way of knowing.

Do something, she pleaded with her guardian silently. But although his hands worked as fast as she had ever seen them, Rajah's poultice was still incomplete.

There was a scuffling of footsteps at the door, and from the corner of her eye Ellishiva noticed Mr. Belanos, an elf, hurrying into the Hall. The fitted black tunic he wore, with its neat row of antique buttons, matched his thick black hair and balm-coated eyebrows. His face was kind and wise, and his brown eyes were warm. He looked like (and, Ellishiva knew from experience, he was) a person with many interesting things to say. Under his arm, she glimpsed a squat, unusual olivine jar. The olivine itself was tinged a strange yellow color, and the whole of the jar seemed to be encased by a red mace of sorts that curled down its sides in uneven, red streaks.

Trailing alongside the elf was a small, round-faced Va'nature girl of about six. A doll dangled from her hand. Mr. Belanos's free hand rested soothingly on top of her head of leonine, fiery red hair—as fine as the lacy network of mace that covered the nutmeg seed. Around her fern-green neck were scatterings of small, tattooed oblong marks in the shape of nutmeg shells. Ellishiva's heart sank. This girl was Amborella Nutmeg, her younger sister.

Hektor and Samara slunk in after them. Ellishiva noticed that her brother still looked as shocked and silent as he had when he'd left. Samara, on the other hand, was out of breath, and it did not take a detective—or, for that matter, a best friend—to know that she must have been telling Mr. Belanos all the details of what had happened on the way over.

Finally, Onuris dashed back in as well, and the Hall became twice as bright.

"Make haste, Belanos!" called Rajah, still mixing the healing paste as quickly as he was able. "I need just a touch more honey on this poultice, Gustav."

"Elli? Elli!" cried the little red-haired Va'nature, slipping from Mr. Belanos's grasp and dashing to her sister's side. Ellishiva struggled to move her mouth, but it was useless. Amborella turned her huge eyes on their guardian. "Rajah, what happened to Elli?" Her lower lip quivered.

"Samara, Hektor, I told you to bring Mr. Belanos, not Amborella," Rajah scolded, his troubled eyes never leaving the mortar.

Queen Neive shot a hard look at Samara, who pretended not to notice, keeping her gaze fixed instead on Mr. Belanos. The black-haired elf quietly joined Rajah on Ellishiva's left side at the Neem Table. Carefully, he set the olivine spice jar atop the wooden surface, next to the odd plants by her ankles.

"Open it, please, Belanos," said Rajah, still not looking up from his poultice-making. "I removed the enchantments earlier. The Silverdine will do nothing more than take note of what is about to happen here."

Mr. Belanos nodded, and a line of concern creased his forehead. Gingerly, he twisted off the olivine jar's lid.

Ellishiva's eyelids were drooping again, but through the red-brown screen of her eyelashes she could see the Silverdine spice dust streaming about the room. Visions of smoke faces and whispers of old voices swam in the faintly glistening vapor as it rose ever higher toward the ceiling until, suddenly, the silvery wisps gathered together—like a puff of shimmering cloud—many feet above the Neem Table. The light it shed was broad enough to rival Gustav and Onuris as it hovered calmly in midair, watching, listening.

"Can you hear me, Elli? Elli?" Amborella was pleading in a small voice next to her ear. "It's me." The tears welled slowly in her little sister's big round eyes.

Ellishiva tried to move, to make a sound of response, anything. But the wetness at the corners of her mouth only dribbled down her jaw, and her heaving worsened at the effort.

"What happened to her, Hektor?" asked Amborella, turning to look at her brother beside her, as though she were sure *he* would know the answer. But Hektor only stood dumbly by the table, motionless.

"Shh. Not now, Amborella," soothed Mr. Belanos, laying a comforting hand on Hektor's shoulder. The he looked pointedly at Samara and nodded. Ellishiva heard her friend take a shaky breath.

"Rajah, I—I think Elli drank some water in the forest and it . . . tasted funny," she began unsteadily, then stopped, stealing a fearful glance at Queen Neive.

Rajah paused in his work and focused on the pale-faced, twitching fairy child.

"Samara, you must tell us everything that happened," Ellishiva's guardian told her best friend seriously. "I can assure you that Queen Neive will not interfere. You will not be punished for it."

"Well," resumed Samara after a long moment, obviously choosing her words carefully before letting them past her lips. "We were running—you know, just playing around, that's all. And we were thirsty, so Elli got some leaf water from a locust tree, but then later . . . something strange happened. The leaves on the tree turned black with—with ravens, and then—then they flew up and disappeared. Elli said the water tasted salty, briny, but I never tasted it." Samara paused, stealing a wary sideways glance at Queen Neive before continuing. "So then we started running again. I was flying ahead, leading her home—safely, you know," Ellishiva heard a tremor creep into Samara's voice. "Then she disappeared, and Atticus found her again first, and when we were coming home she was telling him something about humans and—and a fairy's heart, and I think she saw it, Rajah. I think she was in the human world," she finished abruptly, breathless.

For a moment, Ellishiva felt a flutter of hope. Then Queen Neive spoke.

"Samara!" hissed the queen sharply. "Are you making up stories *again*? And at a time like this? Oh, I have exhausted my patience with you, child."

The hopeful spark died away, ripped apart by the heaving in her chest. If they didn't believe Samara's story, Ellishiva thought miserably, what would they think of hers?

"Now, now, Neive," Mr. Belanos murmured quietly.

"Thank you, Samara," said Rajah, and Ellishiva couldn't tell by the tone of his voice whether or not he had taken the fairy's words to be the truth. "Would you care to add anything to that, Hektor?" he asked.

But Hektor only shook his head. His shoulders fell.

Rajah nodded, and resumed putting the final touches on his poultice. Next to him, Amborella was still whimpering piteously. "Come here, Amber," he said, not pausing in his work this time.

Lady Malinia's feathers ruffled as if to object, but Mr. Belanos touched her arm across the table, hushing her gently.

Amborella tucked herself against Rajah's leg, never taking her gaze off of Ellishiva. "It will be all right, child," their guardian murmured soothingly. "Ellishiva was hurt in the forest. She fell down while she was running and hurt her side, but she will be better soon. You, too, have fallen down running before, have you not?"

Ellishiva had been listening to this lie—that she had fallen in the forest—without being able to correct it for far too long. And, this time, it was the final straw. A black, blazing anger scorched through her like an erupting volcano.

Then a new wave of prickling red needles flashed across her vision, and she froze, reining her fury back into check. But it was too late. The rage scorched on, and it was not her own any longer.

She had let it back in.

As the red flames mushroomed inside of her and she began to drift back to that distant place, however, something odd happened: her own smothered anger came back. Through the burning of her lungs and heart, through the heaving of her aching chest, she dug deep for her resolve, and seized it. She put her foot down.

She fought back.

But the Sixth Element was not so easily frightened off. It met Ellishiva's resistance with a new rage of its own, buffeting against her like a howling wind ripping through the boughs of an old tree. Ellishiva struggled with every ounce of her will to hold her ground, but the strength of her attacker was too great. She could feel the awful creature nudging her, inch by inch, out of her own body, and she knew that she could not keep it at bay forever.

Then she felt something cool and damp spreading over the wound in her side. The pain in her aching body dulled; the heaving in her chest became less ragged. *Rajah's poultice*, she thought.

And, with a final gasp of effort, she pushed back against the Sixth Element.

As though from far away, she heard someone shout, "Step back!" And then Rajah's voice was speaking a loud, powerful mantra, over and over again.

"Tikicchati ima itthatta! Katākāra kando nissesa! Tikicchati ima itthatta! Katākāra kando nissesa! Tikicchati ima itthatta! Katākāra kando nissesa!"

There was a flash of bright green that could only have been the olivine orb at the top of Rajah's staff. And then, like drops of dye diluting in pure water, the vibrant glow of Khlorus dust began to penetrate the red and black fog of Ellishiva's vision. It was followed by a hum that enveloped her completely, as though the entire Neem Table were shaking. Somewhere in the distance, a cacophony of thumping and rattling picked up, as of books falling from shelves, bottles and jars clanking against each other, and parchment fluttering off of desks in a heady tornado of wind.

Ellishiva was aware of her head and feet staying fixed to the table, yet, strangely, the center of her body seemed to be rising—as though something within her was fighting, longing to get out.

And then it did.

With the fire of a thousand green suns, the force inside her doused the hold of the Sixth Element and burst free. It blazed out of the tattooed lines and circles on her body, launching itself upward, and taking her with it.

In mere fractions of an instant the stupendous light had engulfed the great Hall and surpassed it, shooting high into the blackness above Mannahatta. Ellishiva couldn't think—couldn't even try to think. The speeding light shimmered with heat and sound as it rocketed through the sky, absorbing her until she was no longer herself.

She *was* the light.

When it reached the abyss of ether encircling the earth, it stopped. There was a moment of suspension, as if time itself were standing still, and dead silence.

Then it fell, plunging down through all the levels of the atmosphere like a meteor. And the only thing she felt when it finally collided with the ground was a vast and painless burst, as of billions and billions of brilliant green seeds scattering over the tremendous expanse of Earth.

THE FORBIDDEN STUDY

Ellishiva awoke again to a cramp in her side. She stirred and opened her eyes—crusted with sleep—just a slit. Around her, the room was dim, with only the first slivers of silvery, crack-of-dawn light trickling through the vast window in the eastern wall of the Hall of Nature Healing. She was still lying on the Neem Table, she saw, though a thin leaf mattress had been slipped between the hard wood and her body to cushion it. Gingerly, she stretched her stiff limbs, feeling the pinch of her wound again. She let a quiet breath out through her nostrils.

How long have I been asleep? she wondered.

For a long time Ellishiva lay motionless, struggling to unearth the answer to this question. All that came to her, however, were the fuzzy dreams—or had they been real?—of many visitors: Amborella, confessing something about haunting nightmares and her doll. Hektor, staring solemnly down at her. Samara, apologizing and chattering on endlessly, telling her stories about gathering clues from the black market, though what exactly she was gathering them for, Ellishiva couldn't recall. A sobbing Lady Malinia, holding her in her arms like a baby, feeding her soup, giving her warm sponge baths.

She could recall no dreams of Rajah.

Ellishiva pulled the hemp sheet all the way up to her chin and frowned at the high, dark ceiling. In the past, Rajah had scarcely ever left her side. She thought of their quiet walks together, their calm and inspiring lessons in the Arboretum, the mixture of sweet, warm spices—allspice—that was his comforting scent. But wrack her brain as she might, Ellishiva could come up with no explanation for her guardian's new, distant behavior.

There had been other, less familiar dream-visitors, as well. Old, majestic warriors, flying here and there about the Hall on strong, transparent wings. All of them wore the same uniform: a tunic of overlapping scales sewn onto a hemp backing, all of it over coarse, tough leggings and knee-high boots.

One of them in particular floated to the surface of her thoughts. He was a younger version of his elders, perhaps not much older than Ellishiva herself, with an earnest, intelligent, sienna-colored face. Thick, almost leonine white hair hung to his shoulders, and he had a pointed nose and fire-yellow eyes. She could not recall anything that he had said to her—only that his voice was soothing, almost sweet. Ellishiva felt a sudden urge to talk to him, not least of all because he was, like the others, a kinnaran.

"Kinnarans . . . here on Mannahatta," she murmured to herself. "Why?" She frowned up at the ceiling, struggling to think. Around her, the silent intimacy of dawn roamed the Hall with timeless patience.

Then, all at once, she remembered.

Ellishiva sat bolt upright on the Neem Table. The thin strap from her cotton nightgown slipped down over her shoulder, and she tugged it up again automatically. Dark, horrible memories flitted mercilessly through her head: the corrupt locust tree in the woods . . . the pulsing, disembodied fairy heart . . . the human world . . . the Sixth Element . . . the ravens. A spasm pinched her side and she touched her fingers to the bandage there, breathless.

Her first thought was Rajah. He would know what to do, would know what was going on. He *must* know about the ravens, at least. But Rajah was avoiding her, she remembered, biting her lip in dismay. And then Queen Neive's words came back to her.

"Samara! Are you making up stories again?"

Ellishiva stared straight ahead without seeing anything, thoughts churning furiously in her head. If the adults wouldn't believe them, wouldn't help them find the answers . . . where else was there to go?

Her eyes came into focus on a row of old, dusty leather bindings. She blinked, and her heart lifted a little bit. Ellishiva had always been drawn to books—like a bee to pollen, Samara always said. Everything she'd ever needed to know, it seemed, had a book written about it somewhere.

"Ravens," she murmured, slipping off of the Neem Table and walking across the clean wood floor. She paused by the impressive window. Below, a thin gray fog hung over Mannahatta, stretching all the way to the great jungles beyond the island. The dense forest was still asleep; not even a bird broke the flat expanse of the dull sky.

Reassured by the familiar sight, Ellishiva turned away from the new morning and continued across the Hall. The door to Onuris's bedchamber, tucked as it was behind the bookshelves, was ajar. Carefully, Ellishiva peeked in. She glimpsed the firefly dofaun lying at the foot of his bed, breathing evenly. He had fallen asleep in his uniform, with an open book across his chest.

Silently, Ellishiva moved away, coming to stand before the broad, towering wall of books. For a moment, she paused and leaned against it, turning her head and inhaling the nutty scent of aged plant fibers. Then, gently, she began to run her fingers along the diverse bindings.

"Varro," she breathed, tracing her way along the shelves to the Vs. They were, thankfully, at ground level. But after a careful minute of picking through the spines, she was forced to admit that there was no author by that name in the Hall of Nature Healing.

Ellishiva leaned against the shelves again, thinking. The answer came to her quickly, though it wasn't one she liked.

"Rajah's study," she muttered. It was one of the few places forbidden to them in Banyan Tree, and she lingered unhappily where she was, hesitating. Ellishiva hated breaking rules. She'd already tried it once, following Samara to the river, and look what had come of that.

Then a tiny bolt of white-hot pain shot through her wound again. Ellishiva set her jaw.

There was no choice.

Treading quietly, she crept out of the Hall of Nature Healing. She padded down the long, dimly lit hallway, turning sharply at the bend in the L. At the foot of a lone stairway at the end of it, she paused, wishing she could climb the steps to her bedchamber and see Hektor and Amborella. But dawn was already breaking, and her window of opportunity was growing smaller by the second.

Ellishiva pushed on, turning right and hurrying through the great living hall, its fireplace still unlit. It took only moments to creep by it and steal past the empty kitchen.

And then she was slipping through the always-open doors that led into the Arboretum.

The Arboretum was a vast atrium built across several of Banyan Tree's wide upper limbs. Its vast, peaceful greenery engulfed Ellishiva like a familiar embrace. Here, she and the other Va'natures cared for and studied the numberless species of plants that grew within its various sections, from rainforests and desert plains to wide ponds with exotic flowers drifting listlessly on their mirrored surfaces. It also contained the Vivarium, where Ellishiva and her siblings brought new saplings to life. The temperature in the Arboretum was kept carefully under control by the Khlorus spice dust from Rajah's staff. With no visible walls or ceiling, the space had the feel of a rather strange enchanted forest—one that stretched on for miles and miles.

Ellishiva walked quickly through the fernery, passing the ever-unkempt jumble of wooden chairs where they ate their morning meals. A short ways away to her right stood a moss-covered basalt ledge overlooking the east side of Mannahatta, where the elders, and sometimes Ellishiva herself, practiced yoga. Samara had made a hobby of teasing Ellishiva about the discipline's many "bizarre" poses, but Ellishiva assured her it was not the poses but the meditation practice that calmed her thoughts when there were too many of them fighting for attention, and she kept at it anyway.

This morning the ledge was empty of life. Ellishiva let out a long, deep sigh. "He's not awake yet," she breathed.

Encouraged, she turned left onto a twisting pathway that led deeper into the Arboretum. Mist wove its way among the trees, coating the leaves with heavy gray drops of dew. All over the Arboretum, Ellishiva knew, these rivulets of water collected into shallow streams that then came together and poured from the upper limbs of Banyan Tree in a long, shining waterfall. Around her, the greenery was still—not even the faintest flutter of wings in the air, or the smallest whisper of a shadow moving across the ground. She inhaled deeply as she walked, and the sweet scent of unfurled jasmine filled her nostrils.

At last it came into view: the handsome, round tree house built seamlessly into the crown of a high mango tree. At its base, a spiral staircase wound up and around the tree's smooth trunk to the entrance. Its roof was thatched in flax fiber, and its round glass windows were covered in dew.

Please let him not be in his study . . . please let him not be in his study, Ellishiva thought fervently as she crossed the clearing and carefully picked her way up the stairs. At the door she halted, heart pounding, and listened. But there was only silence. She hesitated for another breath or two, wrestling with her conscience.

Then, slowly, she turned the large mahogany knob.

Rajah's private study was a small and comfortable space. The moment she stepped inside, Ellishiva was engulfed by the familiar scent of allspice berries. Just a few steps from her, to the right, stood a broad desk and high-backed chair of ancient wood. The desk was covered in neatly organized objects: reed and bamboo styluses, ink bottles, scrolls of papyrus, sealing wax. Ellishiva's eyes honed in on an olivine jar sitting on the desk's corner—one that was tinted yellow, with a mace-like covering of red stripes. She felt that she had seen it somewhere before. But she wasn't here for spice dust, and in the next moment her gaze moved on again.

Opposite her sat an unlit fireplace, a comfortable armchair resting near its hearth. Above it on the simple mantelpiece was a row of miniature ships in bottles. Next to that, beside one of the round windows on her left, stood a low table framed by two wide planter's chairs. Two or three feet away from them, a gleaming spyglass on a silver stand pointed through the glass toward the eastern sky. A once-magnificent Samarakand rug that had long ago lost its enchanting colors was spread underneath it all, over the circular floor.

And, of course, every inch of the walls was lined with shelves—all of them packed with books.

Ellishiva silently moved to the one nearest the desk and traced her finger along the many bindings. Some were bound with strips of bark; some, wrapped in tattered red linen. Several were fashioned of papyrus, while others wore covers of broad-veined leaves. Their worn spines were embellished with obscure markings, many of them accented with emerald and ochre.

It took Ellishiva only a minute to find the volume she sought: *Dendrology and Therions of the Earths*, by one Reginald Banali Varro. She pulled it from the shelf, fixing the neighboring books to make it look as though nothing had been disturbed. Then she unwound the pliable vine securing its cover, and began turning the yellowed pages with great care, releasing a miasma of ancient dust. Evidently, the book had lain undisturbed for a very long time. Ellishiva pored through it, her brow furrowed in concentration.

Ravens, she thought. *Where are you?*

She turned another page, and her eyes fell upon an illustration that showed the stages of a caterpillar developing in a chrysalis, which was anchored against the whitewashed bark of a birch tree by silken threads. Thoughtlessly, she reached out a finger and traced the image of the chrysalis on the page.

Then, oddly, her fingertip began to glow. Its light grew brighter and brighter, much as it did when she was bringing saplings to life in the Vivarium. A faint wisp of green, like spice dust, rose from the lines of her skin and traced the ink drawing on the page, following the same path that her finger had taken moments before.

The image of the chrysalis began to move, as though something inside of it were struggling to get out.

Ellishiva's eyes felt as though they were about to come out of their sockets. Her mouth dropped open and she didn't bother closing it again. All her attention was on the living paper. Millimeter by millimeter, the insect within the chrysalis emerged until it was fully free. Ellishiva stared at its frail body, which looked almost crushed. Then, stiffly, painfully, it unfolded its gossamer wings and fluttered upward, rising off the page. A fine, glistening powder fell like snow upon the sheet of papyrus that it had left. Ellishiva's heart pounded in her chest as she watched it hovering before her: a splendid—and real—Indigo Morpho butterfly.

Before she could even begin to make sense of what had happened, however, she heard light footsteps coming up the stairs.

Oh no. Ellishiva jerked her head toward the door. A shock of fear rattled through her. *Oh no, oh no, oh no.*

Not even breathing, she clutched the still-open book to her belly and dashed for the only shelter in the room, bumping against one leg of the furniture as she ducked to the floor on the far side of one of the high planter's chairs. Her free hand flew up to cover her mouth as she stared with dread at the doorknob.

The footsteps grew louder. Ellishiva's wide eyes burned from not blinking, and her cheeks grew warm with horror—as though she'd already been caught.

The door opened.

Rajah walked through it and crossed over to his desk, where the Morpho butterfly was still fluttering about carelessly, oblivious. Her guardian's sharp eyes honed in on it, and narrowed. Standing perfectly still, he sniffed the air. Then, slowly, he turned his head.

Ellishiva crouched as low to the ground as she could, willing herself to blend in with the pale wood of the planter's chair, and shut her eyes tight.

"Curious," murmured Rajah quietly to himself. "How did you get here?"

Ellishiva realized that he was talking to the butterfly. Slowly, she opened her eyes. He hadn't seen her . . . yet. Carefully, she peeked up over the curved seat of the chair and glimpsed Rajah inspecting every object on his desk, then turning to his bookshelf.

Silently crouching down again, Ellishiva tried to get ahold of the deluge of questions tumbling lawlessly through her head. Was this her moment to speak to Rajah? To tell him about everything that had happened to her? Would he believe her, or would he accuse her of making up stories like Queen Neive had accused Samara?

Would he listen to her at all, if he knew that she had broken his trust by entering his forbidden study?

A stirring of resentment flared among her thoughts. Why *didn't* she have any dream-memories of Rajah coming to see her in the Hall, when so many mystifying things were happening to her all at once? She bit her tongue. Then again, could she really hold it against her guardian that he hadn't put in an appearance in *her* dreams?

Ellishiva pressed her lips together, and stayed rooted to the floor. As much as she longed to talk to Rajah about everything, she couldn't risk being grounded. Not now. Not when she needed answers about what had attacked her—and whether it was going to attack anyone else.

Across the room, Rajah had picked up the yellow olivine jar with the red stripes. He strode to the door with it. "Some yoga will do me good," he muttered quietly to himself. Then, on the threshold, he turned and held out his hand. The butterfly landed softly in the palm of it. "I shall take you to Nicobar," he said to it, his voice soft. "I am sure Reginald Banali Varro will wonder how you came out of his pages."

Then, with a muted *swish* of his long robes, he left the study.

Ellishiva waited until the faintest of his footsteps had died away completely. She took a few deep, long breaths, touching her wound, which was pinching her with little smarts of pain again. Every cell in her body wanted to bolt out of the study and into the safety of the vast Arboretum again, but she forced herself to stay where she was. She knew how long it took Rajah to do his yoga regimen. For the moment, at least, she was safe.

Refocusing on her task with an effort, Ellishiva lowered her eyes to the open pages of the book again, reading much faster this time. The purplish sky of dawn shed light on the words through the round glass window. Still, it was taking too long. Tensely, she flipped to the index section. Her fingers trailed down the listed names of species, careful not to touch the paper itself this time, only pausing when they finally found what they were looking for.

"Ravens," she whispered, turning to the noted page number. Under her breath, she read: *"Ravens are intelligent creatures. Messengers, they may travel freely to and from the in-between world: the world of Pātāla. They roam the skies at will, grandest and most powerful at night. In the annals of time they have been summoned as spies for dark evil, and have served many renowned sorcerers . . ."*

Ellishiva paused for a moment. "Dark evil," she muttered, her gaze falling pensively on the silver spyglass. In her head, she could still hear the hiss of the locust tree, echoing as though it would never stop. *The Sixth Element is upon you.*

Ellishiva sat poring over the words until the first thin rays of the morning sun crept over the faded rug and glinted on her golden toe ring. She drew in a sharp breath as time caught up with her. Rajah would be finished with his yoga soon.

Scrambling to her feet, she hurried with the book over to the broad desk. Opening a drawer, she found a stack of blank papyrus sheets half-buried under a collection of old olivine orbs. Ellishiva snatched up a sheet of papyrus, sat down in the high-backed chair, and dipped the first stylus she could reach into the nearest pot of ink. Quickly, almost scribbling, she wrote:

Who are you?

What is a Sixth Element, when there are only five: ether, water, matter, fire, and air?

How did you enter our world?

Why do you want us to feel your suffering?

What kind of destruction will happen on the last quarter moon?

Why do you speak Pali language?

It was you who ripped out that fairy's heart? But how? And who gave you life before that?

A faint sound outside made her jump. Craning her neck briefly at the door, she quickly dipped the stylus in the ink one more time, and wrote:

Madagascar Massacre??

She blew on the wet words, fanned the papyrus a few times, and then folded the whole sheet into a rough square, which she tucked away in the only safe place she could think of: the band of her underwear next to her hip, beneath her nightgown. Then she closed the book and returned it to its place on the shelf, muttering, "I bet Jipsin Smilodon would know something about this Sixth Element."

When everything had been replaced exactly as she'd found it, Ellishiva crept over and peeked through the streaks of dew on the easternmost window. Outside, the Arboretum was nearly as still and empty as she had left it. Rajah was nowhere to be seen.

Quietly, she opened the study door and made her escape. The sun exploded on the horizon as she made her way back to the warren. She watched the morning star rise until it was round and burning—a deep, saffron red, like an overripe mango. Ellishiva kept up a steady pace as she hurried along the twisted pathway, halting only when she reached the breakfast fernery. There she paused and, a little breathless, risked a glance up at the yoga ledge.

Rajah was still at his *Surya Namaskara* practice, his front facing away from her and his arms open as if to embrace the world before him. Nearby, the butterfly from the book sunned itself, perched atop the familiar olivine jar. There was something serene about them, posed there in the pale morning light, Ellishiva thought. Something reassuring. Something whole.

For one brief moment, she thought about interrupting him. Then she shook her head and, soundlessly, crept out of the Arboretum, back inside.

Ellishiva moved on silent feet past the kitchen (Lady Malinia, thankfully, was not yet preparing breakfast), down through the comfortable living hall with the unlit fireplace, past the foyer and the stairs to her bedchamber, and back along the L-shaped hallway.

When she entered the Hall of Nature Healing, her heart jumped into her throat.

"Walle? What are you doing here?" she whispered.

Hovering above the Neem Table was a small firefly dofaun, only a bit larger than a house cat. His friendly face was as round as a baby's, with an eager expression and big, bright black eyes. His antennae quivered with excitement at the sight of her.

Ellishiva let out a breath of relief. Then she walked up to him and planted a kiss on his plump cheek. "I'm so glad to see you," she said truthfully, pulling him into a hug.

Walle's wings folded closed, and his lower body shone bright red. Ellishiva grinned and set him down at the foot of the table, then climbed back into the makeshift bed herself and tugged the sheet up to her neck, just in case someone wandered in. "How are you?" she asked.

"Doing well, Elli," said Walle, beaming. "I've been coming to see you every morning. You've been asleep a long time," he added, taking flight again and hovering closer to Ellishiva's face.

"Really? Every morning?" she said, smiling at him. Then the smile became a frown. "How long have I been here?" she asked.

"Um. Over a fortnight, at least," replied Walle. One of his antennae gave a small, nervous twitch. "Er, where were you coming from, Elli?" he asked uncertainly, scratching the twitchy antenna with one of his upper limbs.

For a long moment, Ellishiva did not reply, sizing the little firefly up. Then, "From Rajah's study," she admitted finally.

Walle gasped. His eyes went wide, and his antennae hummed admiringly. "You did that by yourself, Elli? Without Sam?" he breathed. "You are so bold."

Ellishiva felt her cheeks go pink. No one was used to *her* breaking the rules, least of all Ellishiva herself. She *had* been rather bold, she supposed. For a moment, she wasn't entirely sure that she disliked the feeling. Then she caught her own thoughts, and cleared her throat. "So . . . so what's happened since my attack?" she queried, trying for a careless shrug of her shoulders.

"Oh. Strange things, Elli," Walle told her in a low voice. "Sam said that light burst out of you like—like a thousand suns that night." The firefly flailed all four of his upper limbs to demonstrate.

Ellishiva lay quietly where she was, listening to him and thinking about the butterfly in Rajah's study. Finally, she took a breath and asked, "What light?"

"You don't remember, Elli?" gasped Walle. His face was as red as his glowing abdomen now, flushed with awe and excitement. "Mother said that she thought the world was coming to an end. The clouds were churning like—like seas on fire," he gushed, his black eyes going wide again at the memory. Then he gave a little smile, and added, "But not many other dofauns could see the colors at night, 'cause—"

"'Cause you can see night as clear as day," interrupted Ellishiva, a little louder than she had meant to. She winced, then pulled the firefly closer so that they'd be able to speak more quietly.

Walle nodded, and went on in a dark whisper. "Mother was so afraid. Even I was. Oh, and listen to this—some people are actually glad it happened!" His antennae drooped like wet hair around his face.

Ellishiva stared at him, dumbfounded. "Why?" she blurted.

"They've been watching the clusters of foxfire around Central Pond," Walle explained nervously. "Ever since the light came out of your body, the foxfire has been growing bigger and brighter. Ahpa says it will be the best crop of Bluzure spice dust in generations, this coming Foxfire Harvest."

Ellishiva raised her eyebrows. "Your father said that?"

Walle nodded. "Yes, Elli, my ahpa said so."

"Light. From *my* body?" muttered Ellishiva. She looked at him sharply. "Has my name been in *The Times*? Are people talking?" she asked anxiously.

"No, not even your name, Elli," Walle assured her. "Everyone thinks that you just fell and got hurt. I only know the truth because . . . because Sam told me. Nobody else believes her though. Queen Neive says she's making up stories again." He gulped down a gasp of air, and went on. "But *The Times* is reporting the strange weather patterns. Patches of dark clouds have been—have been drifting over Mannahatta unexpectedly and—and some of the dofauns are going crazy with it, Elli. They're saying it's a plague from the human world. Rajah issued a proclamation that said it was just nonsense— just a strange weather pattern. But even he advised people not to walk alone," he trailed off, breathless.

"So people are buying this nonsense," said Ellishiva in disbelief. "And Rajah is lying to them! Why?"

"Don't know, Elli," the little firefly said, shaking his head. "I'm not sure the dofauns believe him, though. If you ask me, I think they're only waiting for the Foxfire Harvest to be over; then they'll all bolt away to some other colony."

Ellishiva nodded grimly. "You've seen Sam, then?" she asked.

"Yes. Well, Sam . . . ," began Walle, his antennae humming nervously again. "Sam was arguing with Gustav. Um, a lot. She kept flying in through the window whenever she pleased," he gestured with one upper arm at the huge wall of glass behind them, "and Gustav didn't like that, so she's not allowed in here anymore, actually. I'm studying under Onuris for part of my hands-on summer lessons, though. How to make elixirs. So I get to see you every day," he added proudly.

Ellishiva mustered a half-smile. "That's great. Maybe you can teach me how to make them, too," she suggested.

"Oh, I doubt that Elli. You know so much more than me," blushed Walle, hiding a giggle with two of his front limbs. His drooping antennae perked up a bit.

Ellishiva loved making Walle laugh. Nevertheless, it didn't take long for the stony look to settle over her face again. "I need to get to Bear Market. To see Jipsin Smilodon," she confided lowly.

Walle gave her a bleak look. "They say Jipsin Smilodon has been setting up his shop in the black market lately," he replied darkly. "I heard it's even more dangerous than it used to be, these days." He gave a little shudder, and the glow from his abdomen dimmed for a moment.

"Why would Jipsin Smilodon be in Aurochs Alley?" wondered Ellishiva, frowning.

"Don't know," faltered Walle. "Maybe the dark clouds are making him go mad like the others. But most dofauns don't have those long, killer canines." He gave a little shudder. Then, obviously trying to sound braver than he felt, he took a deep breath and said, "Elli, we're not allowed in the black market. And . . . and you're already wounded. What if something else happens to you?"

Ellishiva was not eager to dwell on yet another rule that she would, more likely than not, have to break. "Did anyone else come to see me?" she asked, changing the subject.

The firefly's black eyes brightened. "Kinnarans are here, Elli," he breathed, as though he himself could scarcely believe it. "They've been in here almost as much as I have, and they look at you as if—as if you were the Oudleef Tree in the window at Wallaby's Emporium."

"Hmm," Ellishiva murmured to herself under her breath. "So it wasn't a dream."

"They've been arriving from Nicobar," Walle went on, "almost every day, Elli, since—since your attack."

Ellishiva scowled and muttered, "That just proves that something's wrong. People ought to use their common sense about those clouds. It's not safe here." She sighed, a heavy thing that seemed to come from her very bones, and fixed a bleak look on Walle. "I saw terrible things in the forest," she admitted lowly. "Horrible, horrible things."

There was a faint rustling behind the bookshelves nearest the doors.

Ellishiva grabbed Walle by his closest arm. "Onuris must be awake," she hissed, talking fast. "I'll pretend to be in a deep sleep. You go by the window and act like you're just coming in when you see him. Hurry!"

She released his arm and Walle obediently dashed away. Ellishiva went limp on the Neem Table, shutting her eyes tight.

In no time at all, Onuris was flying over to check on his patient. Ellishiva waited until she felt his touch on her forehead and heard him whisper unhappily, "Oh no. Heating up again, are you? Strange little spice girl."

Then, and only then, did she turn her head, rub her eyes, and give a great, convincing yawn.

"Oh my," gasped Onuris. "You keep surprising me, Ellishiva." He glanced over his shoulder in time to see Walle dashing back into the Hall. "Make haste, Walle. Go bring me a fiber sponge! Ellishiva is awake, but she is heating up again, I fear. Terribly strange. I must retrieve the elixir."

Ellishiva watched Onuris flutter up to one of the towering shelves along the wall to her right, amber bottles clinking indignantly against each other as he combed through them for the one he sought.

Walle returned with the sponge, and Ellishiva smiled at him, pressing her index finger to her lips. The firefly grinned impishly back at her, and whispered in her ear. "Elli, you're getting pretty good at lying. Just like Sam."

Ellishiva couldn't tell whether she felt more distressed or pleased by this.

Before she could figure it out, however, Onuris was back at her side, waving an uncorked bottle of amber liquid beneath her nose. The last thought on her mind before the heady scent nudged her off to sleep again was Jipsin Smilodon in the black market—and how to find a way to see him.

* * *

It was the first thing on her mind when she woke up again later that afternoon, as well. Ellishiva lay where she was in the quiet of the Hall of Nature Healing for a long time, thinking. Planning.

When she was as sure as she could be that it would work, she got Onuris's attention and asked if she could be released. The firefly looked at her doubtfully, but although the wound in her side pinched now and then, Ellishiva *was* feeling better, and her fever had gone. In the end, reluctantly, he let her go.

Her welcome back to the warren was a warm one. Amborella threw her arms around Ellishiva's waist, making her wince from the sudden smart of pain in her side, but Ellishiva didn't pull away. Hektor didn't say much, but the relief was evident in his eyes. Lady Malinia fussed over her and added her usual place setting to the others for supper, clucking on and on about her terrible fall.

Ellishiva managed to bite her tongue until the third time the well-meaning dofaun brought it up. Then, spying her moment, she steeled her jittery nerves and reminded Lady Malinia of the teacup that had broken on that terrible night when Ellishiva had "fallen."

Lady Malinia nodded sadly, as at the memory of a lost friend. "It was indeed a fine cup, that one," she sighed.

Ellishiva nodded sadly back. Then, trying to sound as though the idea had just come to her, she suggested, "Maybe we should visit Mr. Belanos's antiquities shop at Bear Market tomorrow. To find a replacement for it."

Lady Malinia brightened up instantly. She began clucking excitedly about how the outing would do Ellishiva good, the quality of the goods in Mr. Belanos's shop, and the delightfulness of Mr. Belanos himself.

Ellishiva stopped listening after the first few sentences. Across the table, Hektor shot her a suspicious look, but she ignored him, her thoughts already skipping ahead to the next part of the plan. Mr. Belanos's shop was not in the black market, but it was as close as she could get to Aurochs Alley without anyone becoming suspicious. And she was going to need every advantage she could get.

The questions for Jipsin Smilodon piled on top of one another in her head. He might not have the answers to all of them. But Ellishiva knew without a doubt that he would be a good starting point to begin gathering clues on the Sixth Element.

THE DETOUR

The next day the wind was warm, and the sky was painted in waves of thin white clouds that looked like floating sandbars.

Ellishiva stood by the great window in the Hall of Nature Healing, holding her cream-colored tunic up halfway, exposing her midriff. Sunlight poured through the glass, catching on her long, loose tresses and her golden toe ring, as Onuris hovered around her, carefully applying fresh strips of cotton gauze to her wound. The air smelled of calendula and balsamo.

"Are you sure you are ready for this outing, Ellishiva?" fussed Onuris as he worked.

"I'm ready. Anyway, it was all Lady Malinia's idea to go to Bear Market," Ellishiva told him, tamping down a little wince of guilt at the lie.

"I suppose," said Onuris, wrapping the thin gauze around her midriff a final time. He did not sound convinced.

"When is Rajah coming back from Nicobar?" asked Ellishiva in as bright a voice as she could muster. Her guardian had left for the distant colony early yesterday to deliver the butterfly she'd brought to life, as he'd said he would, she supposed. Then, before the dofaun could answer, she mustered a little courage and blurted on, "You know, I don't remember him coming to see me here, when I was injured. Do . . . do you think he's upset with me, Onuris?" She strove to keep her voice casual, but the strain and hurt crept into it all the same.

"Now, don't get sentimental, Ellishiva," chided Onuris crisply, keeping his eyes focused intently on the gauze. "You should reflect on the time you've spent with Rajah. He cares for you deeply, but he is very busy in these tiring times." He paused, and one of his antennae stiffened. "How did you know he went to Nicobar?" he inquired suspiciously.

Ellishiva just shrugged, and studied the mysterious dofaun back, wondering what he meant by "tiring times."

At last, Onuris shook his head and continued. "Well, you did not hear that from me. But he is away on important business."

Ellishiva stood mutely, staring out at the bright day, as the firefly began securing the ends of the gauze with tiny pins. "I did have many other visitors, didn't I?" she muttered at last.

"Indeed, you have many admirers," agreed Onuris. "Dofauns, fairies—even kinnarans! But you were ever drifting in and out of consciousness, Ellishiva. I am surprised that you are able to recall anyone at all." He fastened the last of the pins in place, suppressing a faint yawn. Ellishiva wondered if he'd fallen asleep with a book again.

She released the cloth folds of her tunic, letting them drop to her hips so that they overlapped her three-quarter-length trousers. It bulged where the bandage was, and she began fiddling with the material, trying to cover it up. The small noli fastened around her waist on a black string helped a little bit, but not much. Subtly, Ellishiva reached a few fingertips into the pouch. They brushed against paper, confirming that it was still there: the papyrus note with her unanswered questions about the Sixth Element.

Suddenly, through the broad window, Ellishiva spotted something moving in the sky. Gathering too quickly to be stirred by the wind, a patch of dark clouds was churning, turning gray, then black, then gray again. She narrowed her eyes.

"What's happening there?" she asked Onuris, pointing.

The firefly paused in his work of packing up gauze and pins, followed the path of her finger, and frowned. "They have been appearing since you sustained your injuries, child," he admitted grimly. "Without warning, the clouds change into these gloomy patches. The weather patterns of our world are becoming strange. Strange indeed." He gave his head a shake and turned brightly to Ellishiva, but not before she glimpsed the empty look in his sunken eyes. "In any case, you must not let it bother you. Life goes on, after all. There is no sense in worrying about that which it is out of our power to change." He snapped the little wooden box of pins shut with a small, final-sounding *click*.

Ellishiva could tell that he was hiding something. Doubtless, he too must be following Rajah's orders. She pressed her lips together, struggling to understand why the elders were bent on ignoring the danger instead of trying to stop it.

"Do you know when the last quarter moon will rise?" Ellishiva asked, her eyes almost as dark as the churning cloud as she followed its movement in the sky.

"Hmm," began Onuris, thinking hard. "Another half a fortnight, I believe." He gathered up the neatly packed supplies. "Come now, let's hurry. She's waiting, you know," he said briskly.

"Wait. Can you fix my tunic to cover my bandage first, so no one can see it? Please?" asked Ellishiva. She tugged at the fabric by her belly button, but it was no good. "If they see it they'll start gossiping."

"You shouldn't be fearful of what people say, Ellishiva," interrupted Onuris primly, "or that fear will own you."

"You sound like Rajah," grumbled Ellishiva. She continued to tug at the tunic.

Onuris gave an almost-silent huff through his nose. "Let's hurry now, Ellishiva. Lady Malinia is waiting. You know how she frets."

Ellishiva did know. Unhappily, she stopped fiddling with her tunic and followed Onuris out of the Hall.

They found Lady Malinia in the foyer, waiting for them. Her metallic feathers shone brilliantly, and she had dressed for the occasion in a one-piece, flowing tunic that streamed over her feathered body and fell to the floor beneath her clawed toes.

"How are you this fine day, Lady Malinia?" inquired Onuris with a polite nod.

"Very well, Onuris. Very well," she crowed merrily, picking a piece of lint from her feathers. At that moment, Amborella came running up behind her. Lady Malinia turned to the little girl. "My dear, did you finish your dalia porridge?" she asked.

"Yes Lady Malinia. It was so cinna—cinnamony," replied Amborella, juggling the word on her tongue. Then she caught sight of Ellishiva. "Oh, look! A bandage!" She ducked away from Lady Malinia's fussing and ran over to hug her sister.

Ellishiva winced as Amborella latched onto her waist, but made no move to loosen the grip of the small, green fingers. Even being only half awake, she had missed her little sister while she was being cared for in the Hall. She bent and kissed Amborella's fiery red hair, then Dollie Burlap's when the child finally let go and held the stuffed toy up for her turn. Amborella carried it everywhere. The doll's body was hand-sewn of rough burlap. Her eyes were black and white beans, her parted and braided hair was brown reed grass, and her nose and lips had been painted in red-brown henna. A pretty necklace with a pendant of hard, amber-yellow copal dangled around her neck, many tiny objects trapped within its depths.

Ellishiva combed through Amborella's hair with her fingers, braiding it into a rough plait as her sister turned excitedly to the firefly dofaun hovering beside them.

"Onuris, could you give Dollie Burlap a bandage, too?" she asked hopefully. "Please? *Please*?" she added, bouncing on her toes.

"Why, child, she must have an injury first," replied Onuris, somewhat at a loss.

"Um. Yes, but—but she *was* hurt," Amborella exclaimed with conviction. "So she *does* deserve one." Ellishiva thought she heard her sister's voice change as she pressed on, more quietly now. "In my dreams, Dollie told me she was hurt. Many, many times. No one cares for her like I do." Her eyes were suddenly somber, all seriousness.

For a long moment, Onuris gazed helplessly between the doll and Amborella's steady stare. Then Ellishiva saw Lady Malinia give him a pointed, somewhat impatient look. The firefly cleared his throat and pressed the fingertips of his upper limbs together. "You take care of her very well," he replied kindly. "Perhaps a bandage can be arranged another time, my little Va'nature. I have much work to do today. Now, off you go."

"Yes, off we go!" cooed Lady Malinia with enthusiasm, ushering Amborella—doll and all—out the door. "Goodbye, Onuris!"

The firefly turned quickly to Ellishiva. "Now, mind yourself well. I am still not convinced that you are quite ready for an outdoor excursion. If you feel any unease, simply return here to me at once." He looked somewhat relieved to be treating the living again.

Ellishiva only nodded, and followed Lady Malinia out of the warren.

Then there was the muffled stomping of feet thumping down a flight of stairs, and a moment later, Hektor—dressed in his uniform, with his Puluma stick tied to the sling-bag on his back—hurtled past her out of the warren to join them.

"Hey, Elli! Ready for Puluma practice?" he grinned impishly, dashing ahead of Lady Malinia toward the vāhmana at the end of the hall.

"Stop running! Enough foolery! You know very well she cannot exert herself!" scolded Lady Malinia. Ellishiva just smiled at her brother's teasing.

"Have you seen Rajah today?" called Hektor over his shoulder, his voice echoing along the hollow banyan branch. "Is he coming to Bear Market?"

"Not today, dear," huffed Lady Malinia, sounding a bit annoyed. "He has not yet returned from his important business. Now come along.

Follow me to Mr. Belanos," she clucked, regaining the lead. "And stop asking silly questions!"

Behind her, Hektor slapped a hand to his chest dramatically, as though an arrow had pierced it, and pretended to swoon. "Oh, my dearest Belanos, let us have tea," he whispered, batting his eyes, on weak and wobbly knees. Ellishiva pulled the door to the warren shut behind them, her hand brushing over the five-sided pattern of interconnecting grooves carved into its surface as she pulled away. Her other hand, like Amborella's, was latched over her own mouth to keep from laughing. Lady Malinia continued to parade ahead, oblivious.

A minute later, the four of them boarded the vāhmana at the end of the hall—run, as always, by Dorian—and began the long descent down through the huge, hollow aerial root. Hektor—also as always—watched the elf supervisor's every movement with baited breath as he lowered them safely through the root, though Dorian himself seemed not to notice, engaged as he was in conversation with Lady Malinia.

When at last they reached the ground, Ellishiva stepped off of the vāhmana and stood, fixed in place, staring around Banyan Circle. It had been weeks since she had been outside—really outside—and she breathed in the fresh, scented air like medicine. Overhead, between the lengths of aerial roots hanging from the banyan's massive limbs, dozens of free-floating vāhmanas—colorful and dull, dirty and polished, dark and bright—wove through the air. Ellishiva dug her bare feet into the cool earth, relishing the scratchy tickle as she wiggled her toes in the grass.

"Come on, Elli!" called Amborella, who was up ahead, trailing Hektor. Hektor himself threw a grin over his shoulder and waved at her to catch up. Although she would have loved nothing better than to wander off with them and enjoy the day, Ellishiva forced her feet to stay where they were. She pointed at Lady Malinia, who was still lingering by their vāhmana, deep in conversation with Dorian. Her best chance of sneaking away to see Jipsin Smilodon would be in Mr. Belanos's shop, when Lady Malinia was always so fixated on Mr. Belanos himself that she rarely noticed anything—or anyone—else.

"Run along, Ellishiva. Run along, dear," cooed Lady Malinia, catching on to her supposedly good intentions. "I shall be right behind you. Do enjoy yourselves for a moment. Go on! I need a word with Dorian."

Ellishiva fought down a scowl at the delay, but there was nothing for it. She started forward to find Hektor and Amborella, who had just disappeared behind one of the colossal aerial roots. Whispers followed her, just as she had feared, but there was nothing to be done about that, either. Telling herself that they would stop eventually, Ellishiva squared her shoulders and moved on.

A swarm of snow-white mosquito dofauns the size of bees swept out of the thin, untroubled crowd and sang by her ear. One landed on Ellishiva's forearm, and she paused in surprise when his pinchers poked at her green skin—obviously, without success.

"What are you doing, stupid!" squeaked one of the more familiar mosquitoes.

"Sorry Elli, he's new. He escaped the Asylum at Derahdin," apologized another.

"Greetings, Elli!" a few of the others chorused together.

"Come on!" The first mosquito was talking again, dragging the new guy off of Elli's arm. "You should know we can't sting a tree—I mean, a Va'nature. Sorry."

"Come on, swarm. Let's go find a nice, pink fairy!" called the second.

Ellishiva grinned as the cloud of mosquitoes buzzed on their way. A warm summer wind blew through her hair. Nearby, at the edge of the huge pond, four nervous elf girls were lining up for a swim meet. Not far from them, an Aotearoa penguin dofaun with white, black, and yellow plumage was trying to coax her anxious, yellow-eyed, pink-footed chicks into the water for the first time.

Ellishiva reached into her noli, took out the papyrus note, and began to reread her questions about the Sixth Element. Her heart quickened, and her frustration with Lady Malinia grew. How was she going to sneak off to the black market section of Aurochs Alley without Mr. Belanos to act as a diversion?

For a moment, she faltered, remembering exactly what it was she was plotting to do—and how very bad she was at breaking rules. She wished Samara were here. Samara would have an idea. Samara *always* had an idea.

From the pond there came a splash, followed by a flurry of frantic cheeping.

"The water is bad!" came the muffled voice of one of the chicks, burying his face in one of his mother's flippers.

"You need to learn to swim. We do not only live on land," maintained the mother penguin, gently but firmly prying the sobbing chick out from under her wing.

"Elli! Hey, Elli!" Ellishiva turned at the sound of the familiar voice to find a honey-brown elf boy with tight curly hair dashing past her, Hektor and Amborella at his heels. He was wearing a maroon uniform that looked exactly the same as Ellishiva's except for the name and number on the back. He and her brother and sister all looked to be headed toward the entrance to Bear Market.

"Bairon, where's Sam?" Ellishiva called after him, perhaps a bit too loudly.

Bairon shrugged his shoulders. "Don't know!" he shouted, far more interested in showing Hektor and Amborella his new Puluma stick.

Ellishiva began trudging after them in the direction of the high, arched root laden with glossy leaves, thick old vines, and yellow trumpet flowers that marked the start of the market. Her mind was elsewhere as Bairon pulled out a green Puluma ball and began using the curve of the stick to manipulate it skillfully around the legs, paws, claws, and hooves of lucky passersby, who did not appreciate the extra attention.

"Watch it!"

"This is not a Puluma court!"

"Bairon, you're not at Central Pond now. Cut it out!"

Ellishiva ignored it all until, taking a hard swing at the ball as if sending it toward a goalie net, the orange-sized green sphere ricocheted off the hoof of a Malacca mountain tapir, glanced off the emerald shell of a grand Senegal razorback tortoise taking a nap nearby, and zipped past her own temple, out among the hustle and bustle of Banyan Circle.

The thought hit her like a bolt of lightning—or, in fact, like a Puluma ball hurtling past your ear. But she would have to act quickly.

"Oh no," groaned Bairon, trying to hide his Puluma stick behind his back as the turtle craned its head around to spot the source of the disturbance.

"I'll get the péquilla, Bairon!" called Ellishiva, jerking her chin in the direction of the ball.

"I'll get it, Elli. You're not supposed to run," began Hektor helpfully, taking a step in the direction it had gone.

"No! Stay there! I *said* I'll get it!" snapped Ellishiva, dashing off to get a head start on him.

"All right, all right. Don't have to jump down my throat," she heard him grumble as she disappeared into the light crowds.

Ellishiva hurried after the ball, ignoring the pinch in her side as the péquilla bounced onward, accidentally kicked and bumped between the aerial roots by busy residents, farther and farther east. Ellishiva might have caught it once or twice. But it so happened that east was exactly the direction she wanted to go.

At last the crowds thinned to just a stray dofaun here and there, and the péquilla rolled clunkily to a halt. Ellishiva bent to pick it up.

A chorus of snickering caught her attention. There, watching her with scornful eyes from a nearby aerial root, were the four Faviola hawk moth sisters. Each of them was as tall as the wheat-colored elf girl in their company. Their bodies shimmered a rich poppy color in the dappled light, and fragments of sunlight glinted off their transparent emerald wings. As usual, they criticized her in loud, humming voices—as though she weren't there.

"What an ugly bandage!"

"Where?"

"On her waist. She's trying to hide it under her tunic."

"Oh, does the green bookworm want even more attention?" sneered one of the sisters mockingly, and another round of snickering broke out. Ellishiva remembered that her note with the questions about the Sixth Element was still in her hand. She dropped the péquilla, which rolled sullenly away again. As casually as she could, she looped both arms behind her back, gripping her elbows tightly. She tried to ignore them and walk away.

It didn't work. In seconds, the lot of them had her surrounded.

"You know, I heard she was attacked," purred the Faviola in front of her, a malicious glint in her black eyes.

"Why?" snorted the one to her left. "She's just another weird Va'nature."

"Where's your little fairy friend today?" chimed in the elf girl, a nasty edge to her words. Ellishiva set her jaw. It was true; they wouldn't have dared approach her like this if Samara had been here.

Then the thing she'd feared most happened.

"She's hiding something in her hand!" hissed one of the hawk moths behind her.

Ellishiva felt her stomach turn. She had a flashback to hanging upside-down from the rotting branch of the locust tree. Her grip on the scrap of paper tightened and her mind reeled, furiously trying to think of a way out. There wasn't one.

She braced her shaky legs and waited for the inevitable.

"*Ahem!*"

The sound was stern and full of authority. Instantly, the snickering around her stopped. And, just like that, the girls fled, some casting fearful glances over Ellishiva's head, others shooting her final glares as if to suggest that this was not over. Relief flooded Ellishiva's chest as she watched them bolt away, out of sight.

The throat cleared itself again, less menacingly now, and Ellishiva turned to find a tall, thin gelada monkey from the Blue Nile looking down at her. The dofaun's eyes were the rich brown hue of maple syrup. Her fur coat was well groomed, and a ginger-colored tunic fell to her ankles. A long, beaded necklace dropped below the hourglass-shaped patch of pink skin on her upper chest.

"Good day, Headmistress Ulima," said Ellishiva with a deep sigh, loosening her grip on her own elbows and letting her arms drop to her sides again. The note in her hand was badly crumpled.

The headmistress of Forest Academy pressed her paw meaningfully to her throat. On her arm hung a basket full of corn husks, and in her other hand she held the péquilla. Sheepishly, Ellishiva took the offered ball with a mumbled "Thank you." Then Headmistress Ulima raised her free paw and, in lieu of her lost voice, began to finger-spell words.

How do you feel, Ellishiva? she asked. *Lady Malinia said you fell off of a basalt cliff and injured yourself.*

Ellishiva just managed to stop her eyes from rolling. Her fall was getting better all the time. She stowed the crumpled papyrus note and the Puluma ball in her black noli. Then she held up her hands and finger-spelled a response, being careful not to make small mistakes under her teacher's critical eye.

I'm well, Headmistress. Thank you. But I see you've lost your voice again.

The headmistress gave a heavy sigh.

I'm on the "gone mad" list, Elli. A few days ago, a patch of dark clouds appeared, and my neighbors, the Tasmanian wolves, came after me—like mad beasts! I screamed so loud, my voice has not yet returned to me. The other dofauns think I have lost my head; no one will believe me. They simply refuse to take these strange—and dangerous!—weather patterns seriously. She shook her head resentfully, and continued. *You be careful, dear. No one is behaving how they ought, lately.* She scowled off in the direction of the Faviola sisters and their elf minion. *I only came down to dispose of these corn husks. Have you seen a pitcher plant? Some of the children must have thrown a piece of hard wood into ours, and now everything smells like a backed-up latrine. Oh, there's one.*

"Why don't you tell Dorian about it?" Ellishiva suggested, speaking now as she followed Headmistress Ulima over to a tube-like, three-foot-tall turquoise plant with yellow spots growing at the base of a nearby aerial root. "He's the head supervisor. I'm sure he could get you some Bluzure to clear it out again."

I did, dear, replied the headmistress. *You know the process. It's like asking for new school supplies.* She rolled her eyes and lifted the triangular, purple hood of the plant. Its inside was filled with hair and slime—both of which, Ellishiva knew, worked to decompose things fast. Headmistress Ulima emptied the basket of corn husks into it before pulling the hood closed again. Then she continued finger spelling. *He's expecting the Senate from the Imperial Colony of Nicobar to send a new shipment soon.* She sighed and righted the basket on her arm. *I'm afraid I must be getting back. You be careful, dear. Don't wander around by yourself.*

"I won't," Ellishiva assured her, wincing inside as she told yet another lie. She waited until the headmistress had hurried away out of sight. Then she dug into her noli for the crumpled piece of papyrus.

It was pinned underneath the péquilla, which reminded her exactly how long she'd been away already. Fearing that she'd wasted too much time chatting with the headmistress, Ellishiva continued quickly on her way, wondering how many other versions of her "fall" were in circulation.

Half a minute later, she arrived in front of a tall, vine-covered fence. The last time she'd gone over it, she'd been bleeding and unable to move. Ellishiva steeled herself and took a deep breath. She tucked the papyrus note back into her noli again. Finally, she looked around, making sure no one was watching.

Then, quicker than a Puluma ball ricocheting through crowds, she scrambled up and over the fence, into the alleyways of the black market.

* * *

"Please be here," Ellishiva whispered to herself under her breath. Aurochs Alley was even darker and more crooked than she remembered. Dank, bitter scents flitted under her nose like poison. Around her, an eerie silence hung in the air. Shadows seemed to flit about at the corners of her vision, yet when she turned to look, there was no one there. She swallowed hard, wishing she had eight eyes like a jumping spider. The soles of her feet were itching to turn her around and take her right back over the fence again, but she knew that an opportunity like this one might not come along twice.

Ellishiva steeled her shoulders, and scuttled onward up the alley.

Time stretched on—longer, she was sure, than it actually was—as she trudged farther and farther up the twisted street. Ellishiva was just about to give up hope of finding Jipsin Smilodon when she heard a tinkling of bells. She paused, almost not daring to believe it, and sniffed the air. The faint scent of myrrh filled her nostrils.

"He's here," she breathed. Then she hustled forward with new energy, following the smell.

It led to a dead-end alley. Normally, Ellishiva would never venture into such a place. But she recognized the vāhmana hovering low to the ground and the square tent pitched within the boundaries of its worn railings. No one else she knew owned a tent like that, its sides festooned with endless trinkets of varying colors, sizes, and shapes, all of which seemed to be constantly jostling for space.

"Hello? Hello, Jipsin Smilodon?" she called as loudly as she dared. "Are—are you in there?"

For a long, silent heartbeat, there was no reply.

Then, "Ellishiva?" came a low rumble. The flap of the tent was pulled back, and Jipsin Smilodon emerged from it. "My dearest Ellishiva," he grinned down at her. "Such a delightful surprise to see my favorite customer. And here, of all places! How are you feeling?"

The large cat stood on his mighty hind legs, grand and fierce. His eyes were the icy blue of arctic lakes. Like all smilodons, two bone-white saber teeth curled down from his upper lip, extending well past the bottom of his chin. They looked, Ellishiva mused, as though they were too big for his head.

"I'm well, thank you," she replied politely. For a moment she was tempted to ask him what perilous object *he'd* heard she'd fallen off of, but in the end she held her tongue.

She waited patiently as he exited the vāhmana and padded down to her, less fearful now that those fangs of his were here, and on her side. The Jipsin adjusted the coarse, sturdy belt lying diagonally across his chest as he walked. Below it, a fine pleated wrap encircled his waist, and under that was a very long tail. What was visible of his skin was lined with pale golden stripes; his pelt, with white and black spots.

When he came close enough, he saw her bandage, and his face changed. He began to circle around her with a slow, ceremonial step. "Ellishiva, my dear," he said at last, grimly. "You are hurt."

"Strange things are happening," replied Ellishiva softly, grateful that there was at least one dofaun in Mannahatta who was not simply going to pat her on the head and tell her not to trip over rocks. Her fingers trailed absently over some of the rare and exotic objects set out for display in front of the vāhmana.

"Indeed," rumbled the Jipsin. "But you will not dismiss them like the others. You know how to listen very well, Ellishiva. It is one of your strengths."

Ellishiva swung her head away from a cluster of vermillion silk scarves to look at him. There was, she saw, a warm spark in the Jipsin's icy eyes. But when he spoke again, all he said was, "So, what kind of books can I interest you in today?"

Ellishiva turned away from the scarves completely. "I don't think you have books on this subject," she said. The edges of the crumpled papyrus were rough against the palm of her hand. Picking her words carefully, she went on, "I'm looking for some information. I'm willing to barter for it. I could even grow a plant for you."

She spoke as casually as she could, but the Jipsin saw through her in an instant.

"Hm! Desperate, are we?" he began, fixing her with a sharp look.

"You must indeed be looking for something of great importance, to be bartering a forbidden service," he commented suspiciously.

Ellishiva felt her toes squirming. Bartering her skills as a Va'nature *was* forbidden—yet another ugly stone to add to the pile. "Yes I know, but—" she began plaintively.

The Jipsin silenced her with a wave of his great paw. "What information do you seek, child?" he asked quietly.

Ellishiva hesitated only for a moment. Then, in a soft voice that even the shadows would have had trouble hearing, she said, "Do you know anything about a Sixth Element, Jipsin Smilodon?"

For a heartbeat, the Jipsin stood perfectly still. Then Ellishiva saw his tail give a violent jump, and his head darted right and left, scanning the deserted alley. Seeing no one, he dropped to the ground and peered straight into her eyes.

"Child!" he hissed. "The Sixth Element is not to be spoken of so lightly!"

Ellishiva blinked, and took half a step back. "Why?" she stammered. "What's so—"

"Terrible evil!" interrupted the Jipsin, catching her by the arm and tugging her back so that he could continue whispering in her ear. "It was the Sixth Element, I believe, that was responsible for this bandage?" He pointed his free paw at her midriff, and a sharp claw sprang from its tip like a swift dagger.

"I didn't say anything about that," Ellishiva whispered back, truly anxious now. In all the years she had been doing business with Jipsin Smilodon, he had never once behaved like this. "I—I just wanted to know what it is," she managed, blinking her huge amber eyes at him.

Looking back at her, the Jipsin seemed to return somewhat to his senses. Slowly, he released his grip on her arm. "My dear," he rumbled in a low voice, "it is best to leave these matters to the elders."

All of the frustration that had been building up in Ellishiva for the past two days bubbled to the surface. "Rajah isn't even here!" she snapped. "Jipsin Smilodon, *The Times* says that the ice forest is melting. That thing ripped out the fairy's heart. I saw it with my own eyes. Something has to be done," she pleaded earnestly.

The Jipsin stared at her with his ice-bright eyes, but said nothing.

The few remaining threads of Ellishiva's patience frayed, and snapped. "I'm not leaving without an answer!" she declared scathingly, meeting his gaze head-on so that he would know that she meant it—because she did.

"Ellishiva," he began. Then he stopped. His nostrils flared, and his eyes fell shut. Ellishiva waited patiently, sharply aware of her own heart thudding in her chest. When the Jipsin's eyes opened again, they were steady with resolution.

"The Sixth Element is invisible to the naked eye," he whispered, so quietly that she could barely make out the words. "It has been in existence for as long as humans have lived upon this earth. Their greed, jealousy, untamed hatred—these powerful spirits manifest themselves in an element: the Sixth Element." He paused and glanced furtively around them. Then he looked back at Ellishiva, and continued. "This evil has now found an entity with a voice. I fear you are right, that it was indeed the creature that ripped out the ice fairy's heart. I fear, also, that it has found a way into our world. Yet what I fear the most is that the Sixth Element will now continue to take other forms—forms that we cannot fight. This is all I know, child." The Jipsin ran his wide tongue over his dry lips as he finished.

Ellishiva was silent for a moment, digesting what he had told her. "Who could have let her into our colony?" she asked finally, her voice as low and husky as the Jipsin's. An image from just after her attack rose in her mind, of a cloaked, furtive figure couched silently in the corner of Mr. Guo's vāhmana, and before she could stop herself the words were spilling past her lips. "Do you think it could have been Baron Puck?"

The Jipsin lowered his eyes to Ellishiva, and his bleak expression grew even more solemn. "My dear, false accusations are themselves terrible wounds." His gaze darted quickly to the bandage at her side. "Before you make them, I advise you to seek the facts."

Ellishiva felt her cheeks grow warm. She swallowed hard, and quickly returned to the original subject. "So it came from the human world, but—but it knows about ours. How can that be, Jipsin Smilodon? The humans themselves don't know about us," she trailed off, her brow furrowing in thought. "I'd be curious to see how the Sixth Element manifested itself in the first place," she muttered, half to herself.

The Jipsin snorted faintly. "I should think you've read enough human history books on wars and such to sate your curiosity by now, child," he noted dryly. "However, if you require a more vivid image, I am sure you shall find it recorded within the many jars of Silverdine spice dust that your guardian has been keeping so faithfully these many long years."

This was true, Ellishiva reflected. As prefect of the colony, it was one of Rajah's duties to record the great events of the world—human and dofaun alike. Her mind skipped back to the attack in the woods— how the locust tree could have killed her, but didn't. How it knew that a fairy's heart could bestow life, however temporary, on the object that possessed it. How it had spoken in the endangered language of Pali. Somewhere on the uppermost shelves in the Hall of Nature Healing, she was sure, there was a Silverdine jar that knew how all of this could be.

"Yes. I'd like to learn more about the root of this Sixth Element," she mused aloud, quietly.

But Jipsin Smilodon was moving off now, back toward a neat pile of books on display beside the vāhmana. "I believe this is the book you are inquiring about, my girl," he called over to her, picking up a worn-looking volume from the stacks.

For a moment, Ellishiva stayed where she was, confused. Then she realized that the Jipsin must be putting on a show for the benefit of any eavesdroppers in the shadows. Clearing her throat, she walked over to him and took the book. Its title was printed in simple letters near the top of the front cover: *The Unauthorized Biography of Amma*. Her eyes narrowed in on the author's name.

"The Tigress of Sundari?" she asked with raised eyebrows, her curiosity piqued in spite of herself.

The Jipsin gave a wry smile. "Of course. If you can think of anyone else bold enough to write the unauthorized biography of Amma herself, Ellishiva, I shall be most impressed."

Ellishiva opened the book and flipped quickly through its pages. The Tigress of Sundari was questionable to say the least—and in more than one respect.

"It is a rare copy of course. Only a few in circulation," the Jipsin was saying.

The words were out of Ellishiva's mouth before she could stop herself. "I'll take it," she blurted.

The Jipsin smiled down at her. "Alas, child, I am afraid I have already bartered it away to someone else. May I interest you in another trinket?"

Ellishiva felt her face fall with her hopes. Nevertheless, she let her eyes roam quickly over the eclectic collection of styluses, scarves, old books, slingshots, elixirs, nolis, bracelets, and bottles of henna arranged decoratively around the vāhmana. "No, thank you," she mumbled. "I should be going." She stole a glance behind them at the crooked stretch of Aurochs Alley and wished, not for the first time that day, that Samara were there to brave it with her. "Oh," she said, suddenly remembering. "By the way, um. Do you have any olivine?"

"Olivine!" exclaimed the Jipsin, looking at her as though he thought anything in the world might come out of her mouth next. "I'm sure I need not remind you, child, that olivine supplies are closely regulated by the Senate. Any such materials floating around would be illegal." Then he caught the hopeless look on Ellishiva's face, and added, "But perhaps, if it were for a very good cause, I might try to obtain some."

Ellishiva smiled at him. The Jipsin smiled back.

A rumble sounded overhead. The Jipsin glanced up at the sky, and a grim look passed over his face. "When the darkness of this evil is upon you, you have not the power to control your actions, and terrible are the thoughts that fly through your fevered mind," he muttered ominously.

Ellishiva was not sure whether he was talking to her or to himself. However, before she could ask, the Jipsin had sprung into action, quickly pulling covers down the sides of his vāhmana, securing his merchandise. "Now, child," he said as he worked, "you must not linger in this place by yourself. Hurry back to Banyan Tree. And on your next visit, do not come alone. The dark clouds over Mannahatta are making many dofauns do strange things, and they appear without warning." He finished tying down the last cover and glanced at Ellishiva, who still had not budged. "Go! Aurochs Alley is not safe!"

The wisps of cloud overhead began to churn into something larger and, without risking another word, the Jipsin turned his back on her, boarded his vāhmana, and vanished into the pitched canopy of his tent.

In the next moment, a veil of dark shadow crept over the alley. Ellishiva craned her neck up to the sky, watching with an uneasy feeling in her heart as the cloud, like a blanket of thick smoke, moved in.

"Hurry, child! Go!" thundered the Jipsin from within the tent. "*Go!*"

Ellishiva hurried off. Around her, Aurochs Alley was as barren as ever, and yet there seemed to be a subtle, unsettling shift in its crooked nooks and crannies—as though the darkness overhead had poisoned the shadows themselves. "What could these clouds possibly do?" she muttered under her breath. A shiver ran down her spine.

Behind her, she saw the Jipsin's vāhmana rising into the air, as though he didn't even trust himself to remain on the ground at a time like this. The unsettled feeling in the pit of her stomach deepened.

In the distance, someone screamed.

Ellishiva felt her face drain to a pale green. She doubled her pace from a walk to a jog out of the dead-end alley, detouring around through another. Up ahead, she saw the corner that would lead her back to the vine-covered fence. Her jog became a run. She sprinted down the rest of the narrow street and careened around the soot-smeared wall, blood pounding, almost tasting the safety of Banyan Circle on the tip of her dry tongue.

Then a huge, black shape was looming in front of her, barring her path.

For one horrible instant, every muscle in Ellishiva's body went perfectly still with fear. Then she caught sight of the bull's horns. They were polished until their tips shone like the points of silver needles, and each of them was festooned with circles and circles of beads, much like the ones Samara wore around her ankle. This was no hardened criminal out for blood. This was a friend.

"Hello, Geb!" Ellishiva called, relief sweeping over her like water over a broken dam. She gave a cheerful wave, and took a step forward.

But Geb didn't move—didn't even nod back a greeting. Ellishiva slowed to a stop again, and the smile petered out at the corners of her mouth. Overhead, the dark cloud was churning faster than before.

Suddenly, the young bull began to paw the ground. His left hoof made long, dull scraping sounds as it dragged over the uneven cobblestones, like a harvest reaper sharpening his long blade. He lowered his head, keeping his red eyes fixed on Ellishiva. A long strand of saliva fell from his pendulous lower lip, and his black nostrils flared.

He's going to charge me, Ellishiva realized in disbelief.

"Geb," she said, the lone syllable of his name sticking in her throat like sour honey. She cleared it and tried again. "Geb, stop it. It's only me."

The bull's muscles rippled beneath his charcoal coat.

Ellishiva felt her panic rise, and, along with it, her anger. "Geb! What's wrong with you? I said *stop it*!" And, in a last-ditch attempt to drive some sense into him, she yanked the Puluma ball out of her noli and threw it at him as hard as she could. The péquilla ricocheted off his front hoof, and vanished into the shadows.

Geb charged.

Ellishiva turned and ran, sprinting back through the twisted, empty alleyways as fast as her legs could carry her. The wound in her side stung her with every stride. "Stop!" she yelled furiously, desperately, at the crazed bull keeping pace behind her. "Stop, Geb. *Stop!*"

But the hoofbeats continued, grim and lightning-fast, on her trail. Ellishiva could run faster than almost anybody else she knew, but the pain in her side was growing worse. Eventually, he would catch up with her. Her mind working furiously, she tore around another blind corner.

It was a dead end.

Ellishiva barely had time to register this before a powerful gust of wind was sweeping over her, blowing her hair wildly around her face and forcing her to a halt. She reeled around, her heart in her throat, expecting to find herself nose to nose with the honed points of Geb's horns.

But, curiously, the bull had stopped as well. For a moment Ellishiva felt a flicker of hope that he had finally come to his senses—but no. Geb was pawing the ground again, repeating his pre-charging ritual. But why?

It dawned on her that a strange scent had blown in with the gust of wind—one that seemed to ring of crumbled lime leaves and broken cloves. Disoriented, Ellishiva took a step back—and bumped into a body.

Instinctively, she jerked away from it, snapping her head toward the new threat, then back to the crazed bull, then back to the . . . to the . . .

"A kinnaran?" she blurted, bewildered.

But his fire-yellow eyes were fixed on the threat a few feet away, battle strategies shifting rapidly behind them. Ellishiva stared, dumbstruck, as he faced down the burly dofaun without a trace of fear. His white hair shifted like filaments of long pepper spice in the remnants of the wind he must have brought with him when he'd swooped down from the cloudy sky. And, suddenly, it dawned on her that she knew him.

He was the boy who had come to see her in the Hall of Nature Healing—the one with the kind face. The one she'd thought would be interesting to talk to.

"Stay back," he told her in a low voice, still without so much as glancing away from his adversary. Ellishiva realized that her mouth was hanging open. She closed it, and stood stock-still on the cobblestone street. There wasn't much place to run to in a dead-end alleyway, anyhow.

Then, just as Geb was finishing his ritual, the kinnaran unfurled his transparent wings and launched himself at her erstwhile friend.

It was a bold and clever move—and it worked. Ellishiva watched in awe as the kinnaran boy darted over, under, and around Geb, moving so quickly that even she herself could barely keep track of him. The raging bull's hooves skidded as he wheeled about, struggling to figure out which way to charge his attacker.

At last, the boy flew up, spun once in the air, and planted a swift kick on Geb's shoulder. The bull snorted loudly and stumbled. Ellishiva furrowed her brow. Surely one kick couldn't be strong enough to bring down a rampaging bull, even from a kinnaran. And then it hit her.

"Payamar," she breathed. "Read about it."

In front of her, the kinnaran boy had landed on Geb's back and was wrestling the panting bull to the ground, one hand holding tightly to a polished horn, the other putting pressure on what looked to be a very specific point on the thick black neck. Ellishiva continued to stare, transfixed. She noted how light the boy's armor looked, its overlapping pearly scales flashing in the dim alleyway as he moved. She saw the way his tongobiri sword fitted against his back, curving slightly where it rested between his wings, which were folded again now. In seconds, the huge bull was on the ground, all the fight gone out of his limbs.

And, just like that, it was over.

A sudden whisper of apprehension tugged at Ellishiva, now that the immediate danger was out of the way. "He's not dead—right?" she called to the kinnaran anxiously.

The boy had slid off of Geb's back and was now kneeling on the floor, checking the bull's pulse. "No. I only applied a pressure point," he called back. "Don't worry. He'll be up again soon." Then, quick as a flash, he flew up off the cobblestones and landed again, on his feet, in front of Ellishiva. "I'm Maximus," he introduced himself matter-of-factly.

Ellishiva blinked at him. "I—um. I'm . . . Ellishiva. Cinnamon," she managed.

Maximus smiled. "I know who you are," he said.

Ellishiva blushed—which, of course, made no sense, and was embarrassing to boot. Clearing her throat, she asked in a rush, "Was that one of the one hundred and eight pressure points of payamar?"

The kinnaran disappeared, and she blinked again, confused. Then she realized that he was kneeling at her feet.

"What—what are you doing?" she asked, taking a step back.

"Just picking up your péquilla," he replied, standing up again. He moved, Ellishiva thought, as if he were immune to gravity. "I like your toe ring. Only ever seen one like it before. And yes, that was one of the one hundred and eight pressure points of payamar. Here," he handed her the péquilla. "I'm afraid you're going to need something better than a ball to defend yourself," he added, and Ellishiva thought she could see just the faintest glint of mischief in his eyes.

"Oh, yes. Um, thanks," she babbled, taking the péquilla from his hand. It was true, she realized. If the Sixth Element attacked her again, what could she do about it? She was hopeless to defend herself even from her friends, she thought, glancing warily at Geb lying on the ground, let alone her enemies. For a moment she wished she'd thought to ask the Jipsin for an escape potion of some kind—maybe a flying one, so that she could disappear among the treetops in the blink of an eye, like Samara.

"You're not supposed to be in this alley, you know," Maximus was saying. He glanced up at the sky, a troubled look on his brow. Ellishiva looked up, too. The black patch of cloud was beginning to dissipate, winks of sun peeking through the thin parts. She looked over at Geb on the ground. The feverish intensity had finally left his body, and he had dropped off into an exhausted slumber. For a moment, Ellishiva considered waking him, just to make sure he was all right. Then she thought better of it, and let him doze.

Beside her, Maximus sighed. "So what are you looking for out here?" he asked.

"I . . . ," Ellishiva faltered. She couldn't tell if he was especially sharp, or if she was sluggish with shock from the day's events. She wracked her brain for something intelligent to say. "Is—is that choji oil I smell?" she managed finally.

"Yes, actually. We use it on our blades," replied Maximus. He did seem a little impressed, Ellishiva thought fleetingly. Before she could ask to see the blade itself, he was already pulling it out of its carved wooden scabbard. Ellishiva's eyes grew wide. She had only ever seen such a sword in books. The hilt was a simple design of green malachite. Its wavy edges were razor-sharp and shone in the dappled sunlight like ribbons of glass.

"A tongobiri sword," she breathed, unable to keep the awe out of her voice. Nevertheless, her feet took a step backward in spite of herself. There were no weapons in Mannahatta Colony.

"Our duty is to guard the dofauns, and the Va'natures who plant saplings in the human world," Maximus spoke reassuringly, reading her mind once again. He looked thoughtfully at the tongobiri in his hands. "It's dangerous work. Sometimes we're spotted by humans, and creatures who have not yet become dofauns." He sighed again, and returned the sword to its scabbard. Then he leveled his gaze at Ellishiva. "So. You were going to tell me what you were doing here by yourself."

Ellishiva met the look head-on, considering. She had only just met the young kinnaran, and logic told her that it was unwise to share your secrets with strangers. Still . . . Her thoughts flashed back to the blurred memories of him visiting her every day in the Hall of Nature Healing during the fortnight that she had been ill. He had just saved her life, after all. But, more than that, there was something in his eyes when he looked at her. Something steady.

Something trustworthy.

"I came to see Jipsin Smilodon," she told him finally, keeping her voice low and soft, just in case the shadows were listening. "I needed some information."

Maximus nodded, and the glint returned to his eyes. "Well, no wonder you were in such a rush. I'm sure the dark clouds are affecting him, too. I wouldn't want to be around those killer canines when that happened, either." He grinned, showing his teeth. There was a small scar, about as long as her thumbnail, on his chin.

Slowly, she felt herself grinning back at him. "And why are you here?" she asked finally.

"Well, first, because you needed to be rescued," he began matter-of-factly.

"I mean why here on Mannahatta," Ellishiva jumped in quickly, then wondered if that was rude, interrupting him. She winced and bit her tongue.

Maximus studied her for a long minute. When he spoke, however, it was clear that his sudden solemnity had not been triggered by her bad manners. "We're here because of your attack. Because of the Sixth Element," he confided, speaking in the same low, soft voice she herself had used a moment ago. "Your guardian is trying to make it seem like you had an accident so that there won't be widespread panic. He's telling everyone the dark clouds are just strange weather patterns." Maximus threw a grim look at Geb, still out cold on the cobblestones. "Although personally, I'm beginning to think that might not be the best idea," he added, reaching out and giving her elbow a tug.

Ellishiva let him lead her out of the dead-end alleyway. "He—but Rajah left for Nicobar," she faltered. There were so many questions bursting in her head that she didn't know which of them to ask first. "You know what the Sixth Element is? I mean, whose form it's taking?"

"No, we have no idea," replied Maximus. He looked sorry to admit it. "I'm here to ask Jipsin Smilodon, just like you did. I'm sure he told you the same thing he told me. But I think," he went on, bending close to her ear and lowering his voice until it was barely above a whisper, "I think someone let it in. This colony is too protected for it to find a way in on its own. Amma herself made sure it was well hidden. Even most people in Nicobar and the other colonies don't know about Mannahatta."

"Really?" Ellishiva said, fascinated. She stared straight ahead of them as they walked, thinking. But nothing in Mannahatta seemed worthy of being kept secret from the rest of the world. She shook her head once, frustrated. "That doesn't make sense. It isn't as if we have anything important to hide." She glanced back at Maximus, and his fiery eyes were fixed on her intently. Ellishiva swallowed the nerves that were jangling to life in her chest again, and changed the subject. "You've met Walle, right?"

The kinnaran nodded.

Ellishiva took a breath, and went on. "He said that on the night of my attack, light like . . . like a thousand suns burst from my body into the sky." She paused, feeling suddenly foolish as she described it. But she steeled her shoulders, and asked her question anyway. "Did you see anything that night?"

Maximus gave her a measured look. "Well, it's not every day you see an injured Va'nature. You're very strong beings—all of you. And you all heal in different ways. I didn't see anything, because it's daylight in Nicobar when it's night here on Mannahatta. But I can ask around."

"Yes. Thank you. I've been wondering what that light meant." Ellishiva gave him a searching look. He did not seem to think she was crazy.

One more thing to be grateful to the young kinnaran for, she thought wryly.

They reached the end of the street and turned onto another, walking in thoughtful silence. They were not far from the vine-covered fence now, and trickles of chatter began to drift to Ellishiva's ears again. Then, slowly, the shady elves and dofauns who frequented Aurochs Alley's main stretch began to reappear, bartering in low whispers as usual.

She was almost glad to see them, Ellishiva mused. Though, in fairness, that might have had something to do with the well-armed, payamar-trained kinnaran walking beside her.

"Aren't you too young to be on assignment?" she asked him curiously, breaking the silence.

"It was the general's idea," Maximus admitted. Even as they strolled, she could see that his sharp eyes were alert, taking in every detail of their surroundings. "He thought it would be a good way to satisfy the fieldwork component of my summer training. So far, I have to say I agree with him." He gave her a somewhat impish smile.

Ellishiva smiled back. "Thank you for rescuing me," she said, and she could have sworn that he beamed a bit. Then she realized what he'd just said. "Wait. The *general* is here?"

Maximus nodded, but said nothing. Maybe he wasn't allowed to say more, Ellishiva thought. She had seen kinnarans before, rarely, but never a real general. To keep her tongue from asking the youth beside her questions he couldn't answer, she changed the subject yet again. "So . . . did you come to see me? In the Hall?"

"Yes. Every day," confirmed Maximus. "I met everyone. Your friends are kind. But your elders . . ." A frown crossed his forehead. "They refused to talk about what really happened to you. At least, to me. Not to any of us who are still completing our studies. And I truly don't like that." He pulled his gaze away from the alley suddenly, and fixed Ellishiva with a straight, steady look. "I'm glad you came here to seek information from Jipsin Smilodon. You're brave. If there's any-thing I can do to help you figure out what was trying to kill you, I will."

Ellishiva knew, without even a whisper of a doubt, that he meant it. Her heart lifted. Before she could stop them, the words were leaving her mouth. "Can you teach me payamar?" she asked bluntly.

Maximus stopped, and looked at her with raised eyebrows.

"I mean," Ellishiva went on, licking her lips nervously, "only if it's not too much trouble. I just . . . need to learn how to defend myself.

With something better than a ball," she finished flatly.

The corner of Maximus's mouth twitched at the mention of the péquilla. He resumed walking again, a thoughtful look in his eyes.

"It won't be easy," he mused, as much to himself as to Ellishiva. She held her breath. Off to the right, there was a faint clinking as one of the vendors poured a collection of small, obsidian-black carob beans into his palm for a customer to see.

Finally, Maximus continued. "Samara told me about the way you play Puluma with the dofauns. Not many Va'nature can do some of those moves. She told me about your yoga, too—that you can bend yourself like a piece of bamboo."

"Yoga?" Ellishiva interrupted, grinning. How now—someone younger than Rajah who wasn't going to tease her about yoga? It was almost too good to be true.

"Yes, yoga." Maximus grinned back. "Most payamar moves are based on the actions of nature. It's no coincidence that almost all the positions in yoga are named after animals." He paused, looked her over one last time, and then gave a firm nod. "Your Arboretum would be a perfect place to practice."

"Good. The Arboretum it is," said Ellishiva. She waited to see if he would be offended by her boldness, but the grin on his face only grew wider. He even forgot to keep an eye on the shady crowd around them for a moment.

"All right," he said.

Just then, a shrill, frantic cry pierced the vine-covered fence beside them, making them both jump.

"*Ellishiva!*" It was Lady Malinia's voice. Ellishiva winced, and groaned inwardly. Lady Malinia's scream was quickly followed by shorter, almost as worried calls of, "Elli! Elli, where are you?" Bairon and Hektor were on the hunt as well.

Ellishiva cleared her throat and looked at Maximus, trying to ignore them. "So where are you off to now?" she asked.

"Er, Cheeky Canteen." He was trying to keep a straight face, but she could tell by the sparkle in his eyes that he was amused by the manhunt going on behind the fence. "I worked up an appetite taking down our friend Geb."

Ellishiva opened her mouth to reply to this, but was interrupted by another high-pitched, hysterical scream of her name. She shut her mouth again, and rolled her eyes. "I'd better get going, too," she grumbled. The proper exit to Aurochs Alley—the one that led to the main hub of alleyways that made up the east end of Bear Market—was in sight now; she wouldn't have to jump the fence again, which was good. Her side was sore, and she was in enough trouble with Lady Malinia without landing on top of her head, to boot. "See you in the Arboretum, then?"

"In the Arboretum," Maximus confirmed with a nod, still holding down a laugh at Lady Malinia's relentless squawking next door. In spite of herself, Ellishiva couldn't help smiling, too, as she turned and walked away.

After several steps, she could still feel his eyes on the back of her head. She turned again and saw him standing where she'd left him, watching her. He smiled, and waved. Ellishiva waved back.

Then he spread his incandescent wings and rose into the air. A light breeze blew as he swooped overhead, sending her hair tossing about her head. She watched him vanish over the rooftops toward Bear Market.

Ellishiva stood where she was for a moment, breathing in the scent of lime leaves and cloves that he'd left behind. Then she turned and walked back toward Bear Market.

BEAR MARKET

"Are you trying to give me heart failure?" shrilled Lady Malinia furiously.

Ellishiva cringed as she stumbled along behind the rampaging pigeon, arm caught in a grip like a feathery vice, and wished the dofaun would lower her thundering voice. But Lady Malinia only continued to steamroll hectically down the alleyway. "What if something had happened to you? What would I do? What would *Valerius* do, Ellishiva?" she scolded harshly, finally halting in front of the Meads Den, a popular tavern favored by the elders. Several Leshan panda dofauns and a few of the elves loitering in front of the establishment turned their heads to see what the ruckus was about.

Ellishiva felt her cheeks go pink. Behind her, there was a bedraggled scuffling as Hektor, Amborella, and Bairon finally caught up and stumbled to a halt around her, all three of them out of breath.

Lady Malinia was still glaring at her, waiting for an answer.

"What would Rajah do?" Ellishiva muttered bitterly, trying to tug free of her grasp. "What does he care? He didn't visit me in the Hall. I don't see him here, combing the streets for me."

She trailed off when she saw Hektor shaking his head mutely at her, but it was too late. On either side of her, Amborella and Bairon's eyes grew wide.

Lady Malinia's eyes, by contrast, nearly bulged out of their sockets.

"What was that?" she yelled at the top of her lungs, drawing the attention of a group of Simao pink-spotted elephants farther down the alley. "What has gotten into you today?" She tightened her grip on Ellishiva's arm and yanked her close again. "I was kind to take you out, Ellishiva Cinnamon. Don't you dare take advantage of my kindness! Or have you already forgotten that we spared you your rightful punishment for running wild in the forest with Samara? Now mind your tongue!" she snapped.

"I—I—" began Ellishiva, struggling to look contrite. Inwardly she was seething, and her fingers were squeezing the ball in her hand so hard that her knuckles were turning yellow. "I couldn't find Bairon's Puluma ball and Ma—one of the kinnarans helped me get it back." She shoved the péquilla at Lady Malinia to prove that the story was true.

The dofaun's metallic plumage inflated to an indignant tuft. She brushed the péquilla aside with one wing, sending an already sweaty Bairon hobbling after it. "*KINNARAN*?" she roared.

Ellishiva swallowed and cringed backward. Even the dofauns and elves around them jumped. A murmur rustled through the crowd.

"A boy!" shrilled Lady Malinia. "And what were you doing in the black market with him? You're not allowed in there, Ellishiva Cinnamon, as you are perfectly aware! Did he touch you?" Her caretaker seized her shoulders and turned her around, inspecting.

"What? No! Nothing! I wasn't doing anything!" protested Ellishiva, wriggling free of the prodding feathers. A hundred beady eyes seemed to be staring at her. "He just helped me get the ball," she insisted, lowering her voice in a bid to keep the prying ears at bay.

Lady Malinia had no such quibbles. "Oh, if Valerius knew about this," she blabbed on, just as loudly as before. "You have no business with a kinnaran boy, Ellishiva. And at your age!" There were echoes of terror in her words now, and everyone who passed them looked on silently, absorbing the fresh gossip.

Ellishiva stared at her caretaker as though she really had lost her mind. "He rescued me!" she blurted, forgetting to stick to the far safer just-the-ball story.

"Silence!" cried Lady Malinia. Her voice reverberated down the alley.

A surge of emotion rushed through Ellishiva, swamping her in pain, shame, anger, and guilt. Before she could stop herself, Samara's words from the forest were bubbling to her lips, sharp and acidic as unripe cumquats. "This is a *prison* I live in!" she shouted at Lady Malinia, her words ricocheting down the meandering alleyway, which had, in fact, fallen rather silent at the dofaun's earlier command for silence.

Lady Malinia stared at her, so furious that she literally could not speak. Ellishiva continued to glare at her for another long moment. Then she turned her back and began to storm away. Overhead, a pair of teal doves with yellow-tipped feathers fluttered out of the Meads Den, singing merrily, as if to mock her.

She hadn't gone five steps before Lady Malinia was upon her again, her words sharper than ever. "That's it!" she seethed, barring Ellishiva's path. "You want to be like Samara? Well, enjoy your freedom today, because tomorrow you are grounded!"

Ellishiva gaped at her in disbelief. "What?" she cried. She had never once been grounded. Her heart raced. *Not now*, she thought desperately. "You can't do that!" she protested angrily.

"Watch me!" shrilled Lady Malinia, shaking one long, feathered finger in her face. "You are grounded for half a fortnight! Now come with me!" She grabbed Amborella's hand, spun on her heel, and stormed away better than Ellishiva ever could, already lamenting her hard lot in life. "Oh, Hektor, do you see? Do you see what she's doing to me? *And* in public! Flouncing away like a wicked, proud little thing!" She began to sniffle, fighting dry tears. "She will be the one to give me heart failure—you just watch. Oh! She must have hit her head even harder than we suspected."

"I did not fall!" Ellishiva shouted at her back. "*Or* hit my head!"

But Lady Malinia only continued forging forward through the crowds, sniffling piteously and ignoring her insolent, rebellious young Va'nature completely.

Ellishiva trailed behind her at a distance, not daring to break another rule again today. Grounded. And for half a fortnight! It would have been bad enough anyway, she thought with a sick lurch in her stomach, but for it to happen *now*. Now, when she needed her freedom more than ever. Now, when the Sixth Element was threatening to invade the colony, and no one else was prepared to lift so much as a finger to stop it.

She had to find Samara. And fast.

They crossed from the eastern end of the labyrinth of alleyways that was Bear Market over to the western side. In contrast to the eastern half of the market, which was largely made up of practical stalls, the streets of the west end were lined with small, quaint shops of a more permanent nature, each identified by its own unique sign. Many creatures, handsome and humble alike, were wandering from door to door, going about their daily business.

Hektor and Bairon, finally deciding that the coast was clear for now, quietly drew up to walk on either side of Ellishiva.

"You shouldn't have upset Lady Malinia—and in public," chided Hektor in a low, stern voice. "Now I know why you convinced her to buy a new tea set. You just wanted to sneak off to the black market."

Ellishiva scowled at him. "You're accusing *me* of causing a scene in public?" They passed Thyme and Teas, and she shot a paranoid glance at the silver-feathered dodo birds and red-beaked Mascarene parrots chatting amongst themselves in front of it, baskets filled with gold-yellow honeysuckles on their arms. Luckily, the dofauns were too engrossed in one another to notice her, her bandage, or her rampaging caretaker. Ellishiva turned to Bairon. "I see Atticus made you a new Puluma stick," she noted, trying without much success to keep the tightness out of her voice as she admired the smooth, J-shaped bamboo stick on his back.

"You like it, Elli?" said Bairon, his eyes lighting up. "I'm going to break it in at practice later."

"Yes, it's very nice. And I can't wait to see you play. But don't forget—the stick won't win the game for you. You've got to concentrate on your passes," she counseled, dropping her voice to a confidential pitch. "The rest of you will have to work even harder, now that I can't play."

"I am working on them, Elli," Bairon reassured her. Then he dropped his voice as well, and went on. "You know, I have to tell you. Ahpa is saying that you didn't fall—that something attacked you in the forest that day. Do you think it's true?"

"That's just a bunch of lies," interrupted Hektor with a growl. "Rajah said she fell on a stump and cut her side, and she hit her head, hard. Your father doesn't know what he's talking about."

Ellishiva shot her brother an acidic glare.

"What? That's obviously a lie, Hektor. You know she didn't fall," argued Bairon, frowning at him.

"You're calling Rajah a liar?" bit back Hektor.

"No! You're just mad because you think you let it happen, Hektor. Elli knows what happened to her better than Rajah does. It's her body," insisted Bairon. He glanced back at Ellishiva, and the hard look in his eyes softened. "How are you feeling anyway, Elli?"

"I'm fine," muttered Ellishiva, her insides churning with anger at her traitor of a brother.

They passed a few dofauns sitting under the sprawling branches of a weeping boer-bean tree with the words "The Jungle Shack" painted neatly on its trunk. As with the dofauns outside Thyme and Teas, they were engrossed in their lunchtime conversations, some sipping nectar from the tree's hanging maroon flowers, others munching leisurely on the blooms' stiff petals. *Good*, Ellishiva thought; news of the scene Lady Malinia had made back at the Meads Den hadn't traveled this far yet.

Bairon was whispering into her ear again. "Have you talked to Sam?" he asked earnestly.

"No," admitted Ellishiva. "I heard Gustav kicked her out of the Hall the last time she came to see me."

"Sam's a liar!" Hektor cut in sharply. "She forces Elli to do things she doesn't want to."

"Elli, you need to talk to Sam," suggested Bairon, ignoring their unwelcome peanut gallery. "She's been digging around for clues as to what truly happened to you for almost a fortnight."

Ellishiva nodded. "Bairon," she asked, "have you seen Atticus or Banog?"

Bairon shook his head. "I haven't seen Atticus since he gave me this yesterday," he reached behind him and patted the Puluma stick. "And Banog isn't here. But I heard that he's on his way back from Nicobar now, because of your attack."

"Shut up, will you?" snapped Hektor. Bairon gave him a hard stare.

Ellishiva stared, too. Her brother was acting just like the elders, she realized—shading the truth.

"Come, children. Come!" called Lady Malinia from up ahead, pausing with Amborella to glance back at them. "We mustn't keep Mr. Belanos waiting!" All signs of sniffling had vanished from her face, and there was even a light spring in her step as she turned again and waddled on. The upcoming visit to Mr. Belanos had, it seemed, magically cured her bad mood.

"Uh, Lady Malinia?" ventured Hektor, suddenly seeming to realize how close they were to the antiquities shop. "May Bairon and I go visit Ms. Tavia? Atticus gave her some of my acorns."

Ellishiva scowled at him. Next to her, Bairon fought down a grin, and she knew they were thinking the same thing. Hektor hadn't given acorns to anyone, but he would say anything to avoid a visit to Belanos Antiquities . . . at least one that involved listening to Lady Malinia giggle nonstop about nothing for who knew how long.

"Very well, Hektor," said their caretaker distractedly, continuing her beeline through the market. Then her feathers bristled slightly, and she shot a somber look over her shoulder at Ellishiva. "Your sister, however, must remain with me. Oh, and if you chance to run across Headmistress Ulima, do let her know where we are, dear boy. We never settled on a meeting place for Amborella's grammar lesson. Come along, girls!"

Ellishiva glowered at her, but Lady Malinia was already tripping off again, oblivious. Hektor wasted no time making his escape and, giving her an apologetic look, Bairon followed.

Amborella tugged her hand free of Lady Malinia's and came back to hold Ellishiva's instead. Ellishiva gave it a squeeze and shot one last frown at the back of Hektor's head before grudgingly starting forward again, following in the wake of their caretaker, who was almost flouncing now, her grand behind swaying from side to side.

Ellishiva scanned the crowds for a flash of blond hair or a flutter of iridescent fairy wings, but there were none to be found.

"Have you seen Sam?" she asked Amborella quietly, peering into every single shop they passed.

"Yes," replied Amborella, and Ellishiva stopped to glance at her in surprise. "I saw her when we came into the market. She was looking for you, too—like we were. But then she left." She swung Dollie Burlap back and forth, nearly bumping the knee of an elephant bird rushing past, a jar filled with fat, wriggling worms tucked securely underneath her wing.

Ellishiva frowned, cursing her bad luck. She was about to ask Amborella where she'd seen the fairy last when she heard it, crackling like puffed rice from the Lavender and Pine grooming shop: whispers about her fall in the forest. To make matters worse, she was sure she caught something about her being alone in an alley with a boy, as well. Ellishiva passed a hand over her eyes.

Perfect.

"Sam's not in there, Elli," said Amborella, giving Ellishiva's hand a tug. Mutely, Ellishiva trudged forward again, following Lady Malinia's waddling tail feathers.

The aromas of the alley around them intensified, and a few shops later, the rich scent of ripe fruits simmering in a honeyed broth found its way to Ellishiva's nose. She glanced sideways at Siren's Serendipity. The window was filled with cakes, muffins, cookies, and breads delectable enough to make anyone—even if she had a full belly—crave a little decadent something. She glanced back down at Amborella, whose huge eyes were fixed on a display of round dates the size of small apples on sticks. Inside, the treats were stuffed with whipped avanella nut butter, and their outsides were drizzled with red and white swirls of thick, sweetened cream, all of it topped off with a sprinkling of cacao crystals.

"You want a barbee jujube?" Ellishiva asked her younger sister. "Maybe I'll have one, too."

A group of children burst out of the shop, each gripping the stick of a barbee jujube in his small, gleeful fist. When they saw Ellishiva, they stopped in their tracks, staring at her bandage. Ellishiva glared at them.

"You don't even like barbee jujubes, Elli," Amborella reminded her. "You like treenitys best."

"You're right, Amber," Ellishiva mumbled. The children were still staring, and no amount of scowling on her part seemed able to make them stop. "Let's go."

They turned quickly and nearly collided with Lady Malinia's rump. "Wait!" she warned. "We must look both ways before we cross, lest we get trampled by dofauns."

Lest we be rumpled for Mr. Belanos, Ellishiva corrected sullenly in her head.

They stood where they were, waiting for a group of robust rhinoceroses to amble by. The dofauns' thick bodies were covered in coarse white hair, and each of their snouts was embellished with six huge, curving horns. The snouts themselves, however, were smeared and spotted with dried dirt; they had just come from plowing their fields.

Lady Malinia made them wait for the veil of dust to settle before they moved on. Ellishiva continued to scan the streets for signs of Samara without success.

Belanos Antiquities had just come into view, however, when she caught sight of someone else darting into its old oak door. Ellishiva squinted at the figure, making the most of her brief glimpse. It was Baron Puck, carrying what looked to be a box under his cape. And there was something else, too—something she recognized. She only caught a snatch of it when the corner of his cape flapped once in the wind, but she knew it on sight: a yellow olivine jar with red stripes.

The baron vanished into the shop for the briefest of moments. Then, as quickly as he had slipped into it, he hurried out again, disappearing into the crowds of Bear Market.

Ellishiva narrowed her eyes as she followed Lady Malinia's tail feathers across the bright alleyway. Nothing about what she had just seen made sense, but she was hardly in a position to go scampering after him to figure out what he was up to.

A tiny silver carillon on the door chimed as Lady Malinia pushed past it, leading the way into the antiquities shop. "Greetings Mr. Belanos!" she cooed cheerfully.

In moments, the dark-haired elf was standing before them, a characteristically warm smile on his face. Lady Malinia, as usual, wasted no time in reaching her feathered hand up for a kiss. Mr. Belanos took it in his own and gallantly raised it to his lips. "Why, my dear Malinia. How delightful to see you again. You look splendid, as always. The rainbow itself could not match those feathers. And—" he paused for a moment, sniffing the air. "Ah. Nicobar honey balm . . . with a hint of Bactria frankincense, *and* a drop of Samal poppy. Simply delicious, my dear!"

"Why Belanos, you flatter me," tutted Lady Malinia, bringing her other hand to her beak coyly.

Ellishiva rolled her eyes. Which was unfortunate, because that was the precise moment that the elf's bright brown eyes peered over Lady Malinia, and met Ellishiva's.

She winced at being caught, but Mr. Belanos only winked at her quickly, and exclaimed, "Oh my! Look at that. Our poor spice girl is out and about at last." Quickly sidestepping Lady Malinia, he knelt in front of Ellishiva. His sharp eyes took in her bandage, then rose to her face again, sympathetic but steady. "I am glad to see you are recovered, Ellishiva," he said in a low voice that only she could hear. "A gash like that would have killed others."

Ellishiva frowned. Before she could come up with a response to this unusual behavior, however, Lady Malinia was speaking up again.

"Poor spice girl, indeed!" she interrupted with a loud *harrumph*. "I will have you know, Mr. Belanos, that she nearly gave me heart failure this morning."

Mr. Belanos gave Ellishiva a quiet sigh and a hopeless smile. Then he got to his feet, and went back to wait on his best customer.

Ellishiva watched him go with a curious sense of foreboding in the pit of her stomach. In the past, she had always felt a sense of tranquility in the antiquities shop. It was a cozy place, full of warmth, and the scent of the dust that had settled into its nooks and crannies over time had always been comforting to her. Even in the summer months, a hot cup of Mr. Belanos's fruit tea was always a welcome prospect. She glanced around the room at the collection of familiar objects: blue pod wind chimes, a didgeridoo with red and white painted spots, two or three Tibetan tea churns, an ancient pottery wheel, lovely amber bracelets with various tiny objects trapped in their depths, and distinctive umber pottery. Oil lamps of every shape lined the walls, some of them lit and burning with the scents of myrrh and sandalwood. On the counter sat a wooden Sumerian abacus with rows of counting beans—something that Ellishiva one day hoped to barter away from him, when she had something worth bartering with. Nearby, Amborella was having a play conversation with Dollie Burlap, showing her some colorful paintings of ships on the wall.

Ellishiva's gaze strayed past her sister, out the open window. There was no chance of finding Samara, cooped up in the antiquities shop like this. And tomorrow she would be grounded for half a fortnight. She furrowed her brow, struggling to think her way out of this trap.

"Malinia dear, take a look at these Corinth silver teaspoons in this box. I've been saving them for your eyes particularly," Mr. Belanos was saying several feet away. "I'll just pop over to pour Ellishiva a cup of this tea from Madagascar, and then I shall be back to grace you with my undivided attention."

Ellishiva threw him a sharp glance. Just hearing the word "Madagascar" made the tiny hairs on the back of her neck rise. She remembered the words she'd written on her note—the same ones that Lady Malinia had babbled with such horror when she was lying injured in the Hall.

Massacre.

She eyed Mr. Belanos as he crossed over to his Yixing tea set, made of purple clay, which sat atop a low table fashioned from a tree trunk. He beckoned to her. Warily, Ellishiva went over to join him.

"Now I know you haven't tried it before, Ellishiva," said Mr. Belanos, gesturing for her to sit in one of the gnarled, antique chairs beside the table, "but I am wondering if you will favor this particular tea. I am very, very curious. Yes indeed."

Ellishiva sat on the chair's handwoven cushion and narrowed her eyes. But the shopkeeper was doing nothing more suspicious than offering her a cup of tea, something he did each and every time she visited him, and she could hardly interrogate him under Lady Malinia's hawk-like gaze. "Um. Thank you," she said helplessly. "I'll give it a taste."

Mr. Belanos smiled at her, and poured the tea. The liquid that flowed into her small, handleless cup was nearly clear, only slightly tinged with purple. A plume of steam rose lazily from its surface. Ellishiva picked it up, inhaling its unusual scent.

"You know," Mr. Belanos was saying, "a visitor just brought this tea to me. It is a rare and splendid treat. One of my favorites, in fact. It comes from a special plantation on the volcanic slopes of Madagascar, where Rajah himself hails from. He was once the prefect there. As you well know already, I am sure." His words were conversational, but the look he gave her while he spoke them was piercing.

Ellishiva had not known that Rajah had once been prefect of a colony in Madagascar. She narrowed her eyes further, meeting the elf's searching stare measure for measure. This was no casual cup of tea.

He was trying to tell her something.

"Curious thing," Mr. Belanos went on, never taking his eyes from hers. "There has of late been a slight whiff of Madagascar tea about the Muheekantuck River. But, of course, you do not go there."

Ellishiva didn't know what to say. *If only*, she thought, *if only Lady Malinia weren't poring over the box of teaspoons, listening to every word.* Wishing she could read the elf's mind, she lifted the cup closer to her nose. "It smells like Simao sweet grass. And some—some kind of mixture of spices," she decided, giving him an inquiring look.

But Mr. Belanos only nodded once—approvingly, she imagined— and left her to go check on Amborella.

A visitor, Ellishiva thought, and immediately wondered if Baron Puck had been the one to bring Mr. Belanos the tea. Her eyes combed the shop in more detail than before, searching for the other object that the baron had brought in. And there it was, tucked away on a shelf behind two short stacks of old, dusty books: the yellow olivine jar with red stripes.

It must be the history of a Va'nature, she thought, noting its unusual colors. *The enchantments must be off. Otherwise, they wouldn't all have access to it. I should have looked at it closer in Rajah's study.*

Ellishiva turned back to the steam snaking around her face. She sniffed the tea again, absorbing the distinctive aroma, but her thoughts were drifting. There had to be a way to view the Silverdine spice dust in the jar. But the thought of sneaking into the shop while Mr. Belanos was away made her squirm with guilt. Everything that came out of her head lately seemed to be devious, and she was far from being used to it.

Still lost in thought, Ellishiva took a sip of the tea.

The first drops had barely touched her tongue when a lonely wisp rose from the teacup, separating itself completely from the rest. Ellishiva's eyes went wide as it took on a purple hue, and then became even darker—a more familiar deep gray.

The dark bark of a locust tree.

Memories of the day she was attacked bloomed to life vividly in Ellishiva's head. Her hands shook, and tea sloshed over the rim of the cup onto her skin. She glanced at Mr. Belanos, but his back was to her now, and when she looked at the cup again, the vision had vanished, leaving behind only haunting whispers.

The Sixth Element is upon you.

A shudder ran down Ellishiva's spine. She set the clay teacup down hard on the low table. It gave a dull *thunk* in protest.

"Tea for you, Amborella?" queried Mr. Belanos's voice from across the room. "And for Dollie Burlap? Perhaps your dolly favors purple tea from Madagascar, eh?"

Amborella giggled, delighted to be part of the conversation, especially when it included her Dollie Burlap. Mr. Belanos brought her over to the tree-stump table and settled her into one of the gnarled armchairs next to Ellishiva. (The chair was so large that Amborella had to climb up onto it, sitting Dollie Burlap beside her; neither one of them could touch the ground with her toes.) Then he looked at Ellishiva herself.

"Are you all right, my dear?" he asked, noticing the spilled tea. "You look as if you've seen a ghost."

"Oh no, I'm—I'm fine," Ellishiva managed. Her hands were still shaky. She sat on them. "It's just too hot. The tea, I mean."

"I see," said Mr. Belanos, and the piercing look was in his eyes again. "Did you enjoy your first taste of it? Before it burned you."

Ellishiva nodded mutely. The tea really would be pleasing, she thought, if it didn't bring back such awful memories.

"Indeed," Mr. Belanos murmured, handing Amborella and her dolly a cup. "The tea from Madagascar is invariably splendid. Many special things come from Madagascar, you know."

Ellishiva stared at him as he poured some tea for Amborella and instructed her to blow on it before every sip, so that she would not burn herself as Ellishiva had. She wished she understood what he was trying to tell her, but what Madagascar had to do with the Sixth Element she simply couldn't guess.

There was a loud, impatient rattle that sounded very much like a box of silver teaspoons being plunked heavily on a countertop. Mr. Belanos gave Ellishiva a last, wry look, and then strolled off to tend to Lady Malinia again.

Ellishiva glared at his retreating back in frustration. Madagascar. She knew almost nothing about it—not more than she knew about any other place, anyway.

"Elli, you need to talk to Sam," Bairon's words came back to her. *"She's been digging around for clues as to what truly happened to you for almost a fortnight."*

Samara. What had she discovered? Ellishiva turned her stare away from Mr. Belanos's back and directed it out the window, searching the crowds again. Diagonally across the alleyway, a group of children was gathered around Wallaby's Emporium, waiting to submit their year-end report cards to the Oudleef Tree. The Oudleef Tree was perhaps three feet high, and was brought to the colony only once a year, always after school was out. Every year, students lined up to slip their report cards into the well-worn niche beneath its roots. If the Oudleef Tree was pleased with the grades, it shed a leaf that could play the music of a particular instrument, but only at the command of its owner. Flat and as long as a Va'nature's index finger, oudleefs came in red, orange, brown, green, or yellow, and could float along beside your ear any-where you went, if you so chose. An oudleef lasted precisely one year before recycling away into dust, at which point it was time to get a new one. This went on, year after year, until the day a student graduated from her studies completely. Then, and only then, did the Oudleef

Tree issue a music leaf that would live as long as its owner. Often, clusters of students joined their oudleefs together into orchestras to play complicated, beautiful songs. It was said that the Oudleef Tree never forgot a single leaf that left its branches.

Ellishiva saw Hektor and Bairon wedged into the eager throng, along with two of her dofaun classmates, Nazeem and Hodges Wallaby. All eyes were fixed on the Oudleef Tree in the front window. Samara could be out there, Ellishiva thought, camouflaged by the masses.

If only she could get out of the antiquities shop.

Feeling as though tiny ants were nibbling at the soles of her feet, Ellishiva glanced around the room again. Amborella was having a play conversation with her doll. By the counter, Lady Malinia was pointing to another beautiful teapot made of Yixing purple clay on one of the higher shelves. "Why, Belanos, I just love that one! Such a delicate, lovely handle." Lady Malinia was mad about teapot and teacup handles.

"Splendid choice," agreed Mr. Belanos, reaching for a stepladder.

Ellishiva turned her head and stared at the floor, her thoughts racing. She bent her right leg and lifted it up onto the cushion with her, twisting the golden toe ring around and around in circles. It was a habit. As long as she'd had it, the toe ring had never once come off, no matter how hard she tried. She kept her ears tuned sharply to the conversation going on by the counter. All she had to do was pick the right moment . . .

"Oh dear, I fear I do not have enough chits in my noli to purchase it, Belanos," Lady Malinia was saying as Mr. Belanos descended the stepladder and placed the teapot in her hands. "But I shall go at once to the Mannahatta Barter Exchange to obtain more. Is it open, do you think, or are they at their midday meal?"

"Malinia, dear. Please don't trouble yourself standing in line at the Exchange for chits. We will barter instead with a tray of your excellent treenity treats."

Ellishiva stole a glance at the elf through her lowered eyelashes. Her eyes fell on the yellow olivine jar with red stripes, tucked into the corner among the dusty books behind his shoulder. *Come tomorrow, I'll be grounded*, was all she could think.

"Delightful!" cooed Lady Malinia. "I shall bake you a heaping tray as soon as I am able and send it over with the children."

Mr. Belanos smiled at her. "Please, don't trouble yourself baking in this summer heat, Malinia. I am quite content to wait for the treats. You have your hands full these days, what with Valerius being gone so much."

Lady Malinia gave a long-suffering sigh. "Indeed, that is too true, Belanos. I shall perhaps put it off half a fortnight or so, then. Thank you for understanding."

"Of course, of course," replied Mr. Belanos gallantly. "And I am sure you need not tell me in advance, whenever you decide to send them. The girls know where the key to the shop is, after all. Just in case I am out. I'll just wrap this up for you," he added, taking the teapot from her and disappearing into a small storage room.

Lady Malinia waited until he was out of sight. Then she seized the largest of the silver spoons from the box she'd been examining earlier and held it up in front of her like a hand mirror, preening and adjusting her splendid feathers. That done, she made a fake smile, inspecting her red beak for specks of breakfast berries.

"Ahem!" coughed Mr. Belanos politely, reemerging with the wrapped teapot. "You look as fresh as a bouquet of Himalayan rhododendrons. Here we go, my dearest. I am sure you will be very happy with this one."

"Why, Belanos! How thoughtful," cooed Lady Malinia, slapping the spoon down quickly on the counter. Instead of landing in the box it had come from, however, it hit the Sumerian abacus next to it. Beans went flying every which way, bouncing wildly off the countertop and scattering on the floor. "Oh, goodness," gasped the preening pigeon, horrified. Her cheeks went as red as her beak, and she and Mr. Belanos immediately bent to pick them up.

Ellishiva saw the chance she had been waiting for.

"Ah, Lady Malinia?" she began, forcing her voice to sound casual.

"I'm really, really hungry. I didn't have breakfast in the Hall this morning. Can I go get something to eat? I'll stay with Hektor at all times, I promise." She stopped, a little surprised. It had come out just as a lie should—namely, sounding like the truth.

Walle was right, Ellishiva thought with a twinge; she was getting better at this.

"Hungry now? Very well, you need to eat," babbled Lady Malinia distractedly, beans slipping like tiny silverfish through her feathered fingers. "Wait. Take Amber with you. Oh! Perhaps you should wait for me," she added, distressed.

"Oh, Malinia, why worry your pretty head?" interrupted Mr. Belanos smoothly. "Surely, nothing will happen to them. Look, I see Hektor just there, at Wallaby's Emporium."

"Well," blinked Lady Malinia. "Well, I am sure you are right, Belanos. Wait, Ellishiva," she called. Ellishiva was already halfway to the door, tugging a perplexed Amborella along after her by the hand. She paused and glanced back, every one of her nerves on edge. "Do not forgot to look for the headmistress, for Amber's grammar lesson," clucked her caretaker as two more beans scurried away from her clumsy fingertips.

Ellishiva let go of the breath she had been holding. "All right," she agreed shortly. And then the carillon chimed as she and Amborella pushed quickly, blissfully out the door.

As soon as they were out of sight of the windows, Ellishiva stopped. She leaned against the wall of the alley, taking several deep breaths to calm herself. Her insides were changing like the seasons. Lying again, she thought guiltily. Was there something in the tea? Why was Mr. Belanos behaving so oddly?

What had he been trying to tell her about Madagascar?

"Are you okay, Elli? Elli?" There was a small tug at her hand.

Ellishiva didn't answer.

Her sister sidled up to her, tucking herself against her hip. "You know, Elli," she whispered, "maybe that Sixth Element that attacked you tainted your blood." Ellishiva blinked, and stared down at the sweet, red-headed little girl beside her. "I heard these things," Amborella went on, as casual as anything. "It was Rajah, and Mr. Belanos and—and Queen Neive. They were talking about it in the Arboretum, while you were in that deep sleep in the Hall and—" Her whisper grew quieter still. "They said you were speaking things in a dance. I wasn't eavesdropping. I was finger painting. I told Hektor, though, and he doesn't believe me. He said you were too sick to dance." She stumbled to a halt, breathless.

Ellishiva pressed her lips into a line. So the elders were talking about her trance among themselves; they simply wouldn't admit to the rest of Mannahatta that it had happened. She groaned and sank a few inches down the wall. The inside of her head felt like a jumble of water rapids after a storm: one moment filled with tension, another with euphoria. One minute she was the best liar in the colony, the next she was grounded. Maybe her blood *was* tainted, like Amborella had overheard.

But tainted blood or no, *someone* had to do something about all of this. And it wasn't going to be Rajah, she thought grimly.

"You know, Amber," she murmured, speaking mostly to herself, "this is our home, too. They didn't have me read all those extra books to keep me from thinking on my own. The elders are hiding something," she took another deep breath, standing up straight again. "And we need to find out what it is."

Amborella nodded seriously, proud to have a part in such an important mission. Ellishiva gave her a wry smile and squeezed her hand.

Before they could set off to find Samara, however, Hektor and Bairon came running toward them up the alleyway.

"Elli! Look at this!" exclaimed Hektor, grinning from ear to ear as he came to a halt in front of her, one hand reaching for something hidden under his singlet.

Extinguishing her smile like a candlewick, Ellishiva walked straight past him without a word, heading toward the southern part of the market, in the direction of Cheeky Canteen.

"Hey!" Hektor protested, scurrying to catch up with her again. "What has gotten *into* you, Elli? Why are you acting so weird?" he demanded.

"*I'm* acting weird?" Ellishiva halted in her tracks and rounded on him, her eyes blazing. "What's that supposed to mean, Hektor? You know as well as I do that something isn't right. Rajah and Lady Malinia—all the elders are lying to us. Well, if you want to believe them instead of me, that's your business." The words were as cold and hard as ice spilling off her tongue—frostier, in fact, than she'd intended, but she didn't take them back. Next to her, Amborella was looking up at them with wide eyes, her mouth a perfect, tiny "o." Ellishiva forced herself to calm down. She gave the little girl's hand a squeeze. "Come on Amber," she muttered. "Let's go." And with that she set off again, heading deeper into the market.

It didn't take long for Hektor to get over his speechless shock and catch up to them again.

"You've gone mad, Elli!" he shouted at her back.

"You've really upset her." Bairon's voice. He must still be trailing along on her brother's heels, Ellishiva thought. "She *just* came out of the Hall of Nature Healing."

"They should have kept her there," said Hektor coldly. "Listen to her, Bairon. Making up stories like Amber about her Dollie Burlap."

Each of his words seemed to burrow deep into Ellishiva, like splinters that no one could dislodge. Still, she managed to grit her teeth and hold her peace. Amborella, on the other hand, turned her head and stuck her tongue out at their surly brother over her shoulder.

They passed a group of boisterous elf girls gathered around someone's new oudleef, which was nestled in the palm of its owner's hand. All of them were too engrossed to notice Ellishiva or her bandage, she saw with relief. "Play 'Purple Moon,'" commanded the elf girl holding it.

Immediately, the familiar song filled the air, played in the tones of an ocarina flute. Ellishiva felt Amborella's footsteps slow down beside her, and on any other day she would have been tempted to stop as well, possibly to even offer her own oudleef to join the girl's ocarina in a duet. But Samara was still nowhere to be seen.

Releasing a quiet sigh through her nose, she gave the little girl's hand a tug, and they pressed onward through the market.

They wound their way through two more alleys without event. Then, at the corner of the third one, Ellishiva stopped. "More kinnarans," she whispered, feeling her heart skip a tiny beat in spite of herself. She glanced over her shoulder to find that both of the boys were still behind her. "Look. Across the alley," she told them. "Careful. Don't both stare at once."

Blatantly ignoring this last instruction, Bairon and Hektor looked over Ellishiva's shoulder, grinned, and then began waving enthusiastically at the kinnarans in question.

"What are you *doing*?" hissed Ellishiva.

"*I* want to see!" whispered Amborella, struggling to peer around her sister.

"I told you, I was trying to show you something before, Elli," said Hektor, their argument forgotten and all of the original excitement back on his face. "You have to see their weapons, their tongobiri swords. They're just unbelievably itutu."

"You *know* them?" interrupted Ellishiva, pretending to fix her noli so that he couldn't see her eyes.

"Yes!" exclaimed Hektor. "They've been here almost a fortnight now. The youngest is Maximus. He's not much older than us. He came with them to do his summer field training. That one there, waving to me, is Morpheus, and the taller one is Theo. Wait until you see how they can move, Elli. They all do payamar. It's amazing!"

"Who's that one again, speaking to Baron Puck? The one with the white hair down to his shoulders?" asked Ellishiva, still being careful not to meet his eyes. Of course Maximus was friends with all of them. Why shouldn't he be?

"They all have white hair, Elli," Hektor pointed out dryly. "But that one is Morpheus. You should have seen it. He picked me up and tossed me in the air like I weighed nothing! He's the one who gave me this," he continued breathlessly.

"Stop pointing!" snapped Ellishiva, trying to comb through Amborella's hair with her fingers—not the easiest thing to do when her subject was wriggling around like a fish. "How does he know Baron Puck? And what do you mean he tossed you into the air, an—and what is *that*?" she gasped, staring at the thing that Hektor had just brought out from under his shirt. It was curved and flat, carved from a strong piece of light-colored wood. Ellishiva narrowed her eyes, and dropped her voice. "That's a weapon, Hektor," she accused.

"It's not a weapon, Elli. It's a boomerang," protested Hektor, turning it lovingly in his hands. He waited for a hint of approval from her, but she gave none, and after a few long seconds he cleared his throat. "Yeah, Baron Puck and Morpheus have been talking a lot. It's like they're old friends or something. Anyway, look, Bairon got something too," he added, slapping his friend on the shoulder. "Show her, Bairon."

Bairon glared at Hektor.

"Let me see, Bairon! Let me see!" clamored Amborella, standing on tiptoe and pulling at his Puluma uniform. With a reluctant look at Ellishiva, Bairon opened his palm. "Oh my gosh. A human coin! A Spanish piece of eight!" the little girl crowed. She was, Ellishiva thought, obviously proud of herself for recognizing it. "It looks like my gold solidus! But yours is silver. Rajah said my solidus was used in the Roman and Byz—Biz Empire." She pulled a gleaming, hand-hammered coin from her noli and held it out for Bairon to admire. Bairon smiled, and the two put their heads together to compare their treasures.

"Byzantine Empire, Amber," Ellishiva corrected distractedly. Her eyes were on the kinnarans and Baron Puck. "And Bairon's coin is not a Spanish piece of eight. It's a Cathay coin. They must have salvaged it from a boat. Some human ships have been navigating the oceans since the Han Dynasty."

Bairon looked up at her, impressed.

"And Hektor," Ellishiva continued, looking away from the odd meeting taking place in front of them to stare, fascinated in spite of herself, at the weapon in his hands again. "Your boomerang is carved with ancient picture writing."

"I know, Elli," said Hektor with a careless shrug of his shoulders. "It's in hieroglyphics. Sam can read it, I bet. I wonder what it says."

"You still can't read hieroglyphics, Hektor? You were in the same class as she was," sighed Ellishiva, shaking her head. Her eyes strayed back to the kinnarans.

Hektor bristled. "It's not my fault. That class was boring," he complained, squinting his eyes and tracing the glyphs with his fingertips. "I think it's a name. Cla—Ca . . . something."

"You should put that away, Hektor," said Amborella.

"Yes, put it away," agreed Ellishiva shortly. "How do you know it's not a bribe?"

Hektor narrowed his eyes at her. "A bribe for what? Geez, Elli, what is wrong with you today? Calm down."

Ellishiva scowled at him. She herself didn't know what had gotten into her. Why was she standing here, wasting time, while her tiny window of opportunity to find Samara was slipping away? Taking Amborella's hand again, she plunged deeper into the market before her infuriating brother or his friend could follow.

It was teeming now; the crowds had reached their peak. Everywhere, the air was filled with the sounds of merchants bartering and merchandise changing hands. Ellishiva led the way through bizarre and beautiful flowers, fruits and vegetables of unusual shapes and colors, bolts and stacks of homespun cloth, heaps of rainbow horn melon, clusters of fresh red and yellow dates. The riot of colors, bathed in the golden sunlight of summer, was truly endless.

"Fresh carrots for cabbage, anyone?"

"Trade mustard greens here for purple potatoes!"

"Wild leeks! Fresh wild leeks! Need just a few heads of garlic."

Ellishiva held on to Amborella's hand tightly as they snaked their way out of the central hub of chaos into another section of the market. Here the stalls were laden with mounds of spices, and bunches of dried herbs hung from their canopies, turning lazily in the breeze alongside pots, pans, and other cooking utensils. Still, there was no sign of Samara.

Ellishiva was on the point of giving up her desperate search when she heard it.

"Elli! *Elli!*"

The voice was familiar; high-pitched and sure of itself. Ellishiva whirled around, and her face broke into a grin, flushing with delight or relief—it was impossible to tell which.

"I am telling you, it is *good* to have wings!" declared Samara, landing lightly in front of her and Amborella. Her blond hair was pulled into a high ponytail, and there was a noli fastened around her waist. She was dressed in the same orange Puluma uniform as Hektor, ready to go to practice later. "Mannahatta is getting so crowded lately. Have you seen all these newcomers?"

Ellishiva flung her arms around the fairy's pretty neck. "Sam! I've been looking everywhere. Missed you!" she blurted.

"Missed you, too!" Samara agreed, squeezing her back with enthusiasm. Finally, she pulled away and looked Ellishiva up and down. "Do you feel better?" she asked seriously. "I came every day except yesterday. Gustav kicked me out."

"I heard," Ellishiva said with a grin.

"Hi, Sam," chimed in Amborella. "Have you seen Walle or the headmistress?" Ellishiva winced. She had completely forgotten about the grammar lesson.

Samara tapped one finger against her chin thoughtfully. "Walle, yes. He was looking for you. But no, I haven't seen the headmistress."

"Don't worry, Amber. We'll find them," Ellishiva reassured her sister quickly. Then she turned back to the fairy in front of her. "I have so much to tell you. But starting tomorrow, I'm grounded."

"I heard," huffed Samara, rolling her eyes. "A pair of teal doves had too much to drink at the Meads Den. They've been flying around gossiping about it to everyone. And something about a boy. In an alleyway? Anyway, the Faviola sisters heard and the whole thing just exploded, of course. Ugh, Elli. I wanted to punch them!" Samara grabbed Ellishiva's hand and began leading the caravan off through the crowds. "I couldn't believe it. Grounding *you*, of all people! Who does Lady Malinia think she is?"

"I couldn't believe it either," Ellishiva muttered. "I had to bite my tongue, too, or else it would have been longer. She's so moody lately, Sam. You should have seen her face when I told her about the kinnaran." She shuddered at the memory. Then she shook it off, and pulled herself together. "Sam, Walle says you've been digging around for information. Have you found out anything about the Sixth Element?"

"Is that what attacked you? The Sixth Element?" Samara gasped, still pushing her way through clusters of shopping dofauns. "Elli, we have so much catching up to do! But first I have to show you something. I was over at the Tigress of Sundari's office—"

"*The Mannahatta Times*?" interrupted Ellishiva. A bad feeling flickered to life in her chest. "What were you doing there, Sam? Did she interview you?" She narrowed her eyes and gave the fairy's hand a sharp tug, trying to get her to slow down. "Did she ask you anything about me?"

Samara did not slow down. "By the way, where are we going?" she asked airily.

Ellishiva narrowed her eyes further. "Cheeky Canteen. We're supposed to eat," she said, feeling her appetite draining by the second.

"Great! I'm starving!" chirped Samara brightly. And, with a yank that made poor Amborella squeak in surprise, the fairy dragged their small three-link chain away into the market.

CATHAY ALLEY

Ellishiva had still not managed to free her hand by the time they stumbled into Cathay Alley. Her feet felt as though they might never be able to walk straight again. Behind her, Amborella's summer tunic was smudged with dust.

Samara, by contrast, was as light and merry as ever.

"Sam," Ellishiva gasped, struggling to catch her breath. "I'm trying to talk to you—"

"I know, Elli," pooh-poohed Samara lightly, "but we're almost there, and we can catch up over the midday meal. Calm down."

Ellishiva scowled at the blond ponytail swaying back and forth in front of her. The next person who told her to calm down, she thought grimly, was going to regret it.

The alleyway was lined with outdoor eateries. Dozens of them went by as Samara continued to pull Ellishiva and Amborella down the busy street. The Giant Beaver Lodge, Ellishiva noticed, was even busier than usual. Creatures of every sort filled its ground-floor tables and chairs, some chatting amicably with one another, others with their noses buried in the paper. Above, on the balcony, a group of middle-aged fairies snacked on heaps of steamed soybeans served atop old copies of *The*

Mannahatta Times, gossiping contentedly. And there were elves sprinkled into the mix, too, most of them sipping yerba mate from dried gourds.

Before she knew it, Ellishiva found herself standing under a well-worn, familiar sign. Its light wood had turned dark over time with the smoke of dozens upon dozens of cooking fires, but the words carved so carefully into its surface were as readable—and as welcoming—as ever.

Cheeky Canteen.

If the Giant Beaver had been crowded, Cheeky Canteen was packed to the brim. A cheerful din of voices, laughter, and clinking dishes enveloped the three of them as they stood and took in all of the bustling activity. Fairies, elves, and dofauns were huddled together around the long, rectangular tables, catching up with family and friends. Ellishiva noticed groups of kinnarans squeezed in among the masses, too. Most of them were gobbling down large bowls of noodles with relish, stopping only to pass around the condiment tray and fresh jugs of chicory malt. Ellishiva was on her toes, craning her neck to peer at each of their faces, before she fully realized that she was searching for a glimpse of Maximus. She dropped back down onto her heels again, hoping that Samara hadn't noticed. "It's so loud, Sam," she almost shouted into the fairy's ear. "Do you see a quiet table?"

Samara shook her head. "It's been like this since the kinnarans arrived. Oh, look!"

At a table in the middle of the chaos, Walle was waving at them. Headmistress Ulima sat beside him, sipping a cup of tea. Next to her was Bairon's mother, Cassandra, a wheat-colored elf with long dreadlocks that covered most of her back. And squeezed onto the ends of the benches with them sat Bairon and Hektor.

Ellishiva scowled. Leave it to Hektor to head her off at the pass.

"Elli!" Amborella was tugging at her hand. "Can I go see the headmistress?"

Ellishiva looked down at her, and nodded. "Be careful, and don't forget to eat before your lesson," she said, kissing her sister quickly on the forehead before letting go of the antsy little fingers in her own.

"I will, Elli. See you later, Sam!" And with that Amborella scampered off to join Headmistress Ulima.

Ellishiva, on the other hand, was not keen on talking over all the details of the Sixth Element with Hektor breathing down her neck.

Next to her, Samara seemed to read her mind. "Let's wait here. Asia can find us a quieter table," she suggested. Ellishiva nodded in agreement.

But quieter tables were hard to come by, and if their friend Asia was out and about among the guests, she was moving too quickly to be spotted. "Do you smell that?" said Samara with a sniff of longing as a sweet, spicy whiff of acorn-noodle broth drifted their way. "I'm so hungry."

Ellishiva shrugged, watching Mr. Guo ladle soup from one of the hanging cauldrons near the middle of the canteen into bowls. "I'm not," she replied indifferently. Steam billowed up from the freshly filled bowls, and acorn noodles, sliced white mushrooms, and wild green leeks bobbed sleepily to the top of the amber broth.

Samara held a hand to her growling stomach. "I wish we could find—"

"Look! Over there. It's Asia," Ellishiva interrupted brusquely, flailing one arm in the air to get the elf girl's attention.

Surprisingly enough, it worked. Asia paused and flashed them a smile, pushing her black hair out of her almond-shaped eyes and away from her fair, bright face. She hoisted a tray loaded with empty noodle bowls up on one hand and began to pick her way toward them, but was interrupted by a kinnaran reaching out to grab her elbow.

"One more special, if you'd be so kind, my girl!" he requested boisterously. "And two jugs of chicory malt!"

"Yes. Coming right up," replied Asia, expertly keeping the tray balanced as she extracted her elbow and hurried away from him.

"So many kinnarans," breathed Samara, eyeing the sizable group that the patron in question was a part of—all of them crowded around the fire pit.

"Yes," agreed Ellishiva, watching Asia duck and weave toward them with her tray like a world-class dancer, attending to little questions and orders as she went. "The one who helped me in the black market was called Maximus." Even as she said his name, her eyes began combing the crowd for him again.

"Oh, so that was the boy you got caught with," whispered Samara impishly in her ear. Ellishiva did not reply, forgetting to keep the eager, wistful look off her face as her search continued. And, unfortunately, this time Samara noticed.

"Oh my goodness," she squealed, unfolding her wings and fluttering around Ellishiva like a giddy moth. "You like him! Look at you. You're glowing. You like Maximus!"

"Stop that!" snapped Ellishiva, grabbing the loud-mouthed fairy by the wrist and dragging her down to earth again. "I don't know what you're talking about. As if there isn't enough gossip about me without you jumping on the bandwagon and—oh, look what you've done. Now Hektor and Bairon are coming over here. Who is *that*?"

Most of the circle of kinnarans around the fire pit was disbursing, shouldering their tongobiri swords and slapping one another on the back good-naturedly. Where they had been, there stood only two men: one a familiar elf, and the other a stately looking kinnaran, his armor gleaming even in the shade of the canteen's canopy.

"Who is *that*?" echoed Hektor in disbelief, joining them just in time to hear the question. Bairon, as usual, was on his heels. "Who is *that*? *That* is General Iliad!" her infuriating brother continued, holding his head high as though he thought he were a celebrated commander himself.

"I know," Samara glared at him. "He dined with Queen Neive and some of the refugee ice fairies that arrived at Central Pond last night."

Hektor scowled back at her. "Well, Ellishiva didn't know," he muttered sullenly.

"He's talking to Baron Puck," Ellishiva observed, ignoring them. "It looks like they're having an argument."

"The baron is always angry," snorted Samara. She bent closer to Ellishiva's ear. "Besides, I found out, Elli, that on that day when the Sixth Element had a go at you, he was in the forest. That's why he was on Mr. Guo's vāhmana. What was he doing there? Since when does *he* wander around in the woods?"

"Yes, I remember," Ellishiva murmured, an image of Baron Puck with his nose buried in *The Times* stirring in her mind. "He's hiding something," she went on, speaking as quietly as she could without being drowned out completely by the noise of the canteen. "I saw him coming out of Mr. Belanos's shop earlier. He left something in there . . . ," she trailed off, sneaking a wary glance at Hektor—who was absorbed in admiring the kinnaran general—out of the corner of her eye. "Remind me to talk to you about it later," she whispered to Samara, who nodded.

Ellishiva let her gaze stray back to the general. He really was rather impressive, she thought. *Just like in my books.*

The argument ended and Baron Puck stormed away from the general, who did not seem especially bothered by it. Nearly all of his troops had wandered off now. She watched as he shook hands with Mr. Guo, commending him on an excellent midday meal, no doubt. Then he turned—and his eyes fell on Ellishiva.

He bowed.

Ellishiva gaped at him. For once, Hektor made himself useful by pinching her—hard—which snapped her out of it enough that she was able to return the bow, at least, though her knees felt weak and the end result was anything but graceful.

General Iliad winked at her. Then he stood and swept from Cheeky Canteen, following his troop. "Hektor, my lad," he called as he strode past, "remember: the mightiest oak in the forest was once a little acorn that held its ground!" He flicked an acorn at them, and Hektor caught it easily with one hand. Yet Ellishiva couldn't help feeling, as she watched the retreating back of the general, that somehow the message had been meant for her. She stared at his magnificent red cape, flapping softly in the breeze behind him, until he was out of sight, swallowed by the crowds of the market.

"What was that?" Hektor demanded as soon as the grand kinnaran was out of earshot, though his face was beaming with pride at the general's gift. He tucked the new acorn into his pocket with care, as though it were unspeakably valuable. "You call that a bow? Geez, Elli. And I was standing right beside you," he groaned, dragging a hand over his face in embarrassment.

"Did you see that, Hektor?" Bairon interrupted, awestruck. "The general bowed to Elli." He looked at her and grinned. "He must think you're some kind of queen or something."

Ellishiva just stared at him, mystified and dumbstruck.

There was a sharp rattle as someone plunked down a tray of empty soup bowls nearby. "Elli! *Elli!*"

"Ow," squeaked Ellishiva as Asia flung her arms around her and hugged her tightly.

"I'm sorry it took me so long," apologized the elf girl, breathless. "Oh, it's good to see you!" She gave Ellishiva another hard squeeze. "We're so busy today. Well, it's been like this for almost a fortnight, actually. Every table I pass by seems to need something. Hi, Sam!" She released her grip on Ellishiva long enough to give the fairy a hug as well. "Follow me," she told them. "I just cleaned a table for you in the back."

It was tricky enough to navigate the bustling canteen even without a tray of bowls balanced on your hand, but at last they reached a long table in the quietest corner of the eatery. The boys wasted no time plunking themselves down at the end of it, taking off their sling-bags and resting their Puluma sticks on the edge of the table.

"This is perfect!" piped Samara, giving their friend's shoulder a grateful squeeze.

Asia smiled. "I'm gonna bring you our special. It's *amazing* today," she said. Before she could scurry away again, however, Ellishiva grabbed her hand.

"Asia, don't you get a break?" she asked earnestly. "Sit with us for a minute. I haven't seen you in ages. What's been happening?"

The exhausted elf girl plunked herself down on the bench, a look of relief flooding her pale face. "Ahpa has been extremely busy lately," she admitted. "Most days he's had to leave me here by myself while he goes to gather more seaweed from the river." She waved to a small group of patrons behind Ellishiva, gesturing that she'd be there in just a moment. Then she went on. "It tastes different from the kind he used to bring home, though." A little frown creased her smooth forehead. "He says it's special. He's been bringing back all sorts of curious things that have washed up on the riverbank. Our garden in the back is packed with them, and I'm supposed to take inventory of them as well as all the food for the business. Some of it smells strange," she added, wrinkling her nose. Ellishiva frowned.

From the opposite end of the canteen, someone shouted Asia's name. The elf girl sprang up from the bench. "Sorry, I have to go. Be back soon!" She gave Ellishiva's arm one last, cheerful squeeze, then hurried off before any of them could protest.

"Asia!" Hektor called after her. "Can we get a few taftnooks and a round of Lilly Pilly Fizz, when you get a chance?"

"Got it!" Asia called back to him over her shoulder before scurrying away toward the fire pit.

"I'm not touching that seaweed soup," Hektor told Bairon dryly, pulling a handful of acorns out of his pocket and laying them on the table for inspection.

"It still tastes good," Bairon shrugged. "It's just . . . different."

"I think it's what's making the dofauns go crazy," Hektor speculated in a low voice.

Ellishiva cast a sidelong glance at them as they began to debate the details of seaweed poisoning. They sounded as though they'd be at it for a while. She looked at Samara, who grabbed her hand and pulled her down to the opposite end of the table.

"Okay," Samara whispered when they were as alone as they were ever going to be. "Tell me."

And Ellishiva told her, in a hushed and hurried voice, about every detail of her encounters and discoveries since the day of her attack: the locust tree and the human world, Rajah's study and her research on ravens, Jipsin Smilodon and the information he'd given her about the Sixth Element, and her talk with Maximus.

"One thing that puzzles me, though," she admitted, reaching into her noli for the crumpled papyrus note, "is an olivine jar. I saw it in the Hall, and it was in Rajah's study when I snuck in there, too. Should have gotten a closer look while I had the chance." She scowled at her own bad luck. "It looks like a Va'nature spice jar. One with a history recorded in it. I thought he'd taken it to Nicobar with him, but then today I saw Baron Puck bringing it into Mr. Belanos's shop—"

"Wait!" interrupted Samara, her eyes going suddenly wide. "Was it a squat yellow olivine jar with red stripes?"

Ellishiva felt her eyebrows go up. "Yes. How did you know?"

Samara bent closer to her on the bench. "Elli, that was the jar that Mr. Belanos brought in to record what was happening to you in the Hall. I was there when he opened it and released the Silverdine spice dust. There were voices, even screams inside. You know how you can hear the echoes of the memories inside when you open those things?" She paused and caught her breath. "Rajah, Queen Neive, and Mr. Belanos must have been viewing something important in that dust before we all arrived with you that night," she said.

Ellishiva nodded grimly. "I remember seeing it there, too. It was strange that they didn't use my own spice jar to record what was happening to me." She furrowed her brow, thinking. "And Va'nature spice jars have enchantments on them to keep them sealed, Sam. Only Rajah can open them, with his staff." She looked the fairy in the eye. "Do you think . . . ?"

"Yes—no," Samara jumped in, excitement bubbling under her words. "What I mean is, I heard Rajah tell Mr. Belanos that the enchantment had been lifted. Listen, Elli, we all saw the light burst out of you that night. But that was all we could see. It blinded us. The Silverdine in that jar, though—"

"—knows what really happened," Ellishiva finished. A shiver ran down her spine.

Samara's eyes sparkled. "We have to find out what that light from your body did. And what was already recorded in the Silverdine to begin with."

"They're hiding something here on Mannahatta, Sam. I can feel it," replied Ellishiva solemnly. "And I know how we can get our hands on the Silverdine spice dust in that olivine jar."

Samara nodded approvingly. "You know," she said, "I was bartering with the Jipsin for a book, and I saw a sketch of that exact spice jar."

Ellishiva blinked at her. "A book? *You* were bartering for a book?" She narrowed her eyes. "Which one?"

"Oh," Samara shrugged, "nothing exciting. Just some biography—"

"You mean it was you who got that book about Amma?" Ellishiva blurted, shocked and—she had to admit—a little impressed. "Why didn't you take it with you? I want to read it, too, Sam. Is there a sketch of Amma in there?"

Samara waved her hand in dismissal. "I didn't have my noli when I bought it, so I thought I was going to have to wait for Queen Neive to be out on business before I could sneak it into the alcove. I just haven't had time to go back and get it yet," she admitted. "And no, no sketches of Amma. But there are a few of the prefects, and one of them is a drawing of Rajah in his study. He looked a lot younger. It said that he was the prefect of Madagascar. And that was the sketch I saw it in, Elli," she went on, the excitement back in her voice again. "It was that same jar, sitting on the shelf in his study behind him."

"Madagascar," Ellishiva echoed darkly. "I keep hearing that word. Lady Malinia was going on about a Madagascar Massacre when I was in the Hall, and just today it kept popping up in Mr. Belanos's shop. He mentioned it too many times to be a coincidence, Sam," she said, looking the fairy dead in the eye again. "He wanted to make sure I heard it. And if you think that jar has something to do with Madagascar . . ."

"All the more reason to see what's recorded in it," concluded Samara triumphantly.

"It must have something to do with their big secret," Ellishiva agreed. She threw a glance at the far end of the table, but Hektor and Bairon were still engrossed in their discussion, inspecting the acorns between them like fine jewels.

Ellishiva turned back to Samara, whose lips were pursed in the look of concentration she wore when she was considering how best to go about breaking the rules. "We have to figure out how to get into Mr. Belanos's shop," she mused thoughtfully.

"Don't worry. I have a *sweet* idea," confessed Ellishiva, smiling a little in spite of herself. "Will tell you about it later. Was there anything else in that book that was interesting?"

"Yes. There was a sketch of a creature. The caption said her name was Symran," said Samara. "I've never seen a dofaun like her. She had the head of a pretty fairy, but the body of a phoenix." Her best friend's eyes sparkled and her fingers drummed against her noli, worrying the drawstring as she spoke. "But Elli, there's something I've been wanting to—"

"Now, we all know what Rajah has taught us," announced Mr. Guo, suddenly appearing at the head of their table with a tray of steaming soup bowls and chilled gourds of pink Lilly Pilly Fizz. Dried reed straws peeked from the tops of the drinks. His sweat-covered face creased in a broad grin as he looked down at the four of them. "Hot foods on warm days cool the body down!"

"I think he just claims that Rajah said that to stay in the soup business, especially in this crazy heat," Ellishiva heard Hektor whisper to Bairon. Both of them hid their chuckles behind their hands. She frowned at them.

Mr. Guo, meanwhile, hadn't heard a thing. "How do you feel, Ellishiva?" he asked kindly, serving each of them a Lilly Pilly Fizz.

"Much better, Mr. Guo," Ellishiva replied, taking the gourd he handed to her. "Thank you." She was growing terribly weary of that question.

"Wonderful! Then try this. I made it especially for all of you. It's one of my favorite recipes from my cooking book. Dotori guksu with ginger and turmeric broth accented with sliced lotus root and acorn noodles. Drink up now. The broth will make you strong." He gave a well-meaning nod as he served the remaining bowls of piping hot yellow soup. "Asia mentioned that you were curious about the new seaweeds—particularly you, Hektor—but I'm afraid they are in short supply at the moment. Hard to come by, you know."

Ellishiva brought her bowl of soup up to her face. The sharp aroma of fresh ginger cleared her head, but even that couldn't rouse her appetite.

The new seaweeds are hard to come by? she thought, her forehead creasing in puzzlement. *But Asia said he's been out harvesting them for a fortnight.*

"And for you, fairy child!" Mr. Guo announced suddenly, interrupting her thoughts. "For you, I have fixed this especially."

"Oh, what is it?" exclaimed Samara, her wings giving a flutter of excitement.

"I believe," said Mr. Guo with a meaningful look, placing a bowl in front of her, "it will calm you down."

Samara stared eagerly down into the bowl. There, floating on the surface of her soup, was a long, slender scarlet chili pepper. The blood rose to her cheeks. "A red chili?" she cried indignantly.

"Yes, indeed," confirmed Mr. Guo with a grin, patting his round stomach with one hand. "To cool the tongue of the talkative fairy. I have it on good account."

Ellishiva quickly hid her own grin behind her hand. At the other end of the table, Bairon and Hektor snickered and bumped their knuckles together. Samara turned and leveled them with a stone-faced stare.

A moment later, Asia arrived carrying a large bread peel—a flat piece of wood with a long handle attached to one side. On it was a cluster of several six-inch-round discs: thin, crispy flatbreads, all of them doused in a sauce of basil, garlic, and tomatillo, then layered with sliced green tomatoes, julienned ramps, and slivers of pickled green olives. To top it off, the whole thing was smothered in melted, steaming green cheese.

"Eat up!" Asia laid the bread peel with its mouthwatering concoction in the middle of the table where everybody could reach it. Her face was flushed red from tending the fire pit. "Taftnook doesn't taste the same if it's not eaten right away!" From the other side of the canteen, two more patrons called her name, and Asia waved clumsily to them as she hurried away from her friends again.

The boys wasted no time diving in, lifting flatbread pieces of the taftnook from the bread peel, careless of the gooey cheese dribbling from its edges.

Mr. Guo smiled fondly at his daughter's retreating form. Then he took a deep breath, and stretched his own aching back. "Enjoy your meal then, young ones. Glad to see you, Ellishiva. Very glad indeed," he added. Then he, too, lumbered off to attend to the large cauldron bubbling over the open fire pit.

As soon as he was gone, Samara removed the chili pepper from her soup with two fingers and laid it on the table. Then she lifted the bowl and took a drink of the broth from the rim. When she put it down again, several long acorn noodles were dangling from her lips. She caught them with a pair of hashi—two slender wooden sticks—and shoveled them the rest of the way into her mouth.

"So, what were you doing at *The Mannahatta Times*?" asked Ellishiva, stirring the yellow soup in her own bowl with a hashi stick, but not eating it.

Samara set the sticks down so that they lay flat on top of the bowl's rim, and shifted her lunch aside. Her eyes were sparkling with delight. "Oh, Elli," she began, "it's the most amazing thing!" She reached into her black noli and, from it, pulled another one. It was made of a muted, rose-colored fabric, and it didn't look like much, Ellishiva thought. Nonetheless, Samara placed it ceremoniously in the middle of the table for all to admire.

The boys took one disinterested glance at it and went back to wolfing down the taftnook. Samara rolled her eyes at them, then turned excitedly back to Ellishiva. "Well?" she prodded. "What do you think?"

"Um," began Ellishiva uncertainly.

But Samara was already launching into her story. "The Tigress of Sundari gave it to me, to thank me because, well, she was asking me so many questions. You know, about the ice-forest fairy refugees that just arrived. Oh, and she told me the name of the murdered ice fairy, Elli! Her name was Renee. Nobody else knows that because, I mean, it's not even mentioned in *The Times*, but—but anyway, look at *this*!"

She snatched the rose-colored noli off the table and put it between them on the bench. Then she reached into it, mouthed a few silent words, and pulled out—Ellishiva blinked and did a double take. There, on the bench next to the tiny noli, sat a large green ball the size of a honeydew melon. It had to be twelve times larger than the unassuming little pouch it had come from. Its outer skin was made of tough pandus leaves wrapped in fine, strong strings.

At the end of the table, Ellishiva heard the boys gasp. Before she could even look up, they were hovering over her and Samara, wonderment plastered all over their faces.

"That is too itutu, Sam!" exclaimed Bairon.

"How does it work?" added Hektor, predictably.

"You can fit a balón in there?" said Ellishiva, her eyes narrowing. It was common enough for people to carry around the smaller, orange-sized péquillas in their nolis. The much larger balón, by contrast, had never fit into any noli that she had ever seen.

"Yes," gushed Samara. "Isn't it divine, Elli? It's a special kind of noli. Look at its lining." Samara carefully reached into the little pouch, tugging a pinch of its inside fabric out so they could see. It was covered in a thin, shimmering veil of the finest red dust that Ellishiva had ever seen.

On either side of them, the boys leaned their forearms on the table and craned their necks, observing intently. "It's made with Rojorine spice dust," Samara explained, her voice barely below a squeal. "Real Rojorine! Like in a fairy's wand!"

"Sam," Ellishiva began, but her friend was still absorbed in her demonstration. She and the boys watched in awe as Samara snatched the straw from her Lilly Pilly Fizz gourd—easily twice as long as the noli itself—and tossed it into the shimmering red dust.

It vanished.

"See? It just disappears!" crowed Samara, as though she had already done this a hundred times and still had yet to grow tired of it. She let out a satisfied sigh. Then she carefully folded the flap of the noli closed, looked at the boys, and continued smugly, "I can stuff as many things in it as I want, and it always stays the same size. It doesn't even weigh more! Then, when I want to pull something out again, I just reach my hand inside, say its name, and it comes right back. I love it!" She turned to Ellishiva. "What do you think, Elli? Isn't it the most itutu thing you've ever seen? You can borrow it if you like," she added generously. "The spice dust won't come out, or else, you know, I could make a wand. But who needs a wand when I've got this!" she finished triumphantly, finally pausing to catch her breath. She looked at Ellishiva expectantly.

Ellishiva grabbed her by the shoulder and dragged her closer so that she could talk in her ear. "Sam, that's illegal magic," she hissed in a low voice. "Spice dust can only be stored in containers made from olivine. And even then, the olivine is controlled by the Senate of Nicobar. I don't trust the Tigress. She was probably bribing you for information with that thing. And where was Baron Puck when you were talking to her?"

"Oh, I don't know where he was. You worry too much, Elli," shrugged Samara, shaking off Ellishiva's grip lightly. The glow on her face was undiminished. "I didn't tell her anything about what happened in the forest," she added. "I just told her what the Jipsin said about dofauns behaving strangely, with the dark clouds and all. And it's not like she doesn't know that already," she laughed. "She *is* a dofaun."

"Sam, this just doesn't seem right," Ellishiva interrupted, trying to keep her frustration from boiling over. "The Tigress is known for twisting stories and printing sensational headlines. *Plus*, the baron has been acting really suspicious lately. And she works for him." She paused and glanced at Hektor and Bairon, who had wandered back to the other end of the table again and were now slurping up their acorn noodles as loudly as they possibly could. Ellishiva rolled her eyes and turned back to Samara. "There's no way a dofaun like the Tigress would give you something like this just because you answered a few questions about things that everybody already knows," she concluded grimly.

Samara's face tightened. She grabbed the Puluma ball and stuffed it back into the noli.

"Sam," Ellishiva said sternly. "You've got to give it back."

"Yeah, Sam, it's probably a bribe," chimed in Bairon from the far end of the bench.

Ellishiva rounded on him. "Right, because you haven't taken any strange gifts from anyone lately," she scowled. "Where is your coin, anyway?"

"See, Bairon, I told you to shut up!" Hektor snorted, kicking his friend under the table.

"Listen!" Samara broke in loudly. Everyone stopped and turned to her. "I am a fairy without a wand," she said piteously. "I'm surrounded by magic everywhere I go, but I'm helpless to use it. None of you know what it's like for me." She looked down, fixing her regular noli with a bleak look. Then she rallied a bit, and the familiar glint sparked to life in her eyes again. "But—but the Tigress understands. I think she might even be able to get me a real fairy's wand, the way she was carrying on. But then that mean-looking Baron Puck showed up, and . . . and she said I had to leave the office."

Ellishiva stared at her. "I don't like it, Sam."

Samara turned on her. "And how do *you* feel, Elli? Fine, you don't have a wand, but you and Hektor and Amber are *Va'natures*! You're supposed to be planting seedlings around the planet in the human world. Rajah keeps telling you it's not your time, so the Va'natures from other colonies go around doing *your* work!" She crossed her arms over her chest and muttered, "It's a *prison* we live in."

"Oh, give it a rest, Sam," growled Hektor, gathering his acorns from the table and shoving them back into his pockets. "In case you hit your head in the forest like Elli and forgot, you *had* a wand before you tried to steal Queen Neive's journals. It was rightfully taken away from you. So stop whining about it already."

"Oh yeah?" snapped Samara. Her face flushed as red as a ripe strawberry, and she jumped up from the bench. "Are you going to make me?" she shouted.

"Just shut up, both of you!" yelled Ellishiva. Even in the din of the canteen, a few heads turned their way. She scowled and lowered her voice. "All I'm saying is that strange things are happening. Come on, none of you find it odd that all of sudden we're receiving gifts—right after this Sixth Element tried to kill me? We don't know who let her into the colony. It could be anyone. Even people we know. Plus, everyone is going about as if nothing is wrong. The dofauns think the dark clouds are just some strange weather pattern, Rajah is *lying* to all of us—" she stopped, catching her breath, and leveled a dour look at the three of them. "What will we do if the Sixth Element attacks again?" she asked quietly.

There was silence around the table. Ellishiva glared pointedly at Hektor, but he only looked away, fingering the acorns in his pockets. She cleared her throat impatiently. "Hektor," she prodded sternly, "why did that kinnaran give you a boomerang?"

"A weapon!" piped up Samara, jumping at her chance to change the subject. "Itutu! Let's see it, Hektor!"

"There is never anything *itutu* about a weapon, Sam!" Ellishiva snapped at her. It seemed she was the only one who understood that they weren't all playing some jolly little game. She turned back to Hektor. "Rajah will be upset if he finds out," she warned.

Hektor winced, then set his jaw and glared at her to try to cover it up. "It's not a weapon, Elli. What do the kinnarans carry? That tongobiri sword is a weapon. Not this boomerang," he declared.

"Well, for now," jumped in Bairon before the bickering could go any further, "all this talk about gifts and weapons is going to make us late for Puluma practice."

"Right. We should go," agreed Hektor, relief written all over his face. "I need to pick up a few more acorns on the way. Missing a few sizes."

"Why do you even care?" butted in Samara, not bothering to hide the scorn in her voice. "An acorn is an acorn. You're so obsessed with them."

"So what if I am. You got a problem with that?" rejoined Hektor at once.

Samara rolled her eyes and swung her head away from him.

"Nazeem and Hodges must be warming up," Bairon said pointedly to Hektor, obviously trying his best to avoid the bloodshed.

"Yeah, yeah. I hear you," Hektor grumbled. Then he pulled out the boomerang and slid down the bench until he was sitting opposite Samara at the table. "I need you to read some hieroglyphics for me," he muttered, holding it out to her.

"Hmm. Still can't read hieroglyphics, huh?" she said sweetly with acid in her eyes, rubbing it in for all it was worth. Hektor scowled at her. Samara deliberated for only a moment before snatching the boomerang out of his hands, unable to resist the chance to show off, or to humiliate him further. Her fingers traced the glyphs thoughtfully. "Hmm," she murmured to herself.

Ellishiva glared at them both, but they ignored her. From the far end of the table, Bairon gave her an apologetic look.

"It says . . . Cla—" Samara stopped short, and her squinting eyes went wide. "Who gave this to you?" she asked Hektor. "It has the markings of a heart! It's an enchanted wind messenger with love messages!"

"Morpheus gave it to me," replied Hektor, shrugging a little to cover his surprise. "He's one of the kinnarans. He said it was time to pass it on."

Ellishiva glared at them harder. But, if they noticed, she was easy to ignore.

"So, what did I miss?" asked Asia, plunking down on the bench beside Hektor, her face flushed and exhausted. Hektor snatched the boomerang back from Samara and tucked it away out of sight again. Samara crossed her arms over her chest and glowered at him. There was a moment of strained silence. "Nothing, really!" Hektor said at last, unconvincingly.

An elf family got up to leave, and Mr. Guo called for Asia. She sighed, and stretched her legs. "I'll meet you guys at the Puluma court," she said. "I have more tables to clean before I go."

Bairon almost jumped to his feet. "Come on, we'll all help Asia," he suggested, only too eager to disband the tense assembly at the table.

Samara frowned at her purple-colored nails and huffed. "Well, if we must. But then we're all going to Central Pond." She looked pointedly at Ellishiva. "Together."

Ellishiva propped one elbow on the table, dropped her chin into her hand, and pretended not to hear. If they wanted to ignore her warnings, fine. They deserved to be ignored in return. Her mind was racing. There was so much she needed to do with her limited time today; she could sense it. She just didn't know what it was that needed to be done yet. She thought of all the havoc the Sixth Element could wreak while she was cooped up in the warren for the days ahead and shuddered.

"Wonderful!" exclaimed Asia gratefully. "I can change in your room when we get to the Alcove, Sam." She picked up as many bowls as she could carry and set off. Samara and Bairon gathered far fewer of them and trailed, with far less grace, after her.

Hektor lingered at the table for a moment. "So . . . are you coming, Elli?" he asked quietly.

Ellishiva didn't answer. Hektor sighed, shook his head at her mutely, and went to join the others.

The patrons in the canteen were finally beginning to thin out, Ellishiva noticed numbly. All of the kinnarans had left except for one small group tucked against the wall a few tables away. She thought of Maximus—how he, at least, had taken her seriously. Had wanted to help, even. But he wasn't here now.

She felt empty.

For a long time, Ellishiva sat quietly by herself, stirring her untouched soup with a lone hashi stick. She waited for a plume of steam to rise from its surface, wondering if it might turn green like the tea in Mr. Belanos's shop. Then she realized that the soup had lost all its warmth, and its steam along with it. She pushed the bowl away and brought the straw jutting out of the half-full gourd of Lilly Pilly Fizz closer to her lips. Tiny carbonated bubbles clung to its length, sporadically bursting now and then. From the table against the wall, she was vaguely aware of the last group of kinnarans getting up and wandering away.

Ellishiva sighed, blowing a few bubbles into the gourd with her straw.

"Are you going to eat that?"

She glanced up and almost choked on the straw from raw surprise. Maximus was standing beside the table, right across from her, his yellow eyes sparkling with amusement.

"I'm not hungry," Ellishiva replied, dropping the straw from her lips as though it had been a tiny, poisonous snake. She pushed the bowl of soup closer to him. "But—but it's cold," she warned clumsily.

"I think food tastes better cold," he smiled at her, and sat down on the bench. Then he looked at her more closely, and his brow creased in concern. "What's the matter? Why do you look so sad?" he asked.

"I'm not sad. I'm thinking." Ellishiva spoke with her eyes on the soup. "When I'm thinking or reading my face is different."

"Really?" Maximus's eyebrows went up a bit. "How do you know that?"

"Well, Rajah once told me it's important to know what you look like. That is, how your face changes," Ellishiva explained, managing a wry smile. "Or you'll forever walk around in life as if you have a curtain over your head."

Maximus grinned. "I've heard of his wisdom," he said. "He must have taught you many things already."

"Yes, he has," Ellishiva murmured. A little wave of sadness rolled over her. "I miss him. When he's here, I feel like nothing can happen to me." Her voice dropped until it was barely above a whisper. "But something did happen. And now he's gone."

Maximus pushed the soup aside and leaned his arms on the table, bending a few inches closer to her. "Well, that's easy enough to fix," he replied, almost as quietly. "Just think of him and remember the lessons he's taught you. That way part of him will always be with you." He closed his fingers into a light fist and patted his chest once, gently.

Ellishiva's wry smile grew a little. "Now you sound like he does," she chuckled. But there was a warm spot of gratitude in her heart.

"I try," Maximus smiled back, reaching for the soup again. "I'm the youngest son in my family, and trust me, my mother finds ways to make me think of her—especially when the general takes me on long summer trips."

Ellishiva nodded. "Have—" she began doubtfully. Then she cleared her throat and spoke a little louder. "Have you heard anything about Rajah since . . . since you got here?" she asked.

Maximus took a small sip of the soup and licked his upper lip. He glanced behind him quickly to make sure all of the other kinnarans had left the canteen. Then he leaned across the table toward her. "I heard he's with Amma in Nicobar," he said, speaking in a low voice again. "They were having meetings of the elders from all the colonies, but now even the Senate is involved, I heard. I don't know much else yet. The general just arrived last night, and I haven't spent much time with him or the officers who came with him. I'll keep my ears open for more news and let you know when I hear it, though."

Ellishiva looked at him as though he might vanish before her eyes at any moment. There was so much gratitude in her chest that she thought her ribs might crack. "Thank you so much," she said softly.

Maximus's fire-yellow eyes sparkled at her. "That's what friends are for," he replied easily.

Ellishiva smiled. Her gaze drifted across the canteen to Samara, who was doing her best to stack dirty dishes without getting gunk under her fingernails. "Sam's my best friend," she admitted. "We argue sometimes, but I'm not worried. The next time we talk it'll be as if nothing ever happened." She sighed and gave Maximus a weak half-smile.

"I saw your argument," he admitted. "The two of you sounded more like sisters. I have two of them, so I know," he added with another impish grin. "Poor Hektor barely gets a word in with her, does he? She's like—like wildfire."

Ellishiva snorted under her breath. "Maybe she'll at least stop trying to make a wand, now that she has that enchanted noli," she muttered to herself. Then she glanced back at Maximus, and added, "Hektor, on the other hand, is *not* 'poor.'"

Maximus gave a helpless little shrug. "Try not to be so hard on him," he advised, slurping down the rest of the yellow soup. "Brothers are protective of their sisters. Me included. Look," he went on, jerking his chin faintly in the direction of the brother in question as he reached for a slice of the cold taftnook. "He's glanced over at me talking to you a few times already."

Ellishiva rolled her eyes. "I know, I saw. But he's just being so . . . so *stubborn*," she spat resentfully. "He won't believe a word I say about the Sixth Element, and I *need* him now, more than ever since . . . since Rajah is . . ." She trailed off.

Maximus gave her a sympathetic look. "That's rough. Don't give up on him, though. I have an older brother, too. I'm sure Hektor has a lot on his mind. But at least Samara is on our side. An army of three is better than an army of two."

"An army?" Ellishiva mumbled, taking a long sip from her Lilly Pilly Fizz and trying not to feel too pleased that he had just called them an "us."

"Yes. It's hard when you have to battle something yourself," he recited, as though he'd known the words by heart for many years. "But if you have a team to share the work, you can accomplish many things, and much faster. You should try it," he concluded, popping another piece of cold taftnook into his mouth.

They sat there in companionable silence. Ellishiva realized that all the tense muscles from her argument with Samara and Hektor had relaxed again. It was as though she were a brittle sheet of parchment, and this unusual kinnaran's words were like ink soaking into her, lending her strength.

"I do have a lot to do," she said softly, breaking the silence. She pulled out her crumpled papyrus note and smoothed it out in front of her on the table. "And it would be a lot easier with help," she confessed.

Maximus grinned at her and nodded. There was another long moment of silence. Then, "So . . . I heard you like to read books," he ventured, eyeing her note.

"Yes, I do," Ellishiva confirmed. Then she stopped smoothing out the wrinkles in the paper and looked up at him with one eyebrow arched. "You know a lot about me," she pointed out neutrally.

"Oh. Yes, well," Maximus started. The tops of his ears went a little redder.

"I know you love payamar," interrupted Ellishiva, smiling innocently. "Do you like books, too?"

"I like some," Maximus replied, grateful for the change of subject. "At our academy, our teachers encourage us to read at recess, actually. And to practice payamar, too."

They both smiled and chorused, "What good is exercising the mind and not the body!"

Maximus laughed. "I guess our teachers say the same thing."

Ellishiva leaned toward him a little over the tabletop. "Here, the exercise we do at recess is just simple yoga stretches. We have a good headmistress, too. When she gives you something to read or research, it's like—like she gives you a piece of adventure, or—or a mystery to solve." She trailed off, suddenly self-conscious, and sat back again. "I'm talking too much, aren't I?"

Maximus only smiled wider. "No. Not at all. I like listening to you," he said. "You're like a leaf caught up in the wind. You can never tell which direction it will go. It makes you interesting." A curious look came into his eyes. "Once, a long time ago, I heard Morpheus talking to his friend about a girl that Morpheus's twin, my other older brother, knew once." He tilted his head slightly, and quoted, "'What he loved about her most was that she was a girl who was entirely unpredictable.'"

Ellishiva felt her cheeks begin to heat up again. "Really! Twins!" she managed finally.

Maximus shrugged, and reached for another slice of the stiff taftnook.

"Oh, that must be cold," commented Ellishiva. She reached over and pushed the condiment tray closer to him. "Here, put some spices on it. That should make it taste better."

"Oh no, this is good. Thank you," Maximus declined politely. "My mother puts a *lot* of spices on things. They set my insides burning." The corner of his mouth twitched. "My ahpa always says she has a heavy hand with them. I think I'll eat this the way it is."

"Well, you know," suggested Ellishiva, "most spices are not hot at all. It's just the black pepper and chilies that make food hot or spicy. I don't care for those either," she added. "If you ask me, they mask the true flavors of other, tastier spices."

Maximus looked at her, a little surprised. The piece of cold taftnook was still in his hand. He turned and peered at the condiments on the tray, as though seeing them for the first time. Ellishiva smiled at him. "So, tell me about your older brothers. The twins."

"Well," he answered distractedly, inspecting the nearest pot with curiosity, "they tell me that they looked so much alike it was hard to tell them apart."

Ellishiva frowned. That didn't make sense. Before she could ask him about it, however, they were interrupted by a sudden, distant noise, as if a tall tree had crashed to the floor in the forest.

"Did you hear that?" breathed Ellishiva, her eyes wide.

"Yes," Maximus replied curtly. He set the taftnook back down on the bread peel and wiped his mouth with the back of his hand.

They looked around to see if anyone else had noticed, but the canteen and the alley beyond were calm. Hektor and Bairon were drying bowls for Mr. Guo with their backs to them. Samara was wiping tables with Asia, the two of them chatting faster than their hands could swipe at the smooth, lunch-spattered surfaces.

"Stay here," Maximus said shortly. "I'll be right back." Then he rose and walked out of the canteen, hurried past some old barrels and empty noodle racks, and disappeared out of sight, headed toward the forest.

Ellishiva waited ten seconds. Twenty. Sixty. Then, without a word, she tucked her note back into her noli and slipped out into the alleyway after him.

Following the direction he had gone, she trailed carefully down the length of Cathay Alley until it ended, and then pressed on. When she reached the sugar maple that marked the eastern edge of Bear Market, she paused, listening for footsteps and scanning the ground for strange objects. She glanced instinctively around for locust trees, but there were none to be seen. Around her, the woods were eerily silent.

Then, very near, she heard the rough snapping of dry twigs, followed by a low, gruff groan.

Ellishiva's heart skipped a beat, and she dropped silently into the short, thick plants around the base of the sugar maple. The groan sounded again—too big, too deep to be Maximus, she thought. But then . . . who? With a gnawing sense of dread, Ellishiva crept softly nearer through the bushes. Then she took a deep breath, and peered through the leaves.

"Atticus!" she gasped.

The huge bear was sprawled over a patch of broken brambles. His face was scratched, his pristine white fur stained with brown stripes. Ellishiva's stomach turned inside out. There was nothing she could do. Still, she had to do something. She stood up from the bushes and saw Maximus running toward the dofaun, grim determination stamped on his face.

Before either of them could reach the fallen bear, however, the branches above them came alive, lashed by a powerful wind. Leaves churned on the forest floor, and the ground shook. Ellishiva looked up, expecting to be engulfed by a swarm of black ravens at any second. But it was not a crowd of ravens that she saw landing on the lowermost boughs of the tree above her.

"Banog!" she breathed, weak with relief.

The great eagle, who stood as tall as a burly human, folded his mighty amber- and black-feathered wings. She could see the strong claws of his feet cutting into the heavy branch beneath him.

"Don't touch, Ellishiva! Stay away from him, Maximus!" Banog commanded. "He is quite all right, I assure you."

As if to prove the truth of Banog's words, Atticus stirred on the brambles. He looked a bit disoriented, Ellishiva thought, but apart from that he seemed to be himself. Slowly, the white bear lumbered up onto his hind paws, shook his huge head as though to clear it, and began to brush the dirt and green leaves off of his fur.

Above them, Ellishiva saw Banog release a long breath. Then the great eagle tilted his head, surveying her and Maximus. His sharp eyes fixed themselves on the kinnaran. "Well then, let me look at you. They finally let you out of Nicobar, eh?" he said.

Maximus nodded. Ellishiva could see his concern for Atticus mingling with the delight at seeing Banog on his face. Cautiously, he opened his transparent wings and flew up to the majestic bird, who ruffled his own wings in welcome. "I'm so glad you're here, Banog," the kinnaran said earnestly.

"As am I, my boy. As am I," murmured the eagle softly. Then he fluttered off the branch, stirring the leaves again, and landed on the ground in front of Ellishiva. "Hello, my little one," he said simply, though his eyes were full of warmth. Ellishiva managed a smile for him. Banog took in the bandage at her waist. "I take it you are feeling better? I visited you in the Hall many times, but you were in a deep sleep. And then, alas, Atticus and I were obliged to tend to urgent matters."

"I'm much better, yes. Onuris took care of me," Ellishiva answered truthfully, touching her bandage. There was still a knot of dread in the pit of her stomach. But she felt safer with Banog, and there was something soothing about his voice when he called her "little one."

The great eagle turned to Atticus and declared heartily, "Atticus, you are losing your touch!"

"I merely lost my balance," rumbled Atticus groggily. Ellishiva took a step toward him. "No!" he gasped, suddenly sharp and alert again as he swung his huge paws in front of him and backed away from her. "Stay away, child! I will be fine!"

Ellishiva halted, taken aback.

"That's right!" boomed Banog, and his voice, she noticed suddenly, was too casual to be believed. "Keep away from Atticus. He has fallen before, and he knows well how to survive."

Ellishiva studied Atticus's body, and a frown deepened on her forehead. Even from where she stood, the reek of smoke, stagnant water, and burnt animal hair was acrid in her nostrils. And the long brown stains on his fur . . . She swallowed hard. There could be no denying their resemblance to long, slimy lashes from moss. A dizzy feeling spread through her bones and nerves.

The Sixth Element had struck again.

Ellishiva took a step back, but her legs buckled and her body swayed. She would have crumpled to her knees had Maximus not been on hand to catch her.

Seeing this, Banog bent his great head down to her level. In that moment, staring back into his eyes, Ellishiva knew that she was right about her theory. When the dofaun opened his beak, however, all he said was, "Would you like a ride?"

A ride where? Ellishiva thought. But before the words could reach her lips, she felt herself being swept up onto the eagle's broad back by Maximus, who pulled himself up to sit behind her.

Banog spread his huge wings and rose a few feet into the air, until he was hovering above the wounded bear. "Come, Atticus. I know you don't favor a stained coat. We must get you cleaned up," he remarked lightly. And with no more warning than that, he swooped.

Ellishiva covered her mouth, struggling not to vomit on Banog or Maximus. She hadn't eaten anything at Cheeky Canteen, true, but the Lilly Pilly and all its fizz was bubbling up in her throat more than enough to make up for it.

A moment later, the lurching stopped as Banog righted himself again. Weakly, Ellishiva peeked down over his shoulder. Atticus, huge as he was, was hanging from the eagle's mighty talons.

And then they were off.

Off where? Ellishiva wondered again. But as Banog rose through the trees and soared high above the colony, swooping northwest over Bear Market and its labyrinth of alleyways, the answer became all too apparent.

He was taking her back to Banyan Tree.

No, Ellishiva thought, but she could hardly say it. They skimmed into Banyan Circle, past Forest Academy with its well-tended gardens and tall, sprawling, adjoining rain trees, and the tip of the dofaun's wing caught the ribbons of the waterfall cascading down from the Arboretum high above. Ellishiva closed her eyes as the fine, cool spray misted over her face. Then Banog wheeled toward the pond, and she felt Maximus grab her shoulder as they both groped to regain their balance. The eagle's amber and black feathers flapped like moving curtains between the aerial roots as he held them all suspended in midair.

"Ready for a bath, Atticus?" he called. "I am taking Ellishiva to the Hall of Nature Healing. Meet you there!" And without further ado he released Atticus, who splashed—*blam!*—down into the pond.

Ellishiva bit her tongue as the eagle swerved and began to rise among the aerial roots, weaving up through the countless vāhmanas toward the great Hall high above. She would have loved nothing better than to enlist his help, but it was clear from the way that he had tried to cover up the Sixth Element's attack on Atticus that—like all the other elders—he was bent on keeping her in the dark.

Behind her, Maximus squeezed her shoulder and her dark thoughts eased a bit. Whatever happened, she was not alone.

THE EYE OF THE SILVERDINE

"Elli! Elli!"

Ellishiva heard Samara's voice calling her from across the Vivarium and tensed, but forced herself not to turn around. Instead, she kept her gaze focused on the sapling in front of her, its thick, silvery leaves shivering as she transferred it into a terra cotta pot. *Natural,* she coached herself, inhaling a deep, rib-stretching yoga breath. *Be natural.*

She was standing before one of many waist-high planting beds. The Vivarium was divided into four squares, and each of them contained several rows of beds like this one, on top of which saplings of varying heights grew and blossomed all year round. One corner of each square was marked by a small tent with a trellis roof, and every one of those housed a worktable cluttered with pots and tools, along with a flip-top desk and one or two chairs.

"Elli!" Samara's voice was closer now. With studied calmness, Ellishiva finished the transplant, dusting some stray crumbs of dirt off of the pot. Then, and only then, did she look up.

The fairy was flittering toward her on shimmering wings, dashing in from the Arboretum beyond and weaving her way through the square maze of sapling beds. Ellishiva barely had time to brace herself and get a firm grip on the pot before Samara was landing abruptly beside her, grabbing her wrist and dragging her over to the closest trellis-roofed tent. She snuck a furtive glance at Hektor, who was tending to his corner of the Vivarium a little ways away. He hadn't even bothered to glance up at the fairy's entrance.

So far, so good.

"Oh my goodness. *I have never* seen such beauty. And the details!" Samara gushed excitedly, plopping herself down into one of the vine chairs beside the desk. The reed mat cushion on the seat crunched faintly under her weight. She propped her legs up onto the flip-top desk. "Elli, you should have been there. It was the most amazing thing. All the bushels of *acorns* Mr. Guo found by the Muheekantuck River! I was just in time. Mr. Belanos is on his way to Cheeky Canteen to barter for them—like, right now. And soon they'll be gone." She let out a tragic sigh, then hid a smile behind her hand.

"Really!" said Ellishiva, as loudly as she could without sounding suspicious. She looked for a spot of space on the worktable where she could set the newly potted plant, but there was none. With a wary look at Samara's feet, she put it down carefully on the other end of the flip-top desk, where she was sure it would not be kicked. "Those must be truly *rare* acorns for Mr. Belanos to be interested in them."

From the corner of her eye, she saw that Hektor had paused over the new holes he was digging in his sapling bed. She let out a long, silent breath. "I hope this works," she whispered to Samara nervously. "Walle is doing his part, keeping Amber distracted."

Both girls craned their necks to peek over into the adjacent Vivarium square, where they saw Walle entertaining Amborella with a game of Plant the Seed. Ellishiva's little sister tripped, and giggled. "You know, Dollie Burlap, you've been winning a lot lately. It's like you want to take over the whole earth!"

Samara smirked, and turned back to Ellishiva. "Oh, it's gonna work. Trust me," she whispered back impishly. "You've been good the whole time you've been grounded, and today is your last day anyway. It's stupid that Lady Malinia won't let you leave the warren without Hektor, but I suppose we have no choice." She rolled her eyes. "There. He just glanced at us again. It's only a matter of time now, Elli. Oh, and by the way," she added, arching one eyebrow wickedly, "I saw Maximus in Textile Alley earlier."

Ellishiva frowned and wiped her hands on her short, dirt-smudged pants. "Not now, Sam. Keep going. Say—say something normal. And don't mention Maximus."

"So I see Onuris took off your bandage," Samara commented loudly, pushing aside the hem of Ellishiva's tunic to reveal the roughly healed green skin beneath. The mischievous smile never left her face.

"He says I'll have this scar forever," Ellishiva replied with a bleak look at the pale, raised ridge on her side. Then she dropped her voice to a whisper again. "What about the rest of the plan? Have you been inside? Is she finished?"

"She will be soon. The kitchen smells great," replied Samara. "I told her I was going to go wait in the Vivarium so I could watch you work."

Ellishiva nodded. Her eyes fell on the worn rose pouch fastened around the fairy's waist. Letting out an uneasy breath, she stood and walked over to the cluttered worktable to organize the mess. "So . . . did Queen Neive suspect anything? About your noli?" she asked.

Samara shrugged dismissively. "Oh, she suspects everything. I just told her one of the rescued ice fairies showed me how to sew it. She said she was happy that I'm finally learning to be domesticated." She rolled her eyes and blew a puff of air out of the corner of her mouth. "She can keep her stupid wand," she concluded primly before launching into a list of all the things she'd been able to stuff into the noli so far.

Ellishiva only half-listened. Her nerves were on edge. She'd spent her half-fortnight of being grounded as productivity as she'd been able, meticulously planning with Samara (who had snuck in through her bedroom window more than once) how they would leave the warren and sneak into Mr. Belanos's shop to view the Silverdine spice dust in the strange red and yellow jar. She had written a papyrus note to Asia, asking her to show Hektor all the things that her ahpa, Mr. Guo, had collected at the shores of the river one by one, if she had to. Just as long as she kept him there as long as she could. Samara had delivered the note, adding a whispered word of advice to Asia that she should avoid the topic of acorns at all cost, as there were no acorns.

"Maybe we can hide," Samara was saying, and Ellishiva returned her attention to her friend just in time to see the fairy absently lift the surface of the flip-desk with one of her feet, sending the pot with the new sapling in it shattering to pieces on the ground.

Ellishiva left the worktable and dropped to her knees beside the broken pottery. "This wasn't in the plan!" she hissed, gathering the fragile plant from the wreckage.

"Oops. Sorry," muttered Samara, biting her bottom lip. Then the look on her face lightened. "Well, we gotta make it look real, don't we?" she pointed out sagely.

Ellishiva glared at her.

Samara put her feet on the ground and bent forward in her chair so that her forearms rested on her knees, peering down at the fractured mess on the floor. "What type of plant is that?" she asked innocently.

Two of the sapling's stiff, silvery leaves had broken and were bleeding a milky liquid that bubbled to the surface of the wounds like mercury. Without much thought, Ellishiva cupped her hands around the fragile little life. Her palms glowed softly and the leaves mended themselves, becoming whole once more. Then she stood and hurried back to the worktable with it.

"It's an Aak sapling. The plant we harvest Silverdine spice dust from," Ellishiva grumbled, her eyes wandering off to study Hektor in his corner of the Vivarium. "Rajah assigned it to me. It's my hands-on summer lesson. Now he'll know it was injured." She huffed, dug up an empty pot, and began to replant the sapling. Then she dropped her voice to a whisper again. "I think Hektor is falling for it. He's cleaned his hands. Sam?" Ellishiva glanced back over her shoulder, then did a double take. "Sam, what are you doing?" she snapped.

Samara had flipped open the top of the desk and was blatantly rifling through Ellishiva's things. "So what did Banog say about the Sixth Element?" she asked, ignoring the question.

Ellishiva scowled at her, but continued tending to the poor Aak plant. "Nothing!" she said. "They've brainwashed him, too. He won't tell me anything because he thinks I'm still a child." She packed a handful of fresh dirt into the new pot a bit harder than was strictly necessary. No use. It wasn't a good fit.

Samara continued sifting through everything in the desk, tossing aside old nolis, ink bottles, papyrus notes, bamboo styluses, and a diary with an embossed round seal on its cover before picking up a hand-drawn constellation map. "Wow, what's this?" she said, unfolding it noisily.

"Be careful with that!" Ellishiva warned sharply as she settled the sapling's spindly roots carefully into their new pot.

Samara shut the flip-top desk and spread the map on top of it. "So this is the map you told me about. The one that tracks the moon," she noted. Then she let out a low whistle. "The last quarter moon is tonight, Elli. 'Destruction to our world . . .'"

There was a long, tense silence.

Then Ellishiva snatched the Aak sapling up out of the ill-suited pot and strode over to the nearest of the raised beds with it. "That's why I planned the jungle sleepover for tonight. So that we'll have more time . . . if we need it." She took a deep breath and held it for a moment, then let it out again in a rush. "Did you tell Asia? And I—I want to invite Maximus, too," she faltered, her mind tripping over everything that could go wrong again.

"Don't worry so much, Elli. It will all work out," said Samara, reading her mind as usual as she flew over to stand by Ellishiva. But even she didn't sound as sure of herself as usual.

Ellishiva chose another pot and scooped a handful of dirt into the bottom of it, then transplanted the Aak sapling for the third time. That done, she cupped her hand over the plant and a soft light radiated from her palm again. Slowly, she raised her arm, and the little sprout stretched upward, as if drawn by an invisible magnet. Its frail stem grew sturdier, and a few new leaves unfurled from its stem like fresh, tiny yawns.

Satisfied at last, Ellishiva began to pack the rest of the pot with dirt.

"You're so good at that," said Samara admiringly. "Bet you that's why Hektor is so jealous. He can't do half of the things you can do with plants," she noted with satisfaction.

"He just needs to study harder," Ellishiva muttered, distracted as she finished settling the sapling into its new home. "All Va'natures can bring saplings to life. There's nothing special about what I do."

But Samara was already moving on to something more interesting. "Oh, do you smell that?" she asked, lifting her small nose into the air and taking a long sniff. "Cacao, puffed quinoa. The batch of treenitys must be done."

"Right. Shh, here she comes," breathed Ellishiva, setting aside the repotted sapling and snatching up a towel. "Hektor's walking over, too. Stick to the plan. Don't mention anything about the dark clouds."

"Oh Samara, dear!" called Lady Malinia. She was standing in the fernery, her feathers speckled with cacao and flour. "The treenitys are ready to be flown over to Mr. Belanos! And thank you for volunteering, dear. I would gladly take them myself, you know, but there is simply too much to do around here today." She let out a sad, wistful sigh and brushed a feathered hand over her face, smearing her red beak with powder.

Ellishiva took a deep breath, and swallowed hard. Then she mustered her nerve and walked up to her caretaker. "Um, Lady Malinia? I've just finished my potting for the day. May I please go with Sam?" she asked. "We'll come right back to the Arboretum afterward."

Lady Malinia frowned. "No, Ellishiva. I do not think that is a good idea," she said. "Samara can fly, and she shall be much safer that way.

Just the two of you walking around Bear Market? And with these strange clouds floating about? No, it is not safe. Not safe at all." She turned and waddled back toward the kitchen.

Ellishiva clenched her fists and trailed after her, forcing her voice to stay meek and polite. "Oh, please, Lady Malinia? We'll be back before you know it," she tried.

"So much cooking to do around here," the caretaker muttered distractedly, ignoring her.

"If it will make you feel better, Lady Malinia," cut in Samara innocently, "we'll ask Hektor to come along." She fluttered over to stand by Hektor, who was just arriving to join the group, and smiled at him sweetly. "You know we'll be safe with a boy around."

Ellishiva glanced at Hektor, whose eyebrows were bunched together, as though he were thinking hard.

"Yes. We'll be safe with Hektor," she agreed, struggling to keep her nerves under control. "And when we get back, I'll help you with the cooking. I'll peel all the potatoes." She danced around the kitchen in the dofaun's bustling, feathery wake. "And I'll pound the tray of garlic and— and do whatever other chores you need help with," she added breathlessly.

"Um, Lady Malinia?" cut in Hektor suddenly. "We'll be back before your next batch of treenity is finished baking. I promise."

Three pairs of eyes stopped what they were doing to look at him. At last Lady Malinia gave a brisk nod, and turned to Ellishiva. "Very well. You are to stay with Hektor at all times!" She shook a feathered finger at her. "I want you all back here before that batch is finished. And it's already in the oven, mind you! We have guests tonight and I'm not nearly done preparing." Though it was still not yet midday, there was already a tragic, exhausted warble in her voice.

The words had barely left her beak before Ellishiva, Samara, and Hektor were bolting through the warren and out the door.

Before she snapped it shut behind them, Ellishiva heard a, "No, no. Goodness dear, you stay here! Go play with Walle." Lady Malinia had caught Amborella by the hand as she tried to sprint past after them, and the little girl had stopped, sniffling.

"Here, I'll carry Dollie Burlap. Let's go finish our game," Walle said, taking the doll from Amborella.

Then the door closed, and Ellishiva and the others were running for the vāhmana.

It wasn't hard, once they reached the market, to convince Hektor to split up: they would deliver the treenitys, and he would go to Cheeky Canteen to investigate the rare acorn find. They let him watch as they began to turn into the dead-end alley toward Belanos Antiquities, Samara carrying the tray of treats covered with a hand-sewn doily. Hektor even suggested that they keep Mr. Belanos busy until he was done at the canteen—something that, Ellishiva assured him, would be no problem at all.

"I'll say it won't," laughed Samara impishly as soon as he was out of sight. "Not hard to keep Mr. Belanos busy when he isn't in his shop in the first place, eh, Elli?"

"Are you *sure* he's at Central Pond?" Ellishiva asked nervously for the third time.

Samara rolled her eyes, and the treenitys jostled around slightly on their tray. "Yes, I followed your plan exactly. Told him that the refugee ice fairies were waiting to have tea, and he closed up shop early to oblige them. Look," she concluded, nodding her chin at the antiquities shop, which was coming up quickly in front of them.

Ellishiva stopped in front of the door, and looked at the neatly printed, vaguely rectangular bark sign hanging from the doorknob by a string. It read:

Out for midday meal

There was a rustling to her right, and Ellishiva turned to find Samara sneaking a treenity off of the tray and into her noli. "What are you doing?" she hissed. "Cover that back up. There has to be something left on it for him." She glanced behind them to see if anyone else had witnessed the theft, but the coast was clear. "How many have you stolen already?" she frowned.

One of Samara's cheeks was stuffed with the contraband, and there was a guilty look on her face. "He's not gonna know how many we brought!" she protested.

"Yes, he will. We always bring a heaping tray," Ellishiva retorted.

"Yes, but," pointed out Samara, swallowing the treenity in one gulp, "but do you ever leave it there as heaping as you brought it?"

Ellishiva didn't answer. It was true: Mr. Belanos always insisted that they share the first round of treats with him.

Samara smacked her lips and gave a cheerful smile. "You know I'm right, Elli. Don't worry so much. Here, have one." She held the tray out to Ellishiva.

Ellishiva rolled her eyes but, unfortunately, there was nothing in the world more delicious than a treenity treat. Stealing another glance around the short alley, she snuck one off the tray and popped it into her mouth. Samara grinned, and did the same.

"Let's hope Asia can keep Hektor long enough," Ellishiva muttered clumsily as she munched. Another frown came over her face. "I wish he would just believe me about the Sixth Element."

Samara crunched down hard on the treenity in her mouth. "Oh, forget about Hektor," she snorted. "What does he know? He still can't even read hieroglyphics. And he'd spend a whole fortnight digging through a pile of junk if he thought there was an acorn at the bottom of it," she added reasonably.

They both swallowed.

"Fine, you're right," Ellishiva admitted, the sweet, guilt-tinged taste of treenity still on her tongue. "Just—here, give me that, and you fly up and get the key."

Samara handed over the treenity tray, flew up to the top of the door, and pulled a small, shiny object from the base of the carillon hanging there. Then she floated back down with it again. Ellishiva took it from her, handed back the tray, and unlocked the door. The carillon gave a low jingle as she pushed it slowly open.

Inside, the antiquities shop seemed to have a warm glow about it, as if some invisible sun were setting through an unseen window. All around, the dusty objects cast strange shadows over their shelves and on the floor. Ellishiva and Samara stood where they were, taking it in, searching.

Ellishiva spotted it first.

"There!" she whispered sharply. Leaving Samara with the tray, she hurried across the room and slipped in behind the counter. There, on a shelf just above her head, not far from where she'd glimpsed it the first time, sat the yellow- and red-striped olivine jar.

Ellishiva reached up and took it. A tingling filled her body—whether from anticipation or the jar itself, it was impossible to say. "We can't watch it here," she said quietly, with a furtive glance at the windows. "Someone might see us. Quick, let's go into the stockroom."

They ventured back into the room behind the counter. It was not an especially large space to begin with, and the many wooden crates piled at varying heights around the floor made it seem smaller still. Against the walls, close-packed shelves housed a collection of broken pottery fragments, household utensils, musical instruments, and chipped busts of elves and fairies.

The girls settled down on the cluttered floor, and Ellishiva placed the jar on top of a squat crate in front of them. Samara laid the tray of treenity treats on the ground beside her.

Ellishiva reached out and traced the long red streaks on the jar's surface. The lid trembled. She jerked her fingers away again, wide-eyed.

"What's happening?" asked Samara in a loud whisper.

"Don't know. Pretty sure it's not supposed to do that." Ellishiva sat up on her heels, her mind reeling back to the paper butterfly she'd brought to life in Rajah's study. Warily, she leaned closer to the jar, inspecting it. "It has something etched on its lid," she muttered.

"What is it?" demanded Samara.

"It's a picture of a nutmeg seed," answered Ellishiva, frowning. "No wonder the jar is tinted yellow, like the flesh of the hulk. And the red streaks," she went on, everything falling into place now. "They look like the mace that wraps around the seed itself."

"So what does it mean?" interrupted Samara impatiently.

Ellishiva stared quietly at the strange jar for a moment, thinking. Finally, she said, "Amborella's history must be recorded in here. The root of where she came from." She paused, letting the truth of it dawn on her. "It must hold the story of the origin of the nutmeg seed that became her soul."

They sat in silence for a second, staring at the jar. Then Samara gave Ellishiva's shoulder a nudge. "Go on then. Open it," she nettled. "The enchantment is off, remember? Rajah said so."

"Know what I'm thinking?" interrupted Ellishiva, turning to the fairy excitedly. "The first nutmeg tree was planted by Amma on the Isle of Bandalara. It's in our history books. All nutmegs come from that one tree. I bet you something else happened there. Something nobody wants to remember." She bit her lower lip hard, thinking.

"Oh, let's just have a look already!" snapped Samara, darting an uneasy look at the jar. "Open it! I want to see what happened after that light burst out of your body that night—"

"All right, all right!" Ellishiva cut her off, exasperated. She cast one more sidelong glance at the jar and took a deep breath. "Ready?" she asked quietly. Samara met her gaze and they nodded once, together.

Ellishiva opened the lid.

The slight tremble in the jar became a shake. She and Samara sat frozen on the floor, like the carved busts behind them on the shelves, watching with baited breath. Then, like an underwater geyser, a stream of Silverdine spice dust flooded upward into the stale air above them. A soft sea of voices speaking every imaginable language accompanied it, rising and falling like waves lapping at a distant shore.

In moments, the dust had expanded, forming itself into a flat plane that hung above the crate, its edges a blur of silvery dust. Pictures began to form on its misty surface, grainy and hard to distinguish at first, but gradually becoming clearer.

Places that Ellishiva had only ever read about—ancient, human places—began to fade in and out before their eyes.

The Silverdine began with ships. Various types of them rose from the dust, all under construction: dhows with triangular sails, wide square-rigged carracks with rounded sterns, and slimmer, faster galleons with multiple decks and as many as five masts. From these, the Silverdine focused on an old, battered vessel that had made many voyages, criss-crossing the wide blue oceans of planet Earth. Its boards were worn and pitted, lashed by countless waves.

The dust spun again, and a dark stain spread around the vessel. The carcass of a huge whale appeared, bound to the ship by ropes. Sharks snapped and ripped at its torn flesh. Ellishiva's stomach turned. The stain in the water below was its blood.

Once more, the Silverdine spun, and now it showed them rough seas from a great height, with ships bobbing on its surface like toy boats. One carried a terrible cargo—dark-skinned humans, shackled with heavy chains. Some were being lashed with thick wet straps, some thrown off the ship still alive to lighten its load. Their wailing voices cut off abruptly as they were swallowed by the dark waves of the frightful ocean below.

"Elli," gasped Samara in a low, fearful voice. "Is—is that really the human world?" She looked over at Ellishiva and her lips trembled like a flower in a cold wind.

"Every bit of it. If you'd read my books, you'd understand," Ellishiva muttered darkly. "Now shhh. Just watch what's happening, all right?" she said, giving the fairy's forearm a comforting pat.

The Silverdine spice dust was spinning again. This time it showed mankind hunting and slaughtering animals, and a horrible sound filled the room as the victims squealed, bellowed, and howled in pain and fear. Then the humans began to attack each other. Vast battlefields appeared, with ranks of soldiers stretching endlessly away to the horizon. The men wielded spears and maces, broadswords and daggers, bows and arrows. Some carried shields and lances; others wore leather helmets, and still others were arrayed from head to toe in heavy armor, the sturdy plates of metal covering even the horses they sat on.

The dust spun again, and a sea of voices arose once more. A rowdy crowd of humans was gathered around a small table—men and women gambling with pieces of eight, shillings, kwartnik coins, bags of black pepper, cloves and other spices, exotic stones, furs, elephant teeth, ambergris, and seashells. Nearby, unheeded by their owners, trapped animals gnawed at the bars of their cramped cages. Filthy humans sat shackled to each other for sale in markets. Some held their heads in their hands; some dozed, too weary to think of a grim future. Excitement rose in the gamblers. Greed shone from their sweaty faces, and the air was filled with angry shouts and joyless laughter, as harsh as venom in a raw wound.

The spice dust before them spun rapidly again. Great whales lay beached, dotting the white sands of calmer shores. Majestic glaciers collapsed like sand castles into the ocean. Magnificent forests appeared, then blackened and crumbled, ravaged by blazes set by man. Ancient trees, hacked apart, groaned like giants as they toppled. Nests fell, eggs shattered; tiny birds lay helpless on the ground, peeping.

"This is why Amma gave refuge to fairies, elves, and other races," hissed Samara, scowling. "The humans hacked down their forests— their only home."

"Shh," breathed Ellishiva, leaning over to whisper into her ear. "Don't say anything about places. The Silverdine is sensitive. It'll think you're giving it a command. Watch," she added. Turning back to the misty plane before them, she said in a normal voice, "Show us the Isle of Bandalara!"

As if it had ears, the Silverdine spice dust quieted for a moment, swallowing the raucous gamblers in a puff of silvery mist and flattening itself once more. Then a new scene with new men appeared on its cloudy surface. They stood on the deck of a sailing ship, watching the bright rays of the sun spreading across the lush forests of Bandalara Island. The men had long pale hair and large dark hats; their uniforms were dotted with brass buttons, and their shirts sewn with ruffles. They wore trousers that gathered just below their knees over long, white stockings. Even their shoes had buckles.

"Gentlemen!" cried an important-looking officer, and his voice echoed eerily around the storeroom, like a ghost. "For years, we have hidden the treasures of this island and profited from its abundant nutmeg. Now this new empire imagines that it has conquered Bandalara to reap the same reward. Hear me, all of you! This must not happen!" he declared, his voice rising like thunder. "If we cannot profit, they shall not either. Set the plantation on fire! Burn it! Burn the nutmeg trees!"

"Surely we will not burn these trees," came the earnest voice of a younger officer. "Not all nutmegs bear fruit, and those that do take many years to mature. The natives say these trees were here long before their ancestors came to the island."

"We shall grow them elsewhere!" barked the older officer shortly.

"But . . . these environs, this climate. Will conditions be right elsewhere?" protested the young man.

A dark rage came over his superior's face. "I have issued an order!" he snarled. "Destroy this nutmeg plantation! Bandalara must burn! The only thing the new empire will inherit is charred soil!"

The young officer's face fell.

Ellishiva's throat went dry, tightening with fear.

"Why do they destroy?" breathed Samara in astonishment beside her.

"It's called greed," replied Ellishiva, stealing a brief glance at the rose-colored noli fastened at the fairy's hip. "Now pay attention."

The spice dust was swirling furiously. Suddenly, the island was filled with roaring, leaping flames that made the fire in the wide hearth at home seem a mere spark in comparison. Dense smoke blanketed Bandalara Island, blocking the rays of the sun. Then the eye of the Silverdine swooped down through the haze, where animals were running frantically, seeking safety. Some of them were ablaze, squealing, yelping, and howling in pain. Many ran into the ocean. Many did not know how to swim. A swarm of honeybees rose from its hive, only to be vaporized by the raging flames. Their white ashes fell, lifeless, to the baked earth.

The tallest and most noble nutmeg trees in the plantation crumbled like charred biscuits. Above, dark smoke infiltrated the pale, puffy clouds, staining them like soot on white sheets.

The spice dust spun again, revealing a familiar figure with kohl-black hair standing in a clearing ringed by smoke.

"Rajah!" whispered Ellishiva, wide-eyed. "He looks so young."

"Who's that girl?" asked Samara, leaning an inch closer to the scene.

The young Rajah was holding a Va'nature girl in his arms, clutching her raven head to his chest. One side of her face was burnt; the other covered in soot. Injured as she was, however, she fought his grasp with her remaining strength, desperate to go back into the fire, as if she had left something there.

"She looks like the others," Samara murmured. "They all have that same crest on their uniforms."

Ellishiva tore her gaze away from Rajah and the girl for a moment to observe the rest of the scene. Everywhere, other girls with black hair were moving fast over the burning places, flirting dangerously with the flames. She turned back to the girl in Rajah's arms, her uniform burnt and torn, her face distorted with pain. Streaks of tears etched pale lines down her grimy cheeks.

"She's a Va'nature, all right," Ellishiva muttered lowly, "but I can't see her spice mark. She's all burnt."

The scene in the Silverdine spice dust shifted repeatedly as the smoke cleared, blew across the image, and cleared again.

"Look! Two more raven-haired girls. They look like twins," Samara observed immediately.

Ellishiva looked at them as well, her eyes squinting at their tiny forms in the dust. "Coriander spices," she said finally. "I can see the marks on their skin now."

"What are those strange moves they're doing?" Samara wondered aloud. "Why are they going back into the fire like that?"

"That's combative payamar," replied Ellishiva without glancing away from the scene. "They're going in there to save the creatures. They must have rescued scores of them by now. I bet you they saved the lives of dozens of dofauns in our colonies around the planet that day."

Samara looked ill. "This is terrible, Elli."

"There, Sam!" exclaimed Ellishiva, pointing into the dust again. "He's back, look! That's the young Rajah over there by that burning nutmeg tree."

The scene had changed to a hilly plantation scarred terribly by the fire—a grim landscape of charred, jagged trunks. On it, a single towering nutmeg tree still stood. Sections of its burnt bark were aglow with dying fire, and nearly all of its glossy green leaves had crumbled to ashes. Yet at the very top, on a lone limb, lingered a cluster of greenish-brown ones.

And, from it, hung a single yellow nutmeg.

At the base of the nutmeg tree, snatches of darkened bone marked the skeletons of many creatures that had died on the blackened ground, as if they had gathered there to defend it. Amidst the bones lay a tongobiri sword like the one Maximus had shown Ellishiva in the market, along with a burnt set of armor. But there was no body within its protective folds—just a pile of red ash the color of kinnaran skin. And lying near it among the remains, Ellishiva spotted the little crest from the black-haired Va'nature girl's uniform. Slowly, into the dust, the sky began to rain.

A chill sank down Ellishiva's spine. She grabbed Samara's hand. The fairy was shivering, too.

In front of them, young Rajah looked up at the smoldering tree. He was covered in black soot, his face caked with dried blood. There were raw burns on the side of his neck.

"Rajah still has that fire scar," whispered Ellishiva solemnly. "It goes from his neck up to the side of his face. His hair and beard usually cover it."

In the Silverdine, the day darkened. Then lightning split the blackness like shards of brilliant white glass slicing through the sky, and the silence was shattered by a terrible crack of thunder. The wind rose, and sheets of rain crashed down like crystal splinters, piercing the scorched ground. Torrents of charcoal-tainted water streamed from the ravaged land into the gray sea.

Ellishiva watched as the burnt crest from the dead Va'nature girl's uniform got caught up in the current, swept away by the oily, glimmering tributaries until, at last, it sank beneath their mercury surfaces, swallowed by the earth.

The young Rajah began to climb the nutmeg tree, ignoring the tempest around him. He hoisted himself up by the remains of its branches, inch by inch, his hands almost slipping, his feet catching and sliding on the wet wood. When he finally reached the top, he grabbed the remaining limb for dear life, wrapping his arms and legs around it.

Samara leaned into Ellishiva's shoulder. Ellishiva held her hand tightly. Her eyes were fixed on the spice dust. "Look," she urged quietly, "this has to be Amborella's seeded soul."

The young Rajah was reaching for the last remaining yellow nutmeg on the tree. The skin had split half open, exposing a thick layer of creamy flesh. It cradled the hard brown shell inside, which encased the seed of the nutmeg. The shell was covered with a lacy network of fiery red mace the shade of Amborella's hair.

Rajah tried to bend the limb toward him to reach the nutmeg. But no sooner had he clutched it than he lost his grip on the slippery bark and fell to the ground. A jagged stump pierced the young Va'nature's belly, and he screamed with such pain that both girls jumped.

Then, in a soft flash of light, the Silverdine spice dust collapsed, compressed itself into a tight line, and poured itself back into its container with such force that the jar spun round and round, then clattered to a standstill, the lid drawn to the rim like a magnet as it snapped shut into place.

For a moment, both girls were speechless. Then Samara found her voice. "So that's the end?" she blurted.

"I'm afraid it was only the beginning," Ellishiva murmured darkly. She turned to the fairy. "Sam, what we've just seen? This is what Jipsin Smilodon told me, about how the Sixth Element came to be. These bad things, the ones the dust showed us before it took us to Bandalara—those are what continue to strengthen her in the human world. And they never end. I keep reading about them in my history books," she whispered, half to herself. "They just get worse and worse."

The two of them sat in silence for several long seconds, rooted to the floor. A million thoughts were sweeping through Ellishiva's mind.

Then, just outside the shop, they heard the telltale *thump-clack* of a cane.

Ellishiva felt the blood drain out of her cheeks. She snatched the jar from the squat crate. Before she could clamber to her feet with it, however, Samara grabbed her wrist. "Wait! We still need to figure out what the light that came from your body did!" she hissed.

"Yes Sam, but not now. Someone's coming," Ellishiva snapped back in a whisper. "We've got to get out of here." She jerked her wrist away and hurried out of the storeroom. The yellow and red jar was sending tingles over her skin again. Ellishiva peered out into the main room of the antiquities shop, but the coast was clear. Quickly, she crept behind the counter and shoved the jar back into its place on the shelf. Then she turned to bolt away—and ran smack into Samara. The tray of treenitys went flying from the fairy's hands, its contents scattering away across the floor like so many beans from an abacus.

"Great!" Ellishiva hissed. "Look at this!"

"*You* bumped into *me*," Samara bit back as they both dropped to their knees on the floorboards and began to frantically pick up the treats. They had barely gathered a fourth of the mess, however, when the carillon chimed. A dim red light flooded the antiquities shop.

Ellishiva's knees froze on the floor. She glanced at Samara, whose eyes looked as ready to jump out of their sockets as her own.

A tall figure loomed over the countertop, looking down at them. When it spoke, its voice was smooth and shrewd.

"Well, well, well. What do we have here?" drawled Baron Puck. His black cape was blotched with eerie shadows in the red light. "Two peas in a pod."

The girls sat mutely where they were, surrounded by the incriminating mess of treenitys. The baron walked slowly around the counter, taking in every last spilled treat as he went. When he was standing squarely between them and their escape, he spoke again. "Well? Have you lost your voices?"

Ellishiva's tongue felt like stone in her mouth. There was nothing to say.

Baron Puck narrowed his eyes. "I see," he growled. Then, slowly, he pointed his wand at them, the tiny, familiar etches of pentagons on its olivine surface flashing with the movement. Ellishiva recoiled toward Samara and shut her eyes.

"Katākāra kando nissesa!"

There was a burst of red behind her eyelids, and Ellishiva snapped them open again. The baron had lowered his wand so that it faced the floor. Red light was pouring from its tip, and flying up and around in its glow was a small tornado of the pyramid-shaped treenity treats. Ellishiva watched in amazement as those that had crumbled pieced themselves back together again and then, in an orderly procession, the whole assembly returned themselves, neatly stacked, to the tray. Finally, the tray itself hopped into the air and landed on the counter, and the doily fluttered down to take its rightful place over the treats.

Ellishiva caught Samara's gaze fixed sharply on something, and turned back to the baron in time to see him tucking the wand into a hidden side pocket on his vest that was concealed under his cape. A tiny object fell from his person and bounced away from him on the ground.

Before Ellishiva could stop her, the fairy had snatched it up, surging to her feet to disguise the movement. "Since when does an elf carry a fairy's wand, and speak fairy language?" she demanded indignantly to the baron's face.

Ellishiva scrambled up as well, wide-eyed, and kicked Samara in the heel, gesturing at her to *zip it*. But she was too late.

Baron Puck took a step forward, closing the already small gap between them. He leaned down, so close that his nose almost touched Samara's ear, and whispered in a dangerous voice, "You two have been keeping secrets. I suggest you continue to do so."

Then he stood up again, his red eyes peering down at them coldly, as though waiting for a response. Ellishiva managed a shaky nod.

"Well, we weren't doing anything wrong," Samara scowled up at the elf defiantly, her fist closed tightly around the fallen object so that not even a wink of it was visible between her fingers. The baron's eyes flashed at her, but she only glared at him harder and forged on recklessly. "Lady Malinia sent us to deliver these treats and—"

"—and we were just leaving," interrupted Ellishiva bluntly, grabbing Samara by the elbow and shoving past Baron Puck. Seconds later she was hauling the loud-mouthed fairy out the door, leaving the baron standing alone in the antiquities shop.

Ellishiva waited until they had rounded several alley corners before she stopped and turned on Samara. "What was that?" she hissed.

"A distraction," replied the fairy brightly. "Look at this neat broach the baron dropped," she grinned, opening her hand. The trinket was made of ammolite, and its textured surface glittered like dragon skin in the afternoon sun. "He has no idea that I picked it up," she went on with a triumphant laugh. "It's mine now!"

"Sam, that's stealing," Ellishiva growled at her through gritted teeth. "You shouldn't have provoked him like that. That elf is too weird. There's always been something strange about him, and now it's worse. He's *dangerous.*"

Samara brushed her off. "He's nothing to worry about, Elli. What's he going to say? That we were in Mr. Belanos's shop? We were *allowed* to be there," she pointed out reasonably.

Ellishiva shook her head mutely for a moment. But this was no time to build the fairy a new moral compass from scratch. "Do you have the key?" she asked instead. "We'll have to get back in to find out about the light that came out of my body later."

"It's in my noli," Samara assured her, giving the illegal pouch a pat. "Hektor isn't back yet. Where should we go now?"

Ellishiva considered this. "Let's find Maximus," she said at last. "We can ask him about the spice girls and the dead kinnarans we just saw in the Silverdine. Maybe he can help us figure out who the voice behind the Sixth Element is."

The fairy nodded. "Textile Alley then," she said. "Let's go."

They hurried off through the twisted alleyways of Bear Market. Samara, Ellishiva noticed, kept inspecting the broach she had pilfered from the baron.

"Can't you put that away?" she snapped under her breath.

Samara ignored this suggestion. "What is Baron Puck doing with a wand?" she frowned. "That doesn't make any sense."

"Maybe Queen Neive gave it to him," Ellishiva muttered, turning her face up to the sky. There were no dark clouds in sight.

"Ha! I doubt that," snorted Samara. "I've never seen the baron at Central Pond. Not even once, Elli!"

"He said we were keeping secrets," Ellishiva murmured nervously. "I hope he wasn't using makrós to read our minds. Only the elders of the elf race can do that, right? And only to each other?"

"Not true, Elli," Samara corrected primly. "In the *Unauthorized*

Biography of Amma, the author says that Amma, too, has the power of telepathy—I mean, makrós."

"I need to borrow that book," said Ellishiva. They were nearing their destination now, and her eyes began combing the alleyways for Maximus. "The market is empty. Everyone must be staying home." She thought of the brutal black clouds and a grim expression came over her face. "Come on," she urged. "Let's hurry."

The girls made several sharp rights and lefts, passed the nearly abandoned, gray-pillared, mammoth Mannahatta Barter Exchange, covered their ears as they walked by the loud water mills, and finally hung a right into Textile Alley. Located in the northeast section of the market, it, too, was not as busy as it usually was, though a few brave dofauns did wander up and down its length, going briskly about their business.

Ellishiva stopped and scanned the scene in front of her. The alley was peppered with tall mulberry trees from start to finish. On their branches and leaves, millions of silkworms nested snugly, as puffy as cotton balls. From the scores of brown branches streamed endless thin lines of silk, stretching across the alleyway like billions of clotheslines—all of them running directly into the shops, where quilling machines were eternally at work, winding the new silk thread onto bobbins. Ellishiva strained her eyes for a flash of wings, but if Maximus was hovering among the tree-tops, she couldn't see him. Sighing quietly to herself, she gave Samara's arm a tug and the two of them started forward again into the alley.

Shops went by on either side as they walked. In front of some were stacks of cotton; others boasted strung, dried broadleaves and rolls of flax. Each contained unique garments: school and Puluma uniforms, gowns and tunics. Ellishiva peered into every one of them, searching for the face she needed to see. Seamstresses and tailors toiled away, peddling spinning wheels or turning out spools of cotton thread. Some wore padded white bracelets bristling with pins on their fore-paws. In the next shop, the walls were packed from floor to ceiling with colorful fabrics: fine silks and humble hemp, soft cotton and cool linen. Next door, the window was filled with a menagerie of buttons. Some were acorn caps and halves of nutshells; others were gold nuggets and pieces of quartz.

"There's Maximus!" cried Samara suddenly, and Ellishiva jerked her head away from the button display. She followed the fairy's finger to where it was pointing up in the sky and down the alleyway. A familiar pair of wings was buzzing there, accompanied by two others like it.

"Maximus!" Ellishiva called, waving her arms over her head so that she'd be easier to spot. One white-haired head turned, followed by its two fellows, and a moment later the trio began to descend.

Ellishiva ran down the alley to meet them, Samara close at her heels. She had barely stopped when three sets of kinnaran boots landed softly in front of her. And then Maximus's fire-yellow eyes were looking into her own.

"Hi," she said bluntly, out of breath.

"Hi," he answered, and she could see the mischievous twitch of a grin tugging at the corners of his mouth.

Ellishiva wanted to blurt out everything they had just discovered, but the presence of the two older kinnarans standing behind him made her hold her tongue. "Where are you all heading?" she asked instead.

"We're going to the Muheekantuck River," said Maximus. "I was looking for you earlier." Behind him, the shorter of the two kinnarans nudged him in the shoulder. Maximus cleared his throat. "Oh, sorry. This is Morpheus, and Theo."

The older kinnarans bowed to the girls. Ellishiva thought she heard a faint squeal of delight come from Samara's throat. "Good to see you again," the fairy said in a coy voice that could have given Lady Malinia a run for her money.

"Nice to meet you," Ellishiva offered simply, struggling not to roll her eyes. She looked at Morpheus, the kinnaran who had nudged Maximus in the shoulder. "I saw you in the market that day," she noted.

"You gave Hektor his boomerang." She took careful note of his face as she said it, looking for a hint of some hidden motive behind the gift. But Morpheus only smiled at her, completely guileless.

Ellishiva smiled back, reassured. Then she turned to Maximus. "We have to hurry back home, actually," she began, a little haltingly. "But when you get back, um. We're having a jungle sleepover at the warren tonight and—and um . . ."

"What she's trying to say," interrupted Samara brightly, "is that you're invited to come, too!"

"Thank you, Sam," Ellishiva growled out of the corner of her mouth, wrestling with the embarrassed smile threatening to take over her face. She threw a quick glance at Morpheus and Theo.

"Yes, sure. I'd like that," replied Maximus, sounding a little awkward himself. Underneath it, though, Ellishiva was aware of the intense way he was looking at her, as though he had something important to tell her, too.

Behind him, the other kinnarans exchanged a smirk. Then Morpheus nudged him in the shoulder again. "Er, guess we have to get going, too," Maximus told her apologetically.

"All right," said Ellishiva. "See you later, then." Her insides were burning to ask him if he'd heard anything new about the Sixth Element, but there was nothing to do except wave as the three kinnarans began to fly up into the air again.

Next to her, Samara gave a dreamy sigh.

Ellishiva shot her a glare out of the corner of her eye. "Did you have to embarrass me like that?" she hissed under her breath. "I can speak just fine on my own."

"*Sure* you can."

Ellishiva scowled. "I just didn't want to make the other kinnarans suspicious. Besides, I think he wants to tell me something. If I could just think of a way to call him back for a second, without the others . . ." Her brow furrowed.

"Yeah," said Samara distractedly, reaching into her enchanted noli and pulling out a treenity treat. She flicked it into the air with her thumb and turned her face up, ready to catch it with her open mouth.

The answer hit Ellishiva like a polar bear being dropped into a tranquil pond. Quick as a flash, she snatched the falling treenity out of the air.

"Hey!" Samara protested.

Ellishiva ignored her. "I think we should give Maximus some treenity for his trip."

Samara rolled her eyes. "Oh, all right," she grumbled finally, reaching into her noli and rummaging around for the others. "Well? Call him back already! If they get any farther, he'll be out of earshot," she added, mouthing an extra, silent word and pulling out a handful of the treats.

"Okay, okay," Ellishiva snapped, yanking a blank piece of papyrus out of her own noli and holding it out so Samara could drop the snacks in the middle. "Maximus!" she called, noisily wrapping them up. "Maximus, wait!"

Above her, all three of the kinnarans stopped and turned, and for one miserable moment she thought the whole trio would come back. Then Maximus separated from the group, and flew back down to her.

Ellishiva let out the breath that she'd been holding and shoved the crumpled bundle of treats at him. The pyramid top of a lone treenity peeked out from the opening. "Oh, great!" he said, smiling as he reached for the rumpled package. "Thank you, Ellishiva."

Before he could pull it from her fingers, however, she tugged the papyrus—and him along with it—a couple of inches closer. "You got any news?" she asked bluntly.

Maximus shot a wary glance over his shoulder, as if checking to make sure the others hadn't followed him. Then, "Yes. I heard Rajah is coming home this evening," he confided quickly under his breath. "I couldn't say it in front of them, but they're having a meeting at your warren tonight. I have to go now. Sorry. We can talk more tonight, though." The young kinnaran's feet lifted off the ground.

Ellishiva released her end of the treenity package. "Fly in through the bedchamber window, so you won't be seen," she whispered hurriedly after him. "And come back safe. I have a lot of questions for you." Maximus nodded and gave her one last, warm smile.

Then he was gone.

CHAPTER NINE

JUNGLE SLEEPOVER

Rajah had called a gathering of the elders.

He had returned late that evening from Nicobar, just as Maximus had told Ellishiva he would. She had begged to see him as soon as he returned, but Lady Malinia had had other ideas. "Child!" she had squawked in exasperation. "Have some patience! Valerius is *prefect* of the colony! It is not for us to interrupt his important meetings. He shall see to us when he is able." The caretaker had suggested that they would, perhaps, all have breakfast together in the morning.

This did not sit well with Ellishiva. It was the night of the last quarter moon. For all she knew, there might not be a morning to have breakfast *in*.

So she had sent Amborella to the kitchen to make purpleade punch for the sleepover. The kitchen was right next to the great living hall, which had been converted into a dining hall for the important guests. Ellishiva had every reason to suspect that Lady Malinia would shoo her back into the bedchamber as soon as she dared to show her own face around the corner. Amborella, however, was the picture of innocence, and therefore stood a better chance of eavesdropping than anyone.

Jungle sleepovers took place in the bedchamber that Ellishiva shared with Hektor and Amborella. The semi-round room, which occupied a portion of one of the highest, eastward-facing limbs of Banyan Tree, had a high ceiling and four grand windows. Next to each window was a living tree whose trunk had curved sharply—like the outline of a stair step viewed from the side—and whose branches had obligingly bent themselves into four posts. Each of the beds was different. Amborella's and Ellishiva's were made of smooth, dark wood, and had full canopies of thick, overhanging leaves. Hektor's bed, meanwhile, was a lighter shade, and the leaves of his canopy were thinner and more feathery. Despite their differences, however, each bed was bordered on one side by a doorway into a dressing chamber and on the other by a writing desk in front of a window, except that by Ellishiva's there was also a bookcase packed with scores of books.

Jungle sleepovers, however, were not for beds. On such occasions, Ellishiva and her siblings pitched a huge, leaf-covered tent-canopy on a slender tree-trunk post in the middle of the room, like a big green umbrella. Beneath it, with Lady Malinia's help, they hung a wealth of snacks from dangling vines: treenitys, mangoes, pomegranates, sliced coconuts, figs with their stems and leaves still on, and four-inch-long stalks of unpeeled sugarcane. In the center of it all hung a colorful rice-paper lantern that had not yet been lit and, a little ways off, another one that would never be lit at all—which was where Walle slept. On the floor below was a comfy and chaotic mess of tossed tatami mats and handwoven cushions with a few soft, rounded bolsters thrown in, peppering the seating arrangement with bursts of color.

Ellishiva walked over to the middle of the tent-canopy, distracted. Most of the others were already there, all of them decked out in their pajamas. To her right, Hektor and Bairon sprawled on stuffed, purple bags large enough to cradle their entire bodies. Across from them, Samara and Asia had arranged themselves on a heap of colorful cushions. Asia was busy knitting a tabi sock with divided toes and, behind her, Samara sat a bit higher, plaiting the elf girl's luxurious dark hair into neat waterfall braids.

Automatically, Ellishiva reached down and picked up a squat olivine jar with an etching of flames on it. Removing the cap, she stood on tiptoe and tapped a few specks of Bluzure spice dust into the hanging paper lantern. The tent was immediately filled with flickering, cozy blue light. Ellishiva put the jar on the floor again and flopped down next to the girls. Absently, she reached up and plucked a pomegranate from its hanging vine.

"I wonder what's keeping Maximus," she wondered aloud, unable to keep the worry out of her voice. With a practiced hand, she smacked the pomegranate on the hard floor to crack it open, spraying its red juices on the books beside her knee—*The Art of Payamar* and *The Unauthorized Biography of Amma*. Digging her fingers into the new split, she pried back the fruit's thick red-yellow skin, revealing clusters of glossy red seeds underneath. Still distracted, she began picking them free and popping them into her mouth one by one.

"Maybe he's still by the river, Elli," offered Bairon uncertainly, reaching up to pluck a stalk of sugarcane from the vines. He tore the hard bark away with his teeth, peeling it back to reveal a stringy white center. A trickle of sugar juice escaped the corner of his mouth as he chewed it. Next to him, Hektor stuffed three whole figs into his mouth, then turned to show them to Bairon, opening his eyes as wide as he could, like a monster devouring his victims. Bairon almost choked on the sugarcane.

Samara rolled her eyes at them. "Hope Amber comes back with news soon, Elli," she mumbled quietly.

But Hektor had caught the eye roll. "Maximus isn't going to come," he declared scornfully. He lay back on the purple bag, tucking one hand behind his head and reaching up with the other to bounce two hanging figs together.

"Why?" demanded Samara at once. "Did you say something to him, Hektor?"

"He's too busy for this nonsense," Hektor snapped at her. "The only reason I participate is because I sleep here." He plucked the larger of the figs from its vine. "Need to get my own bedchamber," he muttered under his breath.

"You're just upset about the acorns," Ellishiva noted carelessly, and then wished she hadn't.

"*Upset?*" Hektor growled fiercely, his eyes full of cold fury. He pelted the fig at Ellishiva, who dodged it. "You *lied* to me! All three of you—including you, Asia," he added reproachfully.

The elf girl's cheeks turned as red as the pomegranate seeds. She bent her head down closer to her work.

"Hektor, would you stop pretending already?" blurted Ellishiva in exasperation. "We wouldn't have *had* to lie to you in the first place if you'd just believe us! I can see on your face that you don't really think everything's okay. You're just letting Rajah brainwash you. I can't just make this stuff up. The Sixth Element is real. And whoever she is, she's coming tonight," she added grimly, throwing a wary glance out the open window at the darkening sky beyond.

"I heard that the dofauns are afraid to speak about what happens to them when the dark clouds move over Mannahatta," began Asia quietly, not looking up from her work. Her cheeks, Ellishiva noticed, were still pink under the blue glow of the paper lantern. "Some say that if Amma finds out which of them the clouds are affecting, she'll send them to the Asylum at Derahdin." Furtively, she risked a glance up from the sock. "They say terrible things are about to happen," she whispered.

"What you hear at Cheeky Canteen is rubbish—pure gossip," dismissed Hektor immediately. Asia looked up from the tabi sock and frowned at him. He glanced away first, avoiding her stare by concentrating on stuffing more figs into his mouth.

"What I can't figure out is how the Sixth Element found us," began Ellishiva, half to herself. "Maximus said that almost no one knows about Mannahatta Colony, but why?" She struggled with the answerless question for a long moment, then shrugged her shoulders irritably and pried open the other half of the pomegranate. "Everyone knows there are only five elements: air, fire, matter, ether and—and water." She tossed a few seeds into her mouth and crunched down on them, their hard insides getting stuck in the grooves of her molars. "When I was attacked, she said she would arrive by the last quartermoon," she murmured thoughtfully. "The tides are controlled by the moon. I wonder if she was navigating the oceans looking for Mannahatta, and found the fairies of the ice forest along the way." Ellishiva trailed off as the awful memory of the dead fairy's heart beating in the rotting trunk of the locust tree flooded back into her head. She pushed aside the remainder of the pomegranate.

"But why would it be looking for Mannahatta?" chimed in Samara, her fingers still weaving through Asia's hair.

"It must want something here," replied Ellishiva logically. "Why else would it bother to invade us?"

"What do we have that it would want?" wondered Asia, her hands pausing in their knitting as she looked over at Ellishiva, genuinely curious.

"Nothing," admitted Ellishiva. Then she added in a low, quiet voice, "At least, nothing that we know about."

There was a short, heavy silence.

"You mean they're hiding something on Mannahatta?" prompted Samara breathlessly.

Ellishiva gave a grim nod. It made only too much sense.

"Amazing!" Samara gushed excitedly, her fingers flying through Asia's dark hair again. "Maybe it's a weapon to fight the Sixth Element off, and they wouldn't tell us because, you know, they didn't want us to worry," she speculated, gabbing a mile a minute. "The kinnarans are here. I mean, that *has* to be it, right? And maybe we'll get to see whatever it is in person, Elli, because tonight is the last quarter moon."

"Well, I'll be asleep!" growled Hektor through a mouthful of figs, his teeth speckled with brown seeds. He reached a fist out for Bairon to bump his knuckles, but the elf boy pretended not to see.

Samara glared at him. "Is it so impossible for you just to hear her out? She's not stupid, you know!" she snapped. Then she turned back to Ellishiva. "I bet you that's what they're talking about downstairs at that gathering, Elli. Hope Amber comes back with news." She paused, admiring the intricate design of the waterfall braids that now ran halfway around the crown of Asia's head, before resuming her work.

"Sam, you should start to build your own alcove," remarked Hektor sourly. "Then you could be Queen of the Nosy Fairies."

"Why don't you just pack a few more figs into your mouth? They make you look handsome," bit back Samara with a sneer.

"Listen!" Ellishiva interrupted loudly, and four sets of eyes swiveled around to look at her. "We can't do this," she said, fixing Samara and Hektor in particular with a withering look. "We have to work and think together, like an army. We'll never be strong enough to defeat her otherwise." She took a steadying breath and went on quietly. "The Sixth Element attacked Atticus. We're lucky he wasn't killed. Tonight it could strike again. It's obvious that none of the elders are going to tell us anything. I've given up on them." A small knot formed in her throat at the thought of Rajah's neglect, but she swallowed it and plowed on. "They're hiding something from us. Something that has to do with the massacre at Bandalara Island. They've been passing around Amber's Silverdine spice dust, having these secret meetings . . ." She threw a foreboding look at Samara, who looked back at her knowingly. "I wish we knew who she was, the girl who was murdered that day. I bet Maximus would be able to tell us something about it, if he were here." She trailed off, her gaze wandering helplessly back to the empty window.

"Murdered!" cried Hektor. His eyes were popping out of his head the way the figs had bulged from his mouth a minute before. "Are you crazy?" he hissed, dropping his voice to a lower tone. "No one speaks that word in our world!"

"You'd rather ignore it and let it happen again?" retorted Ellishiva at once, and Hektor fell silent, his mouth pressing itself into a line. Ellishiva glared at him for a moment. Then she let the anger out of her chest in a long puff of air. "We can't fear a word, Hektor," she went on, more gently now, her eyes straying to the shimmering pomegranate seeds in the half-shell beside her. "It is what it is. All races bleed the same, love the same, speak the same despite their different languages, and breathe the same air. The moon and the sun belong to no one, and we should share them equally." The speech of the human captain in the spice dust, shouting at his men to burn the nutmeg trees so that no one else could have them, was echoing horribly in her head. She fought down a shudder. "What Sam and I saw on the Isle of Bandalara, in that Silverdine, was pure horror, Hektor. The death, the greed—misery. It *was* the Sixth Element. And now it's here." She took a deep breath, and raised her eyes to her brother.

But Hektor was unmoved. "Don't look at me like that," he snarled. "Whatever you're doing, you're on your own."

A stab of disappointment hit Ellishiva like a slap. Nevertheless, she rallied. "No, I'm not! Everyone else in this room is ready to help me. And so is Maximus," she said defiantly.

"Maximus again?" Hektor smirked. He craned his head around, as if to inspect every nook and cranny in the bedchamber, before fixing his scornful eyes back on Ellishiva. "Doesn't he have to show up before he can help?"

"He *will* help me," Ellishiva retorted fiercely. "And he's full of strength and he has brilliant ideas. I don't need you." She lifted her chin as she glared at him. "Or—or Rajah."

"There. You heard it!" snapped Samara beside her.

Hektor met their glares head-on for a few long seconds. Then some of the fight seemed to go out of his shoulders. He slumped deeper into the purple bag and his gaze drifted off to stare mutely at his figs.

Ellishiva made herself look away from him. She turned to the others. "We've got to find out who the voice is—the one that's giving the Sixth Element its current form. And we need to know who let her into our world," she added quietly, grimly. She glanced impatiently at the bedchamber door. "What's keeping Amber? Rajah must have brought back some news from Nicobar."

"Who let the Sixth Element in?" snorted Samara, tugging on a strand of Asia's hair with a little too much force and making the elf girl miss her stitch. "Think about it, Elli. The baron? Sneaking all over the place? An elf with a fairy's wand? And what was he doing in the forest the day you were attacked?" She resumed her neat plaiting with her nose lifted a little, knowingly, in the air—as if there were nothing further to discuss. "That elf is not to be trusted."

"Elli. You know, I wonder . . . ," chimed in Bairon before Ellishiva could reply. "I heard my ahpa say that, during your sleep, Rajah kept going down to the roots of Banyan Tree. To Chingetti Cellar. He has a hidden study down there, a secret one. Not like the one in the Arboretum. He called it the Bulbdome or something." He turned his head and spat out a few tiny pieces of dried sugarcane husk before turning back to the group, wiping his mouth with the back of his hand sheepishly.

Ellishiva nodded. "Yes, I've heard about that study," she admitted in a low whisper.

"What's your point?" snapped Hektor, glaring furiously between Bairon and Ellishiva. "We're forbidden to go to Chingetti! What does it matter what's down there?"

"Hektor, don't be jealous of Elli because she has a brain," interrupted Samara sweetly. Asia missed another stitch of her knitting and choked, fighting down a giggle. Hektor scowled and chucked the short stem of a fig at them. It missed.

"Bairon," pressed Ellishiva, ignoring the others. "Have you ever been to Chingetti Cellar? What's down there?"

"Nothing much, Elli," Bairon confessed. "I saw it briefly once, with my father. He stores things in there for the Foxfire Harvest. It's just a dark place. It's not unheard of for Rajah to go down there. It's just he's been going a lot more than usual lately."

"Ah, the Foxfire Harvest. It's nearly here. Have you been rehearsing for your dance, Hektor?" inquired Samara with feigned politeness. Hektor's jaw worked, no doubt trying to come up with a biting retort, but in vain. "No? Shame," sighed Samara in the tone of a teacher who is used to disappointment from her hopeless pupil. She shrugged and turned to Ellishiva. "You know what I'm thinking, Elli?" she began, and her fingers paused on the braid in Asia's hair. "Chingetti Cellar is in the roots. And you know where the roots lead."

Ellishiva frowned, thinking. Then her eyebrows lifted as she realized what the fairy meant. Before she could speak the answer, however, Bairon beat her to it.

"They lead to the Muheekantuck River," he said excitedly.

The excitement was contagious. "Bairon," asked Ellishiva, leaning forward on her handwoven mat. "Your ahpa must have hundreds of maps of Chingetti Cellar. Right?"

"Of course, Elli. The shelves in his office are packed with rolls and rolls of maps," Bairon confirmed, taking another big bite of sugarcane.

"You've got to be kidding," broke in Hektor, venom in his words. He glared at all of them in turn, his angry brown eyes coming to rest, finally, on Ellishiva. "Haven't you broken enough rules?" he accused, and she winced. "Don't think I don't know about you and Sam wandering off to the river's edge for olivine to make her an illegal wand. You snuck off to the black market without telling us. You lied to me about the rare acorns at Mr. Guo's place. And now Chingetti Cellar? What do you think you are, Elli? A fairy like *her*? You don't have wings, you know. You should stop trying to fly around in Sam's rotten footsteps."

Samara threw the comb she was using at him. Hektor caught it before it hit him, then scowled and pelted it back at her. Asia snatched it out of the air and gave each of them a disapproving look.

Ellishiva was furious. "What is your problem, Hektor?" she snarled, truly at the end of her rope. The Sixth Element was about to break into their world, and all he could do was insult her friends? She plucked a mango from a vine overhead and began rolling it on the hard floor, partly to release the sweet juices within its skin, and partly to keep herself from chucking something at his head. "No one is going anywhere. We're having a discussion, that's all. Calm down, will you? And don't tell me what to do," she added coldly, giving him a hard look. "If I want to fly, I'll get something from Jipsin Smilodon, and it's none of your business."

She thought she saw Hektor turn a paler shade of green, but it was hard to tell in the blue light of the paper lantern. A sticky silence filled the room for a moment. Ellishiva bit the tip off of the softened mango and spat it out. Then she popped the exposed end of it into her mouth, squeezed the bottom, and sucked out the juice. When the skin of the fruit became dry and wrinkled, she pulled it out of her mouth and tossed it away, letting her gaze stray back to the darkening window. Beyond it, a pale half-circle was rising in the sky.

"The last quarter moon," she breathed, and a shiver went down her spine. "I wonder how she will strike." A twisted image of huge black clouds transforming into thousands of ravens and descending upon Banyan Tree filled her head. She set her jaw, struggling to smother the panic rising in the pit of her stomach. "The elders won't talk to us, but they must know what's going on. Part of it, at least. They've got to have a plan, right?" She glanced around the room, but the faces that looked back at her were doubtful and bleak. Ellishiva's resolve hardened. "I want to hear how Rajah and the kinnarans are planning to keep us safe," she declared, getting to her feet. "I'm going downstairs. Rajah will *have* to speak to me."

"Are you crazy? You'll shame him!" Hektor almost shouted at her, lurching to his feet, too, and moving to stand between Ellishiva and the door. "He has guests!"

"Get out of the way," she growled at him.

Hektor only crossed his arms and planted his feet, his message clear: if she wanted to go down there, she'd have to go through him.

Ellishiva might well have thrown herself at him if, at that moment, the standoff hadn't been broken by the sudden arrival of Amborella, who staggered into the bedchamber clutching Dollie Burlap under one arm and balancing a tray filled with doll-sized mugs in her hands. She gave Hektor a strange look as she passed, but said nothing, resigned, as if he were one of the unsolvable mysteries of the universe. Ellishiva held her ground a moment longer, glaring at her brother, then turned abruptly and followed the little girl as she toddled into the middle of the pile of cushions.

"And where have you been this long?" asked Samara as Amborella deposited her burden on the ground. Ellishiva thought she caught a thread of relief in the fairy's voice.

"The kitchen!" replied Amborella triumphantly.

"Oh, great," grumbled Hektor, shuffling back toward the group as well, and plucking a pomegranate from the hanging canopy. "What immortal purple ambrosia have you brought us now?"

Asia shot him a glare. "Don't listen to him, Amber. Come sit next to me," she said kindly, patting a cushion beside her. "I'm knitting a pair of tabi toe socks for you."

"Oh, joy!" said Amborella, scrambling over to the cushion to look at her impending new socks with bright eyes. After admiring them for a moment, she looked over at her brother. "Did Walle come yet, Hektor?" she asked.

"Do you see him?" retorted Hektor, biting off a piece of the pomegranate's bitter skin.

Amborella pursed her lips into an indignant knot. "You're so rude, Hektor!" she accused, sticking her tongue out at him.

Meanwhile, Ellishiva had pulled her own cushion up next to her sister's. "So what are they talking about, Amber?" she asked anxiously. "Did you hear anything unusual while you were in the kitchen?"

Amborella looked at her, aghast. "Elli! We're not supposed to listen when elders talk in private, unless you are an invited guest!" she informed her, obviously quoting Lady Malinia word for word. "I was just making purpleade punch in the kitchen. It was your idea," she reminded Ellishiva helpfully. Then she turned to the others, her eyes bright again. "Want some? I added something special!" she announced proudly.

"Oh! No, no! No thanks," mumbled a chorus of voices, tripping over each other.

"You know, Amber," drawled Hektor, wrinkling his nose, "Lilly Pilly Fizz is fruity and delicious without any 'secret ingredient.' And stop calling it purpleade punch! That's so ridiculous."

"It's not for you!" Amborella yelled at him, dropping a wooden spoon into the punch and stirring it busily, as if she hadn't heard a word of all the grumbling. "Who's first?" she asked the room at large, cheerfully.

There was an uncomfortable silence.

"Maybe later," Asia suggested softly, not wanting to hurt the little girl's feelings.

"Oh, look! We have eaten almost everything in the jungle," chimed in Samara quickly, gesturing up at the clusters of vines dangling from the canopy. They were still full of food. "I'm absolutely stuffed!"

"I can see that," Amborella scowled at her sarcastically, still stirring her purpleade with purpose.

Ellishiva ducked her head so that she was at Amborella's eye level. "Amber, are you *sure* you didn't hear anything the elders were saying when you were in the kitchen?" she implored earnestly.

Amborella heaved a sigh and gave her sister a look of great disappointment. "No, Elli. I told you, I was just making purpleade punch. Do you want some?" she added hopefully.

"Oh, look! We have a latecomer," Samara cut in suddenly, coming to Ellishiva's rescue. Ellishiva felt her heart skip a beat. She jerked her head around toward the window. But it wasn't Maximus who flew in to join them.

"Oh. Good to see you, Walle," said Ellishiva, trying to curtail her unfair disappointment.

"Walle!" cried Amborella, and a huge grin broke across her face. The dofaun firefly lit up as well, and immediately flew over to her. Amborella clambered to her feet and stood on tiptoe to plant a kiss on the hovering firefly's plump cheek. Walle's abdomen shone bright red.

"Hello, everyone!" he said, waving one of his upper limbs at the rest of the group. "Sorry I'm late."

"How's your mother feeling, Walle?" asked Ellishiva. Walle's mother had fallen ill a few days earlier, when a particularly large black cloud had swept over their home in the colony.

"Much better, Elli. Thanks for asking," Walle said appreciatively. He flew over to her. "Sorry I'm late. I was learning how to make a Bocaveen elixir. Did I miss anything?" he asked in a low, conspiratorial voice that made Hektor frown across the room.

"No, not really," Ellishiva began, casting a wary glance at her brother. Then she lowered her voice as well. "Did you say you're learning to make Bocaveen elixirs?" The firefly nodded at her cheerfully. Ellishiva nodded back, the cogs in her mind turning furiously. With a Bocaveen elixir, they'd be able to change their voices to sound like someone else's. And the vāhmanas in the colony were voice controlled.

Including the one to Chingetti Cellar.

"That's great," she said, trying to sound casual so as not to arouse Hektor's suspicions. "You should keep practicing that one."

Walle's black antennae perked curiously. "You want to change your voice?" he asked, and the "why?" was nearly off his tongue when he was suddenly interrupted by Amborella.

"I made purpleade punch with a secret ingredient, Walle!" she declared gaily. "Want some?"

The firefly's eyes widened. He looked furtively around at the rest of the company, who all rolled their eyes and shook their heads in warning. Hektor immediately stood up and untied as many of the hanging fruits and treenity treats as he could hold, tossing them quickly around the circle into all-too-eager hands. Ellishiva caught another mango.

The others quickly crammed whatever Hektor happened to throw at them into their mouths—anything to avoid having to try Amborella's punch with its added "secret ingredient."

Oblivious to this, Amborella happily plucked a doll mug from the tray, filled it with purpleade punch, and held it out to Walle. The little dofaun accepted it with two of his upper limbs, and took a cautious sniff. For a moment, his face quivered. But Amborella was staring at him hard, and there was no escape. Bravely, he lifted the cup to his mouth and took a sip. He'd barely swallowed before the half-choked coughing began, as though the liquid were stinging his throat.

Hektor and Bairon burst into a fit of giggles for a few seconds before promptly striking up a chant.

"Drink! Drink! Drink!"

"Don't do it, Walle!" Ellishiva warned as quietly as she could, risking Amborella's wrath. "Who knows what it will do to you!"

But the brave Walle only shook his head at her once, grimly. Then he raised the cup and gulped down its toxic contents, spluttering every sip of the way. Ellishiva and the others stared at him, transfixed, until he had wiped the last couple drops of the stuff from his chin. For a breathless moment, everyone waited to see what would befall him. But the seconds ticked by, and the young firefly showed no sign of internal torture. He had somehow survived.

Hektor and Bairon let out a triumphant whoop. "Here, Walle, have a fig," said Ellishiva's brother, grinning as he tossed one over to the lucky dofaun. "Come sit over here by us."

Ellishiva rolled her eyes at them. Then she turned back to Amborella, determined to make a last-ditch effort. "Amber," she started, making her voice sound casual. "There weren't any kinnarans downstairs, were there?"

"Just General Iliad," said Amborella, too distracted by her purpleade triumph to remember that she wasn't supposed to have been spying. "He was just listening to Rajah tell him about his trip to, um—to Yarrabah Colony. But I didn't hear anything else, because they went to Rajah's study in the Arboretum to talk more. Here, Walle, have more punch."

"Yarrabah!" exclaimed Ellishiva under her breath. She shot a look at Samara, who met it gravely. It was clear that they were thinking the same thing. Rajah had told everyone that he was going to Nicobar. He had told them that the dangerous black clouds were nothing to worry about. He had told them that Ellishiva's attack had just been a little fall in the woods. If he had lied about all of this . . . what other secrets was he keeping?

Seething, Ellishiva settled back onto her woven cushion. Across the room, Hektor was slapping a nauseous-looking Walle good-naturedly on the back. She let her gaze linger on him grimly, remembering the way he'd barred her way to the door earlier, and told herself to be patient. He'd be asleep soon enough. And then, she promised herself, she would unearth whatever Rajah was hiding once and for all.

CHAPTER TEN

VISITORS IN THE HALL

It seemed to take half the night for everyone—especially Hektor—to drift off to sleep, and Ellishiva's nerves gnawed at her more with every passing minute. Finally, desperate for a distraction, she dragged her woven pillow out of the "jungle" and over to the broad windowsill nearest her bed, propping herself up with it. On her lap, she opened *The Unauthorized Biography of Amma*, though it was hard to make her eyes focus on the words. Her gaze kept straying up, warily, to the gleaming light of the last quarter moon. It was as bright as she had ever seen it, and it was surrounded by a fine scattering of endless stars. "Like spice dust," she breathed to herself. Below, the firefly-peppered crowns of the trees of Mannahatta Island glowed warm and peaceful in the dark. Faintly, the song of a Nubian nightingale floated to her ear.

Ellishiva sighed, troubled. She braced her elbow on her knee, and rested her chin in the palm of her hand. Thoughts and feelings crowded into her mind, tumbling over one another lawlessly, like a swarm of ants. So much was happening. Her worried gaze found the moon again. *Sixth Element, keeper of the ice fairy's stolen heart, bringer of the dark clouds that fill our skies. Who are you? Whose voice do you speak with, from so long ago?*

Then her thoughts took a different turn. Maximus. She had been hoping to tell him about what she'd seen in the Silverdine, to ask him the very same questions she was wondering now, tonight. But beyond the window, the sky was still and empty. A feeling of foreboding stirred in Ellishiva's stomach. "Where are you?" she whispered to the night.

It made no reply.

Trying to shake the bad feeling, Ellishiva bent her head over the book in her lap once more. She leafed through its pages, pausing on the one with the interesting sketch of Symran—the dofaun with the face of a pretty fairy and the body of a phoenix. Her fingers traced the lines below the sketch as she began to read, silently mouthing the words before her.

"Symran, the most unique of all dofauns, resides at the Himosa. Upon her forehead she wears the Mark of the Earths: three wavy lines. Each of them represents one of the Three Earths. Here, the first two are the color of ash, symbolizing that the First and Second Earths have already been entered into. The third line remains green. When this mark turns to ash like the rest, it will signal the beginning of the Third and final Earth. Then must all creatures of conscience be gravely concerned for the future of this planet and all of its inhabitants."

Ellishiva continued reading in silence for a while, sometimes shaking her head in doubt or disbelief, sometimes frowning down at the pages beneath her fingers, thinking hard. At last she paused and leaned her head back onto the soft pillow, taking in deep, slow breaths of the crisp night air drifting in through the window. "You have to speak to me, Rajah," she breathed to herself finally. "You need to know what I know, what I'm thinking. Now more than ever."

Gently, purposefully, Ellishiva closed the book. She pulled her gaze away from the window, instead letting it drift over to the group sleeping beneath the leafy canopy, sprawled among the mats and cushions. Amborella tossed about in her sleep, her Dollie Burlap clasped tightly in her hands.

Hektor lay on his purple bag next to Bairon, snoring loudly.

Silently, Ellishiva set the book on the windowsill and tiptoed over and between Amborella and Asia until she was standing over Samara. She knelt down.

"Wake up. Sam, wake up," she breathed into the fairy's ear.

Samara rolled over, grumbling vaguely in her sleep.

With a flicker of impatience, Ellishiva nudged the fairy again. "Sam. *Sam*," she hissed insistently.

This time, Samara blinked groggily awake. "Wha—what's wrong?" she managed croakily, propping herself up on one elbow and rubbing the sleep out of her eyes.

"Shh!" Ellishiva lifted her finger to her lips in warning. Then, "Come on," she whispered. "We're going to Rajah's study in the Arboretum. I'm going to make him talk to me this time. Maximus hasn't shown up, and something isn't right. I'm worried." She reached down and helped a wobbly Samara to her feet.

They had just begun to pick their way out of the jungle when a soft red light flickered above their heads. Ellishiva froze and craned her head around. It was coming from the paper lantern where Walle was sleeping. Carefully, she tiptoed back and peered into it. The firefly peered back at her. He looked, she thought, positively sick.

Ellishiva frowned, concerned. "Are you all right, Walle?" she whispered.

"Noooo," moaned Walle quietly.

Ellishiva's frown grew. "Do you want to go home?" she asked.

"Noooooooo," groaned the little firefly pitifully, a little louder this time. Ellishiva glanced around sharply, but Hektor was still snoring on his stuffed bag, oblivious.

"What's the matter with Walle?" whispered Samara, flying over to hover by Ellishiva's ear.

"Shhh," Ellishiva whispered back, slightly panicked. "Just—just grab him before he wakes up the others."

Ellishiva held the rice-paper lantern steady while Samara lifted the sick firefly from his bed. At their feet, someone mumbled, and they jumped. But it was only Amborella, still hugging Dollie Burlap and turning over in her sleep.

"What's wrong with her?" Samara breathed into Ellishiva's ear.

"I don't know. She's been talking in her sleep a lot since she got that doll," Ellishiva whispered back. Then Walle gave another moan and she winced. "Come on. Let's hurry."

They picked their way out of the bedchamber, Samara flying ahead with Walle curled up like a house cat in her arms. Every creak of the floorboards sounded like an earsplitting shriek to Ellishiva as she followed the others down the stairs.

At the foot of the stairs, Samara paused, stroking Walle's wilted antennae with a rueful look on her face. "One more victim of Amber's purpleade punch," she sighed. "I was wondering how long it would be before it took effect." She looked up at Ellishiva. "Do you think we should take him home?"

Ellishiva looked at the miserable little firefly and forced herself to swallow her guilt. As bad as Amborella's purpleade was, there were even bigger things at stake. "No," she muttered, trying to sound firm. "I think we should keep him with us in case . . . in case we get caught."

Samara stared at Ellishiva blankly for a moment. "Isn't that, um . . . mean?" she ventured at last, uncertainly.

Walle gave another long whimper. It was so pitiful that, for a moment, Ellishiva almost relented. Then she caught herself and set her jaw. "No. We have no choice. Not now. Not when we need answers," she insisted. She looked apologetically down at the firefly. "I'm sorry, Walle. Do you think you can hang in there? Please? We did warn you that this would happen."

Walle grimaced, but managed a stoic nod. Ellishiva bent and gave him a peck on the cheek, but he didn't seem to have the energy to glow. "Don't worry. You'll be fine," she promised. "Just try not to speak. It will make you want to vomit."

"Yes, and don't let your guard down, either," warned Samara gravely. "That punch has too many side effects to count."

They were about to tiptoe around the corner into the living area, toward the Arboretum, when suddenly Ellishiva heard faint sounds—words and shouts—drifting down the empty L-shaped hallway behind them. She held out a hand to stop the others from moving and stood perfectly still, listening.

"Hear that?" she muttered under her breath.

"Huh?" said Samara, whose attention was on the wilted firefly in her arms. "What? I don't hear anything."

"Shh," Ellishiva shushed her quickly. Then she pointed down the dim passage that led to the Hall of Nature Healing. "Look. There's light down there. See? It's reflecting off the wall." She set off toward it.

It took the fairy and her bundled-up invalid a moment to catch up. "What are you doing?" she whispered in Ellishiva's ear as she flew along behind her. "I thought we were going to the Arboretum—?"

"We are," interrupted Ellishiva brusquely, not slowing in her stride. "But we should see what's happening here first. It sounds important. We can head to the study afterward."

"Poor Walle," mumbled Samara with a sad shake of her head. "Hang in there."

"Oh, stop fussing. It's not like Amber's punch is going to kill him," Ellishiva muttered, wrestling down the fresh bout of guilt that squirmed to life in her chest. "Come on. The sooner we get there, the sooner we can put him back to bed." She picked up the pace.

A moment later, the girls and their miserable passenger turned the corner to find that the doors to the Hall of Nature Healing were indeed ajar. The light grew brighter and the voices louder as they approached.

"Do you smell that?" asked Ellishiva in a low whisper. "Turmeric. Honey . . ."

"No," admitted Samara, adding in a mutter under her breath, "You and your impossible sense of smell."

"Someone pounding . . . a poultice . . . ?" stammered Walle in a pained voice.

Ellishiva felt her skin begin to prickle as she drew up to the crack in the door, though with excitement or fear, she couldn't tell. No matter how small she tried to make herself, she felt as glaring as a full oil lamp with a moonless night all to itself.

"Well, guess you got your wish, Elli," whispered Samara, fluttering over her head to peer through the crack as well. "All night you've been wanting to eavesdrop on the elders."

They leaned forward, as close to the huge panels of wood as they could get without interrupting the sparkling flow of the crisscrossing rivulets of spice water. In Samara's arms, Walle gave a small, faint whimper. Ellishiva winced, stood on tiptoe, and gave the firefly's drooping antennae a light tug. When he looked down at her, she pressed a finger to her lips. Walle sighed miserably.

The girls peeked through the crack in the doors, into the Hall of Nature Healing. Sections of bright silver roved over the curved walls of bottles and books as Gustav and Onuris busied themselves around the Neem Table in the center of the room. Near the ceiling, a cloud of Silverdine spice dust floated serenely, rhythmically, recording. It, too, gave off silver light. Across from them, on the easternmost wall, soft moonlight poured in through the grand window, glimmering on the jars that filled the shadowy shelves and catching on the carved tops of ink bottles crowded onto the desks of the fireflies.

In the middle of it all, Rajah, Banog, Queen Neive, Mr. Belanos, and General Iliad were all clustered around the Neem Table, shifting and speaking in harsh, low words to one another.

Ellishiva was straining her eyes to see who exactly it was that they were clustered around when Walle let out a low moan.

She and Samara jerked back from the doors. Ellishiva's heart pounded wildly in her chest. Next to her, the fairy's eyes were as round as barbee jujubes. But several seconds went by, and no one came bursting angrily out of the Hall to apprehend them.

Ellishiva's fear turned to frustration.

"Cover his mouth. We'll get caught," she whispered urgently.

"Isn't that why you wanted to bring him along?" pointed out Samara.

Ellishiva scowled at her. "Practice your Hektor imitation some other time, Sam," she snapped quietly. "We have to do something. Put him—" she cast around for a hiding place, but the L-shaped hallway was as barren as it always was. Then her eyes fell on the rose-colored pouch at Samara's hip. "Put him in your new noli," she ordered desperately.

Samara looked at her, aghast. "What?" she said, holding the sick firefly a little closer.

"We *can't* get caught," insisted Ellishiva, forcing the words out between clenched teeth. She looked apologetically at the invalid in question. "I'm so sorry about this, Walle."

Walle blinked at her, as though trying to make sense of what was happening.

Samara sighed and rolled her eyes. "Walle, I'm going to put you in my noli," she explained in a whisper. "Don't be afraid. You'll be fine. But don't touch *anything* in there. Even the Tigress couldn't tell how old this thing is. Who knows what the other owners have put in it."

Another little spasm of guilt wormed to life in Ellishiva's chest, and she had to bite her tongue to keep from taking it all back. Walle stared at Samara in horror for a moment before drumming up his courage. Then, steeling his antennae, he nodded, all six of his limbs clutching his stomach.

Samara gave him an encouraging smile. Then she opened the enchanted noli and stuffed the suffering firefly in. Ellishiva watched his body shrink, just like the Puluma balón, as he disappeared into its mysterious depths. She looked at Samara and opened her mouth, poised to tell the fairy to take him back out after all. Before the words could find their way out, however, they were interrupted by a roar from the Hall.

"How could this happen!" bellowed the loud, deep voice of General Iliad.

Swallowing her conscience, Ellishiva turned back to the crack between the doors. Inside, the bright silver lights of the firefly dofauns had stopped roaming the walls, frozen for a moment by the echoes of the general's furious outburst. Around the Neem Table, the bodies had shifted, but it was still impossible to identify the figure thrashing about on its surface. "That's Theo," breathed Samara, who had fluttered over to peek through the crack again as well. "The one at the foot of the Neem Table, next to the general."

"I remember. We just saw him this afternoon at Textile Alley, with Morpheus and Maximus. But—ugh. Do you smell that?" whispered Ellishiva, her nose wrinkling up like a prune. A head above her, Samara nodded, and she knew that the fairy was remembering the same thing she was: it was the same foul, rotting scent that had accosted them in the forest that day, right before the locust tree had attacked.

"I can't hold him much longer!" Theo's hoarse voice called out, his hands gripping the legs of the writhing patient lying on the table before him. The leggings, Ellishiva saw, belonged to a kinnaran.

Maximus, she thought, and her heart leapt into her throat. But try as she might, she could not see the injured warrior's face through the crowd of bodies that surrounded him.

"I have him secured," declared Banog, rising off the floor and pinning the kinnaran's shoulders to the table with his huge, strong talons.

"His wings are badly damaged," assessed Mr. Belanos grimly. He, too, was struggling to hold the writhing kinnaran down.

"Damaged? There are no wings left!" bellowed the general.

Rajah leaned over to examine the bloodied legs of his patient on the Neem Table and, at last, Ellishiva could see the wounded kinnaran's face.

"Morpheus," she breathed, both horror and relief flooding through her at once. "But then . . . where is Maximus?"

Above her, Samara shook her head grimly. "I don't know. Morpheus's armor is on the floor," she said. The words had no sooner left her lips than Onuris swept down and picked up the stained, heavy pile of boots and scales. The mound was nearly as big as the firefly himself, yet he lifted it effortlessly, flying quickly away again to deposit the bloody things out of sight behind the bookshelves. "Wow," murmured Samara appreciatively. "Onuris isn't that strong, usually. He must have drunk a Somanar elixir."

Meanwhile, the general had not finished his rampage by a long shot.

"*How did this happen*?" he roared again, fixing his fiery gaze on Theo.

The exhausted young kinnaran winced. "I did my best, General, but—" he began shakily. Then he trailed off, apparently lost for words, trapped in the horror of a memory. His armor had been ripped apart in several places, and there were nasty blisters on his face, neck, and arms. Nevertheless, his determined grip on Morpheus's kicking legs never slackened.

"What do you think happened to his armor?" whispered Samara.

Ellishiva did not reply. Few things were powerful enough to rip through armor like that. And only one had pledged to attack on the night of the last quarter moon. She shot a meaningful look at the fairy above her.

Understanding dawned on Samara's face. She pressed her thin lips into a line. "You were right, Elli," she murmured, reaching down to hold Ellishiva's hand. Her gaze strayed back to the grotesque scene in the Hall. "It's happening. Just like the Sixth Element said it would."

"This is her third attack," Ellishiva whispered back, remembering the discovery of Atticus outside Cathay Alley on the day before she'd been grounded. "Maybe the three of them—Theo and Morpheus and . . . and Maximus—were trying to stop the Sixth Element from getting into our world again and then this—" she swallowed, trying hard not to think the worst about Maximus's absence. "And then this happened," she finished quietly.

Onuris flew over and began applying a healing paste to Theo's bloodied blisters while the latter continued to hold down his fellow's writhing ankles. On the Neem Table, Morpheus continued to moan and thrash about worse than ever, like a fish flipping on a riverbank. Then, as they watched, he began to cough violently, and white foam spewed from the corners of his mouth.

"Elli," whispered Samara, her voice trembling, "that's what I was telling you about. That was what you looked like after the attack, when it was you on the Neem Table."

"With foam coming out of my mouth? Really?" Ellishiva whispered, aghast. "I thought I was vomiting."

"Theo, *what happened*?" demanded the general yet again. But Theo only stared at the tortured kinnaran on the table, as though his ears had ceased to hear anything but the other soldier's pain.

"Come, Iliad," intervened Queen Neive firmly. "Let the rest of us take care of this." She put an arm around the general's shoulders and led him away from the sordid scene, over to the large window. There they stood, whispering in voices that were too low to hear. Ellishiva saw the general press his fingers to his temples. Through the window, pale moonlight winked off the scales of his armor. At the table, Rajah was mixing white mud with dried red berries in a familiar stone mortar while Theo, Banog, and Mr. Belanos continued to hold Morpheus fast. It seemed an eternity before her guardian at last finished his task, and bent to apply the poultice to his patient's wounds. As he did, the injured kinnaran groaned louder.

"Theo, why did you leave Mannahatta Island?" asked Rajah, his voice calm and steady.

"Morpheus insisted!" blurted Theo. He stole a nervous glance toward his superior by the window.

"You are the commanding officer, not Morpheus! And you were told to remain on the island!" snarled the general gruffly from across the room before Queen Neive could stop him.

"But General, Morpheus insisted!" Theo protested, fissures of desperation in his voice. "He said he understood her and that it smelled like—like the tea plantations at Madagascar!"

Madagascar. Ellishiva's ears perked sharply at the word. She tugged on Samara's sleeve to get the fairy's attention. "That's what Mr. Belanos said the Muheekantuck River smells like these days: Madagascar," she hissed under her breath. "And the tea he gave me to drink was from Madagascar, too. Rajah was the prefect of the colony there . . ." She trailed off, her eyes studying the general, who had turned back to the window. His fingers were pressed to his temples again, and he no longer seemed to be listening to Queen Neive's whispered words of reassurance. In the reflection of the glass, Ellishiva could see something like heartbreak on his face. She frowned. It seemed strange that a general, who had surely seen many of his troops wounded in battle before, would let himself become so emotional over one casualty.

Or were there, in truth, more casualties than she could see?

Ellishiva's stomach lurched. She tugged again at Samara's elbow, fighting a wave of panic. "Sam, something has happened to Maximus. I can feel it. He must still be out there, somewhere."

"Well. Maybe not, Elli," replied Samara, doubt lurking beneath her words. "They haven't said he's dead or anything . . ."

"Of course he isn't dead. He's alive," insisted Ellishiva unsteadily. "I know he is. The Sixth Element must have captured him."

"You think?" began Samara uncertainly.

"Yes," snapped Ellishiva, distressed. "Now shh. Let's listen."

She leaned close to the crack in the doors again. Overhead, Samara warily followed suit.

"Tell me, Theo," Rajah was saying, his eyes focused on Morpheus as he continued to apply the mudpack to the kinnaran's wounds. "When you were on South Island, did you hear anything unusual? A voice, perhaps?"

"Yes. A woman's voice. Speaking in Pali language. But—but it came from nowhere. No body, no face." His voice shook, and he glanced at the general's turned back as he spoke. "It was sad, wailing. As if in agony. It sickened my insides just listening to it." He buckled slightly, nearly losing his grip on Morpheus's ankles, and a nauseated look passed over his face. In an instant, Onuris was by his side, holding a tiny open bottle under his nose. The kinnaran breathed in deeply, and seemed to find his knees again. He gave the firefly a grateful nod.

"I'm going to the river," declared General Iliad in a stony voice. He had dropped his hands from his temples now, and he was gazing fiercely out at the moonlit night, as though wanting nothing more than to charge out and destroy it.

"Patience, Iliad. We cannot go there now," Rajah counseled evenly, never taking his eyes from his patient. "We have a life to attend to here. Morpheus needs you."

"I agree," chimed in Banog. "Let us wait for daylight, General."

General Iliad turned violently away from the window, making Queen Neive jump. "I have orders, Valerius!" he roared, striding to the Neem Table and slamming his huge hands down on its smooth surface. He glared ferociously at Rajah like a dofaun driven mad by the dark clouds. "We are here to protect the child, and I will use everything in my power to do so!"

Rajah did not flinch, and his steady hands did not pause as they continued to tend to the young kinnaran fighting for his life on the table in front of them. "Patience, Iliad," he said again.

"What child?" breathed Ellishiva. The dread in her stomach churned into an awful sense of foreboding. "Sam, what are they talking about?"

But Samara only shrugged her shoulders and shook her head. Neither one of them could drag their eyes away from the scene unfolding in the Hall.

Queen Neive left the east window and rejoined the others. "Are you sure the creature is on South Island?" she asked Theo, her face drawn and stern.

"Yes! Yes, my lady," confirmed Theo anxiously.

"This is the third attack, Valerius!" exclaimed the general. "One on the First Spice Child, Ellishiva Cinnamon. Two: Atticus, barely saved by Banog. And now this creature is attacking kinnarans—on a last quarter moon, no less! The child whispered of this, you said. The Sixth Element is gaining strength and killing in both worlds. There may be nothing left by the next quarter moon if we do not act now!"

Ellishiva swallowed in the darkness of the hallway. Her thoughts were stuck, like a gnat in honey, on the first thing that the general had said. *The First Spice Child . . .*

"Elli? Elli?" Gradually, she became aware of Samara's bony elbow nudging her in the shoulder. "*Elli . . .*"

"Shhh, Sam. They'll hear you," hissed Ellishiva, swatting her away.

"Fine, fine," huffed Samara. She floated down a bit, so that her mouth was next to Ellishiva's ear. "Elli, why is he calling you the *First Spice*? There are loads of other Va'natures, right? In other colonies?"

Ellishiva shrugged irritably and bent closer to the crack between the doors. She was wondering the same thing, and she hung on the general's every word, determined to ferret out the answer somehow.

"How did the creature penetrate this colony?" General Iliad was saying. "*You* must know, Valerius. This is *your* colony. You are account-able for it! *No one* was supposed to find the child Ellishiva Cinnamon! We swore an oath, all of us in this room! We swore to Amma that she would be kept a secret!" The general's voice was barely under control, and his yellow eyes were shot-through with specks of red the color of his body.

Rajah did not reply, continuing to tend to Morpheus as if the kinnaran leader had said nothing.

Ellishiva pulled back into the dark of the L-shaped hallway. Her heart was pounding so hard she thought it might crack her ribs. "*I am what's hidden on Mannahatta?*" she breathed. Her brain struggled to grasp the meaning of the impossible words.

Samara floated down to stand beside her. "What?" she whispered.

She rolled her shoulders in frustration, as though nothing in the world could make less sense. "Why would they be hiding you?"

Ellishiva shook her head mutely. That was indeed the great mystery. She peered back into the Hall, looking for the general again, but her eyes snagged on something else instead.

In a dark corner, a head with pointed ears was silhouetted against a shaft of moonlight, craning itself over the mess of letters on Gustav's writing desk.

"What is *she* doing here?" hissed Ellishiva, narrowing her eyes and nudging Samara to look as well. "Fishing for a story for *The Mannahatta Times* again? *Now*?" Another thought struck her. "Do you see Baron Puck anywhere?" she whispered, scanning the shadows of the Hall.

"No, I don't see him," replied Samara, and Ellishiva thought she heard a faint flicker of guilt in the fairy's voice. "I don't know why she's here. I guess she must have been having tea with the rest of them before all this happened. You know how Rajah always includes everyone."

In the Hall, the figure was emerging, finally, from the shadowy desks in the corner.

"You have a point, Iliad," purred the Tigress of Sundari, padding smoothly across the floor on her soft hind paws, like oil slinking over wood. Her lush fur was pale pink and patterned with flowing, creamy white and tawny stripes. "The Sixth Element could not have breached the colony's borders without assistance. Perhaps," she went on, her voice light and dangerous, "this creature's helper is even closer than we think. Something—no, *someone* had to lend her strength and guide her." Her glassy yellow eyes fixed themselves intently on Ellishiva's guardian.

A cold silence fell over the Hall at her words. Even Rajah paused briefly in his ministrations, though his eyes never left the injured Morpheus.

At last, the queen of the fairies spoke. "My dear Tigress," declared Queen Neive with distaste. "Such speculations are not worthy of decent ears. Nor even of the ears that grace your tasteless tabloid,

I should think." The look she shot the Tigress could have frozen steam in midair.

The Tigress ignored her completely, as though the queen's words had no more effect on her than a passing breeze. The buttons on her softly draped silk tunic glinted at her neck and wrists in the silver light as she padded gracefully over to the Neem Table and boldly laid one perfectly groomed paw on the general's shoulder, as though she alone understood and supported him.

Queen Neive watched silently, a deep frown on her lovely forehead. Mr. Belanos raised an eyebrow. The Hall of Nature Healing seemed to hum with tension—so much so that even the fireflies hovering above the scene, who were always the picture of calmness, seemed disturbed.

With his back to the doorway, Ellishiva could not see Rajah's face, but she thought it odd that he could remain quiet in the face of such awful accusations. Surely he couldn't let the Tigress get away with such a thing. Yet the seconds ticked by, and still her guardian said nothing. The frustration built up in Ellishiva until, finally, the words spilled from her lips without her permission.

"*Defend yourself,*" she whispered, loud enough that a faint echo of the words bounced around them in the L-shaped hallway.

"Shhh!" Samara prodded her in the shoulder sharply, horrified.

But it was too late.

In the Hall, Rajah stood perfectly still for a moment. Then he turned his head slightly to the right, as if he were about to peer over his shoulder at the giant doors where the girls were concealed. But he didn't. Instead, he lifted his chin a little and gazed purposefully at the Silverdine spice dust hovering above the Neem Table. Overhead, a thin wisp of dust broke away from the cloud and drifted toward the doors.

No one else in the room noticed.

Ellishiva jumped to her feet. "Hurry! Sam, come on!" she whispered urgently, yanking at the fairy's pajama leg. "It's coming. It's going to record us. We'll get caught! We've got to go. Now! Hurry up! Get Walle out!"

Samara did not need to be told twice. An instant later, the two of them were dashing down the L-shaped hallway as though it were a Puluma court. As they ran, Samara plunged her hand into her noli and muttered, "Walle!" In the next moment, the firefly was being pulled from the rose-colored pouch by his antennae, a trail of shimmering red dust wafting down behind him. He gasped and sputtered in surprise. Samara hugged him to her tightly to muffle the sounds.

They swerved around the bend in the hallway, Ellishiva in the lead. Ahead, she could see the stairs to the bedchamber where the others were sleeping soundly, oblivious. For a moment, she desperately wanted to climb them, to burrow deeply into the cushions of the jungle sleepover and pretend that everything was just as it had always been. But the thought had barely graced her mind before General Iliad's words were echoing through her head again.

. . . the First Spice Child, Ellishiva Cinnamon . . .

There was something about herself that she didn't know. Something important. Something that could only be found in her own spice jar, in the history of herself. And her spice jar, she knew, was kept in one very safe place.

Rajah's study.

Her guardian would be busy in the Hall for some time—that much was clear. And there could be no telling when another chance like this might come up. Ellishiva set her jaw.

"The Arboretum," she whispered to Samara over her shoulder. Then she sprinted past the staircase to the bedchamber and tore into the great hall beyond, running as fast as her legs would carry her. She had barely turned the corner into the kitchen, however, when her eyes were blinded by a bright light shining directly in her face. Her bare feet slipped on the polished floor and she slid, skidding forward despite her cartwheeling arms. Before she could stop herself, she was bumping into something soft . . . and feathery.

"And what are you doing in my kitchen at this time of night?"

snapped Lady Malinia, a sour scowl on her face. In front of her, she held a lamp—the source of the blinding light. Though the lamp was only lit by one tiny firefly, it threw a huge black shadow on the cupboards behind her. A white kerchief was wrapped around the dofaun's head, and a long, worn linen nightgown dropped nearly to her talons.

Ellishiva, gasping for air, heard Samara land clumsily on the ground behind her right shoulder.

The groggy caretaker did not appreciate her charge's lack of response. "Well?" she demanded in a clipped tone, leaning over Ellishiva. "You know the rules for jungle sleepovers. No wandering about after bedtime! Especially when we have guests! So, what have you got to say for yourself? Speak up, child!"

Ellishiva opened her mouth, but no words came out of it. She was too out of breath to say anything. Her chest heaved from the sprint—up and down, up and down.

"Oh, Lady Malinia," piped up Samara, coming to the rescue. "We're so, so sorry. But it's, uh—it's Walle. He isn't well at all, so we flew. I mean, we ran. I mean, we rushed over here to bring him to you!" She held the bedraggled firefly out in front of her with both hands.

"Yes," gasped Ellishiva, finding her voice at last. "It's Walle, Lady Malinia. That's why we're here. We were sleeping, and he started tossing and moaning in his bed. He needs your help. You—you've cured all of us of Amber's purpleade punch before."

Lady Malinia frowned and set the lamp down hard on the kitchen table, jostling the firefly within. For a moment, Ellishiva was sure she heard a high-pitched grumble about there not being any peace around here and putting in for a transfer to another limb. Before she could mumble an apology to the little creature, however, Lady Malinia was taking Walle from Samara's outstretched arms.

"Oh my!" tutted the caretaker sympathetically, her attention shifting completely to the whimpering firefly. "You poor thing! Oh, she's done it again. Too much huacatay in her purpleade. I *told* her not to add it to the Lilly Pilly Fizz. Ellishiva, get one of those mugs." She gestured to a spot above the washbasin, where various clay mugs of all sizes hung from wooden hooks. Ellishiva had barely pulled the smallest down from its perch before her caretaker was tacking on extra instructions. "Quickly now, fill it halfway with rainwater."

Ellishiva obeyed, her heart still beating fast. From the corner of her eye, she saw Lady Malinia gently lay Walle down on the kitchen table, then reach across the smooth surface toward what looked to be Samara's waist, where the rose noli hung unsuspectingly by her hip. The fairy immediately recoiled, a look of horror on her face.

But Lady Malinia was not out to confiscate the pouch. Instead, her feathered fingers closed around her own burlap noli, which was plopped on the tabletop not far from where Samara was standing.

"I saw that face, fairy child," clucked the dofaun pigeon shrewdly. She tugged open the burlap noli and pulled out a small, dried brown pea pod. "My own old noli does me very well, thank you. They don't make them like this anymore, you know," she added with a long-suffering sigh.

Samara swallowed and shifted her noli out of sight behind her.

Lady Malinia took no notice. Carefully, she shook the pea pod close to her ear, listening for something. Ellishiva strode over and placed the mug of rainwater in front of the dofaun, and then stood by, watching. With a firm nod, Lady Malinia split open the dried pod. From its depths she extracted one tiny, round, white seed, and dropped it unceremoniously into the water. Instantly, it began to bubble and hiss, much like a fresh gourd of Lilly Pilly Fizz.

"Now, dear," she cooed to Walle, supporting the young firefly's tiny shoulders with one of her broad, feathered hands, "sit up and take this." She held the mug of fizzing water up to Walle's mouth until he had swallowed every last drop of it. Then she patted his back gently but firmly for a little while, clucking reassuringly. Ellishiva watched and waited.

Not a minute had gone by before the firefly's drooping antennae perked up, and a look of surprise came over his face. Then, suddenly, he let out a gigantic belch, followed by a thunderous fart. The bitter stink of huacatay filled the air, like a pot of boiling marigold flowers.

"Whew!" cried Samara, waving her hand back and forth in front of her nose. "And to think I had you in my—" she stopped short, biting her tongue before it could give away the secret of her noli.

"None of that, Samara!" chided Lady Malinia sharply. "I suppose you'd like to tell me that fairies do not belch or fart. Or that you, of all creatures, are too fancy-fancy for that! Dear little Walle," she added sympathetically, turning back to the firefly and gently stroking his head and wilted antennae with her soft hand. "Pay her no mind whatsoever. You will be glowing again very soon, dear. I promise."

Samara giggled, and Ellishiva caught the note of relief in the sound. "Sorry, Walle. Just playing with you," she said with an innocent grin.

Lady Malinia was true to her word. Only moments later, a soft red glow kindled in the firefly's abdomen, and then began to strengthen. His face filled with relief. Then it filled with something else.

"The latrine," said Lady Malinia with a pointed look at him, "is just down the hall."

Walle blushed a little, and glanced at Ellishiva. She mustered a smile and a nod for him, encouraging him to go. He shot her a grateful look before scampering off around the corner as fast as his wings could carry him.

Ellishiva turned her head to stare out of the kitchen's open double doors, into the Arboretum beyond. Her mind was throbbing with the fresh memory of the scene she had just witnessed in the Hall of Nature Healing, and time was trickling away. If she could only think of a way to get past Lady Malinia . . .

"Are you hungry, girls?" her caretaker was asking. She strode across the kitchen and began rummaging about in the pantry. "I could use a bite myself. We've plenty of fresh snacks. I've been cooking all day." She finished digging around and came back to the table, a loaf of banana-fig-acorn bread and a jar of avanella nut butter cradled in her wings.

Samara put on her most innocent face. "Lady Malinia? Can I have some of your delicious treenity treats, please?" she asked, taking great pains to sound sweet and polite.

"Oh yes, dear," replied Lady Malinia, setting the bread and butter on the table and bringing out a few earthenware dishes and a knife. All of her annoyance from before had been forgotten. "Help yourself. Just look in the pantry. Ellishiva had the idea to make extra batches for the sleepover. Oh, and Mr. Belanos told me he greatly enjoyed the treats that the two of you dropped off earlier today. Thank you both for delivering them for me." She waddled over to the cupboard and back, this time toting along a pitcher of almond milk with some glasses, before settling down on a bench next to where Ellishiva was still standing.

Ellishiva watched a grin break over Samara's face as she fluttered over to the pantry and opened the door to a whole heaping tray of fresh treenitys. The fairy threw a glance over her shoulder to make sure that Lady Malinia wasn't looking her way. Then she began to stuff the pyramid-shaped treats into her enchanted noli. Ellishiva frowned, frustrated at being stuck in the kitchen at a time like this. She wondered absently if, given the chance, Samara would stuff even a pile of pitcher-plant guts into her noli, just because she could.

Her thoughts were interrupted by the scrape of clay on wood. Ellishiva looked down to find that Lady Malinia had pushed a plate with one slice of thickly buttered bread over to her, and was preparing two more for Samara and herself. Ellishiva took a deep breath and nudged it back across the table to her. "I'm not hungry," she began haltingly, struggling to come up with the magic words that would allow her to escape. "I'm, uh. I'm—"

"Goodness dear, you're not having hot flashes like me, are you?" interrupted Lady Malinia suddenly. She sidled over to the edge of the bench and began mopping Ellishiva's face with the bunched-up hem of her nightgown.

"No, I—I'm fine!" gasped Ellishiva in a muffled voice from beneath the cloud of cloth. It took a good ten seconds before she finally managed to wriggle free of the dofaun's well-meaning wiping. "I'm just sleepy," she finished, letting out a great yawn to prove it.

Samara sidled up to the table, looking pleased with herself, and took a great bite out of the slice of buttered bread.

"Here, have some milk with that, dear," urged Lady Malinia, pouring milk for all three of them into short glasses as though she hadn't heard Ellishiva—which, Ellishiva knew from experience, she probably hadn't. "A teaspoon of turmeric will see to it that we all sleep soundly, and the almond milk makes us wake up with a functional brain," she added in a singsong voice, scooping a heaping spoonful of the bright yellow spice into each cup.

Ellishiva watched the dofaun carefully stir the mugs of milk, her blood boiling with frustration. She felt as though an eon had drifted by since she'd stumbled into the kitchen. Then Walle flew drowsily back in from the hallway, and Lady Malinia had to start the whole milk-preparation process over again.

Ellishiva turned her own cup around and around in her hands while she waited, her pinky finger tapping the glass and her toe ring tapping the floor. A slew of questions was tumbling messily through her head. Why had the general called her the First Spice? Why were they hiding her? Who—or what—were they hiding her from?

There was only one thing that could tell her. And it was sitting, unguarded for the moment, in Rajah's study in the Arboretum.

"I'm *so* tired," Ellishiva said again, louder than before. Maybe if she could get Samara to help, they'd be able to sneak away faster. She stretched her hands above her head in a fake yawn, caught the fairy's eye, and jabbed her raised index finger meaningfully in the direction of the open double doors.

Samara, who was in the middle of swallowing a large gulp of yellow milk, noticed and gurgled in surprise.

"Oh, yes. Yes, of course you are, dear," said Lady Malinia distractedly. "It is quite late. Quite late indeed."

Walle had dutifully drained his cup of milk and now lay dozing on the table, one set of limbs under his head, the other resting contentedly on his belly. An idea struck Ellishiva. Not the best, perhaps, but it would have to do.

"Come on, Walle. This table is too hard to sleep on," she cooed, gathering the firefly up in her arms and stroking his antennae soothingly. "Let's go back to bed, Sam. See you in the morning, Lady Malinia," she said, letting out another huge, fake yawn for effect. "Thank you again for baking the extra treenitys."

"Yes, dears. Off you go," clucked Lady Malinia, yawning herself as she gathered up the dirty dishes and put them in the big washbasin. "Have a good night's sleep now, all of you."

They walked out of the kitchen without looking back. As soon as they had turned the corner at the far end of the living hall and were standing at the foot of the stairway to the bedchamber, Ellishiva stopped and bent her head toward Samara's ear. "You're starting to act like Hektor, hoarding all that food," she muttered, shooting a pointed glance at the rose-colored noli. "Here. Hurry up and take Walle upstairs, but don't fly. That way Lady Malinia will think they're my footsteps. Walle, you go and rest. I'll explain everything to you later, okay?"

The little dofaun nodded obediently.

"You want to sneak out to the Arboretum, to Rajah's study, don't you?" accused Samara. "I knew you were up to something. Honestly, Elli, sometimes I'm afraid of what you're going to want to do next." She took Walle from Ellishiva's arms with a loud sigh. Nevertheless, Ellishiva thought she heard the faintest note of pride in her friend's voice.

"Hurry up. Meet me in the fernery by the breakfast table as soon as Lady Malinia goes to bed again. And don't walk back, fly. We don't want her to hear footsteps."

Samara nodded and disappeared up the staircase with Walle in her arms.

Ellishiva turned back to the living hall, keeping her ears perked toward the kitchen, waiting for the clink of dishes in the washbasin to fade away. Waiting for her moment . . .

CHAPTER ELEVEN

DEEP ROOTS

A low fire was still crackling in the hearth when the girls stumbled into Rajah's study a short while later, its sleepy flames making shadows dance over the chairs and the silver spyglass. On the low table by the round east window, several abandoned, half-full teacups had lost their last wisps of steam.

"So where do we start?" asked Samara, breathless from their sprint across the Arboretum. They had slipped out of the warren the instant Lady Malinia had waddled back to bed, and the elders' business in the Hall of Nature Healing was far from finished. Not even the whisper of a breeze had followed them to the study. For the moment, they were safe.

Ellishiva eyed the rounded walls of books, and felt suddenly overwhelmed. "Don't know," she muttered, out of breath herself.

Samara gave her a sympathetic look. "Long night," she summed up succinctly. Then she added in something closer to her usual cheerful voice, "Well, at least now we know why Rajah has been treating you differently, right? Hiding you, keeping you here against your will—"

"Fly up," interrupted Ellishiva, who was hardly in the mood for one of Samara's singular pep talks. Her chest rose and fell; she could feel the blood pulsing in her temples. "Go to the other end of the bookshelf.

That part, over there. Look for anything with Amma's name on it. Or anything that has to do with Nicobar or—or anything that says 'First Spice.' Wait!" She grabbed the fairy's wrist before she could fly off. "Don't forget to look at all the spice jars closely. Mine's in here, I know it. Check the top shelves. I'll go through Rajah's desk."

Samara nodded curtly. Ellishiva nodded back, took a deep breath, and released her wrist. On a mission, the two of them set out to divide and conquer the secrets of the study.

For a long while, nothing caught their eye. Ellishiva searched every cranny of Rajah's desk, too distracted to care about the tornado she was leaving in her wake. Drawers were left half open, and scrolls of papyrus and short stacks of books fell to the floor unheeded. An ink bottle by her elbow toppled onto its side, setting a dark stain spreading over an important-looking journal. Meanwhile, at the far end of the room, Samara was rooting carelessly through shelves, knocking books to the ground and leaving everything else in jumbled, messy piles, as if an earthquake had just rocked the mango tree house.

By the time Ellishiva looked up from the search again, Rajah's study was in shambles.

"Nothing. I can't find anything!" she huffed, panicked. She kicked a fallen book aside, adding in a mutter under her breath, "At least these aren't coming alive on me tonight." She yanked a half-open drawer out of the desk completely, turned it upside down, and inspected the bottom for any hidden papyrus letters that might have been taped onto it. Its few remaining contents spilled out to join the mess on the floor. Ellishiva tossed it aside and pulled out another drawer, this time sending the several old, empty olivine orbs that had once crowned Rajah's staff rolling out across the study as she flipped it over. Still, there was nothing to be discovered.

Frustrated, Ellishiva glanced over at Samara, who was hovering near the top of one of the bookshelves. The fairy was muttering things to herself as she leafed through the pages of a book. Not finding anything, she simply tossed it carelessly over her shoulder, where it landed with a *thunk* in a pile of its similarly disappointing fellows.

Ellishiva drew a deep breath and shifted on her feet. Her bare toes bumped one of the fallen olivine orbs, and she frowned. Without knowing quite why she did it, she bent and picked up the orb, and quickly stuffed it into her noli.

"Find something?"

Samara's voice was practically in her ear. Ellishiva jumped, nearly bumping her head on the heavy desk. She straightened up and turned to find Samara standing right behind her, her eyes scanning the impressive mess around the desk. The fairy sighed. "I'm not sure exactly what Rajah did to be this far on your bad side, but remind me never to make the same mistake, will you?" she said matter-of-factly.

"Don't sneak up on me like that!" hissed Ellishiva, pinning her friend with a withering look.

"What? It's just the two of us in here," protested Samara defensively. She let her gaze stray back to the disaster zone around the desk. "Just keep taking out all your pent-up rage on this stuff instead of me, okay?" she grumbled.

"Did you find my spice jar?" Ellishiva asked brusquely, forgetting to apologize.

Samara crossed her thin arms over her chest. "Maybe. What's it look like?" she asked.

Ellishiva shrugged irritably. "I don't know. I've never actually seen it," she admitted. "Maybe it's brown, though. Like cinnamon. Since Amber's looked so much like a nutmeg seed, I mean. Look, why don't you fly up to the top shelf, just here," she pointed, "and see if you can find anything there. Maybe hidden behind those books—"

"I was just there, Elli!" huffed Samara, exasperated. "Can't you see for yourself that I combed all of those shelves?" She gestured widely at the wreckage on the shelves before fluttering over to the planters chairs and plunking herself down in one heavily. A huge yawn escaped her and she rubbed her eyes.

"Don't you fall asleep on me!" Ellishiva snapped, scowling. "We're not done here yet." She glared at the sulking fairy until Samara dragged herself, pouting, off of the planters chair and trudged back to the bookshelves again. Grimly, Ellishiva went back to ransacking desk drawers.

Only minutes later, Samara found it.

"What's this?" The fairy was crouched down examining something obscured by books, not far from the planters chair she'd been sitting in earlier. "Here, Elli. Come see!" she called, a ray of excitement in her voice. "It's an olivine jar, a brown one. Ugh, this thing weighs a ton."

"Where?" said Ellishiva sharply, tossing the drawer in her hands on top of the others on the floor and hurrying over to Samara.

"It's different than the others," the fairy was saying as she dragged the olivine jar off the shelf, and even at first glance Ellishiva knew she was right. To begin with, it was larger than usual. Its lid was not simple and flat like Amborella's; rather, it was tall and carved to resemble the bust of an unusual creature. At its base, the carving had been embossed with a seal.

Ellishiva knelt on the floor beside her friend, the olivine jar between them, and bent her head to examine their discovery. "This is it," she whispered, her voice shaky.

"Are you nervous?" asked Samara, trying for a lighthearted laugh. But her voice was unsteady as well.

"Of course I'm nervous. I'm about to see my past—my roots," Ellishiva said quietly. As she spoke, the warm breath of her words was drawn, like a wisp of smoke, into the jar. "I don't know what it will hold, where it will take me. They say I'm the First Spice," she went on, shaking her head in bafflement, "but what does that mean?"

The girls stared mutely at the jar for a few seconds, the low light from the fireplace casting shadows over their faces. Then, finally, Ellishiva roused herself and reached her hand out toward the lid.

Immediately, the lines on the skin of her palm spewed thin trails of green spice dust. She and Samara had barely had time to marvel at them before the bright wisps were drawn quickly into the jar like Ellishiva's breath.

Ellishiva yanked her hand back as though she were afraid the carved creature on the lid would bite her fingers.

"Oh my goodness!" gasped Samara. Her eyes were wide, her face radiating wonderment. There was no trace of a yawn in her now.

"Just like the butterfly from the book," Ellishiva murmured, half to herself.

Samara turned her huge eyes on her. "What?" she demanded.

Ellishiva winced a little. "I was going to tell you," she mumbled, "but I wasn't sure what was going on, and then so many other things started happening." She stopped and shook her head once, sharply, as if to rid it of useless excuses. "It happened here, in this study. I was looking through a book and I touched a picture and—" she faltered for a moment, remembering. "And I brought a Morpho butterfly to life."

Samara stared at her, drop-jawed, for a long moment. "*What?*" she gasped, swatting Ellishiva in the shoulder. "How could you not tell me this? Elli, you have Khlorus in you. You're made with *Khlorus spice dust*! That's why they're hiding you!" She paused for a much-needed breath and then forged on, almost giddy. "You're made with the same spice dust as the Supreme Being, Amma!" A broad grin broke across the fairy's face, and her blue eyes sparkled mischievously.

Ellishiva shook her head, trying hard to keep it from pounding. "I'm still not sure," she muttered. Then she took a deep breath and made herself think. "It doesn't make sense, Sam. Why is this dust coming out of me suddenly, just like that?"

"I don't know, but we can find out!" said Samara, who was practically bursting with enthusiasm. "Touch it again, Elli! Go on, don't be scared. I'm right here with you."

Ellishiva hesitated for a long moment. But reckless though the fairy's suggestion seemed, there appeared to be no way around it. Bracing herself for the worst, she slowly reached both of her hands forward and clasped them around the jar.

Without warning, the carved lid flew off and clattered to the ground. Ellishiva waited, breathless, for the Silverdine to rise into the air as it had done from Amborella's jar, but nothing came. She was just opening her mouth to point this out to Samara when a bright green flash nearly blinded her. It took a few seconds before she realized that the spice dust was spewing from her hands again. This time, however, the Khlorus was not rising in mere wisps. This time, it was pouring from her palms in currents, like the rays of the sun itself.

Ellishiva released her grip on the spice jar and stared in baffled silence at the magic spilling out of her before her eyes, endlessly—as though it came from a bottomless source. In moments, Rajah's study looked like a shaken snow globe, only with tiny specks of glowing green spice dust drifting around instead of snowflakes.

"Well. This is different," muttered Ellishiva. The scene around her was so impossible that it made her head swim. Her knees felt weak, and she was suddenly very grateful that she was sitting down.

"You're unique. That's for sure," concluded Samara gleefully. She stretched out her hands to try to catch the falling green spice dust, looking as though she'd love nothing better in the world than a bucket to collect it all in.

Ellishiva was still trying to make heads or tails of the whole thing when she felt the tug. "Sam," she started, but the fairy was completely engrossed in her efforts to capture some Khlorus. The tug became a pull, and the pull became relentless. Ellishiva sucked in a deep breath, ready to scream for help, but it was too late. Next to her, she heard Samara gasp.

And then the spice jar was dragging her in.

It seemed to take an eternity to move through the vortex, though in reality she knew the trip could not have lasted more than a few seconds. At last, the spinning halted abruptly, leaving her breathless and dizzy on a strange-feeling ground. Ellishiva sat stock-still where she had landed, blinking furiously at the blackness around her. One thing was clear: she was no longer in the study. Nor did she have any idea how to get back.

"I'm inside my spice dust," she breathed into the silence. "And it's definitely not Silverdine."

Before the panic could settle into her stomach, however, a lone, green light appeared not far from where she was sitting. It darted about, embroidering the darkness like a lone firefly searching for an invisible destination. Somehow, the sight of it calmed her. She remembered why she was where she was.

And she remembered where she was trying to go.

Ellishiva got to her knees, then to her feet. Above her, the green light was flitting just out of reach.

I need to fly, she thought. And just like that, she found herself rising into the strange atmosphere. It did not seem surprising, as if she'd somehow already known she could fly all along. In front of her, the green light had stopped its frantic darting and seemed to be watching her like a curious bird. Ellishiva looked back at it.

Take me to my birth, she thought. And almost of their own accord, her fingers reached out and touched the light.

The explosion was infinite, blossoming into a galaxy that sent billions upon billions of stars cascading in brilliant showers around her. In seconds, her entire body was covered in Khlorus spice dust, glowing a shimmering green.

And she was moving.

Like a comet, she flew through time and seasons. Voices in many languages swirled in and out of her ears. Visions of places she did not know but had somehow seen many times before flashed around her. When the maelstrom of memories at last gave way, she found herself flying over a gargantuan tree, its branches giving off an aura of soothing light. It towered above a lush forest, planted in the exact center of an island that was surrounded by an endless turquoise ocean. The scent of a crisp arctic breeze filled Ellishiva's nostrils, and an infinite calm spread through her. She felt strangely warm . . . tranquil.

Then, suddenly, the movement stopped. Ellishiva blinked, and opened her eyes to find her shimmering body standing in the middle of Banyan Circle—or at least, what she imagined it would have looked like long ago. The ground beneath her feet was moist and the land around her felt wild—empty and untouched. Overgrown shrubs and vines wound their way up the tree's usually clean aerial roots. Not far from where she stood was a rough, untamed version of the vine arch that was now the entrance to Bear Market, nearly unrecognizable without its heady, yellow trumpet flowers. Ellishiva stood perfectly still, taking it all in. Around her, the empty evening whispered in and out of cracks and shadows, as though waiting for something.

A speck of water touched her forehead. Ellishiva craned her neck up and saw endless pearls of raindrops swelling on the tips of the leaves of Banyan Tree. High, high above, its crown disappeared completely into misty gray clouds.

"I'm on Mannahatta. This is our Banyan Tree," murmured Ellishiva. She inhaled deeply, smelling something. "Cinnamon," she whispered. Her eyebrows lifted and she turned, searching for the source of the scent. Then she stopped, frozen.

A creature was standing near the vine entrance to Bear Market. In his hand he held a wooden staff crowned with an orb filled with Khlorus spice dust. The orb gave off a bit of green light; nevertheless, its bearer seemed to be squinting into the dimness around him. Ellishiva crept closer.

The dofaun lifted the staff, then brought its tip down firmly on the ground. "*Vitarita āloka!*" he commanded, and the Khlorus in the olivine orb glowed brighter.

Ellishiva knew that voice.

"Banog?" she called, no longer bothering to keep to the shadows. A smile usurped her lips. "Banog, is that you?"

No response. A chilled breeze rippled the eagle's soaked layers of amber and black feathers as he stared piercingly past her into the dimness—at what, she could not say. Frowning, Ellishiva strode directly up to him and reached her glowing green hand out to touch his wing. But her fingertips passed through him as though he were made of air. So did the rest of her body. She stopped trying to get the eagle's attention as she realized, heart pounding, that he could neither see nor hear her.

"This is all in my mind," she breathed, mesmerized.

"Is that you, Perseus?" Banog called suddenly, and she jumped. "We are quite safe. This is no hunt. We no longer live in the human world. Indeed, we are as far from the reach and rage of mankind as we are able to be."

"Perseus?" Ellishiva muttered to herself, confused. The name was not familiar. She looked around, bending sideways to peer beyond the vine archway into the empty space that had not yet become Bear Market. But there was no one there.

Banog spoke again. "The child has not eaten all day. Have you brought her any food?" The great eagle dusted his feathered fingers together, businesslike, and a few lingering, shimmering specks of Bluzure spice dust wafted down onto the moist ground at his feet. Where they landed, a path of vibrant green moss bloomed, leading away from where Ellishiva stood.

She followed it.

It led her just a short ways away, to a little clump of wild-looking shrubs. There, nestled on the ground among the lowest branches, was a small, woven basket filled with folds of something. Ellishiva furrowed her brow and bent down to peer inside. Then she jumped back, her mouth falling open in surprise.

From underneath a damp cotton blanket, a plump little green leg pushed itself free like the frond of a new fern. It shivered for a moment as the cold wind swept over it, and tiny bumps rose on the soft, new skin. On one of the little foot's tiny toes gleamed an intricate ring shaped like a golden lotus.

"My toe ring?" murmured Ellishiva, stealing a puzzled glance at her own feet. Then she knelt beside the basket, looking into it more closely this time. The baby's face was ringed by a mass of mussed-up curls, rust brown and coiled like tightly rolled quills of cinnamon. Her cheeks were full and carried a tinge of pink, just like the new leaves of a cinnamon tree. Near her ears and neck, many faint brown circles ran like tattoos over her skin. Her chubby legs kicked off most of the blanket, revealing a line of deep emerald green running up the center of her body. It stopped just below her collarbone, where it spread out in a tracery of delicate lines, like the veins on a leaf. She wore nothing save a soft linen napkin secured by burlap twine.

Ellishiva took a moment to examine her own grown-up feet and hands. Then she looked back at the baby. "I was chunky," she muttered.

She was still watching her in fascination when Banog himself came over to join them. Seeing the child tossing restlessly, the great eagle carefully lifted one of her tiny, green hands to her mouth. The baby's lips found two of her fingers and she began to suck; her other hand reached up to grasp the curls of her hair. She blinked her amber eyes at the dofaun curiously. Banog sighed and began to tuck the baby back under the blanket again.

There was a small sound behind them, so faint that Banog didn't even hear it. Ellishiva turned her head and her mouth fell open a second time.

"A snow leopard!" she gasped. In a moment she was on her feet. Since the dofaun could not see her, she began to circle around him with slow steps, letting the awe and curiosity show openly on her face. She had never seen a more magnificent creature in her life. The leopard was easily as tall as Banog. He stood on his mighty hind legs, his glossy white coat dotted with spots of black and gold. In one of his forepaws, he held something that Ellishiva had only ever seen in books: a three-pronged trident, its golden barbs gleaming in the dim light of Banog's staff. From the base of its prongs hung an olivine jar.

The snow leopard stood watching his comrade tend to the baby for a long moment. Finally, he spoke. "My apologies for taking so long, Banog." He took a deep, tired breath and tucked the trident into a sheath fastened on his back. "I was at the lake. The fairies intend to name it 'Central Pond,' it seems. They were having a difficult time sculpting their home. Basalt rocks, everywhere. It was quite the challenge, carving such things into their new alcove. But it seems that they will be all right now." He stretched and adjusted the sturdy belt lying diagonally across his chest.

Banog snorted. "Your altruism is admirable, Perseus, but there is still work to be done here, if we are to finish securing this colony before Amma arrives." Ellishiva pulled her gaze away from Perseus to find that the eagle was once again holding the large olivine jar in his feathered hands. He poured a handful of glittering Bluzure spice dust out into his palm, then strode over to do the same for Perseus. The snow leopard did not object.

Then, as if by unspoken agreement, each dofaun tossed the enchanted substance into the air with a gesture as graceful and commanding as a maestro conducting an orchestra.

Ellishiva watched, entranced, as the Bluzure worked its magic around her. The spice dust glowed blue, scurrying purposefully up and around Banyan Tree. It wove through the vine archway where they stood and flew beyond it like a swarm of honeybees, into the unformed landscape of the future Bear Market, making sense of madness. Everywhere, all at once, the Bluzure swallowed sharp rocks and undergrowth and tangled vines, clearing the ground and dotting the colony with rare and exotic plants and flowers.

Ellishiva had no idea how long she stood there marveling at the transformation of her home. At last, however, she again became aware of the dofauns that had changed it all.

Banog and Perseus were standing in front of the basket with the baby in it, both of them staring mutely, expectantly, at the sky. Banog spoke first. "I cannot wait to hear why Amma brought this child to life," he muttered quietly.

Ellishiva frowned and stepped closer to them.

The eagle made a sweeping gesture toward the basket, and a vein of aggravation crept into his voice. "Look at her. She is only a baby, just like my younglings. The humans caged them, ravaged their feathers for prized adornments. Now they are gone. And your cub's pelt, Perseus," he went on, his eyes hard with anger. "It has probably been made into a floor mat, or hung in some dwelling, perhaps to impress visitors. The finest warm coat of a snow leopard of Mirkush, rarest among furs. What purpose, what sense can there be in bringing a child like this into such a world?"

Ellishiva felt a shiver race down her spine. Before Perseus could reply, however, the conversation was interrupted by the sky.

High, high above, a blinding light burst from the massive crown of Banyan Tree. It was so bright that, even watching from her spice dust as she was, Ellishiva could barely stand to look at it. Next to her, both Banog and Perseus shielded their eyes.

Then, from the radiance, a gleaming creature as large as Banog swooped down toward them. Its wings were broad, and its feathers glistened like spun gold in the searing light. Suddenly, Ellishiva realized that she had seen it—her—before. She had the body of a phoenix and the face of a pretty fairy. On her forehead, between her eyes, were three tiny, wavy lines: two the color of ash, and the third green. She was pale as she came to hover before them, her brows knit together in exhaustion, beads of sweat glistening on her forehead. In the cool, crisp air, the breath streamed from her nostrils in puffs of crimson-colored cloud. She shuddered as her golden claws touched down upon the earth, as though the ground itself were unbearably hot.

"Symran," breathed Ellishiva in wonderment, gazing at her. "I've read about you. 'Rarest of the dofauns . . .'"

Next to Ellishiva, Banog and Perseus had bowed their heads. "Salutations, Supreme Amma," they said together. The words were spoken quietly, with deep respect, Ellishiva noticed. And as soon as she turned her head back to Symran's lowering wings, she could see why.

Amma's bearing was unmistakably regal. For a moment she towered above all of them, sitting astride Symran, the oversized hood of her long white cloak obscuring her face. Then she jumped effortlessly from the exhausted dofaun's back and landed barefoot, light as a feather, on the moist forest floor. As she strode toward them, the untamed weeds in the wide circle around the great banyan tree transformed into a carpet of tender green grass, very much the way it looked in present-day Banyan Circle. Just before she came to a halt in front of them, Ellishiva caught a glimpse of something glinting on the first joint of her second toe, and did a double take.

It was a golden ring adorned with an intricate lotus flower, identical to Ellishiva's own.

Before she could begin to make sense of it, however, the Supreme Being spoke. "I see the child is calm." Her words were brusque and to the point.

Banog dipped his head again, respectfully. "Everything is as you willed it."

Ellishiva watched Amma carefully as the Supreme Va'nature inspected the new colony. Even without the boost of Symran's back, she was tall, like Queen Neive. Through the deep shadows of the cloak around her face, Ellishiva thought she could see a flicker of light reflecting in Amma's glassy amber eyes.

"Take off your hood," Ellishiva breathed, as though her will had some kind of power over the past. "I need to see what you look like. Please . . ."

But Amma was no more able to hear her than Banog and Perseus had been. The Supreme Being gave a curt nod, perhaps in approval of the new colony. Then she spoke again, and her imperious voice echoed among even the tallest branches of Banyan Tree high above them.

"No one shall know of the existence of this First Spice Child," she decreed, "save those who live within this protected colony. She herself will not know of her origins, nor of her gifts, and none will encourage her to seek them. She will grow and live like any other Va'nature. Here shall she dwell until the day when she matures in wisdom and is ready to fulfill her destiny."

Amma raised her right hand so that the palm faced the vine arch nearby, and a burst of shimmering green Khlorus spice dust spewed from her skin. In moments, yellow trumpet flowers were blooming among the intertwined leaves, releasing a sweet, familiar fragrance into the night air.

Ellishiva stared, wondering vaguely if she, too, could do that. Her conscious thoughts, however, were all revolving madly around a single question.

My destiny?

Next to her, Banog cleared his throat, bringing her back to her senses. "With all respect, Great Amma, it is the duty of Va'natures to venture forth into the human world to plant their seedlings. Will this special child be confined to Mannahatta alone? Who will care for her?"

Amma did not look at the great eagle when she spoke, as though she were not answering him at all, but merely continuing her speech from before. "Here she shall perform her duties, giving life to and nurturing seedlings. However, unlike other Va'natures, she must never leave this island, nor venture into the human world. Those Va'natures who are raised alongside her shall, too, abide by these rules."

Ellishiva glanced down at her toe ring, then up at Amma again. "Sam was right?" she whispered disbelievingly. "This really *is* a prison? One they built for *me*?"

Amma was not yet finished. "Banog," she commanded, still not looking at the dofaun she addressed. "You will distribute her saplings into the human world where they are needed—in forests, mountains, plains, and valleys far and wide. From this day forward, your base colony will be here, on the Isle of Mannahatta. Valerius Allspice, most trusted among Va'natures, will be the child's guardian. He is on his way here now."

Ellishiva saw the words bubble out of Banog's throat against his will. "Rajah Valerius Allspice?" he blurted, shocked. He and Perseus caught each other's eyes briefly, and a grim look passed between them. Banog's claws dug deep into the earth. Perseus's long tail jumped violently.

Ellishiva stared at them, puzzled.

"Amma," began the eagle carefully. He was striving to make his voice sound humble, but his talons were still digging into the soil fiercely. "Are you sure there is no one else to be the guardian of this precious child?"

"Someone other than Rajah Valerius?" Amma's tone was still businesslike, but there was an edge to her words that made it clear how ridiculous the suggestion was to her.

Banog hesitated for a moment. Then he plowed on recklessly, as if worried that his window of courage might snap shut on him at any moment. "Death came to children from our world for the first time under his care—"

"You question my judgment?" interrupted Amma, and now her voice was like thunder, shaking Ellishiva to the bone. Both of the dofauns bowed their heads and fell immediately silent. But Amma had no intention of letting them off so easily. "Have I not been benevolent to every one of you in my colonies?" she rumbled. "Think you that your doubtful whispers do not find my ears? I know you fault Valerius for the children who were murdered in the human world on the Isle of Bandalara—or what you called it with its more colorful gossip name, the Madagascar Massacre. Yet Valerius did nothing wrong. He shall make a fine guardian for this child, as he has for so many Va'natures in his care before her."

Banog and Perseus kept their heads bowed, not daring to reply.

Madagascar Massacre. Ellishiva felt the hairs on the back of her neck rise at Amma's words. It felt as though an arctic storm were sweeping through her as the pieces finally clicked into place. Images of what she and Samara had seen in the Silverdine of Amborella's spice jar rose sickeningly in her mind again.

It was several seconds before she could focus on the Supreme Being again. Amma was still standing over the dofauns, her hooded head high, as though daring them to challenge her again. But no more doubts or protests were forthcoming. At last, her anger seemed to abate.

"I must leave this place now," she said.

Ellishiva heard a twig snap and turned to find Symran struggling to rally herself. Despite the rest, the weakened creature was still breathing heavily. Pulled by curiosity, Ellishiva walked up to her, so close that she was only inches from the dofaun's face, and saw that the warm breath escaping from her nose and mouth was the raw color of amber, as if a fire was smoldering within her. Then, suddenly, Symran's strained eyes focused—and stared directly into Ellishiva's.

It was as though a bolt of white-hot lighting shot through her. Ellishiva stumbled backward and fell, landing flat on her backside, shocked.

"Impossible. You can't see me," she muttered. But she was not quite sure that she believed herself.

Just then, Amma walked over to Symran and placed her open palm by the creature's beautiful face. The dofaun inhaled deeply, and Ellishiva could see the fine, vaporous wisps of green Khlorus spice dust flowing into her, giving her strength. In moments, her trembling had ceased and she stood tall on her clawed feet, ready to take flight. Without a word or a touch, Amma leapt onto Symran's glistening back in one fluid motion.

Can I do all of this? wondered Ellishiva for the second time, her eyes wide as she gazed up at the two of them.

Amma was speaking again.

"Give the child a name, Perseus," she ordered. There was no fondness, no distaste in her words. It was simply a task that needed to be done, like anything else.

Ellishiva walked tentatively back over to the basket, where Perseus was crouched, his face no longer fierce. He looked down at the baby. At the sight of him, the child reached up her hands and kicked her fat little legs in delight, smiling. Her amber eyes sparkled even more from the reflected light of the trident.

The whisper of a smile caught on the edges of Perseus's mouth. "Forgive me, Great Amma, but this is no ordinary Va'nature child. She is your only—"

"Give her a name, Perseus!" commanded Amma coldly. Then she added, emotionless, "I am no mother."

Ellishiva felt a pang in her chest, as though the Supreme Va'nature had just inflicted some nameless wound on her. But, of course, that made no sense. "We don't have mothers or fathers," she muttered to herself, shrugging her shoulders as if to brush the ache away. It didn't work.

"Do not fail me at this critical moment, Perseus," Amma continued. "Cataclysmic destruction brews in the human world. The power of the Sixth Element grows, and it will not be long before it threatens our world. When the time arrives, the child must be prepared." Then she touched Symran and spoke a word that no one but the two of them could hear. The lotus toe ring on her foot blossomed, releasing a cloudy tornado of Khlorus spice dust. Without so much as a wave, Symran rose into it, high among the uppermost limbs of Banyan Tree.

And then they were gone.

Ellishiva stood exactly where she was for a long time, trying to remember how to breathe. Her stomach was tying itself into a tight, heavy knot beneath her heart. In her head, Amma's final words played over and over, like an oudleef that had forgotten how to heed the command to stop.

When the time comes, the child must be prepared.

"That's the only reason you gave me life?" she whispered. "To face the Sixth Element?" The ache in her chest bloomed into a stabbing, soul-wrenching sense of betrayal. She looked up to where Amma and Symran had disappeared. The dense gray clouds from before had gone. Through the branches of Banyan Tree, a full moon was shining fiercely among a defiantly bright entourage of constellations, putting the dark night around it to shame.

It took her a moment to realize that Banog and Perseus had begun talking in low voices again. The eagle dofaun had joined the snow leopard by the basket, and both of them were gazing at the gurgling baby within with grave looks on their foreheads. "What is this Sixth Element, Perseus?" asked Banog quietly. "Has she truly brought this little one to life purely so that she may face this evil?"

"Not now, Banog," rumbled Perseus with a disturbed shake of his head. "We will speak of it later. The child requires food. Some berries, perhaps. Go. You will be able to find them faster than I on your wings, in the light of such a moon. I will stay with her."

Banog hesitated for a moment, gazing at his companion with sharp, uncertain eyes. Then he gave a curt nod, and flew up into the canopy of the jungle, leaving the snow leopard with the baby in the basket.

Perseus watched until the eagle was out of sight. Then he let out a long, slow breath, and settled down beside the basket, whose lone inhabitant was beginning to pout and sputter. Ellishiva saw the great cat cast about for something with which to entertain her. At last, he pulled the trident from the sheath slung across his back and began to roll its long handle back and forth in his huge paws, setting the gleaming prongs at the top spinning.

The fussing from the basket stopped at once, replaced by a curious coo.

"O-o-oh, little one, you like that?" Perseus cooed back, his nurturing voice sounding strange to Ellishiva's ears, coming from such a fearsome-looking creature.

In the basket, the baby giggled. Perseus smiled and leaned down to her, his long fangs as benevolent as a white picket fence. He continued to spin the trident between his paws like a baby rattle, and its tips winked faster in the moonlight, making bright reflections dance in the baby's amber eyes.

Ellishiva sat down on the other side of the basket, hugging her knees tight. Next to her, the baby's tiny hands flew wildly up in the air and latched onto one of the snow leopard's thick, wiry whiskers.

"Oh my!" exclaimed Perseus, pulling away slightly. "Easy there, little one. You have quite a grip!"

Ping! The baby's small fist yanked out the whisker and brought it to her open mouth.

"No, no! You cannot eat that!" scolded the great cat softly. Ellishiva noticed how gently Perseus tugged the baby's fist—still clutching the whisker—away from her mouth, her tiny hand almost lost in his enormous paw. She imagined him acting so with his own cubs, and a dull pang hit her as she remembered Banog's words—how the cubs had been hunted to death in the human world. *You must miss them so*, she thought sadly, watching him.

Perseus was still spinning the trident. "You are fond of this, aren't you?" he murmured, laughter in his eyes as he gazed down at the baby. "Well, little one, it seems I am to give you a name. You are a curious one, clearly enough." He paused, and a thoughtful look came over his features. "I wonder . . . I wonder, since you favor my trident, if it is fitting that I name you after my cub. I had named her after my courageous mother, for this trident once belonged to her, you know," he said, though the baby did not know this at all. "Her trident found me one day, when I needed it most." The snow leopard's tail jumped a few times, as at a bad memory. He gave a sigh that seemed to come from the pit of his heart, and closed his eyes briefly. When he opened them again, there was a raw sadness in them that Ellishiva had never seen. "But it was too late," he finished quietly.

There was a long, deep silence, as though the earth itself were mourning with the dofaun. At last, Perseus let out another long breath and spoke to the baby again.

"Your home will be among the clouds, on the limbs of this great banyan tree," he told her, pointing to the crown above them with his trident. The child gurgled and a dribble of saliva ran down her double chin. The snow leopard wiped it away carefully with the corner of the blanket. "My mother, too, dwells atop an enchanted place, on the crown of the Mirkush Mountains. So, like her, you shall be called Ellishiva." He smiled, and his voice grew louder, more confident. "I name you Ellishiva Cinnamon of Mannahatta!"

As if they had heard him, the petals of the lotus flower ring on the baby's toe opened. Green Khlorus spice dust emerged, like millions of shimmering strands of corn silk, and streamed around her body. On her skin, the dark green, branching lines glowed. For a moment, the snow leopard's ice-blue eyes were alight with wonder. Then his face fell, and the eyes darkened with worry. "My dearest Ellishiva," he rumbled huskily, "I fear for you. I fear what is to come of your destiny."

Ellishiva sat huddled where she was for a long time, hearing his words bounce through her mind as though it had suddenly become hollow. Yet as she sat, hugging her knees and gazing at herself as a baby, something odd happened. A new feeling swept through her. The ache from Amma's cold words intensified, then faded, replaced by Perseus's kindness, by the familiar way that Banog continued to call her "little one" to this day. She thought of what Maximus had told her, about the worth of having Rajah and his many lessons to depend on when she needed them. Her feelings toward Rajah were as tangled as the twisted vine archway standing just a little ways away from her. Still, he was the only father she had ever known. These were the things she understood. These were the things that—good or bad—made her what she was.

Ellishiva settled her chin on her knees and gazed at the dofaun on the other side of the baby basket. Perseus. He had given her her name, and yet she did not know who he was. She frowned. For every discovery she crossed off her list, it seemed another question sprouted, unveiling even more mysteries to be solved. And this one, she could sense, was not as trivial as it seemed.

Who was this snow leopard of Mirkush?

Before she could ponder the question further, a warmth scented with allspice and old papyrus enveloped her, gently pulling her away to Rajah's study once more.

CHAPTER TWELVE

A SAPLING REACHES FOR THE LIGHT

"Wake up! You're in so much trouble. Are you gonna sleep all day?"

Ellishiva groaned and stirred. Her head felt as if it were filled with a thick fog. Groggily, she cracked open her eyes.

Hektor was standing at the foot of her bed, his back braced against one of the posts, glaring. As she blinked at him, confused, he raised a crisp, juicy apple to his lips and took a huge bite. "Sure wouldn't wanna be Ellishiva Cinnamon right now," he said.

Ellishiva sat up, dazed. Under the sheet, something bumped her knee. She reached down and felt her noli, stuffed with the olivine orb she had stolen from Rajah's study. A quick glance at the center of the room revealed that the jungle sleepover had been disbanded. To her right, Amborella was sitting at the edge of her own bed, engrossed in a low, serious conversation with Dollie Burlap. It was day, but how? When?

Hektor's charming voice brought her back to the present. "How was your beauty sleep?" he inquired, the words dripping with sarcasm.

"Hektor. I was in my spice dust—" Ellishiva stammered, still trying to make sense of where she was and what had happened. "There's

Khlorus in me. Khlorus spice dust! And—and Amma brought me to life because of the Sixth Element. She knew about it all along. Knew it would threaten our world and—and I'm supposed to stop it. Oh, and," she blurted on breathlessly, the memories coming faster now, "and I heard them talking. What happened on the Isle of Bandalara *was* the Madagascar Massacre! We have to figure out who died there—"

"*We?*" interrupted Hektor, bringing her rambling to a screeching halt. "Are you actually comparing yourself to Amma? *Look* at you, Elli! You've become Sam: sneaking around, eavesdropping, stealing, lying. What's *happened* to you?" he shook his head as though he were a professor at Forest Academy and she had just failed her biggest test.

Ellishiva stared at him for a moment, reality crashing over her again like cold water. "I have to see Rajah," she said coldly.

"Rajah's not here. *You* probably drove him away again," accused Hektor bitterly. "He went back to Nicobar. Amma sent Symran for him and everything. Lady Malinia was really upset."

"I did not drive him away," bit back Ellishiva fiercely. "He's the one running away from me. Before my attack he never avoided me like this." She paused and pressed her fingers hard against her temples, willing herself to take a deep breath. "How did I get here?" she muttered finally.

"Two of General Iliad's kinnarans found you *sleeping* in Rajah's study and brought you home. You're so grounded," Hektor informed her, crossing his arms and taking another bite of the apple. "You're not allowed to leave Banyan Tree, not even for the harvest. Rajah told Lady Malinia so himself. There're kinnarans in the hallway and posted around the Arboretum, all here to make sure you don't escape."

"What?" Ellishiva burst out, her voice almost a shout as a stew of panic bubbled to life in her stomach. "Now? *Again?* What is this, the Asylum at Derahdin?"

"You deserve it!" Hektor shouted back at her. "Not only did you break into Rajah's *forbidden* study, you trashed it! Do you have any idea how much trouble you're in?"

Ellishiva was about to snap something back at him when she was interrupted by a brief spike in the conversation next door. She stopped short and turned to Amborella, who was still on her bed, talking to her doll. She scowled. "What's wrong with Amber?"

"How should I know? She's convinced that doll is alive," grumbled Hektor.

"Rajah should be here," muttered Ellishiva resentfully. She turned back to Hektor. "What happened to Sam?"

An impish smile appeared at the corners of her brother's mouth. He pulled a copy of *The Mannahatta Times* out of the pocket of his tunic and thrust it at her. Ellishiva snatched it up and unfolded it. At once, her eyes fell on a headline printed across the top in bold black letters:

Danger in Mannahatta—Young Fairy Tells All!

Her heart sank. Below the headline, sketched in red, was a rather striking image of Samara.

At the foot of her bed, Hektor took another satisfied bite of his apple. A trickle of juice ran down his chin.

"I knew it. I *knew* the Tigress of Sundari didn't give her that noli for nothing," snarled Ellishiva under her breath. She tossed *The Times* away from her and fell back against the headboard, thinking. "Maybe," she ventured finally, speaking in a whisper to herself, "maybe this could be a good thing."

"I'll say it is," snorted Hektor. "She's grounded, too. Forbidden to leave Fairy Alcove. We probably won't have to put up with her for a whole fortnight, at least."

"I didn't mean it that way," Ellishiva snapped at him. "People believe *The Times*, even though most of the time they shouldn't. At least now they'll know they're in danger."

"I've never seen Queen Neive so furious," mused Hektor smugly, ignoring her. There was an almost wistful look on his face, as though he were revisiting a particularly fond memory. "She said Sam is an embarrassment to all fairies. I heard she won't even let her mingle with the guests that are arriving at Central Pond for the Foxfire Harvest." He took another loud bite of the apple.

"The Foxfire Harvest can't happen!" Ellishiva declared grimly. "It's too dangerous. All this time, the Sixth Element has been growing stronger. She has to have been. And she's not going to ignore us forever." She frowned and pressed her lips into a line, thinking hard. "If Rajah is in Nicobar, I'll have to warn the general instead. You said he's here, out in the hall, right? He'll listen. It's his job to protect me—"

"Out in the hall?" Hektor scoffed. "Don't be ridiculous, Elli. He has more important things to do than babysit you. It's just a few of his troops that've been posted here. And they're not supposed to talk to you." He rolled his eyes. "As if we'd cancel the Foxfire Harvest. Everyone's been preparing for it all summer," he added scornfully.

Ellishiva felt the panic in her stomach spread. "Hektor, please. You have to listen to me," she pleaded, leaning forward on the bed to look him in the eye. "I've read about this in my books. In a war, when an enemy wants to attack, they always pick the moment when they can do the most harm, hurt the most people. The Foxfire Harvest is the biggest gathering we have. It's bound to be a target. And everyone will go, no matter how uneasy they are. The dofauns refuse to admit that they're being affected by dark clouds because they don't want to be sent to the Asylum at Derahdin, and no one is going to want to miss out on the biggest harvest of Bluzure spice dust in—in as long as anyone can remember, Walle says—"

"Oh, stop talking nonsense, Elli," interrupted Hektor in disgust. He took one last bite of the apple, then chucked the core at a small pitcher plant in the corner of the room by his desk. It hit the soft rim and bounced off, rolling away across the floor.

"The colony is in danger, Hektor!" insisted Ellishiva, her voice rising in frustration. "I can't believe the dofauns *still* aren't taking those clouds seriously. What, are they waiting for a catastrophic event before it finally sinks into their heads? Because that's exactly what the Foxfire Harvest is going to be—*catastrophic!*" She drummed her fingers on the bed in agitation, glaring at her brother, who continued to glare back at her, unmoved.

There was a flurry of small footsteps, and suddenly Amborella was standing by her bed, holding Dollie Burlap by the hand. "I want to be a songstress someday, just like Asia," declared her little sister breathlessly, swinging the doll. "We cannot wait to hear the singing at the Foxfire Harvest. The very idea makes us eufrolic!"

"That's eu-*phor*-ic, Amber," corrected Ellishiva absently, keeping her eyes on Hektor.

Amborella nodded and repeated the word into Dollie Burlap's ear as the two of them flounced off again, back to her own bed.

Belatedly, the little girl's words sank in. "'We?'" muttered Ellishiva. She and Hektor frowned at Amborella, who was once again wrapped up in conversation with her doll.

Hektor shrugged it off first. "Nothing is going to happen at the harvest, Elli," he insisted, returning to the argument at hand. "And nothing happened on your big scary last quarter moon yesterday, either. You were wrong," he concluded triumphantly.

Ellishiva gaped at him. "*Nothing happened* on the last quarter moon?" she blurted, furious. "Haven't you seen Morpheus and Theo?"

"Just Theo," said Hektor dismissively. "And he looks fine to me. He was talking to Atticus—"

"What about Maximus?" interrupted Ellishiva, almost yelling. "He completely vanished last night, Hektor!"

"So what?" Hektor bit back bluntly. "He probably just went back to Nicobar. Why do you care so much about him? Obviously, he doesn't find *you* interesting enough to hang around for."

"He's my friend. *He* listens to me, unlike my own brother!" Ellishiva snarled. On impulse, she crumpled the copy of *The Mannahatta Times* in front of her into a ball and pelted it at Hektor's head. He dodged it easily. "His words are more precious than every acorn you've ever picked up all put together!" she added scathingly.

Hektor stared at her for a moment, speechless. Then a scowl overtook his face and he pushed away from the bedpost he'd been leaning on. "I'm leaving," he said curtly. "And I wouldn't go telling any more lies to Lady Malinia, if I were you. One more stunt like last night and her heart failure is going to be on your head!"

"Hektor, don't you dare walk out on me!" Ellishiva shouted at his retreating back, furious. "Where are you going? Come back!"

"I'm going to meet Nazeem and Hodges," Hektor snapped over his shoulder. "They're having a rehearsal for our Foxfire Harvest dance routine, and I'm not going to miss it because of you. Come on, Amber. Let's go. Lady Malinia wants you downstairs for midday meal."

With a worried look at Ellishiva, Amborella crawled off her bed with Dollie Burlap and padded across the room, disappearing into the descending stairwell. Hektor followed her without a backward glance, tugging the bedchamber door firmly shut behind him.

Ellishiva was tempted to shout one last insult at his back, but practicality won out. "If you see Walle," she yelled at the closed door, "tell him I have something for him!"

"Why? So you can corrupt him with your lies?" came Hektor's faint reply. "Enjoy your solitude!"

Ellishiva glared at the shut door. Anger simmered hotly on her tongue, but there was no one left to scold with it. Finally, she flopped down hard on the bed again, clenching handfuls of the sheets as though they alone could keep her tethered to the earth. Hektor's bitter words pinged around her head, painfully sharp, like splinters that no one could dislodge.

For a long time, Ellishiva lay where she was, squeezing her eyes shut against the world. Then, slowly, she began to listen to the sound of her own breathing.

Within solitude, pulses life. It was a yoga lesson, something that Rajah had taught her. Yet Rajah was so far away . . .

Maximus's words from the day they had sat together in Cheeky Canteen came back to her. *Just think of him and remember the lessons he's taught you. That way part of him will always be with you.*

Ellishiva steadied herself and remembered. Her closed, scrunched eyelids relaxed, no longer fighting against the dark. As the minutes passed, her panicked breathing changed, becoming slow and purposeful. Inch by inch, she felt her face transforming. The worried lines on her forehead, the locked joints of her jaw and her fingers—all of them surrendered to the measured, steady rhythm of her breath.

At last, Ellishiva opened her eyes. She crept out of bed and walked into her bath chamber. Over the washbasin, she looked at her image in the mirror, and saw exactly what she expected to see. "There will never be a curtain over my face, Rajah," she murmured. Then she lifted the side of her pajama top. From the smooth green canvas of her skin, the Sixth Element's nasty scar glared up at her. "A scar on a tree is a record of what has happened," she whispered, her amber eyes growing hard with resolve. "I won't let this happen again. To me or anyone else."

She dropped the tunic and strode from the washroom, back out into the bedchamber. In moments she was at her writing desk, snatching up a sheet of papyrus and a quill. She wrote:

Dear Sam,

I hope you are well. I've been grounded to Banyan Tree again. I don't know for how long this time. There are kinnarans here, guarding me to make sure I don't escape. This truly is a prison—something you've been telling me all along . . . but don't worry about me. I'll be fine.

Hektor showed me the headline in The Times. I told you not to trust the Tigress. Still, maybe it's for the best. At least now the colony has been warned.

There is <u>so much</u> I need to tell you about what I saw in my spice dust. The *most important thing, though, is that it won't be enough just to find out who the Sixth Element is: from now on, I need to discover what I can do as the First Spice to defeat her.*

Oh, guess what? Banog was in my history, back when I was born! And there was someone else, too—a snow leopard called Perseus. He's the one who named me Ellishiva, but I've never even heard of him. One more mystery to figure out. I want to ask Jipsin Smilodon. He knows everybody. I don't think he's in Aurochs Alley anymore, though. Do you know where to find him?

I wish I could see more of my past, but there's no way Rajah will keep my spice jar in his study or in the Hall of Nature Healing now. He's bound to hide it where he thinks we can't find it. I bet you it's been moved to his other hidden study—the Bulbdome, down in Chingetti Cellar. We've got to find a way to get down there. And once we do, we can head from there to the river's edge to find Maximus. I haven't heard that anyone else is searching for him. Have you?

Anyway, until I find a way to escape Lady Malinia and the kinnarans, I'm going to practice as much yoga and payamar as I can in the Arboretum. I wish Maximus were here to teach me the pressure points, but there must be a book on them somewhere. When the Sixth Element attacks again, we have to be ready!

Reply soon. <u>And only through Walle</u>.

Your best friend forever,
Ellishiva

P.S. Burn this after you read it. If you can think of a way to get me out of here, I could use the help. We need to warn the general before it's too late . . .

Whether by chance or because Hektor had decided to have a small bit of mercy on her after all, Walle did show up at the warren that afternoon, and it wasn't difficult for Ellishiva to convince him to deliver the letter. And that was only the beginning. In the days that followed, while both she and Samara remained grounded, the obliging firefly flew back and forth between Banyan Tree and Fairy Alcove countless times, delivering numerous papyrus notes and making sure that everyone was still in the loop.

Ellishiva stuck to her plan, spending every moment that she could in the Arboretum practicing yoga and payamar. She ventured to the thickest part of it, the lush rainforest section, as far away from the kinnarans guarding her as she could get, just in case. Still, occasionally one would fly by overhead, checking in on her. Ellishiva watched them carefully, but the general was not among their ranks.

She was amazed to discover how easily payamar came to her. Maximus had been right: the connection between it and yoga was undeniable. Her attempts to make the Khlorus spice dust spew from her hands at will were more difficult and more tiring. Still, eventually they began to pay off as well, and healing the snapped twigs and branches of the trees around her grew steadily easier from the practice.

Only coaxing the silken strands of Khlorus spice dust from her toe ring—as she had seen Amma do in her spice jar—remained an unsolved puzzle.

A few days before the Foxfire Harvest, Ellishiva dangled, her mind focused but heavy with thought, from the end of one of the long epiphyte vines that grew along the smooth, lateral branches of a kapok tree. The tree itself was more than one hundred feet tall, and its canopy was dotted with scores of hanging pods that looked like green papayas. Ellishiva barely noticed them. She and Samara had not yet been able to come up with a way to see the general, and every note they'd tried to send to him through Walle had come back unopened. Lower-ranking officers kept heading him off at the pass, the firefly had told her apologetically.

They were running out of time.

"Elli! Elli!" Ellishiva glanced up at the sound of her name to find Walle flying up to hover in front of her. Despite her troubles, she dredged up a smile. "Good morning," she said.

"Good morning," the firefly replied, rather more cheerfully than usual, she thought. "First letter of the day!" he announced. Ellishiva looked down to find a square of folded papyrus clutched in his two lower limbs.

"Oh good," she said, a flicker of hope kindling to life in her the way it always did, despite the days of disappointment. "Hold onto it for a second. Let me just untangle myself."

The dofaun nodded, then flew up to land on the limb above her, watching patiently as Ellishiva climbed up the vine—something she could do much faster than before, since she'd begun her self-training.

"Today," she explained to Walle as she climbed, "I want you to be harder on me than usual. A lot harder. The more impossible it is for me to catch you, the better. Pretend I'm a swarm of fire-wasps hunting you down, like when a patch of dark cloud appears above."

Since her training had started almost half a fortnight ago, Walle had been helping her, leading her on grueling obstacle courses through the Arboretum that got tougher every day. "If you say so, Elli," agreed the firefly obligingly.

"Only way to get better," Ellishiva replied. She had reached the top of the vine now, and was hanging from the tree branch by one hand.

"Elli?" asked Walle. "Why haven't you asked the kinnarans who're guarding you to teach you payamar, instead of learning from books? Wouldn't you learn faster that way?"

"I'm not allowed to talk to them," admitted Ellishiva. "But you know, Walle, I don't really need the books, even. Everything I need to know, I can learn from this Arboretum. Each plant in here has had to figure out a way to reach for the light in order to survive, right?" She swayed a bit on the branch and smiled at the dofaun. Then she swung herself up and straddled the limb to sit beside him. "So what's going on out there? Have you seen Baron Puck?"

"Bear Market is empty," explained Walle, his cheerful manner giving way to something bleaker. "Mother, Ahpa, and I visited some of our dofaun neighbors yesterday. They're afraid to go out into the streets, but they're still going to go to the Foxfire Harvest. They think they'll be safer if they're all together. Plus, they want to gather their share of the Bluzure spice dust." He paused for a breath. "I've been seeing the Tigress everywhere, Elli, but not Baron Puck. No one seems to know where he's disappeared to."

Ellishiva nodded grimly, not surprised. "Well, keep an eye out for him, if you can." She tugged at one of the dofaun's arms, and together they began making their way down the trunk, Ellishiva springing from limb to limb like a monkey, the bottoms of her feet like magnets on the bark. "Have any more kinnarans arrived from the other colonies?" she asked finally, leaping the last few feet and landing effortlessly on the soft ground.

Walle dropped, too, coming to hover beside her again. "I think so," he speculated. "At least, it seems like more of them have been patrolling since you got caught in Rajah's study."

Ellishiva blew a strand of hair out of her face and nodded. "Got my books?" she asked, moving on to the next subject.

"Sorry, Elli. There aren't any more payamar books in the Forest Academy library," apologized Walle, looking genuinely disappointed to bring bad news. He reached under his wing and pulled something out. "But Headmistress Ulima sent you this instead. She's leaving this evening to visit her cousins in Blue Nile Colony. She said to tell you that, without you, the library is just collecting dust over the summer months."

Ellishiva took the book that Walle held out to her and read the title. An eager smile broke over her face. "Oh, good. An updated version!" she enthused, quickly flipping it open to the title page. "*Conquerors of the Great Seas, Volume IV: The New Blood of the Dutch East India Company.* It even has new sketches! Look at all these new fleets, these flags," she continued, leafing through the pages.

It took a minute or two before she became aware of Walle watching her with twinkling eyes, obviously trying very hard to keep from giggling. Ellishiva sighed and set the book aside against the tree trunk. Unfortunately, it would have to wait.

"You ready?" she asked, stretching her arms. "Remember, as fast as you can. Oh, wait! Didn't you have a letter for me?"

In answer, Walle grinned, dangled the folded square of papyrus in front of her nose for a moment, and then dashed away into the wild rainforest with it before Ellishiva could snatch it from his grasp.

Ellishiva tamped down the smile budding at the corner of her mouth and focused, narrowing her eyes on the target. Then her toes plowed into the dirt and she sprinted after Walle.

The sultry, steamy heat of the rainforest rushed over her face; twigs and branches lashed at her limbs as she flew through and around them. She latched onto vines, swung past trees, and vaulted over shrubs and rocks and the gushing drains of the Arboretum. Up ahead, the steady rumble of Banyan Falls was quickly growing into thunder, and the rising mist from its turbulent waters was moving in thick and fast.

"Wow!" yelled Walle, panting as he stole a quick glance back at her over his shoulder. "Every day you're so much stronger, Elli!"

Ellishiva grinned and plunged on. Walle made it as difficult as he could for her, just as she had asked. Nevertheless, she was gaining on him, inch by inch. The firefly dashed under the curve of a bent, fallen trunk and Ellishiva followed, dropping to her knees and sliding, her hands over her head as she leaned her body all the way back like a new sapling in a windstorm. She could feel her skin grazing the ground as she flowed smoothly under the arch like water, coating her back and hair in dirt. No sooner had she emerged on the other side than she rolled onto her feet again, still hot on Walle's trail. A sense of triumph began to pulse through her. This time—finally—the capture would be hers.

Then, suddenly, Walle turned sharply into a stretch of jungle smothered in heavy mist. Ellishiva snagged a vine and swung after him without a second thought. Thick fog from the waterfall moved around her, churning in the wind. By the time she realized where they were, it was too late.

"Oh, no!" she shouted. "Not here, Walle!"

Ahead, Walle grinned mischievously at her and quickly dashed up into the safety of a carob tree.

Ellishiva dropped from the vine and slammed to a halt on the ground, standing stock-still. A new gust of wind shifted the mist around her, and through its pale tendrils she saw that her suspicions were correct: she was in the middle of the Lapita pitcher-plant vivarium, a nursery for young vegetation. Many of the young plants were already taller than she was. All around her, their smooth, tubular traps shivered with life as they soaked in the rolling mist, their many-colored skins bewitchingly beautiful. Had they been mature pitcher plants, Ellishiva might have been content to sit and gaze at them for hours.

But there was one key difference between the mature, gamete pitcher plants in the colony and these wild younglings.

For a moment, nothing happened. Ellishiva was just beginning to think she might have escaped their notice when the long tendrils in the black soil beneath her feet began to move. All around her, the triangular hoods above the shimmering, tubular traps craned upward—and pointed themselves in her direction.

Ellishiva ran.

At her heels, the tendrils of the plants rose up through the dirt like waves on a rough, black sea. Ellishiva dodged them frantically, staying on her feet despite her twisting path of zigzags. The edge of the vivarium had just come into view when a root surged up beneath the ball of her left foot, throwing her into the air. She screamed and flailed her arms, desperately grasping for a stray hanging vine, but the air was empty.

The next thing she knew, she had landed in a dark, squishy space filled with blobs of white slime and long, fat, squirming hairs—the inside of a pitcher plant's tubular trap. Ellishiva gasped in surprise, fending off the worm-like hairs. Around and under her, pieces of half-digested insects swam in a paste of red and green goo. Above her, she saw the hood slowly closing as the pitcher plant prepared to settle down for a chewy feast.

Ellishiva fought with all her strength against the sticky slime and tangled hairs, but to no avail: yoga and payamar were not much use against pitcher plants. She tried pushing Khlorus at it from her palms, but the wisps of green dust were quickly sucked up by the slimy walls around her, making the plant even stronger.

A spark of panic flared to life inside her. It was joined almost immediately, however, by another spark—one that was direly convinced that she hadn't gone through all of this just to end up as a pitcher plant's afternoon snack. Gathering her resolve, Ellishiva shoved back against the tube's tightening clutches—not with the outside of her, this time, but with the inside.

There was a burst of energy that seemed to singe through every vein in her body. Instinctively, Ellishiva corralled it all into one place, and focused hard on her toe ring. The carved lotus blossom stretched open, and just a handful of thin green strands zipped out of it, stinging the walls of the gooey tube around her like tiny zaps of lightning.

The pitcher plant spat her out.

Ellishiva spluttered, but knew better than to waste time catching her breath. She was on her feet again before she'd even finished wiping the slime out of her eyes, darting away between other hungry young pitcher plants toward the safety of the jungle beyond. A triangular hood lashed out in front of her and she bent backward like a bamboo tree, avoiding it easily.

"Wow!" called Walle's voice from somewhere high above. "That move was amazing, Elli!"

But Ellishiva barely heard him. Every muscle in her sweaty, slime-covered body was clenched in concentration, humming in time with her mind and her instincts, so that all her senses were perfectly synchronized and working in harmony to defend her. Writhing roots pitched up through the ground at random and she sped automatically through several moves of payamar, somersaulting, twirling, bending, and dodging away from the attackers as needed.

She had nearly reached the edge of the vivarium when a long, fat tendril curled tightly around her waist and yanked her off her feet. For a split second, Ellishiva froze, caught in the awful memory of the locust tree. Then it released her and she was falling through the air again. This time, however, she knew what was coming. As she plummeted toward the tube trap below, Ellishiva's arms shot out and latched onto the pitcher plant's open triangular hood. All her muscles came alive, and an instant later she was swinging herself safely away from the slime-filled opening.

The pitcher plant jerked, slamming its lid closed again and catching her hand in the movement. Ellishiva pulled and tugged, but the grip of the plant held fast. Inside the tube, she could feel the worm-like hairs beginning to slurp eagerly at her fingers. Worse, the roots of the other plants were slithering up behind her. Fear tugged at her ribs. She couldn't fend off all of them . . .

When faced with fear, change your ways.

The words came whispering through her suddenly and, with them, her focus flooded back. Ellishiva set her jaw and channeled the feeling toward the toe ring. The lotus flower burst open anew, and strands of Khlorus spice dust spewed from it again—only this time there were more than a handful of them. The bright green streaks of lightning shot through the air around her, stinging the approaching roots until they recoiled back into the safety of the earth. The pitcher plant with her hand in it gave a piercing hiss and jerked violently, and the next thing she knew, Ellishiva was sailing through the air once more, over the Lapita vivarium boundary, far from the grasp of the pitcher-plant roots.

She landed with a thud on her back. It knocked the wind out of her, but the ground was soft enough, at least. Since she could no longer sense danger, she lay where she was for a moment. A groan of exhaustion escaped her nostrils. Blearily, she cracked open her eyes.

Walle was hovering above her, his mouth open in awe.

Ellishiva let out another groan and shut her eyes again.

"Wow," the firefly breathed. "That was incredible!" There was a short pause. Then one of his limbs wiped a glob of goo off her arm and he added, a little impishly, "Yuck! You've been slimed, Elli!"

Ellishiva sighed, opened her eyes again, and pushed herself into a sitting position. "You're telling me," she muttered. There was a bad taste on her tongue. She grimaced and spat half a mouthful of slime out onto the ground beside her before tackling the task of scraping the sticky, smelly goo off of the rest of her. "You weren't supposed to *kill* me, Walle," she accused.

"You said as hard as possible," shrugged the firefly innocently. "Anyway, it wasn't *really* dangerous, Elli. I would have rescued you."

Ellishiva shot the pint-sized firefly a dubious glance. Then she remembered what *had* rescued her in the pitcher plant, and her fingers paused halfway through combing an insect-filled blob of green goop from her hair. "Oh! It worked. It finally *worked*. Did you see it, Walle?" she gasped, her voice rising in excitement. "My toe ring. It opened! I *made* it open. When I was being attacked."

"Yes, there was Khlorus everywhere, Elli!" chimed in Walle happily. "From your hands, too!"

Ellishiva stared at the slime-coated lotus flower on her foot, her thoughts racing. "It works," she murmured again. "Now I just need to figure out how to control it better. The way Amma controls hers."

"Like you said, Elli, practice is the only way," offered Walle sagely. His big eyes brightened. "I've been practicing making my Bocaveen elixir, too. Like you wanted," he informed her proudly.

Ellishiva wrung a last glob of bug-goo out of her long hair, and smiled at him. "Good. We'll need it soon," she said. Then she dropped her arms to the ground and raised one expectant eyebrow at the firefly.

"Do I get to read my letter now?" she asked.

Walle blushed pink and handed it over.

Ellishiva took it and began picking at the seal. "That *was* a good test," she reassured the firefly, because it was true. "You know, we should do that again. There are loads of species in this Arboretum that can defend themselves. They'll be better teachers than a kinnaran could ever be," she resolved. Then the hard edge left her voice. "I would have liked Maximus to teach me the pressure points of payamar, though. He's not like the others."

"We'll find him, Elli," Walle offered kindly, picking up on her sadness. Then, to cheer her up, he suggested, "We could head to the shooting-poison pincers from the bixin pods, after the midday meal. If you think you can handle it."

A smile tugged at the corner of Ellishiva's mouth again. "I accept your challenge, my good firefly. Just let me open this first," she said, breaking through the rest of the seal holding the papyrus letter shut. She unfolded it, and Samara's scrawled writing spilled across the page.

Dear Elli,

I don't think it's a good idea to warn Queen Neive. What makes you think she'll believe us? She hasn't even visited me in my room since she grounded me. Trust me, if you say the Foxfire Harvest can't go on, she'll just tell you that you're causing trouble to get attention.

I agree that we've got to do something before the Sixth Element strikes again, but all the elders are still trying to make it look like nothing is wrong in the colony. They're never going to cancel the Foxfire Harvest. It would cause too much panic.

I finally heard some news about the general. He'll be here at Fairy Alcove for the harvest, but finding him alone is still going to be hard since he's surrounded by fairies and other kinnarans all the time. Remember, they wouldn't even let Walle deliver our letters.

I also heard from one of the fairies that Banog has gone to Nicobar to meet up with Rajah. Oh, but the good news is, even though we can't stop the Foxfire

Harvest, I've thought of a way to sneak you out of Banyan Tree so you can be here for it! Well, Walle came up with it, actually. Don't be afraid, you'll be fine. And you __have__ to come to the harvest, Elli. It's the only way to warn the general. He won't listen to anyone else.

Your best friend forever,
Samara

Ellishiva looked at Walle. "You came up with an idea to get me out of here?" she asked, impressed. "What is it?"

Walle grinned and turned around, folding his wings up so she could see. There was something hanging on his back. "Is that . . . ?" Ellishiva narrowed her eyes. "No. Absolutely not," she said, crossing her arms stubbornly over her chest.

"Don't worry, Elli. You'll be fine," Walle assured her, lowering his wings over Samara's rose-colored noli and turning around to face her again.

"This was your idea, huh?" commented Ellishiva dryly.

"Well, technically you came up with it, Elli," Walle pointed out, his face the picture of innocence.

"I am not getting into that," insisted Ellishiva.

"Calm down, Elli. It's perfectly safe," said Walle reassuringly. "Sam fixed the strings so it's nice and snug and flat. Nobody has noticed it yet. Even you hadn't! And I've been wearing it since yesterday."

"I am not getting into that noli!" persisted Ellishiva. "There must be another way."

"There isn't," said Walle. "Unless you've thought of one?" Ellishiva was silent. The firefly nodded as if she'd just proven his point, and continued. "It was comfortable inside the Rojorine spice dust. Plus, even though I felt sick that night from Amber's punch, I saw and heard everything. Sam says you've already been inside spice dust before any-way. She says how different can it be? Trust us, Elli," he finished, patting her on the shoulder with one of his upper limbs. "You'll be fine."

Ellishiva didn't answer. As much as she hated to admit it, there was nothing left to argue about. Not when the alternative was staying locked up in Banyan Tree, leaving General Iliad uninformed and unprepared for the attack. Mutely, she bent her head back to the letter, and finished reading the postscript.

P.S. Still no sign of Maximus, but I got the map of Chingetti Cellar from Bairon. As for Jipsin Smilodon, I know just where to find him . . .

FOXFIRE HARVEST

"I'm sorry, Elli."

Ellishiva looked up to find Amborella standing beside her bed, gazing at her with big, pitiful eyes. She sighed and shifted a few books out of the way. The little girl clambered up onto the mattress and settled herself at Ellishiva's feet. "Lady Malinia says we'll be back after the concert," she explained apologetically. "She says Hektor should still get to perform his dance because, um. Because it isn't him who's grounded."

Ellishiva tilted her head to the side slightly. Two days ago, the reminder of her punishment would have made her angry and frustrated. Not anymore. "Don't worry about me, Amber," she replied, gesturing at the stacks of books around them. "I have lots to read. Just make sure there's always a kinnaran in your sight, okay?" A frown creased her forehead and she leaned forward to look directly into her sister's eyes. "Promise!"

"Okay. I promise, Elli," agreed Amborella seriously. "It won't be the same without you." The little girl leaned forward a bit herself and lowered her voice conspiratorially. "Lady Malinia is worried because you didn't come down for breakfast and midday meal, but I'm not supposed to tell you that," she confided. Sunlight from the open windows caught in her red hair. Her lips, Ellishiva noticed, looked parched.

Nodding, Ellishiva dug a clamshell of bee balm out of her noli. "Come closer," she instructed, and Amborella scooted a few inches nearer to her on the mattress. Ellishiva opened the clamshell and dabbed a bit of balm onto her sister's dry lips. "How have your dreams been lately?" she asked gently.

"Um. They're getting worse," Amborella admitted, the words muffled as she tried to speak without moving her mouth. "Dollie Burlap is telling me to do things and . . . and I don't want to, Elli."

Ellishiva frowned. She snapped the clamshell shut and wiped her finger on her trousers. "What does she want you to do, Amber?" she prodded softly. "I know you'd rather tell Rajah, if he were here. But you can tell me instead, for now. What do you think?"

A troubled look flickered over Amborella's face. "I can't tell you what Dollie said," she mumbled, her already low voice dropping to a whisper. "It's a secret!"

"Well, if you say so," Ellishiva whispered back, keeping her words calm and steady. "But don't forget, even though Dollie Burlap is special, she's still a doll. And dolls are supposed to be friends, not give you nightmares." She sat back again, and looked at the little girl thoughtfully. "You know, maybe you should let her sleep with me sometime. I'd like to hear what she has to say."

Amborella only stared at her mutely. Her thin lips gave a tiny twitch. Ellishiva sighed silently through her nose. She would have to try again tomorrow.

Just then, Hektor stepped out of his bath chamber. He was all dressed up in a cream-colored tunic and three-quarter-length khaki trousers. Ellishiva watched him silently, reproachfully, as he stood by his bed trying to fasten a second choker of strung acorns around his neck.

The sight of the necklace made Amborella forget her troubles. "Hektor!" she called, bouncing a little on her knees and making a few books slide around the mattress. "Can I wear it? Please? It will match my wristband!" she declared, showing off the braided bark band with a single acorn that he had made for her.

A smile tugged at the corner of Hektor's mouth. Without a word, he walked over to his sisters and fixed the second choker around a delighted Amborella's neck. Then he hesitated and glanced at Ellishiva.

She looked away, returning her eyes to *Conquerors of the Great Seas, Volume IV*.

A moment later, the first acorn choker landed lightly on the page she was reading. For a moment, a dull ache invaded Ellishiva's heart. But there was too much at stake, and the wounds her brother had inflicted on her were too deep to be healed with acorns.

"I don't want your gifts," she muttered coldly, pushing it away. She didn't even look up.

Hektor said nothing, but left the necklace where it was as he took Amborella's hand and helped her off the bed.

"Don't worry, Elli. You won't be alone," her little sister assured her as they headed for the door. "The kinnarans are downstairs, and so is Onuris and—and Gustav. See you later!" she called, waving Dollie Burlap cheerfully by the hand.

Then they were gone.

As soon as their footsteps had faded out of hearing, Ellishiva shoved the book aside. She took the orb she had stolen from Rajah's study out of her noli, then pulled the sheet over her head to conceal them both, just in case.

Safe under the makeshift tent, Ellishiva held the orb in both hands, studying it. Though it had been empty when she found it, it was now filled a quarter of the way with Khlorus spice dust, something that had taken her almost the whole fortnight to accomplish, because only wisps of the stuff could be called from her palms when she wasn't healing something or defending herself—all of which was beside the point.

How did it work?

Ellishiva blew over the orb, but nothing happened. She frowned and tapped it, traced its smooth surface with her fingertips. No sparks; nothing stirred. Before the frustration could take over, Ellishiva took a deep breath. She stopped prodding the thing, sat back on her heels, and thought. What did Rajah do, when he was controlling his staff?

The answer came to her almost immediately. Cautiously, Ellishiva bent close to the orb once more. "*Vitarita āloka,*" she murmured close to its surface.

Inside the olivine, the dust stirred and glowed green.

"Elli!"

"*Pidahati āloka!*" Ellishiva hissed. The green light went out and she shoved back the sheet in time to see Walle flying in through the open window.

"Walle, you're here. Good!" she said, a little too loudly.

Fortunately, Walle didn't notice. "Yes! Come on, let's hurry!" he urged, dashing off into Ellishiva's bath chamber, out of view of the windows.

Ellishiva slid out of bed, tucked the orb under her mattress, and stuffed a few pillows under her sheet to make it look as though she were taking a nap, just in case anyone came to check on her. Then she hurried after the firefly.

"Ready?" asked Walle as soon as she crossed the threshold.

Ellishiva nodded. "Remember, fasten the noli in front of you so that I'll be able to see."

In answer, Walle set the noli on the floor and tugged it open. A thin sheen of red Rojorine spice dust shimmered on its inner lip.

Without hesitation, Ellishiva stuck her toe into it and shrank, swallowed in seconds by the red dust.

She was aware of Walle fixing the noli to his belly and dashing out of the bedchamber again, turning south from the window toward Fairy Alcove and Central Pond. Most of her attention, however, was commanded by the inside of the noli itself.

All around her, countless grains of Rojorine sparkled like a miniature galaxy. Yet the specks of dust that drifted by were not stars, but soft, rubbery orbs in varying sizes. Some were clear, revealing the objects within; others were cloudy. They floated aimlessly in the surrounding space, lazily bouncing off of one another now and then. In one, Ellishiva caught a quick glimpse of some yellow slime toads. "Heyyyyy, sweetness. Think you could get us out of heeeere?" they whistled as they rolled by. Ellishiva frowned and scrunched her nose at the smell their orb left in its wake.

A moment later another red sphere went by, this one holding flickers of a burning fire.

The orb Ellishiva herself was in was a transparent one, but she didn't waste much time gawking at the scene around her. Walle had convinced her to venture into the noli a few times the day before, for practice, and she was already familiar with the noli's strange ecosystem. Instead, she immediately rubbed her long hair against the side of her rubbery orb, creating static. Like a magnet, it flew past wrinkled clothing, Puluma equipment, colorful boxes, treenity treats, and several of Samara's other collectibles before coming to a clinging halt, finally, against the wall of the noli's lining.

Here, unobstructed by the countless globes of floating objects, Ellishiva could see and hear everything.

The southernmost edge of Bear Market was disappearing beneath them, giving way to a broad path bordered by two rows of stately date palms. Near the end of it, Ellishiva noticed a familiar dofaun leading a tour.

"Two of Amma's many gifts to this planet are corn and sugarcane," Headmistress Ulima was explaining to a group of young children, her voice restored to its usual strong, clear self. In one paw she held sample saplings of the crops; in the other, an ear of corn and a stalk of sugarcane. "These crops will define the future of the earth for centuries to come."

Ellishiva remembered participating in a field trip just like that one, leading up to the Foxfire Harvest when she was a little girl. But the fond memory was quickly overshadowed by her fears for the day. She pressed her lips into a line, and hoped that the group of children below would be safe.

Ahead, the intense green waters of Central Pond were coming into view, hemmed in by thick, native forests. Ellishiva looked to her right and saw the Puluma court with its two towering walls. Perched atop these was a scattering of children, chatting and laughing. To her left, the circular, moss-covered basalt structure of Fairy Alcove rose into the air, the pointed rock spires on its uppermost story jutting regally toward the sky like the rim of a king's crown. At its foot, the meadow where the Foxfire Harvest was traditionally held stretched westward, bright and buzzing in the sunlight.

"The crowd is almost as big as it was last season," Ellishiva muttered to herself with a sinking heart as she took in the dofauns, elves, and fairies already mingling among the white yurts with pointed tops pitched below. Flags from Nicobar, each emblazoned with three plants and a jade tree, listed from the roofs of the temporary round buildings in the scant breeze. The meadow and the adjoining green expanse of Central Pond were alive with sound and color. Citizens of every age and background gathered to participate in traditional crafts and do-it-yourself lessons. Everywhere she looked there were clusters of friends and acquaintances, all of them mingling cheerfully in an array of feathers, hides, furs, and skins. A pleasant, burbling hum of snorting, laughter, grunting, and chirping drifted up to her from the crowd.

Ellishiva glanced again at the pond beyond the meadow and frowned. "Where are the floating lotus flowers?" she murmured to herself. The pond's empty surface glistened like ice in the sunlight, and the clusters of Bluzure plants crowded around it looked unusually dull and soggy gray.

Walle veered left, and suddenly the stone crown of Fairy Alcove was looming up before them again. At ground level, the alcove was surrounded by a wide moat crisscrossed by bridges. In the space between the water and the walls, elaborate gardens had been planted, and thin waterfalls cascaded down from chinks in the rock high above. Over the curved face of the basalt, epiphyte plants bloomed like a lovely mask. Broad ferns, sprawling moss, and exotic orchids in shades of white, purple, yellow, and green blended seamlessly together like a vast tapestry. From the alcove's uppermost spires, thick, broad-leaved ivies fell toward the ground, ending at varying heights.

Walle approached the moat and dashed over one of the crisscrossing bridges, then zipped high into the air again, speeding toward the vast stone archway that marked the main entrance to Fairy Alcove. For the first time, Ellishiva saw what Samara must take for granted. She felt she had her own wings as she admired the many sculptures carved into the stonework of the arch: hundreds upon hundreds of fairy figures. At its highest point, one such sculpture, larger than the others, had been chiseled with such exquisite detail that she seemed almost alive, her gatekeeper's wand poised over her head as if granting a wish, or guarding against evil.

They flew just beneath her into a vast entrance hall.

"It's nice and cool in here," remarked Walle, knowing that Ellishiva could hear him. He dashed down the long hallway, giant columns of smooth rock speeding by on either side. Each column, Ellishiva noticed, housed a glowing oil lamp set into a carved-out hollow. Several fairies passed Walle going the other direction, the shades of their skins ranging from fair, like Samara's, to pale pink, buttercup gold, or deep, sandalwood blue. They seemed to be dressed for the occasion, and their silken robes flowed freely about them in a rainbow of shimmering hues. When they spoke, their voices were as clear as crystal chimes.

"Lovely to see you again, Walle."

"Welcome, Walle."

At the end of the hallway was a grand, sprawling staircase. Walle flew up the steps and then turned down a long, curved, open-sided corridor lined with many doors, behind which, Ellishiva knew, were the fairies' bedchambers.

But Samara's room was not on the lower levels, and a moment later Walle turned sharply again, swerving through someone's open garden terrace into the hollow center of Fairy Alcove. Ellishiva gasped as he shot high into the air, revealing another view of the alcove that she'd never dreamed she'd see. Above, the clear blue sky looked almost like a dome housing the large, garden-bordered pool far below. Here and there, brilliant green lily pads that were big and sturdy enough to hold Atticus drifted across the water's still surface, looking like pie crusts with crimped edges. In between these, white lotus flowers dotted with tiny, as-yet-unlit oil lamps floated about. Wooden stages, like rafts, had also been added to the mix for choice members of the audience to watch the performers at close range later that evening.

Ellishiva took it all in, then glanced up at the rounded sky again. She felt as though she were suspended in a deep, tropical cave.

Walle was still rising past tiers and tiers of semi-circular terraces covered, like the outer walls of the alcove, in moss and orchids. Behind the terraces, as there had been on the lower levels, were more bed-chambers. Through several open doorways, Ellishiva could see fairies primping for the festival: tying wraps around their bodies, air-drying their henna-wet hands, fixing flowers in each other's hair. On a few of the terraces, groups of friends blew into delicate flutes and even recited poetry from scrolls.

Ellishiva tried to picture Samara reciting poetry and sipping tea on a terrace. The image was so absurd that she snorted, choking on her own laugh. No wonder her friend was always getting into trouble.

At last, Walle turned onto a terrace with waist-high vine rails all around it. Before Ellishiva fully realized where they were, he was speed-ing through an open door into a violet-colored bedchamber. Then a hand was reaching into the noli, and a familiar voice said, "Ellishiva."

Instantly, the Rojorine orb pulled away from the lining and rose toward the noli's opening, where it collapsed in a cloud of shimmering dust that blinded her. Ellishiva blinked and rubbed her eyes. When her vision came back, she saw that she was lying on a frilly, messy bed.

And she wasn't alone.

Ellishiva sat up next to Samara, who grinned at her. In the next moment they had thrown themselves into a rib-crushing hug, one so powerful that in a few seconds Walle had been sucked into it as well.

"Told you . . . it would work!" gasped the little firefly from where he had been squashed between them, just before they let him go. He smiled and sucked in a deep breath.

Samara's bedchamber was on the western side of the alcove, its window facing the meadow, the Puluma court, and Central Pond. It was a big enough space for just one girl to live in, and the stone walls were lined with bookshelves—though you'd be hard-pressed to find a book on them, Ellishiva thought wryly. Instead, the fairy had packed the shelves with dozens of finely carved, brightly colored, and unusually shaped chests—a collection that had been her hobby for almost as long as Ellishiva could remember. There weren't many levels left between this terrace and the uppermost one, where Queen Neive had her quarters and dined with important guests, and Samara hadn't always been in such a high room. However, after the incident with the almost-stolen journals, Queen Neive had moved her here "so as to keep a better eye on the exasperating little minx."

Ellishiva leaned back on her hands and smiled at the minx in question. Samara was decked out in a lovely, classic, and short pink wrap that dropped to her thighs. Her wrists were festooned with dozens of thin, beaded wristbands, and there were even a few rings on her toes. "You're all dressed up," Ellishiva commented, arching one eyebrow.

Samara snorted. "Queen Neive picked it out herself. She wanted to make sure I wasn't going to alarm any of her dignitaries." She rolled her eyes. Then she brightened a bit and leaned in closer to Ellishiva and Walle. "She said I'm not grounded for the night! I can't leave Central Pond, but it's better than nothing. Do you realize we've been grounded for almost a *fortnight*, Elli?" She sighed, and shook her head. "It's just not fair."

"I know, Sam," Ellishiva commiserated. Then she pulled her legs up so that she was sitting cross-legged on the mattress and scooted closer to the fairy. "So you got the map of Chingetti Cellar?" she asked in a low voice. "Can I see it?"

"Yes, Bairon finally brought it to me a few days ago," Samara confirmed, climbing off the bed and crossing to her desk by the window. She pulled the map out of a drawer and handed it over.

Ellishiva spread it out on the wrinkled coverlet and bent down over her crossed legs to examine it closely. She barely noticed Walle and Samara hover up to peer at it over her shoulders, too. Her forehead creased in concentration and her fingers traced the lines of Banyan Tree's sprawling root system, her fingertips hovering just above the surface of the papyrus at all times—just to make sure the drawings didn't get any clever ideas about coming to life.

At last, she spotted it.

"Look. This vāhmana, here!" she declared, tapping the spot with her fingernail. "It leads into the main hub of the roots, and from there it can go north, east, west, or south." She looked up and over her shoulders at her partners in crime, her eyes triumphant. "South is the one we'll take to the river's edge. To get to South Island."

"Great!" gushed Samara without hesitation. "When do we leave?"

Ellishiva pulled the constellation map out of her noli and opened it on top of the first. Excitement and panic were vying for control over her nerves. "I don't know. The next last quarter moon will be here soon, but we have no way of telling if that's important anymore. Or if it was ever important," she mumbled, her eyes following the paths of the constellations. She sat up straight again and began refolding the maps. "Still, we can't afford to delay for long, just in case. What about the general? Any news?" she asked. "Still no word on Maximus?"

"Still no Maximus," confirmed Samara, watching her closely. "But I overheard some of the fairies saying that the general is supposed to hold a meeting in one of the yurts down in the meadow. Not sure which one, though."

Ellishiva nodded. "That narrows it down, at least." She tucked the newly folded maps into her noli. "Maybe we can try following some of the kinnarans. They're bound to have news of his whereabouts." She stared off across the room, thinking. Then her eyes fell on a small sapling with thick red leaves sitting in a pot on Samara's desk. "Wow, Sam. Dragon's Blood?" she commented, impressed. On their own, her feet climbed off the bed and walked to the desk. She bent to get a closer look at the little plant. "Are you going to nurture it so you can harvest your own Rojorine spice dust? Where did it come from?"

Samara waved her hand dismissively. "Gifts from visitors, Elli. There have been a *lot* of them lately. Queen Neive saw to it that I got this one. She's been trying to curse me with manual labor since I lost my wand. But she should know I'm not going to rough up my hands digging around in the dirt," she finished primly, admiring her neatly trimmed nails, which were decorated with flower designs for the occasion.

"She was probably trying to trick you into it," Ellishiva speculated, tamping down the smile that tugged at the corner of her mouth. "These plants take hundreds of moons to mature before you can harvest true Rojorine from them. I'm sure you have better things to do." Her gaze strayed to a handful of barbee jujubes sitting next to the pot and her stomach grumbled. Without thinking, she picked one up and took a bite. Then another.

Several seconds went by before she noticed the firefly and the fairy staring at her.

"You're welcome," quipped Samara shortly, raising one eyebrow and crossing her arms.

Ellishiva felt her cheeks go pink. "Sorry. Hope you don't mind," she apologized sheepishly. "I haven't been eating much lately because . . . well,

I've been trying to avoid Lady Malinia. Hektor keeps saying I'm going to give her heart failure. I think I've become a burden on her and Rajah since all of this started." She looked down at the half-eaten snack in her hand and set it roughly on the desk again, her appetite suddenly gone.

Before her reveries could swallow her up, however, they were interrupted by the dungchen. Ellishiva leaned close to the nearby window and peered out. Up on a small garden terrace shaded by a lone chinar tree, two fairies were blowing into identical silver trumpets twice as long as their bodies. The sound of the horns echoed over the island, powerful and soothing at once, like a pair of singing elephants. The fairies paused to catch their breaths, blew into the dungchen a second time, and then flew away.

"Good. It's time for afternoon tea," breathed Ellishiva. She turned from the window, and looked at Samara. "Let's go find the general."

"I should go back to the harvest," chimed in Walle, unfastening the rose noli and handing it back to the fairy. "Otherwise Amber or my parents will come looking for me. But I'll keep an eye out for Jipsin Smilodon or the general when I'm down there, Elli."

"Thanks, Walle," said Ellishiva gratefully. "Let's meet back here in Sam's room after afternoon teatime to swap information, okay?"

The firefly dofaun smiled and saluted her. Then he dashed out the open window to rejoin the festivities far below.

Ellishiva looked at Samara. "Ready?"

"Ready," confirmed Samara, tugging the noli open again. Ellishiva crossed the room in three strides and stepped into the shimmering Rojorine spice dust. Before she'd even had time to rub her hair against the bubble that formed around her, Samara had fastened the noli to her waist and was flying out of the room even faster than Walle had done, though she went the roundabout way through the center of the alcove so as not to look suspicious.

Before they rose over the crown-like top of the structure, however, Samara swerved sharply. Ellishiva's heart leapt into her throat, but it needn't have bothered; a moment later the fairy had landed among the intense purple flowers of a sprawling jacaranda tree on one of the lower terraces. Several wide swings hung from its thick lower branches, suspended by twined orchid vines. Ellishiva opened her mouth to ask what the matter was before she remembered that Samara couldn't hear her. Luckily, the fairy read her mind.

"Sorry," she apologized, sounding as though there were a rather loud laugh wedged in her throat, "but I really have to see this."

Ellishiva stared through the noli lining at the scene below, and groaned inwardly. "Why am I not surprised," she muttered.

On one of the gigantic lily pads near the edge of the pond below, Bairon and Hektor were reciting poetry, entertaining the crowd of pretty fairies around them with deep voices and dramatic flourishes. At the moment, Hektor seemed to be ending a long speech. "Yet taught by time," proclaimed Ellishiva's brother, bowing to his adoring public with feeling, "my heart has learned to glow for others' good, and melt at others' woe."

A scattering of dainty, delighted applause broke out.

"Admirable," praised one fairy with a nod of approval. "The young Va'nature clearly knows much about Homer."

Not missing his chance, Hektor bowed low before her and swept her hand up in his, planting a gentlemanly kiss on the delicate fingers. A ripple of tinkling giggles bubbled through the little crowd.

"It's no good," Samara choked, tears of laughter in her eyes. "I'm sorry, Elli. You really can't expect me to resist something like this." They shot out of the jacaranda tree toward the group, Samara waving both of her arms wildly over her head to attract attention. "Hektor!" she called, much louder than necessary. "What are you doing?"

Ellishiva could almost feel the collective eyes of Fairy Alcove honing in on the disturbance. In front of them, Hektor froze in a half-bow and looked toward the familiar voice hollering his name. The blood drained from his face.

Quite suddenly, it was so silent that Ellishiva could have heard a leaf drop.

There was a long, shocked silence. Finally, the fairy whose hand had just been kissed found her voice. "Samara, Samara," she chided gently, shaking her head. "You know that is no way to speak to someone. These kind boys are our guests."

Samara pulled a perfectly straight face. "My deepest apologies, Ambika," she replied in the same soft, fluty voice. Anyone else, Ellishiva reflected, would've believed that she actually meant it. "Good sir," she went on seriously in the same proper voice, fixing her gaze on the horrified Hektor, "I beg you forgive my unseemly outburst. The power of your poetic genius struck me so, I could not contain my rapture."

A murmur of approval went up around the alcove. Ellishiva saw Bairon shove his fist into his mouth to keep from laughing. In front of him, Hektor opened his mouth, and then closed it again. He stared mutely at Samara.

With a smirk so faint that Ellishiva was sure no one but the three of them could see it, Samara inclined her head to him slightly and flew gracefully away.

"Hektor," groaned Ellishiva, her stomach aching with laughter as they sped away. Then the laughter faded, and only the ache was left. She heaved a sigh, suddenly sad. "We'd have figured out who the Sixth Element is by now if you'd helped us instead of fighting us," she muttered bleakly.

The noli swung as Samara crested the top of Fairy Alcove and dove downward toward the meadow again, shaking Ellishiva's Rojorine orb free of the pink lining. By the time Ellishiva created enough static to return to the edge again, they were dodging through the crowds of the Foxfire Harvest. Samara zipped past the Faviola sisters, who were perched on top of a huge bison dofaun, fanning themselves with their iridescent wings in the sunlight. Everywhere, on every tongue, was speculation about the upcoming harvest of the Bluzure spice dust.

At the edge of the meadow, Samara swerved into the narrow shadow behind an abandoned yurt and landed. She glanced around furtively— left, right, and even up. Then she paused for a long moment, listening. Finally, deciding the coast was clear, she hunkered down in the yurt's shadow and pulled Ellishiva out of the noli.

"It's so hot out here!" she huffed under her breath as soon as Ellishiva was sitting beside her. She swiped the back of one hand dramatically over the gathering beads of sweat on her forehead.

Ellishiva ignored the comment. "You have to walk now," she whispered. "We'll never be able to hear anything if we're above the crowds. Start by the pond next to that cashew tree, where the kinnarans are." She pointed at the tree in question, its thick leaves shielding the orange-colored "apples" to which the nuts themselves were attached. "I saw their faces when you flew by. They look worried about something."

"Okay, okay," grumbled Samara. Ellishiva nodded and stepped back inside the noli. Samara drew it shut.

"On second thought," the fairy reflected innocently, "there's really no point in walking all the way over there, Elli. Flying is much cooler. I'll just land on an upper limb of the tree. They'll never see us coming."

Ellishiva scowled, but there was nothing she could do trapped in the noli. Samara fluttered over to the cashew tree and perched silently on a fruit-laden branch. Swallowing her annoyance, Ellishiva turned her attention to the group of five kinnarans at the tree's base. Two of them were crouched on the ground, clearly worn out and distressed.

"What happened?" asked one of the standing kinnarans, concern in his voice.

"You look like you just ran around Central Pond a few times," added another gruffly.

On the ground, the sitting kinnarans' white hair was plastered to their faces with sweat. One stripped off his armor and untucked the hem of his shirt from his trousers, battling the heat. "Mannahatta Colony is in grave danger!" he told them, wiping the back of his neck with his sleeve.

The standing members of the group crowded in closer.

"What happened?"

"Are you sure?"

"Does the general know of this?" The third standing kinnaran silenced the others with a wave of his hand. "Where is he?"

"We left the general by the river's edge," the second kinnaran on the ground spoke up finally, his voice much quieter than the other's. "Canoes are drifting back to human villages empty. The Sixth Element is drinking their blood and leaving the headless bodies to wash up on the riverbank."

There was a long, ominous silence. Ellishiva's stomach turned.

Finally, one of the standing kinnarans rallied enough to ask, "Have they found Maximus?"

"No," replied the sitting soldier, perhaps even more quietly than before. "No sign of Maximus."

The first kinnaran who'd spoken ran his hand roughly through his hair. "I don't know why they won't just tell these poor citizens that Mannahatta is not a safe place."

On the floor, his companion nodded mutely and gazed off at a small shrub beside the nearest pond, the tips of its long-leafed branches trailing in the cool water as if it were drinking. "Where did all the lotus flowers from the ponds disappear to?" he wondered aloud.

Inside the noli, Ellishiva frowned, eyeing Central Pond, which gleamed flatly in the sunlight nearby. There was a chill in her blood from what they had said about Maximus, but she forced herself not to dwell on it, storing the information away for later. Here, now, the kinnaran was right: usually there were plenty of lotus flowers dotting the pond at this time of year, like speckles on a nuthatch's egg.

"So many residents here on Mannahatta," the quiet kinnaran below was murmuring, still staring at the empty pond before him. "There may not be enough of us here to defend them all."

Another silence. Then the kinnaran who seemed to be the most in charge patted his bedraggled comrade on the shoulder. "Come on," he muttered gruffly. "Let's get the two of you something to drink."

Ellishiva watched as all five of the kinnarans set off across the meadow, the three rested ones helping their exhausted companions to their feet. She waited expectantly for Samara to pull her out of the noli again, but the fairy only fluttered down from the cashew tree and into the milling crowds a short ways away, doubtless unwilling to face Ellishiva before doing at least a little bit of walking first. Ellishiva crossed her arms impatiently and tried to pay attention to the conversations around her as elves, fairies, and exotic dofauns bustled by: Malacca mountain tapirs with broad white and green bands running down the middles of their black, stocky bodies; a family of thick-necked, strutting Mongolian horses with roan stripes; a flock of Philae shelgeese with iron-gray and teal feathers swooping overhead. None of them had anything interesting to add to what the kinnarans had said beneath the cashew tree.

"I'm not sure how much of this walking I can do, Elli," Samara mumbled, slipping into the shadow of another yurt and pulling Ellishiva out of the noli again at last. "Some of us aren't Va'natures, remember?" she added pointedly.

"It's nice and cool inside your noli," Ellishiva said, unable to resist just a tiny jab of revenge.

The fairy rolled her eyes and groaned. "Ugh, do you *have* to rub it in? I'm dying out here in this heat." She looked up at the fiery sun in the clear sky as though it could stand trial for its crime.

Ellishiva eyed Samara until the fairy looked ready to listen again. Then she said, "It sounds like we're just going to have to wait for the general to come back from the river."

"We don't know if he *is* coming back from the river today, Elli," huffed Samara, fanning herself. "The kinnarans didn't say he was. Why is it so *hot* all of a sudden?" She glared up at the sun again.

Ellishiva had begun to sweat too, but there were more important things roaming through her head. "Come on, let's get back to your room," she suggested. "It's past afternoon teatime. Maybe Walle's heard something we haven't. We can keep an eye out for Jipsin Smilodon on the way—"

"Smell that?" sneered a prissy voice overhead.

Ellishiva and Samara jumped. In the blink of an eye, the four Faviola hawk-moth sisters had touched down in the hidden space behind the yurts, surrounding them. As usual, they were dressed in impeccable outfits, and their beady eyes were gleaming wickedly.

"What a stench," agreed a second sister. "And it's not the heat!"

"It must be coming from the Va'nature," chimed in a third, covering her nose and mouth with the tip of one wing. "Ugh, she smells like a steaming pitcher plant. Disgusting."

A chorus of snickering flitted around the group. As usual, Samara bristled and took a step forward, but this time, Ellishiva held her back. "Allow me," she muttered, taking hold of the rose-colored noli.

Four pairs of moth eyes widened as Ellishiva herself, not her "fairy defender," stepped forward. Without preamble, Ellishiva reached into the noli and whispered, "Yellow slime toads." The bubble containing the foul-smelling creatures she'd seen earlier immediately rose to her hand, and she flung its inhabitants out in a half-circle in front of her. The Faviola sisters shrieked and squealed as the toads landed on their heads and shoulders, releasing a sulfur-scented slime from their glands. In moments, the hawk moths were splattered in the stuff from head to foot. They retreated in chaos, one or two of them casting shocked, fearful glances at Ellishiva as they went.

"I think stinky yellow is your color!" Ellishiva shouted after them. Then Samara grabbed her by the elbow and dragged her away toward a different cluster of yurts before they could be discovered. They stumbled to a halt, breathless, and then burst into giggles, clutching their bellies.

"I didn't know I had those things in there!" gasped Samara gleefully.

"I'm sure there are a lot of things in that noli that you don't know about, Sam," replied Ellishiva, wiping tears of laughter from her eyes.

Then she let herself back into the noli again, and Samara flew away.

The afternoon was wearing on by the time they arrived back at the bedchamber. They had discovered the Jipsin's vāhmana tethered to one of the large common terraces on the upper levels of Fairy Alcove, near the two dungchen, but the Jipsin himself was not in it. Nor did anyone nearby seem to know when he'd be back. At last they'd been forced to return to the room—a bit later than they'd meant to—to wait.

Samara yanked Ellishiva unceremoniously from the noli and then sprawled out on her bed with a cool, damp towel over her face. Ellishiva let her be. She sat quietly in the chair by the desk, staring up at the terrace above and thinking. She wished that Jipsin Smilodon would return so she could ask him about Perseus, the snow leopard. Since Rajah and the others had turned their backs on her, he was the only elder left that she could talk to freely. She frowned and leaned her forehead against the glass. Maybe he'd been the only elder she'd ever really been able to talk to.

"I'm so glad I have wings," whined Samara dramatically from the bed, pressing the cold towel to her face. "Walking—ha! I don't know how you do it, all the time, every day . . ."

Ellishiva barely heard her. She stood from the chair to get a better look out the window, gazing down into the meadow below. To the left of the wide, bustling space, the waters of Central Pond were eerily smooth, and silent. "Even the hippos are quiet today," Ellishiva murmured to herself, disturbed.

"Elli, are you even listening to me!" demanded Samara's piercing voice, breaking into her thoughts.

Ellishiva turned from the window, startled.

Samara had flipped onto her belly. One of her legs was bent upward, waving a dainty foot in the air. The damp cloth had been tossed away onto the pillows, and she was glaring at Ellishiva with a wounded look on her face. "What did you do all that time you were in the Arboretum by yourself? You're acting like a different person!" she accused.

Ellishiva shrugged irritably. "I'm just disappointed that we haven't been able to talk to the general yet," she muttered. Then she remembered who she was talking to. If she couldn't discuss it with Samara, who was she going to tell? Expelling a long breath, she crossed the room and plunked herself down at the foot of the bed.

"It's nothing top secret, Sam," she sighed. "You already know about the payamar. The only other thing was just . . . Maximus told me once that in Rajah's absence, I should reflect on the lessons he's taught me. So I have been, and it gave me strength. It's that simple. I'm not different. I've just learned to think of myself differently. Like the trees in the Arboretum, reaching for the light to survive." She shrugged.

"Ah. I see," said Samara, straight-faced. "Told you Maximus was weird," she added under her breath.

Ellishiva rolled her eyes. "You asked," she pointed out dryly. She reached past the fairy and picked the damp cloth up off the pillows, dabbing her own neck and face with it. "And he's not weird. Elders aren't the only ones with anything intelligent to say," she added.

Samara snorted. "Do elders *ever* have intelligent things to say?" she muttered, stealing a resentful glance at a mandatory portrait of Queen Neive hanging by the door.

Ellishiva ignored her. She tossed the damp towel away again and took a deep breath. "Okay, here's the plan," she said, getting down to business. "Walle still isn't back, which means either he was here on time and we missed him, or he couldn't get away. I'm going to stake out the Jipsin's vāhmana. At least that way I'll be able to catch him as soon as he gets back. Drop me off behind the chinar tree up there, and then you can go and find out when the general is expected to return, or if he's already back. If you spot him, come back and get me right away." She paused, and her eye fell on the potted sapling sitting on the desk. "Oh. Can I take your Dragon's Blood sapling with me, to barter with? I have another one in the Vivarium at home. I'll give it to you as soon as—"

"Please! Take it!" interrupted Samara, scowling at the plant in question. "Can't believe how long it takes Dragon's Blood to mature.

Anyway," she added, sitting up on the bed with a gleeful glint in her eyes, "who needs Rojorine when you can make Khlorus! Oh Elli, I can see it now. We'll set up a shop at Bear Market and—"

"A *shop*?" scoffed Ellishiva. She pinned the fairy with a stern look. "Sam, you're probably the only fairy in the colony whose hands have never touched dirt. We are not *selling* Khlorus spice dust in Bear Market. That's so wrong . . . and *greedy*! What is wrong with you?"

"All right, all right," grumbled Samara. "Sorry I asked." She fell back on the bed again, grabbing the damp towel and dropping it over her face. Ellishiva sighed, knowing she'd probably hurt her feelings. Well, there was only one way to deal with that. Creeping silently up to the edge of the bed, she picked up a pillow and walloped the wallowing fairy in the stomach. Samara squeaked and was up in a split second, snatching a pillow herself and smacking Ellishiva upside the head with it. Before long they were rolling around and laughing, the whole little tiff forgotten.

"Ready to go?" said Ellishiva finally, smiling as she tossed her pillow away from her, back into the pile on the bed.

"Aren't I always?" Samara smiled back. Ellishiva got back into the noli, taking the Dragon's Blood sapling with her, and Samara dropped her off behind the chinar tree on the upper terrace, not far from the Jipsin's vāhmana. Adjusting the earthen pot under her arm, Ellishiva turned to wish the fairy good luck.

A sudden, loud snore from the nearby vāhmana interrupted her. She looked at Samara, wide-eyed.

The fairy grinned at her. "If I spot the general, I'll come back to get you at this same spot," she whispered. Then she glanced toward the vāhmana and pinched Ellishiva's arm in excitement. "Good luck!"

Ellishiva nodded and watched her fly away before shifting the sapling in her arms and tiptoeing off in the direction of the snoring. Jipsin Smilodon was resting on a long planters chair near the far side of the vāhmana, lying on his side so that his face was turned away from her.

Ellishiva paused when she reached the chair, not sure how she should wake him. The dofaun's long tail jumped slowly in his sleep, and his belly moved in and out with his breath like a bellowing fireplace.

She was steeling herself to reach down and shake his shoulder when something caught her eye. Crouching down silently, she squinted at a mark on his flank that she had never seen before—a hieroglyphic. Ellishiva hadn't studied hieroglyphics yet, but she recognized this one from the handful that Samara had taught her: *the House of Horus.*

Of their own will, her lips moved. "You were a pet for the pharaohs," she breathed.

The words had been no louder than the breeze. Nevertheless, the Jipsin's jumping tail froze into an arch. Ellishiva crouched down lower, fixed to the spot. A shiver ran through her body. She glanced up, checking for dark clouds, but the blue sky was empty. Her heartbeat slowed. Then her eyes dropped to the earth again, landing on something by the front legs of the planters chair, and her heart changed its mind, taking a flying leap up into her throat. Her hand jumped to her mouth. She sank to her belly and edged closer to the objects, crawling along using her elbows—which was no easy task with the plant in her arms.

The strange things were two long, bone-white tubes . . . tubes that had been shaped to look like canine teeth. There was nothing extraordinary about them except, of course, that usually they were in Jipsin Smilodon's mouth.

Ellishiva pressed her lips tightly together to keep any sounds of shock from escaping them. She sat up straight on her knees and looked at the face of the sleeping Jipsin. Without his huge canines, he was a different creature. Elegant, sweeping whiskers stretched out from either side of his nose and . . . Ellishiva squinted and leaned closer. Yes, there, among the left cluster of them, was a space where one was clearly missing.

Suddenly, the Jipsin opened his huge, icy blue eyes.

Ellishiva gasped and fell back onto her palms. The earthen pot in the crook of her arm fell to the ground and cracked.

"Why, my dearest Ellishiva," rumbled the Jipsin warmly, pushing himself up on one forepaw. His voice, deep and regal, sent a shiver down her spine. It was familiar.

"'I fear what is to come of your destiny,'" she whispered, rooted to the ground as she stared at him, utterly bewildered. "Perseus the snow leopard. You're the one who named me! I came here to ask you—I mean, to ask Jipsin Smilodon—who you were!"

Perseus opened his mouth, then seemed to think better of it, and closed it again. He cleared his throat.

But Ellishiva was gaining confidence now. "You named me. I remember. You named me after your cub and your mother. I saw it all in my spice dust." She pushed herself to her feet. "All this time, you were pretending to be someone else?" she said, baffled. She took a step back. "Why?"

"Come back, Ellishiva," sighed the snow leopard. "I am not going to bite." He threw a wistful glance at the long, false canine teeth on the ground. Then he gave an immense yawn that showed his real deadly fangs, along with his rough, curling pink tongue.

Ellishiva hesitated for just a moment, struggling with betrayal and curiosity. Curiosity won the battle. She dropped down next to the planters chair again. "Well," she blurted, glancing at the fake teeth again herself, "I always thought those were too big for your head."

The snow leopard graced her with a wry smile. "Come and sit here by me," he said, patting the space in front of him with his paw.

Ellishiva climbed up and tucked herself into the crook of his bent forepaw, letting her back and head sink deep into the warm fur of his belly. The snow leopard looked down at her with a smile in his eyes, as if she were a cub snuggling into its rightful place.

"Something is troubling you, child," he said gently. His ice-blue gaze took in the cracked pot of the Dragon's Blood sapling on the ground.

"You've come to barter, I see."

"Oh. Yes," said Ellishiva, suddenly remembering the other reason she'd sought him out. "I was going to ask you if you could trade me something. Well, I don't know what, exactly, but something that could make me fly? I'll put it together if I have to. I just hope it's not too many ingredients. I don't like mixing things. Well, you know me and elixirs," she chattered on comfortably. "And I'm not bartering my toe ring," she added, smiling at their well-worn joke.

The snow leopard smiled back at her. Then he pulled a serious face. "I heard you were grounded," he said.

"I heard you were a smilodon," Ellishiva retorted playfully. Then she, too, grew serious. "Why did you disguise yourself?" she asked.

There was a tense silence. Ellishiva kept her eyes on the dofaun, waiting patiently for his answer.

At last, Perseus sighed. "It was the only way to see you, Ellishiva," he admitted softly. "Some choose to devote their lives to status and duty. I surrendered rank and shelter for something that was stolen from me, but now is found again: hope. You, Ellishiva Cinnamon, are my hope."

The words kindled sadness and warmth in Ellishiva at once. She remembered what Banog had said to Perseus in her spice dust—the awful story of the snow leopard's missing cub. When she looked up at him again, the lines around his blue eyes seemed older and deeper. Understanding, Ellishiva changed the subject to take his mind off of old wounds. "So is this where you escape to when nobody knows where you are?" She smiled at him.

Some of the sadness left Perseus's face. He chuckled. "Indeed. The flock of customers following me around Bear Market can be over-whelming sometimes. Although now that our friend Samara has found me out, I may need to seek another spot."

Ellishiva snorted. It was true; a secret in Samara's hands was not a secret for long.

Perseus gave a great, rumbling sigh, and grew serious again. "I sense that many things are burdening you, Ellishiva. Speak to me. Answers are never found by allowing questions to dwell within."

He was right, of course. Ellishiva took a deep breath and all the pent-up words from the past weeks came spilling out of her mouth.

"I don't know, Perseus. It's just . . . so much is happening at once. Mannahatta Colony isn't safe, but the elders won't listen to me and won't do anything about it. Rajah is never around. Lady Malinia says I'm going to give her heart failure. My own brother doesn't believe a word I say. And my sister has been talking to a doll. And *then* I discovered that Amma brought me into the world just so I could face this Sixth Element, who's nearly killed me once already. And I'm still not even sure what she did to my body that day." Ellishiva stopped, breathing hard. She wiped the sweat from her upper lip.

Next to her, the snow leopard let out a long, weary breath. "It is much to lay upon your shoulders, I know. I have always been afraid this would happen." He turned his piercing ice-blue eyes downward on her. "Ellishiva, your destiny has been forged. Now it is up to you to write the path for this journey."

The snow leopard rose from the chair and walked into his vāhmana. Ellishiva followed, scooping up the cracked earthenware pot as she went.

"Come here, child," Perseus beckoned. "I have something for you. But the key, I am afraid, has been . . . misplaced." He smiled wryly. "I would not be the least surprised, however, if it has found its way into the hands of your friend Samara. Her collection of chests is quite impressive. I can think of no one else who might have finagled it away from me."

Ellishiva started to smile, then caught herself. She cleared her throat and tried to put on her bartering face. "I brought this Dragon's Blood sapling for trade," she began, then trailed off, eyeing the broken pot uncertainly.

"I see," rumbled Perseus, a twinkle in his eyes. "Amazing how many curious objects once in my possession return to me again. I shall take it off your hands, Ellishiva, since I suspect that Samara would thank me for it. But the trade I really want from you today is your word that you will tell no one of your . . . discovery, of who I truly am." He took the bedraggled sapling gently from her hands and gave her a conspiratorial wink. "I have rather grown to like this Jipsin Smilodon fellow, you see."

Ellishiva grinned at him. "Agreed! It'll be our secret." She leaned to the right, peering around him at the object sitting at his heels. "So . . . what's in this chest?" she asked.

"Let us say that it will enhance the journey ahead," replied Perseus elusively. He set the Dragon's Blood plant carefully on a shelf, and then turned to look her in the eye. "But be warned, Ellishiva. You must only open this chest when you feel that you require assistance most. To use that which lies within, you will need one more thing. But I assure you, that shall never be more than a hand's reach away. Listen to the Khlorus in you, always. It knows your purpose, and there is nothing you will need on this journey that it cannot provide. Fear not, child," he added, noting the look of consternation on her face, "for when the time is right, that which you need will come to you."

"Um. All right," Ellishiva replied, puzzled, her eyes straying to the brown chest on the ground, its lid and sides etched with strange, intricate designs. She knelt and picked it up, hugging it to her chest. It was the size of a watermelon, but nowhere near as heavy.

Perseus nodded his approval. Then he turned and led the way down the steps of the vāhmana again, back onto the terrace. "The kinnarans who stood guard over you in the Arboretum tell me that they have never before seen such vigorous payamar practice," he said conversationally, ignoring the look of surprise on Ellishiva's face. "I confess, I am quite curious about that. How did you grasp and perfect such difficult skills on your own, during your time of punishment?"

Ellishiva shook off her annoyance. Even kinnarans, it seemed, were not above gossiping. "I just thought of something Rajah taught me once," she admitted. "'The goal of every seedling, once planted, is to reach the light.' And I just decided that, well, if the trees could do it . . . ," she shrugged.

"Admirable, child," said Perseus, impressed. "You shall accomplish a great many things with such thinking." He sighed deeply, and set one huge paw lightly, fondly, on top of her head. "I know he has not always been there for you of late," he acknowledged, "but Rajah has always had your interests at heart. Reflect on his lessons, as you are. They were taught to you for a purpose."

Ellishiva felt lighter in more ways than one as he lifted the paw from her head again. Reassured, she turned and asked him about the subject all the other elders seemed to fear most. "Perseus, about a fortnight ago, I looked into Amber's spice dust. I saw the fire at Bandalara in the human world, and I saw . . . I saw all the children and animals that were murdered that day. But there's something I still don't understand." She frowned, and tilted her head a little. "Do you know why they call it the Madagascar Massacre? Shouldn't it be the Bandalara Massacre instead?"

Perseus gave a sigh that seemed to come from the depths of his belly. "You've been quite busy, I see," he muttered, half to himself. Then he fixed her with a look filled with sadness and continued quietly. "The pain Rajah suffers from that atrocity haunts him to this day, Ellishiva. He was always a wise Va'nature, whose dutiful heart stood strong in the face of hardship, as though it rested upon the pillars of the great Hypostyle Hall of Karnak themselves. Now his sorrow holds him captive, torturing him with the woes of one who was once under his protection."

Ellishiva was thoughtful for a moment, letting this sink in. "He was the prefect of the colony there, on Madagascar. Wasn't he?" she prodded finally.

"Indeed he was," confirmed Perseus. "And the name of the colony he led there, on that island, was Madagascar." He paused, letting the pieces click together in Ellishiva's mind before going on, a ray of bitterness in his eyes now. "Gossip requires colorful names to survive, child, as I am sure you have learned by now. So it was that the murders at Bandalara came to be known as the Madagascar Massacre."

Ellishiva was quiet for a long time. Finally, she mustered her voice. "Can you tell me what you know about the Madagascar Massacre?" she asked, her voice low and serious.

Perseus shook his great head slowly. "I was not there when it happened, Ellishiva," he admitted. "The only one who can tell you what you seek to know is Rajah himself. It would not be fair of me to repeat to you what I heard—rumors and gossip. Words, too often, can inflict wounds where they should do good."

Ellishiva looked at him. She had the sense that he was trying to tell her something that went deeper than the words themselves. Perseus returned her gaze, as steady as the chinar tree they were standing beneath. Not far away, a cricket chirped.

At last, the great cat spoke again. "Ellishiva, though I am an elder," he murmured, "I will not stop you from seeking out the things you need, so that you may do what you have been put upon this earth to do."

"You mean . . . I should follow my instincts," Ellishiva summed up, understanding dawning on her.

Perseus nodded. "Trust them and you will never fail. Trust all your senses. Already you are a great listener. It is one of your many strengths. *Observe*, Ellishiva Cinnamon, and you will never be the hunted."

Ellishiva let the words seep into her and knew that they would never be forgotten. She turned to the snow leopard again. "Perseus, I have to go find the general," she confided, her voice steadier and more confident than it had been a mere hour ago. "But I need you to stay the night here, if you can. Please? Don't leave. Not until the harvest is over."

The snow leopard raised an eyebrow at her. "Is that your instincts at work?" he asked.

"Yes. That, and I've read too many books about war," Ellishiva admitted. "Enemies attack at gatherings. They know that celebrations like the harvest are the best times to do the most harm with the least amount of effort."

"Wise words," muttered Perseus. He looked up at the empty sky as though searching for dark clouds. "I will stay the night, Ellishiva. Go then. Continue your search for the general. If I see him myself, I shall inform him that you require an audience with him."

"Thank you, Perseus," Ellishiva replied, following his gaze. Above them, the sky was taking on the purplish hue of evening.

At that moment they heard a familiar voice drifting over to them from another terrace, not too far away. Ellishiva sighed through her nose and tried to hush the regret that welled up in her chest. It was good that Samara had returned so soon, she told herself.

Next to her, Perseus sensed her hesitation. "Go, child," he urged gently. "Go, and use my gift well. Quickly, behind the tree. She will be here in a moment . . . bearing a vāhmana of a different sort for you, unless I am much mistaken."

Ellishiva nodded and started for the wide trunk, the brown chest clutched in her arms. Then the snow leopard's words sank in and she paused in her tracks, glancing back over her shoulder at him. "You know about her noli?" she asked, impressed.

Perseus grinned. "The Tigress, too, must obtain her wares from somewhere. Though I confess, I never would have bartered it to her had I not known what she was going to do with it." He stretched, and Ellishiva imagined that he looked rather pleased with himself. "That noli was not easy to come by. Most spice dust can only be stored in olivine containers, as you know. But this one belonged to someone rather special. Very special indeed."

Torn, Ellishiva stood where she was for a moment, longing to ask him more about the origins of the unusual noli. But then Samara's voice sounded again, closer this time, and she was forced to swallow her questions for a later time.

Perseus smiled at her fondly. "Hurry off then," he said. "And do not forget what I have said to you this day."

Ellishiva's chest was bursting with emotions: excitement that she was on the path to something real and important now, relief that Perseus was here to talk to and to offer her guidance. And more than anything, a new determination to find the general burned in her heart.

With a nod of gratitude, she waved goodbye to the snow leopard and hurried off to wait for Samara behind the tree.

BLACK RAIN

Back in Samara's bedchamber, Ellishiva set the brown chest from Perseus on top of the bed. "Well?" she said, turning to the fairy.

"Try these," replied Samara eagerly, fishing a heavy ring of keys out of her noli and thrusting it at her. Ellishiva eyed them wearily for a moment; there had to be at least thirty or forty of them squeezed onto the silver ring. Still, better options weren't exactly throwing themselves at her feet. With a sigh, she began inserting them into the chest, one by one.

A few minutes later, however, the last of the keys stuck in the lock without success. "Great." Ellishiva pulled it out and tossed the whole useless bundle back to Samara, second thoughts about the accuracy of Perseus's memory running rampant through her head. "You don't have any others?"

Samara lifted her nose primly into the air. "Don't be ridiculous, Elli. This beautiful collection of fine chests," she gestured to the full book-shelves around them, "is impeccably organized. Every key I've ever owned is on this ring." She jingled the bunch of keys in the air for a moment before restoring them to their rightful place in the noli.

Ellishiva ran a hand through her hair and stared at the locked chest.

Samara picked it up and shook it a few times, but nothing made so much as a rattle within. Finally, Ellishiva spoke up. "Well, there's no time to figure it out now," she declared, frustrated. "But I don't want to leave it behind. Sam, would you keep it in your noli? Just in case?"

The fairy was only too delighted to oblige.

"Thanks." Ellishiva's mind was roiling with thoughts. She began to pace the room. "Did you find out anything about the general?" she asked. Then the scent of sweetened hot cacao invaded her nostrils and she paused, surprised, next to the only table in the room—one that, apparently, had been laid out with a small feast in the short time that they'd been away. Restless, Ellishiva leaned over and opened the lid of the nearest pot, revealing cumin-seed biscuits and cinnaquill—sticky cinnamon rollovers with flaky, moist coconut—all of them still warm from the oven. Next to them, the perfume rising from a plate of sweet potatoes baked in their jackets and spiked with cloves made her stomach rumble in spite of herself. "Sam, I don't think you can call this a prison," she grumbled, putting the lid back on the pot with a dull *clink*. "They practically treat you like a queen here. And you've been grounded *how* many times?"

"I have connections," dismissed Samara regally, examining her neat fingernails. "Some of the fairies feel sorry for me, so they bring me news and good food. Anyway, Queen Neive can't let me starve. And besides, Elli, I'm not the one grounded tonight. You are!" she concluded triumphantly. She fluttered over and peered past Ellishiva at the feast. "Do you see any taftnook here? I requested that for supper."

Ellishiva scowled at her and crossed her arms. "Well, they can ground me all they want, but I am *not* going back to Banyan Tree until I find the general. What did you find out about him, anyway? Where is he?" A curl of steam from the sweet potatoes found her nose again, sweet and irresistible. Quickly, she plucked one of the plump, soft cloves from the dish and popped it into her mouth, letting the oils spread, tingling, over her tongue as she chewed it slowly.

"Not going back, huh?" grinned Samara. "You know this makes you an outlaw *and* a runaway, right?"

"Did you find out anything about the general or not?" insisted Ellishiva.

Samara rolled her eyes and took a huge bite out of one of the cinnaquill. "He'll be on Queen Neive's terrace when the concert starts," she said, the words garbled by the bread in her mouth. "I heard some of the kinnarans talking."

Ellishiva nodded slowly. It was better than nothing. Still . . . would it be soon enough? She picked another clove from the yams and set it on her tongue. "Maximus smells like cloves," she murmured to herself distractedly.

"What?" said Samara sharply.

Ellishiva blinked. She'd barely realized that she'd spoken out loud. "I—I mean his sword," she offered haltingly. "It's coated in choji oil, which is . . . made from cloves."

Samara sighed and rolled her eyes. "Elli, I know you like him and just aren't telling me. Confess!" she commanded, brandishing the half-eaten cinnaquill with one hand and pouring herself a cup of hot cacao with the other.

"Don't start with me, Sam. Too much is happening. I don't know how I feel about him," protested Ellishiva. "Wish there was a book on this stuff," she added in a mutter under her breath.

"Love isn't an *appointment*, Elli!" gushed Samara, flying up out of her chair. She posed gallantly in midair and recited, even more dramatically than usual: "'Love doth appear on your doorstep, knocking like a wind of the night, and you must open, yes—open your heart! For being deeply loved by someone must give you strength, whilst loving someone deeply must give you courage." She swept her arms out wide over her head and swooned backward, as if fainting into the embrace of the sky.

"Oh, shut up!" interrupted Ellishiva, striving in vain to smother a grin. She cleared her throat. "You're so ridiculous. Where did you hear that from?"

Samara grinned. "Hektor was reciting it on that lily pad earlier."

Ellishiva bit her lip to keep from laughing. "You know, if you'd put half that much effort into reciting your quarter-term presentations at the academy . . ."

"This is no joke, Elli," interrupted the fairy with a flourish. Then the teasing tone fell out of her voice and she floated down into the chair again, cocking her head. "*Has* a Va'nature ever fallen in love?" she asked, genuinely curious. She packed the last bite of the cinnaquill into her mouth and began licking her fingers.

"No," Ellishiva scoffed. "Of course not. Not *that* way. Geez, Sam, where do you come up with this stuff?"

The fairy shrugged. "Dunno," she admitted simply, her mind already drifting away to a different subject. "Come on, help me eat this. There's too much."

For a few minutes, they busied themselves devouring the feast. Ellishiva picked at the cloves until none remained in the sweet potatoes. Her mind was far away, thinking.

Finally, Ellishiva stretched and roused herself. "Have you seen Baron Puck lately?" she asked, digging the well-worn, folded papyrus note bearing her list of questions about the Sixth Element out of her noli.

"No, I haven't," replied Samara, dabbing her thin lips with a napkin and then tossing the smudged cloth into the now-empty pot on the table. "And I don't expect to, either. He never comes to the Foxfire Harvest. I don't think I've ever even seen him here at Fairy Alcove."

Outside, the dungchen sounded, followed by the cheerful clacking sound of dozens of coconut-shell clappers.

"The concert is starting!" cried Samara. In the blink of an eye she'd flown over to her balcony and was leaning over the railing, peering down at the lily pad-filled pool below.

"We're not here for a concert," Ellishiva huffed, stomping out to the terrace after her. "We're here to answer the questions on this list!" She waved the note in the air. Samara threw a quick glance at it over her shoulder, then made a noncommittal sound and leaned back over the terrace on her elbows again. Ellishiva scowled at her back. "Wish Maximus was here instead of you," she muttered.

Samara didn't hear her. "It's so dark," she commented whimsically, craning her neck back to gaze at the sky over the alcove. "Looks like the moon and stars went into exile or something."

Ellishiva folded the note and stuffed it roughly back inside her noli. "I need a hooded cape," she said tersely. "Before someone recognizes me."

"Oh, Elli. Right *now*?" whined Samara. "It's the opening act! Look, the Macrah dance is starting!"

"Yes, *now*, Sam," Ellishiva snapped quietly. "Since when do you care about Hektor and his stupid dance? It's not like we haven't seen it eighty times before."

"Okay, okay," Samara relented, disappearing quickly into the room again. She hadn't been gone a handful of seconds before Ellishiva heard her gasp. "Elli! Come here. Look! They're stealing Bluzure!"

Ellishiva hurried back into the bedchamber, where Samara was hovering by the large window that overlooked the pond and the meadow. She shouldered her way in beside the fairy and craned her neck to get a good view of Central Pond, around the rim of which clusters of foxfire plants were glowing in the dark. The fairy was right: here and there, dofauns, young elves, and stray fairies were hovering among the plants, dusting the glowing blue spice onto large sheets of papyrus and pouring the result quickly, clumsily, into jars. Once in a while, sparks of red light went up from the wands of patrolling fairies, sending the thieves skittering away.

"Everyone is acting so strange," mused Samara in a muffled voice. The fairy had left the window and was rooting through her closet for the hooded cape again.

"No kidding," Ellishiva muttered back darkly. A shiver went down her spine and she, too, came away from the window, drifting back to the doorway where the brightly lit pool in the center of Fairy Alcove was partly visible. Floating among the lily pads, near the front of a small group of elves, Ellishiva could just make out the iridescent feathers of Lady Malinia perched on one of the wooden stage rafts with Amborella at her side. Not far from them, on the center stage, Hektor and the Wallaby brothers—Nazeem and Hodges—were dancing, their bodies alert and fluid as they moved to a thudding Macrah rhythm. In spite of herself, Ellishiva edged closer until she was back at the balcony railing. All over the floating lily pads and on the surrounding terraces, spectators cheered and danced to the beat along with the performers. She watched as the Wallaby brothers flipped in unison while Hektor, between them, began spinning on one of his hands, drawing a roar of approval from the crowd.

"Here. I know it's not your color," said Samara, materializing out of nowhere and thrusting a lavender hooded cape at her, "but it's the only one I own that isn't flashy."

Ellishiva took the cape and slipped it on, drawing the hood over her head. The pale purple fabric brushed Samara's noli as she arranged it to hang neatly around her shoulders. "You know, I'm pretty sure I saw an orb of fire in your noli when I was in there, Sam," she commented, studying the fairy's face for any hint of guilt.

But Samara was just as surprised as Ellishiva herself had been. "Really?" she said, her eyebrows rising in surprise. "Walle didn't see anything like that. I certainly didn't put anything fire-like in it. Of course, I didn't put those yellow toads in there, either," she added, grinning to herself as she slipped into a crimson hooded cape of her own.

Ellishiva opened her mouth to reply, but was interrupted by a dull hum under her skin. She frowned and glanced down.

"Wow!" gasped Samara, and before Ellishiva knew what was happening, she was being yanked toward the fairy by the collar.

"What! What's the matter?" she whispered urgently, glancing quickly over each of her shoulders.

But Samara wasn't looking behind her. Instead, her eyes were scrutinizing Ellishiva's skin. Her thin lips were pursed in a knot, as if she were trying to decide whether or not she was seeing things. "No, nothing," she mumbled finally. "Thought I saw something glow, but—"

This time it was Ellishiva who seized Samara's collar. "The marks around my neck?" she said, feeling her heartbeat pick up its pace. "Are you sure?"

Samara shook her off. "No. No, it was nothing," she dismissed, turning to look down at the performance over the balcony again.

Ellishiva was unconvinced. In her side, the wound was aching faintly. "Come on, we've got to find the general. Hurry," she said in a clipped tone, turning away from the terrace.

"But Elli, Asia's about to come on," whined Samara. "She's the main event—"

"Not now!" hissed Ellishiva. She stormed back, grabbed Samara by the wrist, and dragged her out into the curved hallway.

As they crept along, keeping out of the warm glow of the oil lamps as much as they could, the sound of the dungchen filled the night once again, announcing the act that everyone had been waiting for. All around the alcove, the squeaks and chirps, growls and grunts, whispers and laughter of the crowd faded away into perfect silence.

"Let's just have a quick look," said Samara, grabbing Ellishiva's elbow and dragging her onto a nearby terrace.

"No!" Ellishiva hissed at her, but it was too late: a few spectators from neighboring balconies had noticed their sudden arrival and were eyeing them with curiosity. She had no choice but to press her lips together and wait for their attention to be drawn elsewhere again.

In the center of the pool below, a new stage raft had appeared, bearing a large lotus. As they watched, the flower began to unfold, each huge petal taking on a different hue as it did so—sapphire blue, moss green, poinsettia red, ocean turquoise, coral pink—until the last of them finally fell onto the surface of the water to reveal a single, smaller white cluster of petals inside. For a moment, the audience held its breath. Then the white bud bloomed open, revealing Asia herself within. She stood perfectly still, letting the gasps of awe and wonder from the crowd unfold around her.

"Wow! She is so beautiful," breathed Samara wistfully. "Wish I had her voice."

"Your voice is one of a kind, Sam," Ellishiva grumbled through her teeth, but she had to admit the fairy was right; Asia did somehow look even more stunning than usual. Her long black hair had been smoothed back into a gleaming bun at the base of her neck, encased with cream-colored lilies of the valley. Her lips had been dabbed with shimmering pink achiote spice. The kimono wrapped around her was made of fine nacre silk painted with cherry blossoms, and its trailing sleeves fell all the way to her tiny feet. But lovely as she was, the ripple of admiring whispers quieted instantly when she opened her mouth to sing.

Asia's voice was so melodious that it seemed a presence in itself, waltzing into the dark night to bless the enraptured crowd. She sang a song of love, betrayal, and rebirth in the Nara tongue, accompanied by the deep, resonating sound of several oudleefs. It was, as always, mesmerizing—mesmerizing enough, Ellishiva noticed at once, to draw the full attention of the fairies on the neighboring terraces away from her and Samara.

"Come on. We've seen enough," she whispered curtly, dragging an unhappy Samara back into the hallway by the elbow. They filed past tall, torch-bearing columns, rising higher and higher toward the queen's own terrace.

They had nearly reached it when a shadow loomed across the path several yards in front of them.

"Someone's coming!" Ellishiva hissed, instinctively pulling Samara behind one of the columns with her.

"Who—?" Samara began.

"Shhh!" Ellishiva snapped under her breath, clamping a firm hand over the fairy's mouth. Moments ticked by. The ambiguous shadow came closer, and closer still, until at last Ellishiva could make out its identity. Her stomach gave an unpleasant flip.

It was Baron Puck.

Samara squirmed under her hand, wanting to see too, but Ellishiva pressed down harder, holding her in place until the baron had turned the corner.

"What was that?" whispered Samara indignantly when Ellishiva finally let go.

Ellishiva ignored her, preoccupied. "That smell," she muttered, narrowing her eyes. Cautiously, she crept out from behind the pillar . . . and felt something wet under her feet. Quickly, she knelt on the floor and touched the trail of shiny spots. She brought her fingers to her nose, and then recoiled. "Blood!" she grimaced, wiping her hand on a dry part of the floor. "The baron is bleeding!"

"The *baron*?" Samara repeated, aghast. "That was—"

"Come on," Ellishiva stopped her bluntly, careful not to step in the blood as she led the way down the hall, following its trail. It took a mere half a minute to catch up to him. Signaling for Samara to follow, Ellishiva hid behind another pillar and peeked around its curved side, listening sharply.

The baron was talking to someone in a hooded cape. "Is she safe?" asked the voice within the hood urgently. "Where is the wand?"

"That's a fairy's voice," Samara breathed into Ellishiva's ear. "I can't see her face."

The baron was stooping slightly, one hand clamped over what must be a wound on his upper leg. "The wand was—" he began in a labored voice. Then the music from the concert swelled in the background, drowning out the rest of the sentence.

Another hum pulsed underneath Ellishiva's skin, and this time there could be no denying the green glow that shone briefly from the marks on her neck.

There was no time to think. Ellishiva grabbed Samara's hand and dragged her back the way they had come, not caring that they were blowing their cover. "We have to find the general. *Now!*" she shouted over the blaring music.

"There!" squeaked Samara in a shocked voice, pointing at one of several sprawling staircases up ahead. Ellishiva shot toward it, her blood booming louder than the echoing beat of the concert in her ears. She reached the steps and turned sharply, charging up them three at a time until she burst, finally, out onto the quaint, green expanse of Queen Neive's own huge terrace. Several attending fairies paused in their duties, staring at her in surprise. A moment later, Samara appeared next to her shoulder, breathless.

"Do you see the general?" Ellishiva barked at her, not caring that several more heads turned her way as she scanned the vast plateau of gardens for him.

Samara flew up a short ways to get a better view. "I think so. Way over there! Another kinnaran just landed beside him and is whispering something in his ear—oh no!"

To Ellishiva's horror, the general rose into the air and followed his soldier off the edge of the terrace, disappearing into the black night.

She was about to sprint across the terrace, shouting his name for all the world to hear, when a third, electrifying hum shot through her. The marks on her skin lit up like hundreds of tiny fireflies, shining brilliant green light into the darkness around her. Several stunned fairies gasped.

"Khlorus," breathed Samara above her, awestruck.

Before anyone could move, however, there was a commotion, and suddenly a flood of fairies and kinnarans was flying by, arcing over the top of the alcove toward the meadow below. Ellishiva rushed to the outer edge of the terrace and peered over, Samara at her heels.

The meadow was in chaos. Everywhere, the citizens who had chosen not to attend the concert ran or flew for their lives. Yurts were crushed, fireflies in lanterns were tossed aside, trapped in their containers, and heaps of Bluzure spice dust lay abandoned around Central Pond like glowing ant nests. And above it all, driving the madness onward, the cause of all this destruction . . .

Ellishiva's stomach dropped like a stone. She jumped over the railing, latching onto some of the hanging vines. "Follow me!" she shouted over her shoulder at Samara. "We've got to get to the dungchen!"

"What's happening Elli?" cried Samara frantically, hovering at the railing.

"Fly! *Move!*" Ellishiva bellowed at her, springing down from vine to vine until she landed, hard, on the dungchen terrace.

Samara landed uncertainly beside her, her eyes still darting and frantic.

Ellishiva could see the green glow from the marks on her neck and shoulders growing stronger, brighter. She dragged Samara over to the dungchen and shoved her toward the mouthpiece of the far one, latching onto the closer one herself. "Blow!" she yelled over the growing roar of noise coming from both within and beyond the alcove. "*Blow!*"

As one, they inhaled huge, chest-swelling breaths and blew hard into the dungchen. Then they did it again and again—until Asia finally stopped singing in the alcove and the thundering beat of the oudleef instruments ceased.

In the music's wake, a terrible symphony arose from Central Pond—a maelstrom of horrible, frenzied screams, grunts, chirps, snorts, and squeals, rising inexorably into the dark sky and flooding into the safe haven of Fairy Alcove itself.

In the meadow far below Ellishiva, Central Pond had become a swirling pit of darkness. Flying up from its depths as if through an open gate, iridescent creatures as big as Banog but with fire-red eyes called and screamed, clotting the sky with beaks and feathers. Then, like a calculated attack from one of her human history books, thousands of black splinters dropped from their claws and fell toward the spinning void of Central Pond below. The pond swallowed them whole and, for a moment, all the world seemed deathly silent.

Then, with a rumble like a thousand herds of charging buffalo, the splinters mushroomed to the surface again—as long as lances now—and exploded into the air. They plummeted to the earth like arrows, as if shot by an archer with hundreds of arms, glimmering in the dark like black rain.

Ellishiva shoved away from the dungchen, scaled the vine-covered basalt wall, and was standing on the inner lip of Fairy Alcove's uppermost level before Samara—even with wings—could catch up. "Ravens!" she bellowed, her voice echoing around the circular space below. "The Sixth Element is here! *Keep the ravens at bay!*"

Her words sparked an eruption of movement within the alcove. She turned and sprinted back to the outer edge of the terrace. Below, the waters of Central Pond glistened like tar. All around its edge, the bountiful clusters of foxfire plants had ignited, forming a ring of fire. The long, lance-like black splinters poured to the ground in an endless storm, and fairies and kinnarans dodged them in midair as they waged war against the screaming ravens with indiscriminate ferocity. Everywhere, the sky was filled with glints of black feathers and flashes of deadly red spells.

"Elli!" Ellishiva turned to find Samara yanking at her sleeve, trying to drag her back toward the inside of the alcove. The fairy's eyes were round and huge. Ellishiva glanced into the round hollow beneath them and saw why.

The pool below had devolved into a riot chaotic enough to rival the scene outside. Wooden stages had been overturned in the water. Everywhere, dofauns, elves, and fairies were screaming and crying amidst a sea of fear and pain. Dozens upon dozens of gaily clad creatures trampled each other as they ran for dear life, though where they were running to Ellishiva couldn't guess. Those who could fly did not make it far beyond the alcove before being intercepted by the ravens.

Transfixed by the horror of the scene, it took Ellishiva a moment to realize that Samara was still tugging at her arm. She followed the fairy's pointing finger to a specific spot in the middle of the chaos and her blood froze in her veins.

"Lady Malinia!" she shrieked. The caretaker was lying unconscious on a wooden stage in the pool below, her beautiful feathers being trampled by dofauns and elves alike as the never-ending mob fought to gain safety. Not far from the raft, Amborella had fallen into the water and was struggling to keep hold of a lily pad. Its huge green leaves jerked and shook under the weight of the stampede.

Ellishiva turned back to the fairy at her side. "Sam, go help Amber!" she yelled into her ear. "I'll get Lady Malinia!"

Without a word, Samara disappeared over the edge of the terrace. Ellishiva latched onto another solid network of vines and swung after her, bounding from terrace to terrace. A huge black splinter nearly grazed her shoulder and she cursed. The assault outside must be gaining ground.

She had nearly reached the bottom of the alcove when a familiar hiss flooded the dark night.

"Find her! I want no one else. Find the First Spice! Come to me, spice girl, and I will spare the rest!"

Ellishiva nearly lost her grip on the vines. She glanced around to see if anyone else had heard the Sixth Element's demand, but no one had. The voice was speaking only in her mind.

A squeal—also familiar—drew her attention sharply back to the pond again. Amborella was losing her grip on the lily pad. Nearby, Samara was struggling to make her way down to her, fighting against a tide of distraught, outgoing white mosquitoes and honeybees.

Pressing her lips into a grim line, Ellishiva bounded down the last two levels of terraces and then swung from one final vine over the heads of a large part of the crowd to land on the corner of one of the less crowded wooden stages. She glanced up and her eyes locked with Hektor's. Her brother was perched on the edge of a half-sunken raft a short ways away. As if reading each other's thoughts, they began to hop toward one another across the stages and lily pads, dodging the crowds as best they could.

Ellishiva had nearly reached him when another splinter came down inches behind her heels, severing the tip of the lily pad she was standing on. Before she could plunge into the water, however, Hektor had grabbed her arms and dragged her onto his wooden stage, which bobbed under their weight. Nor was that the end of it.

"Move!" Ellishiva yelled, throwing her weight to the side and dragging him with her as another black spike hit the stage, splitting it in half like the shell of a pistachio nut. The broken raft tossed on the rough water, and Ellishiva and Hektor abandoned ship, leaping to another bobbing stage covered in a mess of spilled crates nearby.

"Where's Lady Malinia?" shouted Hektor as soon as he'd caught his breath.

"Over there on that stage!" Ellishiva shouted back, pointing. Only one battered wing tip of the unconscious dofaun was visible through the throng of panicked creatures now. Around them, black spears continued to puncture the alcove, and the screams of fairies and dofauns were deafening. Ellishiva felt her stomach turn. It was unstoppable.

Come to me, spice girl, and I will spare the rest.

Drawing a deep breath, Ellishiva set her jaw, and looked at Hektor. "Go help Lady Malinia! I'm going to the meadow!" she told him.

"No, Elli!" cried Hektor, and in his eyes she could see all of her own stubbornness reflected back at her. "Stay here!"

"I'll come back!" Ellishiva barked. She turned to sprint away, but a hand clamped down on her upper arm like one of Banog's iron claws, dragging her down among the crates. "Let go, Hektor!" Ellishiva hissed at him, trying to kick free of his grip. But Hektor only held her harder.

Above them, a fresh swarm of ravens swooped over Fairy Alcove. Ellishiva watched in horror as they dove at random, snatching up anything that moved in their talons and flinging their victims onto the basalt rocks and terraces at will. Bodies splashed into the pool as the huge splinters continued to fall like rain. The battlefront had moved inside now, and fairies shot fiery Rojorine spells at the attackers, knocking them out of the sky. Before long, the water around Ellishiva was peppered with bobbing chunks of burning black feathers.

"I have to go, Hektor!" she screamed, furious. "It's the only way she'll stop killing!"

"She'll kill *you!*" Hektor shouted back, his voice fierce and desperate.

She had no choice. Forcing her guilt down to be dealt with later, Ellishiva bent her arm and tapped him on a spot at the base of his neck—one of the pressure points of payamar. Hektor gasped and his hold on her slackened for a moment. Seizing her chance, Ellishiva wriggled out of his grasp, but she hadn't hit him hard enough, and before she could escape Hektor had latched onto her ankle with both hands, making her fall flat on her belly. She struggled and kicked at him, the blood thundering in her head as she fought to get free. A dead raven fell into the pool nearby, rocking the raft.

"No, Elli! I won't let you!" shouted Hektor doggedly.

And then, quite suddenly, his grip went slack.

Ellishiva glanced over her shoulder at him, and the rest of the world dimmed into a vague, distant fog. "*Hektor!*" she screamed. A huge black splinter had stabbed straight through the crate behind him and punctured his upper chest, spearing him like a brochette. She could see its sharp point oozing a toxic yellow substance where it jutted out from just below his left shoulder, poisoning him.

"Hektor!" Ellishiva gasped again. "*Hektor!*" She crawled to him on her hands and knees, ignoring the rocking of the stage, and took his head in her hands. It was as limp as an unwatered tulip.

A surge of pure anger shot through her. She yanked the black lance out of her brother's chest and hurled it away into the water, nostrils flaring. Inside, her chest felt ready to burst. She bent over Hektor and, acting on instinct, pressed her hands to the open wounds on his back and shoulder.

At once, a green wave of Khlorus spice dust pulsed from her palms and sank, like water on a desert floor, into his body. The yellow poison on his skin sizzled and snapped, crackling away into nothing. With her hands, Ellishiva could feel his blood purging the toxins from his veins, as well. Under the energy pouring from her fingertips, the broken green skin on his body closed and mended. The bleeding stopped.

Finally, Hektor gave a moan and stirred. He'd barely lifted his head half a foot, however, before he collapsed again, exhausted, onto her lap like a sleeping baby.

Ellishiva wiped her hands on her short pants and looked around. Her heart was pounding like a monster on a rampage. In her lap, Hektor moaned weakly. She shot her gaze around the alcove, just daring a raven to be within reach, but her eyes fell on Asia and Bairon struggling to climb up the railing of a nearby terrace instead. Asia's beautiful kimono had been bunched up around her knees, the long sleeves tied in rough knots to keep them from getting in the way.

Shifting Hektor off of her lap, Ellishiva clambered to her feet and cupped her hands around her mouth. "Asia! *Asia!*" she hollered with every ounce of strength her lungs could muster. "Bairon!"

On the terrace, the elf girl and boy swung their heads around sharply. Bairon spotted her first and signaled to Asia. Together, they abandoned their attempt to scale the terrace and jumped onto a broken wooden stage below, picking their way over wreckage and damaged lily pads toward Ellishiva.

"Get Hektor out of here!" Ellishiva ordered Bairon as soon as they reached the crate-filled stage. "Asia, go help Lady Malinia. She's over there!"

Before the bewildered elves could respond, however, someone else was shouting her name. "Elli!" She looked up to find Samara swooping down to them, deftly dodging a splinter as she came. "Amber is safe," she announced, tapping her noli. Then she saw Hektor, and the blood drained out of her face.

"Sam, help Asia and Bairon get Hektor out. All of you, don't forget Lady Malinia! I need to go."

Almost before the words were out of her mouth, Ellishiva was bounding away, not waiting to hear or see anyone's reaction this time. She was choking with rage. As soon as she reached the edge of the pool, she stopped and looked up. Perched on a terrace high above, a lone raven was watching the attack with cold, beady eyes. It would do. Without hesitation, Ellishiva raised one arm in its direction, so that her palm was facing outward, and concentrated.

A lone spot of green light bloomed among the sea of red and black.

Above, the raven saw and left its perch. Ellishiva leapt up and got hold of a strong vine. Her racing heartbeat and her pumping blood were neck and neck as she watched it approach, waiting for her moment . . .

An instant before the raven's talons could close around her, Ellishiva kicked away from the terrace and, using the solid vine, swung herself onto the evil creature's back. She locked her knees behind its neck as it cawed and banked left, then stabilized. It had what it wanted, after all; so much the better if she wanted to come willingly. Quickly, they began to rise out of the pit of chaos that had become Fairy Alcove.

A fresh rain of splinters plunged by as they crested the uppermost basalt terrace, and Ellishiva unthinkingly reached out her arm, focusing on the nearest one. Almost immediately it changed its course, flying into her hand, where she wielded it firmly like the lance it resembled. Below, the raven cawed at her, but continued on its course, straight toward the vortex of Central Pond. The wind planted tiny ice crystals on her face and skin, making her shiver. *When faced with fear, change your ways. When faced with fear . . .*

In the sky around her, the black rain of huge splinters ceased. For a moment, Ellishiva was puzzled. Then she realized that the Sixth Element must be keeping her word. *Come to me, spice girl, and I will spare the rest.* The reinforcements of ravens, too, were being held in check where they rose from the depths of the black pond, though a great number continued to wreak havoc on the ground and in the air below. Ellishiva squinted down into the meadow. Kinnarans, fairies, elves, and dofauns were still fighting for their lives. Some carried the weak and wounded to safety. She spotted Atticus and Perseus crouched back to back, fending off more than their share of attackers. Still, little by little, the defenders were losing ground.

Steeling her nerves, Ellishiva spurred the raven on faster.

Before they could reach Central Pond, however, they flew over a battle where the invaders did not have the upper hand. Ellishiva glanced down to find Queen Neive and several kinnarans making short work of several corralled ravens. Unfortunately, at the same moment Ellishiva looked down, the queen looked up.

A jolt of surprise passed over her blood-spattered face. Then, "Get back here, Ellishiva!" she yelled, firing a stream of red light at Ellishiva's raven. Its tail feathers went up in flames and it began to shriek, swooping through the air in circles while Ellishiva tightened her grip on its neck, struggling to hold on. She was almost right above the fire-encircled pond now and, through the dizzying swoops of the raven, she could see that its surface had taken on a black shine as something new gathered within. As she watched, red slits began to appear in the darkness, just as they had on the trunk of the locust tree in the woods. And, finally, in the middle of it all, a pulsing silver light began to grow.

"The ice fairy's heart," Ellishiva breathed, almost losing her grip on the writhing raven underneath her.

The marks on her skin glowed brighter than ever before. Below, the dark waters of Central Pond began to sweep upward, coiling higher and higher like ten thousand twisting anacondas. Dread and determination warred inside Ellishiva as she watched it rise. In her grip, the black splinter that she had managed to hold on to glowed green and then disintegrated into a spear of light, consumed by the Khlorus within her.

"Do it now, Ellishiva!"

Ellishiva jerked her head to the side and was stunned to see the general hovering in the air not far from her, fighting off three ravens that were picking viciously at his armor, struggling to keep him away. "Now! Focus!" he yelled at her, severing one of the ravens' heads with his tongobiri sword.

Before Ellishiva could reply, the hiss of the rising creature in the pond below filled her head again.

"Come to me, First Spice, for we are one. We are sisters."

"Now, Ellishiva! Do it *now!*" bellowed the general, sending another of the huge birds around him plummeting to the earth below.

Ellishiva struggled to steady herself on the jerking raven, but it was impossible. Thoughts ricocheted through her head like loud echoes in a hollow cave.

When faced with fear . . .

Come to me, spice girl, and I will spare the rest . . .

Change your ways . . .

We are one. We are sisters . . .

When faced with fear, change your ways. Change your ways.

Everything she had been taught, everything she had taught *herself* in the Arboretum, came together within her like a gathering storm. A few feet away, the general sent the last of his attackers plunging to the ground, dead. Under her, the raven tossed and screamed. The green shard of light in Ellishiva's palm became blindingly bright. In her head, every thought disappeared, save one.

I am stronger.

And with that, she jumped off the raven toward the rising horror below. Khlorus surged through her veins, lending her strength. Ellishiva threw the shard of light into the writhing darkness, a stream of blinding green spice dust following it into the heart of the monster like an endless tail.

Instantly, the water collapsed into a black hole again. The shadows on its surface twisted as if in pain. Ellishiva was inches from the swirling blackness when a pair of heavy, armor-covered arms snatched her out of the air. It was the general, she realized, dazed.

A horrible screeching sound filled the meadow, and the hiss filled Ellishiva's head once more, angrier than she had ever heard it before.

"It is not over, First Spice. Face me on the last quarter moon in the river, or all shall perish."

Then all the Khlorus Ellishiva had sent into the black depths of the creature seemed to burst to the surface of the water again, sending green rings of light rippling over Central Pond. In its wake, the earth gave one tremendous rumble. Then it was still.

Ellishiva swallowed. Then she swallowed again. She had never felt so utterly exhausted in her life. Above her, the general cleared his throat. With an effort, she managed to look up into his sweat-drenched, blood-smeared face.

"I heard you were looking for me," he said.

Ellishiva stared at him for another second. Then she dropped her head onto the shoulder of his armor and let him carry her home.

DEEP SCARS

Summer was nearly over, but there was no relief from the sweltering heat. In the hallways of Banyan Tree and Fairy Alcove, the tents that had been set up to care for the injured had only just begun to be taken down. Still, the keepers of the Hall of Nature Healing—Gustav, Onuris, and Rajah—continued to work day and night, making home visits to the many victims of the attack.

Although Ellishiva had saved his life, Hektor's wound still troubled him, and he remained in the Hall where Rajah and the fireflies could keep a close eye on him. Lady Malinia, on the other hand, was already back on her feet, and the first words out of her beak, once she'd regained consciousness, were to insist that Ellishiva not leave the warren. But she had added that Ellishiva's friends could visit her, and Ellishiva suspected that the order was intended to keep her safe, rather than to hold her to her previous punishment of being grounded.

There was no question that Mannahatta had changed forever. The feeling of safety that had wrapped its wings around her all her life had been shattered, and many of the citizens who had survived the attack were leaving the colony for good. Nor was what had happened being kept a secret. Indeed, headlines across the colonies of the world—from her own *Times* to *The Nicobar Post*—spoke of nothing else: *"Massacre on Mannahatta," "The Wrath of the Sixth Element."*

Each day, Ellishiva scanned *The Mannahatta Times* for her name, but it seemed that even the Tigress of Sundari had been too caught up in the chaos to notice what she had done.

Busy with his rounds of caring for the sick and wounded, Rajah was just as hard to get ahold of as ever. In his absence, Ellishiva continued her work in the Arboretum, disappearing so deeply into various sections of it that even Walle and Samara had a hard time finding her. Which, of course, was exactly what she wanted. Many questions weighed heavily on her mind, and it was easiest to think about them when she was alone. One in particular puzzled her more than the others.

"Face me on the last quarter moon in the river, or all shall perish."

The Sixth Element had once before threatened destruction on the last quarter moon. Yet there had been no grand attack that night, and she had struck instead at the Foxfire Harvest—which had not taken place on the night of a last quarter moon. In fact, all the evidence suggested that the Sixth Element didn't care about the moon cycle at all. But if the last quarter moon she referred to wasn't the real moon in the sky . . .

Then what was it?

Ellishiva spent hours puzzling over this question without success. As she did, she wandered through the foliage, looking for trees with broken branches and spotted, yellow, or dull leaves. The seedlings in the Vivarium were no longer a challenge for her. Here in the huge landscapes of the Arboretum, her newfound skills sought worthier challenges. Ellishiva trained her focus—the care and pressure of her touches. Always, the broken branches mended; the leaves regained their former luster, shining brilliantly anew in the sun. One day she stumbled across a crushed bird's nest next to a freshly fallen birch. That one had taken much longer to fix than the others. Nevertheless, she had knelt beside the tree, laid her hands on its whitewashed trunk and, finally, the lotus toe ring had bloomed halfway to help her, adding just a few swirls of its green, silken threads of light to the Khlorus flowing from her palms. Slowly, the tree had righted itself, planting its strong roots in the black earth once more, its branches laden with new leaves. And tucked among the limbs sat the bird's nest: whole again, and waiting for new tenants.

Ellishiva was pleased about the toe ring, and she continued to practice on bigger and bigger trees, nudging the ring to bloom a little wider and to add a few more of its silken strings to her own Khlorus each time. She had come far, and she knew it. Nevertheless, her greatest test was still ahead, and somewhere deep inside herself she knew that the toe ring would need to burst open and spew not just a handful, but millions of its powerful, glowing strands—just as she had seen Amma's do in her spice dust—if she were to stand a chance of defeating the Sixth Element once and for all.

After a few days, she returned to the Lapita pitcher-plant vivarium. For a few minutes, she sat crouched down between the shrubs at the edge of it, her heart beating a steady rhythm in her chest. Wet strands of her long hair clung to her face and shoulders from the thick, rolling mist. Her shorts and her thin-strapped top were covered in dirt from a long morning of tending to withered tree roots. In the vivarium, the pitcher plants rustled warily, as though they could sense an intruder. Ellishiva waited patiently. Around her neck, the light weight of Hektor's acorn choker breathed with her—in and out.

As soon as the pitcher plants had settled a bit, she jumped to her feet and sprinted straight into the patch, quick as a flash of lightning. It was a few seconds before the surprised plants thought to send their roots after her, and even when they did, Ellishiva dodged them all with ease. Even when a tendril at last succeeded in tossing her high up into the air, she was able to gracefully control her descent again, landing far away from their wide, hungry mouths.

A minute later she exited the patch, slime-free and triumphant. Panting, she bent to rest her palms on her knees. The acorn pendant swayed softly, still hanging securely around her neck.

"The beauty of a tree is not its flower, but watching it grow."

Ellishiva snapped upright again and jerked her head toward the voice. A short ways away, Rajah was standing still among the trees, watching her. The Morpho butterfly she had brought to life sat perched on the orb of his staff beside him, opening and folding its wings lazily.

Ellishiva pretended not to notice the butterfly. "Wh—what are you doing here?" she said, still a little breathless.

"Observing you, for the moment," replied Rajah, gently. "You have indeed been reaching for the light." He opened his arms wide.

Part of Ellishiva longed to run into them, as she had always done all her life. But another, stronger part of her was stiff and angry. She stood where she was and stared at him.

Rajah lowered his arms. In his hand, his staff shook a bit. The butterfly stretched its wings at the disturbance.

"I see you've felt my absence," he murmured. "A hug or a kiss from my full moon is not to be expected." He looked away from her for a moment, up at the high canopy of the Arboretum as if composing himself.

My full moon. Ellishiva felt a dull pang in her chest. She hadn't heard the endearment in so long that even his voice sounded strange to her. She swallowed and wiped her sweaty face with the back of one dirt-smeared hand.

"Come walk with me, Ellishiva," requested Rajah, calm again. Ellishiva hesitated only a moment before she obeyed, falling into step beside him as he strode off, away from the pitcher plants. "There are still a great many lessons I need to teach you. Too many for anyone to absorb in such a short space of time. The events unfolding in our peaceful colony are so shocking and unexpected that even I cannot fully comprehend them." He gave a sigh that seemed to come from the bottom of his soul and looked at her askance. "Someday, I hope, you will understand that my actions were only to protect you."

"Why?" Ellishiva blurted angrily, halting in her tracks. Next to her, Rajah stopped also. Their eyes locked. "I was in my spice dust, Rajah, as you know. I saw why I was born. Not because someone wanted me out of—out of *love*, but because Amma needed me to be a—to be an instrument. A weapon against the Sixth Element." She let out a bitter, painful breath. Her lips trembled and she could feel her nerves beginning to go limp like Amborella's Dollie Burlap.

For a moment, Rajah said nothing. Ellishiva watched as his chest fell and rose, and fell and rose again, as if his heart were struggling to burst free of it. At last he said, in a low rumble, "You are brave, Ellishiva. I know of what you did at Central Pond. You have cultivated your inner strength to serve you well. All on your own." He took a deep breath and fixed her with a stern look. "But one must never walk into a storm blindfolded. That which is needed to defeat the Sixth Element now, more than all else, is patience."

He turned and walked on, leading the way down the path ahead. Ellishiva followed in silence. The long, lovely vines draped between the tall trees did not enchant her as they usually did, nor did the bees buzzing from flower to flower, nor the faint chirps of baby birds tucked into nests high above. Her mind was seething with dark thoughts.

Suddenly, the Morpho butterfly swooped down past her right ear in a flash of bluish-green iridescence. For just a brief instant, the darkness inside Ellishiva was suspended as she watched the light wink off of its body, listened to the soft, strong pulse of its wingbeats. Then life came crashing back to her, and she remembered that there was no longer any room for such beautiful, fragile creatures in it. Scowling, she brushed at the side of her head. The butterfly flew away and landed on Rajah's staff again, eyeing her warily with wilted antennae.

The elder Va'nature could not have seen the exchange. Nevertheless, he gave another sigh and murmured as he walked, "Patience, dear child.

I too must abide by it. You are called by destiny, and I, by duty. Duties I must follow, whether I would or no."

"My destiny," snorted Ellishiva resentfully. Her scowl deepened as she stared at his back. "Who gave me my destiny? Where has she been? Amma. Where has she been all this time? Why hasn't she come here even once to speak to me?"

Rajah did not reply right away. Rather, he looked up at the canopy above them, and then down to the vegetation at the edge of the pathway. His gait slowed and he leaned over to touch one of many golden fruits the size of large papayas that hung together against a backdrop of glossy leaves and vines. "Look at the size of these granadillas," he murmured. "Rare indeed. We must give some to Mr. Guo. Perhaps he can make a granadilla fizz of them and add it to his recipe book." He gently plucked one of the fruits, still attached to its long vine, and brought it to his nose. Then he held it out for Ellishiva to smell as well.

Ellishiva didn't even glance at it. Her eyes were fixed on her guardian, and her insides felt as though they were on fire. Even now, when he stood before her again at last, he was just as far away as he had been when he was in Nicobar.

Slowly, Rajah withdrew the granadilla. He looked down into her eyes, meeting her stare with one of his own. "Fear or rage must never be what motivates you, child," he counseled at last, and there was something tired in his voice. "Do not blind your eyes from the inside." He turned and began striding down the path again. "We used to practice yoga every day, you and I," he said without turning his head. "I suggest you continue it, along with your payamar."

But Ellishiva was not about to be put off so easily. "Tell me about the Madagascar Massacre," she demanded, the blood simmering through her veins. "What really happened on the Isle of Bandalara? Who died there?"

This time, Rajah froze in his tracks like a garden statue amidst the lush vegetation. Ellishiva braced herself for a long argument, but when at last he spoke, her guardian did not avoid her question a second time. "Terrible things happened on Bandalara, child," he told her quietly, not looking back at her. "Many creatures, many Va'natures from our world perished that day, fighting to rescue the nutmeg seed from the fires that the humans set. We succeeded, though at a heavy cost. Amma herself planted that last nutmeg seed—now become the first one—in the human world. From it, all other nutmegs are descended."

Ellishiva nodded, her suspicions confirmed. "You saved that seed yourself. That was the tree you fell from, the one that gave you the scar on your neck."

"Yes," confirmed Rajah, and this time he turned his head to peer down at her, his eyes sharp and curious. "I see you have sought out spice dust other than your own in your investigation."

Ellishiva did not reply.

Rajah pressed the fingers of one hand to his temples for a moment, letting his eyelids fall closed. When he opened them again they were soft and nostalgic. "Remember when you were younger," he began, mustering a half-smile that seemed to hold as much pain as it did joy, "you used to cover this same scar with any broad leaf you found in the Arboretum, telling me not to worry, for it would go away. But what did I always answer you, back then?" He paused, and his green fingers absently drifted up to touch the scar in question.

Ellishiva felt a tiny crack work its way into her armor of anger as she looked into his eyes. In them, there was a familiar tableau of loss and grief. It was, she realized, her own pain reflected back at her.

She took a shaky breath and answered, "'A scar on a tree is a record of what has happened. Learn from it. And when faced with fear, change your ways.'" As she spoke, her hand touched her own fresh scar on her midriff.

Rajah nodded and took a step closer. Ellishiva made no move to stop him as he reached out his hand to comb a lock of her messy hair behind her ear, nor when he gently brushed his thumb over her dirt-stained cheek, leaving her skin clean again. For the first time since the night of her attack, she allowed herself to feel how much she'd missed his touch—his calm, wise words. She waited for him to speak again, hanging on the shadow that still lingered in his eyes.

"Our home colony was Madagascar," explained Rajah quietly, though he seemed to be talking to himself as much as to her. "We were simply carrying on with our duties on Bandalara, nurturing new seedlings for the good of all life on this earth. When the humans came and set the plantation ablaze, we were trapped—dofauns, Va'natures, kinnarans, elves, fairies, and others too. Our children were so young . . . so brave. So many perished, that day . . ." He trailed off and his eyes were far away, seeing something that she could not.

"That's why they call it the Madagascar Massacre," whispered Ellishiva.

"Yes. Rumors live longer when they have nice names," said Rajah, an edge of bitterness in his voice. "I will forever be haunted by those words, Madagascar Massacre. And now it seems I have another such pair, Mannahatta Massacre, to keep them company."

They stood in silence for a long moment, staring up at the swaying tree-tops above. A sudden gust of wind rippled through the high branches, shaking the leaves and sending a startled flock of yellow-bellied birds bursting out across the vast Arboretum.

"The Sixth Element has taken someone's voice," Ellishiva murmured at last, thoughtfully. "Do you know who it belongs to?"

For the briefest of instants, she thought she saw Rajah's shoulders tense. Then he gave another weary sigh and she was sure she had imagined it. "My dearest full moon," he said, lowering his tired eyes to meet hers again. "Some questions are better left unanswered." He set his hand on top of her head.

Ellishiva pulled away, frowning. "Is Maximus alive?" she persisted, trying a different question. "Did they find him yet? Have they looked in the roots underneath the colony?" The roots were a theory of hers. Maximus had been missing for so long, and he had disappeared without a trace. It seemed more likely with every passing day that, fleeing the Sixth Element, he might have wandered into the huge system of roots that ran beneath Mannahatta Island and gotten lost down there.

Rajah's grip tightened on his staff. Inside the orb, Khlorus spice dust whirled up restlessly, startling the Morpho butterfly, who fluttered over it for a few moments, eyeing the glowing dust warily. "The general and the others are still looking for Maximus," Rajah told her curtly. This time, there was no mistaking the tension in his shoulders. "They will find him, not you. *You*, Ellishiva, should not be looking for a boy." He spoke the words with finality, banging the tip of his staff against the ground once, like a gavel. The Morpho butterfly fluttered around the orb in protest. "In any case," her guardian went on, his voice cool and businesslike again, "I sought you out for a reason, Ellishiva. You are needed in the Hall. Come with me." He turned and set off briskly toward the kitchen entrance to the warren without another glance at her.

Ellishiva followed silently on his heels, holding her tongue with an effort. Questions tumbled over one another in her head. How could Rajah show so little compassion for the missing kinnaran boy? She furrowed her eyebrows. Lady Malinia had also had a strange reaction to Maximus, she remembered, when she'd mentioned him in the market that day. What was it all about? Could it have something to do with the tension she'd seen between Rajah and the general in the Hall, on the evening of the last quarter moon?

Her most pressing question of all, however, could not seem to help bubbling to her lips.

"Why do you need me in the Hall of Nature Healing?" she demanded of her guardian's back.

Once again, Rajah did not glance back when he replied. "The spear that pierced Hektor during the attack seems to have left a small splinter deep in his chest. That is why his recovery has been delayed. I need you to dislodge it for him."

Ellishiva bit her bottom lip as they entered the warren, crossed the living area, and turned down the L-shaped passage toward the Hall. It made sense; Hektor had been lying in his sickbed for days now without improvement. An echo of the rage she had felt on the night of the attack bubbled up in her, and she forced herself to press it down again, blowing it out of her with a deep yoga breath.

They walked through the living spice-water doors of the Hall of Nature Healing. Within, the room was almost silent; even the fireflies were not hovering here and there on gently humming wings. A cloud of Silverdine spice dust drifted peacefully near the ceiling, recording. In some far corner of the Hall, something steadily dripped—*splat, splat, splat*—on the hard wooden floor.

And in the center of it all, Hektor lay on the Neem Table, as still as the scene around him.

Rajah approached her brother's side and bent, checking on his patient. At once, his face grew grave. "Come, Ellishiva," he whispered urgently. "He is bleeding again. We must not waste time."

Ellishiva joined him at the table, but froze when she saw Hektor. His eyes were closed and his breathing was shallow. There was no question that he looked worse—frailer and paler—than he'd been when she'd seen him the night before. A dull pain began to spread through her, as though she were feeling with his nerves and not her own.

Then Rajah's hand was on her shoulder, as steady and calm as she had always known it to be, lending her strength.

"Ellishiva," he said solemnly. "All your life I have taught you many things, and now the time has come to use one of great importance. Place your palms on your brother's temples."

Ellishiva took a shaky breath and obeyed.

"Good," Rajah encouraged quietly. "Now close your eyes and focus your mind on mantra number twenty-eight. Remember, what have I always told you to do in times of joy or sorrow?"

"I must feel that joy or sorrow as my own," recited Ellishiva in a low voice.

Rajah nodded. Ellishiva closed her eyes and concentrated. Inside her, a strong feeling—one that she was beginning to associate with the power of Khlorus—began to stir.

"Now," whispered Rajah's distant voice, guiding her like a flicker of light at the end of a long tunnel, "say the mantra three times."

Almost without her, Ellishiva's lips began to form the ancient words of wisdom that he had taught her so long ago.

"Tikicchati ima itthatta! Katākāra kando nissesa! Tikicchati ima itthatta! Katākāra kando nissesa! Tikicchati ima itthatta! Katākāra kando nissesa!"

The power within her was growing—not violently, like a storm, but with the steady strength of a rising tide. It flooded through her veins, as soothing as spring rain, washing away the aching pain she felt—that Hektor felt, lying still on the table before her.

"Open your eyes, Ellishiva," instructed Rajah's calm, faraway voice.

Ellishiva lifted her eyelids slowly, as if waking from a deep dream. Her palms were spewing Khlorus more powerfully than they ever had before—dust as strong and vibrant as that which Amma had used to revive Symran in her spice jar. And yet, strangely, this did not surprise her. She felt like the sound of Rajah's voice—as calm as a vast, silent sea without a wrinkle.

"Continue," instructed her guardian. In the back of her mind, Ellishiva mused that his gaze as he watched her was far sharper than his quiet, soothing words. "Repeat the mantra, but do so only in your mind this time."

Ellishiva nodded and her lips never moved as the mantra repeated itself, over and over again, in her mind. Her measured breathing matched its rhythm, calling upon the deep wells of power and compassion that dwelled within her.

She looked down at Hektor's face.

As she did so, the marks around her neck began to glow, softly at first, and then a bright, fierce green. Like the mist from Banyan Falls, Khlorus engulfed Hektor's body, blazing like green fire when it reached the wound in his chest. And suddenly, she knew. As if she had known it all along. As if it were no more difficult than breathing.

Ellishiva opened her lotus toe ring.

The cornsilk strands of bright green light spiraled upward and found Hektor's injury immediately, as though they had been following a map. There was a small, intense flash of light.

Then, as if someone were pouring the youth and strength back into him, Hektor stirred on the Neem Table.

"You may let go now, Ellishiva," said Rajah. His voice was heavy with exhaustion and relief, but there was something else in it as well. Something, she thought, like pride.

Obediently, Ellishiva relaxed, but the Khlorus dust continued to twirl in the air around them. Rajah inhaled a long breath. Then he took Ellishiva's head gently in his hands and pressed both thumbs between her eyebrows, as he used to do when he wanted to tell her something important. "Remember this, Ellishiva," he murmured, looking straight into her eyes. "The mantras are mere tools. You have the power to control Khlorus without them. Listen and observe, and you will awaken the inner eye of wisdom. Always, it will give you strength."

Then he released her and, just like that, took up his staff and left the Hall, the Morpho butterfly trailing along after its stolen perch.

Ellishiva watched him go. Her instincts were screaming at her—screaming something that she didn't want to hear. Rajah was hiding something. A lifetime of studying his face made that clear. An ache, much like the one she'd felt when Amma had denied she was her mother, rolled through her. For so long, she had believed that Rajah's teachings had purpose, had meaning. Well, she had been right, hadn't she? Ellishiva thought bitterly. Amma had brought her to life to confront the Sixth Element, and Rajah's lessons had been preparing her to do exactly that.

She closed her eyes. Whatever his reasons, Rajah was right about one thing: anger did nothing but blind you from within. In her heart, the seed of acceptance had already been planted, and it was sprouting. There was no going back to change the past, so there was no point wishing things had been different. All she had the power to do was to go forward . . . to write her path as best she could.

Even if it was a given destiny.

On the Neem Table, Hektor inhaled a deep, loud breath. Ellishiva opened her eyes and looked down at him. He was eyeing his healed wound with wonder, his eyelids—sticky with sleep—blinking in the light of the remaining strands of Khlorus that still twirled all around them. Then he set his head back on the table again and saw Ellishiva standing over him.

For a moment, neither one of them said anything. Then, hesitantly, Hektor reached one hand up toward her. His finger touched the acorn necklace he had given her, still tied securely around her neck.

Ellishiva smiled down at him wryly. "I hope you believe me now, Hektor," she said, a spark of mischief in her eyes. "Because if you don't, I'm going to have to kill you myself."

THE JOURNEY INTO CHINGETTI

Though she rarely saw him after healing Hektor in the Hall, Ellishiva heeded Rajah's words. In the days that passed as she and the others were preparing to put their new plan into action, she practiced both payamar and yoga in the Arboretum, finishing one and beginning the other until they began to blend together seamlessly, like rain falling into a river.

The morning of the plan dawned cool and clear. Ellishiva sat on the yoga ledge overlooking the vast eastern side of Mannahatta's jungle. She had woken before the others to come here . . . to prepare herself. Now she was nearing the end of her last pose: the tree pose of Vriksasana. Her eyes were closed and the sole of her left foot was tucked up against her inner right thigh while her other foot sank into the thick moss beneath her. It oozed up between her toes, soft and tingly at once. She imagined that her toes were old, strong roots, digging into the depths of the earth as her hands stretched above her head like branches.

When at last she finished, she opened her eyes to find that the orange sun of the new day had risen in its full glory. Her heart felt full and warm as it basked in its light. She inhaled, listening to her breath as it filled her lungs with the sweet scent of yellow kahili ginger flowers. The fallen blooms were everywhere, scattered across the mossy walkways of the Arboretum and the breakfast table in the fernery below—where, she noticed, Samara, Hektor, Bairon, and Asia were just settling down to eat and talk, all of them still dressed in their pajamas. Performing just one Sun Salutation to end her practice, Ellishiva headed down to meet the others.

It wasn't long before their voices became clear to her ears.

"So, anyone figured out what we're going to do with Amber?" Samara asked the table at large. She gave a tremendous yawn and rubbed the sleep from her eyes with one hand as she shoveled a helping of thick, creamy dalia porridge into her bowl. "We can't take her with us into the cellar."

"Let Elli figure it out," dismissed Hektor, yawning himself. He reached across the table and dragged the porridge away from Samara.

"Shame that Elli couldn't heal your head at the same time she healed your wound," the fairy grumbled, rewarding him with a cross look. But Ellishiva noticed that her tone wasn't quite as sharp as it had been before Hektor had been wounded in the attack.

"I think Amber is upset," interrupted Walle timidly. He was holding a battered orb filled with Bluzure spice dust in two of his upper limbs. His other two upper limbs were polishing it absently with the sleeves of his nightshirt, over and over. "I didn't drink her purpleade last night."

"For the good of the cause, Walle," interrupted Bairon kindly, giving a full bottle of the toxic punch on the table beside him a pat.

Walle turned slightly pink, but managed a weak smile.

"Are you going to eat *all* of that?" Samara was nagging Hektor as Ellishiva arrived at the table.

"Don't start with me, Sam. It's too early," Hektor griped at the glaring fairy. He drizzled some maple syrup into his huge bowl of porridge and began stirring it with his index finger. "Elli, what should we do about Amber?"

"Maybe she won't wake up," suggested Walle. He shot a nervous glance toward the warren.

"We do have spoons, you know," said Samara to Hektor, a disgusted look on her face.

"It tastes better this way," retorted Hektor, deliberately licking his finger.

"Amber will wake up," Ellishiva said to Walle, ignoring them. "I'm amazed she isn't already here." Pulling up a chair, she took a seat next to Asia, who gave her a warm, sleepy smile. Ellishiva smiled back and reached for a huge scarlet strawberry lying in a nearby bowl of fruit. With her other hand, she picked up one of the two small amber bottles sitting on the table in front of Walle and brought it up to her eye for inspection. "So these are the Bocaveen elixirs? They're finished?"

"Yes, Elli. Except for the duba root," replied Walle. "I've been practicing a lot," he added earnestly. "Onuris showed me how to make it."

"Amber has been behaving so strangely lately," murmured Asia. A frown creased her pretty forehead as she peeled the skins from the trio of loquats in front of her.

"I'll say," agreed Bairon, dragging the dalia toward him and scooping more porridge into his bowl. "You never know what she's going to say or do these days."

"That doll is giving her nightmares for some reason," Ellishiva agreed, mirroring Asia's thoughtful frown. "It started after my attack, I think."

"She's been carrying it around too long," snorted Samara. "Why doesn't someone make her get rid of it?"

"Rajah gave it to her," said Ellishiva softly, remembering that long-ago day. But this was hardly the moment to get sentimental. Clearing her throat, she pulled out a checklist from the noli at her waist. "All right. Let's go over the plan one more time."

"It's all under control, Elli," chimed in Bairon at once, all confidence. "Walle's got my father's old orb right there, and it should control the vāhmana fine—once the Bocaveen elixir changes Hektor's voice to sound like his. Walle mixed Ahpa's hair into the formula already. The new map of Chingetti Cellar is right here. It's been updated for changing roots. I checked. Ahpa will never know it's missing." He passed a rolled piece of papyrus over to her. "And—" Bairon faltered for a moment, eyeing the bottle of purple liquid beside him warily. Then a brave, determined expression came over his face. "And I'm going to drink Amber's purpleade punch to make me sick. Mother is away visiting my aunt, so Ahpa will have to leave the vāhmana unattended now and then to come home and check on me."

"Wow," said Ellishiva, impressed. "That sounds like everything."

"You're so brave, Bairon," Samara added admiringly. Bairon beamed a little and sat taller in his chair. The fairy turned to Ellishiva. "I've got the chest the Jipsin gave you ready to go, Elli," she added, giving her enchanted noli a pat.

"Good. If we can ever find the key . . . ," Ellishiva muttered, checking another point off her list. She turned to Asia expectantly.

The elf girl cleared her throat with a delicate *ahem*. "Walle and I are ready to be the lookouts. Yesterday we kept track of which elders were where at what times. Tonight, during the second jungle sleepover, we will go to the kitchen to bring up the evening meal. Since we did it last night, too, Lady Malinia should not suspect that the three of you are gone . . ." She trailed off, looking at Ellishiva for approval.

Ellishiva smiled at her. "Perfect," she confirmed. The elf girl gave a sigh of relief.

"Elli, when are you planning on dusting me and Hektor with Khlorus?" interrupted Samara. "The roots of Banyan Tree stretch past the borders of the colony, and if you want to go all the way to the river . . . ," she made a helpless gesture with her hands. "He and I won't be able to go beyond the colony border without it. Unless you want to fight the Sixth Element alone," she added, joking about life-and-death situations as only Samara could.

The muscles in Ellishiva's neck tensed slightly. She hadn't yet told the others that she planned to—that she *had to*—face the Sixth Element alone. "I know, Sam," she sighed, deciding just to answer the question. There was nothing the fairy was looking forward to more than being doused with Khlorus. "We'll do it after we get to the cellar."

"Great. Can't wait!" chirped Samara, glancing gleefully at Hektor across the table.

Hektor just snorted and shoveled another spoonful of porridge into his mouth. "Remind me why we're going to the river again?" he asked groggily with his mouth full.

"That's where I—we have to face her," replied Ellishiva, catching her stumbling tongue at the last second. She snuck a glance at Samara and her brother, but neither of them seemed to have noticed.

"Right. I know the last quarter moon's not far off and all, but, Elli," protested Hektor through another mouthful of porridge, "what if it's all a trick? The Sixth Element said she was going to bring 'destruction to our world' on the *last* last quarter moon, and nothing happened. Then she hit us at the harvest instead."

"Exactly," agreed Ellishiva. "Which is why I don't think that the last quarter moon is really the—well . . ." She hesitated, then took a breath and blurted, "Maybe she's not talking about the actual moon in the sky. She's just so . . . so unpredictable. You know? I just need to follow my instincts. They will never fail me."

Five blank stares from around the table were her only response.

"It's just a thought," mumbled Ellishiva, turning her gaze back down to the list in her hands before her cheeks could grow warm.

A few quiet seconds ticked by. Then Asia, taking pity on her, changed the subject. "I hope Ahpa comes back soon so we can reopen the canteen," she sighed. There was a little ray of worry in her eyes. "I still don't understand why the Senate had to summon him to Nicobar."

"Don't worry about Mr. Guo, Asia. He'll be fine," dismissed Samara in a classic botched attempt at being comforting. "The inquiry will be over soon. They just wanted to examine the inventory of things he's been collecting by the river."

"I know, Sam, but I wish he could have just sent the list instead of going in person. I miss him," replied Asia sadly. She turned to Ellishiva. "Elli, are you sure Rajah didn't take your spice jar to Nicobar when he went?"

Ellishiva shook her head. "No, he needs it here himself. His study in Chingetti Cellar—the Bulbdome—is the safest place to put it without moving it to a different colony altogether," she reasoned, picking the last plump strawberry from the bowl of fruit and pinching its stem off with conviction. "Amber's spice jar has disappeared, too. And he knew I was looking at it. Both of them must be down there now." She popped the strawberry into her mouth and frowned thoughtfully. "There's something strange about my spice dust. I think—maybe because I'm the First Spice—it can take me to things that happened before I was born. Or even after where I am now."

"You mean like a time jump?" gawked Bairon, his eyes wide with awe.

"Yes. Maybe. I'm not sure," replied Ellishiva. "It took me into the element of ether when I was there last time. It was strange," she trailed off, thinking. Then she shook her head, forcing herself back into the present, and looked down at the last scribbled point on her checklist. "Has anyone been able to find out anything about the baron?" Since his secret conversation with the mysterious fairy in the alcove on the night of the attack, the suspicious elf had all but disappeared.

There was a general shaking of heads. "No. But I did hear a rumor," ventured Bairon finally. "I think I heard Ahpa telling Mother that he took the baron and Mr. Belanos down to Chingetti a couple nights ago."

"I bet you it was the baron who let the Sixth Element into the colony," muttered Samara darkly from her corner of the table.

"You're just upset that you made the headlines of *The Times* that day," Hektor pointed out bluntly.

Samara scowled at him.

"Well, we can't rule him out. Someone had to let the Sixth Element in, and we did see the baron in the forest on the day when she first attacked.

He's been acting strange ever since," said Ellishiva reasonably. "Rajah is good friends with both of them, too—the baron and Mr. Belanos. They all came here together from their last colony," she trailed off for a moment, thinking. "I have this feeling that Rajah knows more about the Sixth Element than he's willing to admit. He's been acting strange, too . . . like he's trying to protect someone. Maybe it's the baron," she speculated, though the words didn't taste quite right on her tongue. Absently, she reached into the fruit bowl for more strawberries, but they were gone. She inhaled a breath and let it out through her nose. "Finish up, everyone," she urged the table. "We have a long day ahead."

"You'll all be okay in the cellar. Right?" asked Bairon. He looked at Ellishiva and there was worry in his eyes.

Ellishiva wished she had something reassuring to say, but she didn't. She looked back at him apologetically. "It's the only thing we can do, Bairon," she said in a low voice. "With any luck we'll discover more about the Sixth Element in the Bulbdome. Things that can help us defeat her. And Maximus could be down there somewhere, too. We have to at least try to find him before we head to the river."

Bairon's look grew bleaker, but he pressed his lips together and gave her a firm nod anyway. "At least you won't be alone," he commented.

Hektor pushed his empty porridge bowl away from him and leveled a look at her down the table. "I'm with you, Elli. All the way," he said in a voice as solid as basalt rock.

Ellishiva looked into his steady eyes and her heavy heart grew lighter. Hektor's new attitude was music to her ears, giving her back all the strength he'd once tried to wrest away from her, and then some.

"Aren't you afraid, Elli?' asked Asia softly.

"No, Asia," Ellishiva told her, giving a firm shake of her head to prove the point. Nevertheless, a faint shiver ran down her spine all the way to her toes.

Before anyone could say another word, a head of tangled red hair bounded into the fernery.

"I'm ready to go to the cellar!" announced Amborella, hopping breathlessly into the last remaining chair at the breakfast table.

For a long moment, no one said anything. Walle looked particularly uncomfortable. Finally, Ellishiva sighed and pushed back her seat a bit. "Amber, come sit over here with me," she beckoned, patting her lap. Amborella immediately bounced over, scrambling up onto Ellishiva's knees. Ellishiva brushed her sister's fiery red hair away from her face with her fingers and gazed into her big, eager eyes.

This was going to be harder than she thought.

"You have a very important part to play today," she began, trying to pick her words carefully. It didn't work.

Her little sister leveled a flat look at her and then asked bluntly, "Are you going to leave me, Elli?"

Ellishiva fought down a squirm of guilt. "Asia will be here with you, and so will Walle," she said, trying to sound reassuring. "They need your help to be our lookout. And later Bairon will come by, too."

"I don't want you to go without me! What if you get scared?" whimpered Amborella, her lips pursing in a pout.

"Well," stalled Ellishiva, casting around for a way out. Her eyes fell on the burlap doll hanging, as usual, from her little sister's hand. "You know, if I had Dollie Burlap with me, she could keep me company," she tried. "But I don't want to take her from you."

Amborella tugged the doll up and hugged it against her stomach. Around her, the table held its breath.

"I—I can't let Dollie Burlap go with you. It's too dangerous. But—" she added quickly, before her audience could let out a collective groan. She reached behind the doll's neck and unhooked the necklace with the pendant of amber-like yellow copal filled with many trapped, tiny objects. "Here. You can take this," she offered generously, holding the token out to Ellishiva.

Ellishiva looked at the necklace and then at Amborella. Her eyes burned suddenly as she wondered if she'd ever see her sister again.

Quickly, she blinked back the tears before anyone could notice. "Would you put it on for me?" she asked Amborella.

Amborella nodded, squashing Dollie Burlap between them as she reached up and fastened the necklace around Ellishiva's neck, on top of the acorn choker. "Now you won't be scared," declared Amborella, nodding with approval at her plan.

"Thanks, Amber," said Ellishiva, giving her a half-smile that almost immediately faltered. There was a faint, odd tingling around her neck. She touched the amber pendant, then shook her head and cleared her throat. "All right," she said to the conspirators around the table, whose faces were now openly relieved. "Let's go find some duba root to finish these Bocaveen elixirs."

* * *

Late that evening, after hours of careful preparation, Ellishiva, Samara, and Hektor crept out to the vāhmana in the hall beyond the warren.

Ellishiva hadn't stopped all day. From the moment breakfast had ended she had been needed here, needed there, sought out for approval on this, questioned on that. Nor had everything gone exactly to plan. Walle had been called away home suddenly in the afternoon, and Ellishiva had been forced to mix the duba root into the Bocaveen elixirs herself. She had followed instructions, but mixing elixirs was not her strong point, and there had been no way to test them in advance—something that made her more than a little nervous. Then Bairon had had to stay until Walle came back, which had delayed their departure. After that, however, things had begun falling into place again. Lady Malinia had let Asia and Walle bring dinner up to the bedchamber without coming in to check on them herself, and Bairon hadn't been gone long before Dorian was forced to leave the vāhmana to tend to an emergency at home.

Ellishiva, Samara, and Hektor had wasted no time seizing their chance.

They stole into the vāhmana as silently as shadows. Samara withdrew the olivine orb filled with Bluzure spice dust that Walle had been polishing earlier from her noli, and snapped it into the root-claw holder where it belonged. The Bluzure immediately twirled to life in the orb, awaiting instructions.

Meanwhile, Ellishiva pulled one of the two amber bottles of Bocaveen elixir out of her own noli and shoved it at Hektor. "Remember what Walle said," she warned in a low voice. "Don't smell it. Just drink it down!"

Hektor nodded. Ellishiva stared at him, holding her breath as he yanked the cork out of the bottle with his teeth and spat it out on the floor again. He took a sip.

Both Ellishiva and Samara jumped as he began to choke and cough violently.

"This is nasty!" he gasped at last, struggling to swallow.

"Oh, just man up!" hissed Samara. "Unless you'd rather we throw ourselves down Banyan Falls and hope we magically land in the Bulbdome that way."

"Ladies first," sputtered Hektor, scowling at her.

"Enough!" snapped Ellishiva, peering nervously out at the still-empty hallway beyond. "Hektor, that orb isn't going to listen to you unless you sound like Bairon's father. You have to drink the whole bottle."

Hektor turned his bleak, watering eyes on her. "Are you sure I volunteered for this?" he mumbled.

Ellishiva saw Samara opening her mouth again and waved her hand to shut her up. The fairy pursed her lips and crossed her arms, glaring. Ellishiva turned back to her brother. "Hektor," she began, striving to sound encouraging, "you've always dreamed of operating a vāhmana. This could be the only chance you get," she pointed out.

Hektor stole a quick look of longing at the waiting orb of Bluzure and Ellishiva held her breath. Finally, with a determined glare at the amber bottle, he tilted his head back and drained the rest of the elixir—all, that was, except for the last gulp. Right before it could disappear into his mouth, he gagged, and the bottle itself slipped from his fingers, shattering into pieces as it hit the hard floor. The remaining mouthful of elixir splattered everywhere, sizzling and staining the wood with caramel-colored streaks.

"Now you've done it," snapped Samara sourly, rolling her eyes.

But, for once, there was no biting retort. Ellishiva looked at Hektor, and her heart dropped through the bottom of her ribs. Her brother's face was turning an unhealthy shade of dark green, and as he coughed, he clawed furiously around his mouth as if scratching at an unseen rash. Ellishiva was about to throw the plan to the winds and scream for help, convinced she'd accidentally mixed an elixir of death, when she saw why Hektor was really grabbing at his face. She clamped a hand over her mouth and her eyes stretched open as wide as they could go. Next to her, Samara's eyes were likewise about to pop out of their sockets.

"I—I don't feel right, Elli," groaned Hektor when the coughing fit finally stopped. Only his voice was no longer his. It was Dorian's.

And that wasn't the only thing that had changed.

"I'm really sorry, Hektor," managed Ellishiva in a strangled voice, torn between guilt and laughter. "I must have added too much duba root." Beside her, a high-pitched wheeze escaped through Samara's fingers, which were laced over her mouth like a grate. The fairy's shoulders and chest shook.

"Don't worry. Your face—" started Ellishiva, but she was rapidly losing control herself. "Your face will go back to—back to normal!"

"My *face*?" gasped Hektor. His hands flew up to his chin again, grasping at what had become a mass of curling white tendrils that stretched all the way down to the collar of his shirt. Instantly, the shock in his eyes turned to fury. "You turned me into a root!" he almost shouted at them.

"Shhh!" Ellishiva managed, thinking hard. "Calm down. It's going to wear off eventually! Here." She reached into her noli and pulled out her clamshell of bee balm, which she began to rub over the lower half of Hektor's face. "This should help with the itching, at least."

Hektor scowled, but let her apply the balm. "Will you tell her to shut up?" he snarled, glaring over her shoulder at Samara.

"Sam, that's enough!" said Ellishiva, forcing herself to pull a straight face. "Get over here and help me with this. Dorian isn't going to be gone forever."

It took another long moment for Samara to compose herself. At last, she uncovered her pink mouth and wiped the tears of laughter from the corners of her eyes. "I'm sorry, Hektor. Really," she apologized, seemingly sincere despite the lingering quiver in her voice. She pulled out her own bee balm and began helping Ellishiva, something that seemed to make Hektor feel better, though he still did his best to avoid looking at the fairy's face.

"Okay, let's refocus," said Ellishiva finally, snapping the clamshell shut and tucking it back into her noli. She gave Hektor a completely serious look. "Are you ready?" she asked.

Hektor nodded. Running his fingers uncomfortably through the root-beard one last time, he straightened his shoulders and turned to the waiting orb of Bluzure spice dust. "Chingetti Cellar!" he commanded in the voice of Bairon's father.

The vāhmana dropped.

Ellishiva kept her eye on the orb of Bluzure spice dust as they descended swiftly through the aerial root, past Banyan Circle at ground level, and into the depths of the earth. Any moment, she thought, the orb might realize that Dorian's voice was one swallow of Bocaveen elixir short of its true self and come to a sudden, rocking halt, leaving them stranded who knew where.

But she needn't have worried. The vāhmana continued to fall, and the interior of the root around them darkened into shades of amber, until at last it slowed and finally jerked to a full stop right where they were supposed to be. Samara put the Bluzure-filled orb back in her noli and, with a steadying breath, Ellishiva led the way off of the vāhmana.

They were in Chingetti Cellar at last.

Ellishiva could sense how vast it was more than she could actually see the vastness, at first. Above her, the darkness was as high and heavy as dense rain clouds masking the stars on a moonless night. Under her bare feet, the old, mud-brick paving was rough and cold, and the air in the cavernous space was chilly. On either side of her, Samara and Hektor huddled closer.

"Take out your Khlorus orb, Elli," muttered Samara in her ear.

Ellishiva nodded, and reached into her noli. Earlier that day, she had finished filling the empty olivine orb from Rajah's study with Khlorus for this purpose. Although she didn't need olivine to use Khlorus herself, they had decided it was safer to put some in the orb. That way, if something happened to Ellishiva, Samara and Hektor would still be able to use the light. Pulling it out of the noli, Ellishiva lifted it close to her face.

"*Vitarita āloka*," she breathed, and the dust within the olivine stirred to life, shedding a dim green light over their surroundings.

As one, all three of their mouths fell open.

The massive space around them was a honeycomb of caves and doors. The latter, Ellishiva thought, looked huge and ancient. Most of them were red-brown, with intricate etchings of strange symbols carved into their faces, though great patches of black moss obscured some of the picture writing. A faint wind swished and whistled softly around them, and in the distance Ellishiva could hear the roar of Banyan Tree's great waterfall. She sniffed the air, just to be sure. "Wet leaves, moss, bracken, and bark," she murmured. "It can't be far." The words were barely above a whisper, yet her voice echoed gently around them, dancing with the wisps of wind. She pulled the map of Chingetti Cellar that Bairon had given her from her noli.

"This is *huge*," breathed Hektor, awestruck. His voice was still Dorian's.

"What are those dark holes beside the doors?" wondered Samara. "More caves? Deeper ones?"

"Those aren't caves, Sam," Ellishiva mumbled, eyeing the map. "They're hollow roots. It looks like they run underneath all of Mannahatta Island. Like tunnels."

"Should we go down one of them?" Hektor asked.

Ellishiva fought the urge to say yes. Down one of these tunnels, she felt sure Maximus was waiting. Still, she knew it wasn't practical to begin the search for him yet. Not before they were as prepared as they could be first. Not before they had visited the Bulbdome. "Not yet," she said finally. "But let's check the south root tunnel to make sure there's a vāhmana there that can take us to the river's edge. It should only be a small detour on the way to the waterfall. Come on. This way."

They set off.

"This place is like a whole other colony," whispered Samara behind her shoulder as they crept along the mud-brick floor, huddled in the glow of the Khlorus orb. "There's so much space."

"Where do you think these doors lead?" marveled Hektor, his voice half his own again now. Ellishiva glanced back to see him craning his neck at them instead of watching where he was going. "There must be hundreds!"

"Wow, look at that one," breathed Samara, her eyes fixed on a wide panel decorated in elaborate designs of malachite and silver. She spread her wings and rose a few inches off the ground as if to go examine it, but Ellishiva grabbed her wrist.

"Don't you dare!" she snapped. "We have to stay close."

The fairy opened her mouth to protest, then caught sight of something over Ellishiva's shoulder and dropped to the ground again. "What's that?" she squeaked, pointing.

Ellishiva followed the direction of her finger. In the distance was what looked to be a shimmering blackness, like tar pouring down from a great height. "What's what? You mean that glimmer?" she asked. Samara nodded nervously. Ellishiva rolled her eyes, and released the fairy's wrist. "That's the black pool that the waterfall falls into, where the Bulbdome is. We're going there after we find the south root. Here, Hektor. Hold this."

Ellishiva pushed the open map into Hektor's hands and brought the orb close to the papyrus, inspecting it. "According to this, the south root should be a few hundred yards from the vāhmana we just left. Keep an eye out for the numbers above the tunnel entrances. They're destination markings. The one with the longitude and latitude of the southern tip of Mannahatta will be our vāhmana. Got it?"

Hektor and Samara nodded at her.

Ellishiva turned and started in the direction of the tunnel, taking long strides and counting to herself as she went. For a minute they walked in silence. Samara, Ellishiva noticed, stuck a little closer to her than before.

Then, "Wait!" commanded Hektor under his breath, grabbing both of them by the shoulder and stopping the procession in its tracks. "I heard something." His voice was more his own than Dorian's now. Ellishiva started to say something, but he quickly set a finger against her lips, shushing her. He stared at a place in the blackness for several long seconds. Then, before Ellishiva could stop him, he pulled an acorn out of his pocket and threw it into the dark. It ricocheted off one of the large doors with a sharp *crack* and veered away from them in a series of increasingly faint tapping noises, as if it were bouncing down an unseen stairway.

The three of them stood frozen for a long moment. Then Ellishiva turned on him.

"What are you doing, Hektor?" she hissed. "Keep that stuff in your pockets! Do you want us to get cau—"

"Get down!" Hektor interrupted her, yanking both of them onto the cold mud-brick floor with him. "Put that out!"

There wasn't time to think about it. "*Pidahati āloka,*" Ellishiva breathed to the orb. The Khlorus went dark.

A second later, the grand doors that Hektor's acorn had ricocheted off of cracked open slowly, just wide enough for someone to peek out.

"Rojorine," breathed Samara, so quietly that even the echoes couldn't catch the word.

The door opened a little more and two figures crept out, closing the huge panel behind them. Both of them were dressed in hooded cloaks that concealed their faces, yet when they spoke, their identities were as clear as day.

"What if he has come to harm? Surely he would not have gone without telling us." That was Baron Puck. A dim red glow from the fairy wand in his hand lit his path as he led the way toward the stairwell.

"We know not what may have come up," murmured the other voice, and this one, Ellishiva realized with a start, belonged to Mr. Belanos. "We must stick to Valerius's plan, Baron."

"Yes, yes. I suppose," muttered Baron Puck.

The two figures vanished down the stairs, taking the faint Rojorine light with them.

As soon as they were gone, Ellishiva sat up on her knees. Her heart was pounding. Next to her, Hektor had a guilty look on his face. She scowled at him. That had been far too close.

"Was that Baron Puck?" whispered Samara, incredulous. "With *Mr. Belanos*?"

"That's what it looks like, Sam," muttered Ellishiva.

"Then he's on our side after all," marveled Hektor. "He's helping Rajah!"

"Even if he is, we can't stay here and wait for them to come back and catch us," Ellishiva growled at him. She nudged the stunned fairy next to her in the shoulder. "Come on, Sam. Snap out of it. *Vitarita āloka!*" The light in the Khlorus orb flared to life again. She, Samara, and Hektor continued on their way, this time in utter silence, treading as lightly as they could over the mud-brick floor. A tingle of nervousness prickled at Ellishiva with every door they passed. There was no telling who or what might burst out of them next.

At last, Ellishiva spotted what they were looking for. "There!" she whispered as loudly as she dared, pointing at the archway ahead. "That must be the one!"

"It is!" confirmed Samara excitedly, fluttering a foot or two off the ground to get a better look. "I can see the markings over the entrance, just like you said. And there's something back there."

"The vāhmana," nodded Ellishiva, more sure of it with every step. "Hurry up. Let's just check that it's a working one and head to the Bulbdome."

Strong winds blew into their faces as they entered the gigantic, hollow root, sending Ellishiva's hair tossing wildly around her face. The inside of the rounded wood, she could tell, had been eroded by these powerful gusts of air over time; a wavy ripple pattern ran along its smooth surface, like wet sandbars on a beach. Grabbing hold of most of her hair with an effort, Ellishiva held the orb aloft and peered into the tunnel in front of them.

There was the vāhmana, sitting without a canopy like a lonely, square-shaped boat, right where it was supposed to be.

"Come on. Let's make sure it works," instructed Ellishiva, no longer bothering to whisper. Even shouting, it was hard to hear her own voice over the wind.

But Samara and Hektor were already striding ahead of her. With a sigh, Ellishiva followed them onto the wooden deck of the craft. Apart from the missing canopy, the rest of it seemed to be in decent condition.

"Elli, look!" She turned and caught sight of Samara fluttering over to the console table in the back of the vāhmana, Hektor at her heels. Ellishiva left the railing she'd been examining and joined them in a huddle by the stern.

"Look at it. It's brand new!" gushed Hektor, leaning close to a polished olivine orb packed to the brim with Bluzure spice dust. His voice had returned completely now, but the beard of roots continued to dangle from his chin. He looked between the girls excitedly. "Someone must use this a lot. Otherwise why would they keep the orb so full?" He leaned forward as if to pick the olivine sphere up, then caught sight of his reflection and jerked his head back, startled.

Ellishiva bent down to examine it in his stead. "You're right," she muttered. "It wouldn't be filled this much for nothing. This must be the vāhmana to the river's edge," she trailed off as another nudge to begin the search for Maximus tugged at her heart. But no, the practical thing to do was wait. "Well, it looks like it should work when we need it," she commented with a sigh, giving the orb a tap of farewell.

A green spark shot from her fingertip and touched the olivine, making all three of them gasp and pull back. Inside the orb, the thick mass of Bluzure spice dust began to whirl. Then, suddenly, the vāhmana jerked forward toward the deep tunnel ahead, knocking their feet out from under them. The Khlorus orb fell from Ellishiva's grip and their only light went out.

"Wait!" Hektor shouted as he hit the floorboards. "Elli, make it stop!"

"I can't reach it!" cried Ellishiva, struggling to regain her balance and find the fallen orb at the same time.

"Just tell it to stop!" Hektor yelled at her.

"I can't! It responded to my touch, not my voice!" Ellishiva yelled back.

The vāhmana turned slightly and dropped, plunging into the utter darkness of the huge root.

"Do something, Elli!" shrilled Samara nearby. "We're not supposed to go to the river's edge now!"

"I know! Will the two of you calm down?" Ellishiva shouted. Something round and heavy hit her knee and she snatched it up, barking a quick "*Vitarita āloka!*" at the Khlorus orb. A fluctuating green glow lit the deck. "We'll just ride it to the first stop and come back," she decided. "Okay?"

Two heads nodded mutely at her. The vāhmana was speeding over shallow water now, and the spray of a tiny wave splashed over the railing, making the orb in Ellishiva's hand slippery. She shoved it into her noli for safekeeping; better to put up with the faint light it gave through the pouch's lining than to lose it altogether. Seeing this, Hektor crawled over and handed her the folded map she'd forgotten to take back from him earlier. Ellishiva tucked it into place behind the orb. The vāhmana jerked and the floorboards dug uncomfortably into her knees. "Come on!" she shouted, grabbing Samara by the hand and dragging her up to sit on the bench in the front row.

Hektor followed suit, seating himself in the row behind them.

"It won't be long," Ellishiva yelled reassuringly.

Unfortunately, the vāhmana seemed to disagree with her.

It shot through the crisp, cool air of the hollow root, sending a sharp wind whistling past their ears. As it flew, the space around them grew until it was five times the size of Atticus. The white walls became dappled with patches of moss, and now and again a beautiful, twisted whorl in the wood rushed by.

"Are we almost there?" shouted Samara in her ear.

"It can't be much farther," Ellishiva shouted back. But there was a note of uncertainty in her voice.

The water beneath them swelled into a gushing stream. Uncaring, the vāhmana picked up speed. Hundreds of smaller hollow roots branched off from their large one in all directions, every one of them piping still more water into the main root. In no time, the stream had become a torrent that pummeled the vāhmana's wooden bottom and sent buckets of water and spray over the railing.

"Elli—" started Samara, gripping her elbow like a vise.

"Hold on!" hollered Ellishiva as a large wave crested the prow and flooded the deck, washing her last hope of a quick turnaround overboard. The vessel ducked and swerved, rose and fell, veering sharply to the left and then the right. Ellishiva gritted her teeth and clamped her fingers down on the sturdy bench, clinging to the wood for dear life. Once, the vāhmana shot out into an echoing cavern housing a vast, bubbling pool, and for a second she thought they might have reached the end. But no—a moment later it was wheeling at an impossible angle into another root. Cold water gushed over them freely now, and even shouted conversation had become impossible, drowned out by the howling wind. The orb in Ellishiva's noli flickered wildly, and she struggled to keep her eyes open. Water streamed over her face, but she couldn't risk releasing her grip on the bench to wipe it away.

Then the vāhmana plunged beneath the water altogether.

Ellishiva held her breath. Through bleary eyes, she saw Hektor and Samara doing the same, their cheeks popping out like puffer fish as they, too, craned their necks to see around them. A handful of bubbles escaped Hektor's mouth when he opened it to try to speak, and he immediately snapped it shut again.

Just when Ellishiva was beginning to think they would have to abandon ship, the vāhmana burst to the surface of the water again. Everyone gasped for air as a flood poured from its sides over the railing. It charged at breakneck speed down the root a little ways farther, then slowed and finally stopped.

For a moment they sat in silence, sodden from head to toe, their fingers still gripping the benches for dear life.

"Whoa," offered Hektor at last.

Ellishiva and Samara responded with a shaken, halting laugh. The water was calmer now and the wind had fallen. A chorus of trickles and drips could be heard in the distance. Ellishiva gazed farther down the dark root, which had become a little too small for a vāhmana to pass, and felt her instincts tug on her heart again—as though they had arrived where they were meant to be. And for the moment, at least, no one was proposing an immediate return journey to the cellar.

By unspoken agreement, Ellishiva and the others clambered, barefoot and soaked, off of the vāhmana. One by one, they landed with a splash in a shallow stream of cold water. A tingling chill ran through Ellishiva's body as it engulfed her toes, strengthening her suspicions that there was something to be discovered here. Without a word, she pulled the water-slicked olivine orb from her sodden noli. "*Vitarita āloka*," she mumbled, and its dim, flickering light grew bright and strong.

"Where are we?" wondered Hektor beside her, shivering as he looked around.

Ellishiva's heart sank. She reached into the noli again and pulled out the map. It was soaked through, and as she carefully unfolded it and plastered it against her thigh, it was clear that many of the lines had been washed out.

"Hektor, you should have given it to me instead," griped Samara, peering at the drenched papyrus over Ellishiva's shoulder. "Now it's wet."

"My fault, Sam. I put it in my noli without thinking," replied Ellishiva quickly, determined to cut off the argument before it started for once. "Come on. Let's see what's up ahead, since we're here," she added, nodding in the direction of the dark tunnel.

"Um. I don't know, Elli. We don't have a map anymore," protested Samara, sneaking a dirty look at Hektor. "Shouldn't we go back now? Before we get lost?"

"We won't go far," said Ellishiva in a tone that left no room for argument. "Hektor, bring the orb from the vāhmana, just in case. And Sam, put it in your noli to make sure it stays safe. I don't want to touch it again until we're ready to head back."

Giving her matching uneasy looks, Hektor and Samara obeyed. For a moment, Ellishiva was tempted to give in to their caution and turn back. But Perseus's words from the Foxfire Harvest were whispering in her mind, refusing to be suppressed.

Trust your instincts, and you will never fail.

Holding the orb of Khlorus aloft, Ellishiva led the way into the dark root.

For a long while, they plodded along in silence. The passage here was neither as tall nor as wide as it had been earlier. In the rounded walls, Ellishiva could smell the fresh water of the Muheekantuck River mingling with the faint saltiness of seawater. Behind her, Samara tracked their path by marking *x*'s on places where the root had scars, which seemed to be a bit drier than the rest of it.

As they walked farther and farther into the tunnel, Samara and Hektor following doggedly on her heels, Ellishiva began to realize that she couldn't keep her secret—that she alone must go on to face the Sixth Element—from them much longer. The creature had made it clear that it wanted her and her alone. Her spice jar had told her that this was her destiny. She couldn't let them become casualties in her war.

Nevertheless, she fully expected them to fight her every step of the way.

Steeling herself for a bitter argument, Ellishiva took a breath and began, "Hektor, Sam . . . there's something I need to—"

"Wait!" interrupted Hektor sharply. Ellishiva stopped in her tracks and turned to look at him. They had arrived in a hollow hub of the root system, and the Khlorus orb cast green light over several new paths forking off in different directions. Hektor was staring intently toward the entrance of a narrow one to their right. "Did you hear that?" he whispered.

Ellishiva listened closely. Sure enough, a faint sloshing seemed to be coming from the tunnel in question.

Without a word, Hektor began to tread silently toward the noise. Ellishiva followed, every one of her nerves on edge. Samara slowly brought up the rear. But her brother moved faster than both of them, and it wasn't long before he disappeared up ahead into the blackness.

"Hektor?" Ellishiva whispered as loudly as she dared. The name came back to her like so many ghost-whispers: "*Hektor . . . Hektor . . . Hektor . . . ?*" She shivered. "Hektor, stop! Come back. We can't see you . . ."

"*Can't see you . . . see you . . . see you,*" echoed the ghost-whispers.

Ellishiva stopped walking. Her heart was pounding wildly. The root systems under Banyan Tree were alive and changed constantly. What if Hektor had fallen down an unmarked one, swallowed whole by the darkness without a trace? What if the thing that had been making the splashing sounds had caught and gagged him up ahead, and was now just lying in wait for her and Samara? What if—

"*Elli!*" The sound of her name ripped through the root like thunder, making her jump out of her skin. Beside her, Samara produced a sound that was half-squeak, half-scream. "Elli!" Hektor yelled again, and this time it was clear that he wasn't hurt. "Elli, here! Get over here! Fast!"

Urging the orb to glow brighter, Ellishiva ran toward his voice. The Khlorus cast huge shadows over the gnarled walls around her as she rushed through the root, Samara at her heels. When she reached Hektor, she stopped so suddenly that the fairy nearly crashed into her.

"Maximus?" she breathed.

Maximus sat in the shallow water, slouched against the root wall like a heavy, wilting sunflower. Hektor was on the ground with him, struggling to hold him upright. The young kinnaran's armor was gone; his clothes were in tatters. One of his sleeves had been ripped from his filthy shirt and bound around his eyes. His hollow face was barely visible beneath the dirty tendrils of hair plastered in streaks over his cheeks and forehead. He looked as though he lacked the strength even to moan in pain.

Ellishiva shoved the Khlorus orb into Samara's hands and dropped to her knees in the running water beside him, heart pounding, eyes taking him in. What was left of his shirt seemed to be as thin as gauze. She pulled her damp tunic—the outermost layer of her clothing—over her head and tucked it around his emaciated shoulders and chest. For a moment she was tempted to remove the blindfold, but then she hesitated, worried that this time the yellow eyes beneath would not be fearless, but afraid. Instead, she cleared her throat.

"I knew you weren't dead!" she blurted, then winced. It was hardly what she'd planned her first words to him to be. All these weeks . . .

The dazed kinnaran stirred with an effort, and reached an unsteady hand out cautiously toward her. Automatically, Ellishiva caught his dirty fingers in her own and guided them to her face. Even now, seeing him in such a state, his touch calmed the chaos within her.

"Ell—Ellishiva?" he managed painfully.

Ellishiva felt a pang in her chest and pressed his fingers harder against her cheek. "You're badly hurt," she mumbled.

Maximus didn't have the strength to reply. She stared at him, aching and at a loss.

"Make him better, Elli."

She blinked and looked up. Hektor, still propping up the kinnaran, was staring at her as if he didn't know what she was waiting for. For a moment she was confused. Then the memory of healing him in the Hall flooded back to her, washing away the feeling of helplessness that had been weighing down her heart.

What *was* she waiting for?

Quickly, Ellishiva leaned forward and pressed her palms against Maximus's temples. She shut her eyes and took several deep breaths, repeating the healing mantra over and over again in her mind. After only a few seconds, a glow stronger than that of the Khlorus orb began to filter through her eyelids. Cautiously, she cracked them open.

Green spice dust was flowing from her hands and from the marks on her skin. Around her, the root was as bright as if it had been lit by three grown fireflies. Hektor pulled back as the Khlorus swirled around Maximus, filling the injured kinnaran with strength of his own. As they watched, he sat up by himself and his wings moved. He gasped in a huge gulp of air, as if he hadn't really breathed in weeks and was trying to make up for it.

Behind her, Samara produced a muffled squeal of delight. Ellishiva turned to find her staring at the olivine orb in her hands, which was now shining like a miniature green sun, filled to the brim with Khlorus. The fairy's eyes were wide with excitement, and Ellishiva could tell that she was itching to shove the orb into her noli. She pinned Samara with a withering look and, with a sigh, the fairy relented—probably because she knew that the disappearance of their only light source would hardly go unnoticed.

Ellishiva turned back to Maximus. "Can I take off your blindfold?" she asked gently.

"Yes. Go ahead," replied Maximus. He sounded dazed and a little wary, as though he were worried that once the blindfold was off, everything would turn out to be a dream.

Ellishiva scooted closer to him in the water and began to unwind the blindfold.

"Why did you put it on in the first place?" asked Hektor while she worked. "Did something happen to your eyes?"

Maximus shook his head faintly. "It was so dark down here. After the first few days, I started to lose my strength from straining so hard to see." He sighed. "Covering your eyes can lead to inner vision. They train us to fight blindfolded," he trailed off, pausing for a moment. Then he added in a shakier voice, "I did fear, however, that the Sixth Element might have stolen my sight forever with her poison."

Ellishiva finished unwinding the bandage and pulled it carefully away from his face. "And has she?" she asked, already knowing the answer as she gazed at him.

Maximus looked back at her for a long moment, his warm yellow eyes sparkling in the light of the Khlorus. "No," he replied finally, the words low and grateful. "Thanks to you."

Like a distant echo from a place she didn't want to think about, Rajah's warning whispered in her ear. *You, Ellishiva, should not be looking for a boy.* She shoved it down, an unwanted mosquito pricking at her happiness, and smiled at him.

"I thought I'd gone mad," Maximus went on hoarsely, glancing around at the rest of the group. "Thank you all for—for finding me."

"What happened to you?" asked Hektor.

Maximus turned to him, getting a good look at the white beard of roots for the first time. A knowing look came over his face. "Bocaveen elixir?" he commiserated. "Never could get that one right myself."

The corner of Hektor's mouth twitched up. He shrugged one shoulder and reached up to stroke the beard's wispy ends. "Think it's growing on me, actually," he admitted.

Maximus grinned at him. "Don't worry. It'll go away," he said reassuringly. Then his face fell and his bright eyes grew cloudy. "Does anyone know what happened to Morpheus and Theo?" he asked the group.

"Morpheus was hurt. Badly," Ellishiva told him. "But he's much better now. I haven't seen him or Theo much. I think they've been out looking for you."

Maximus nodded, visibly relieved. "I thought they were dead, that the Sixth Element had killed them both on South Island that day," he confessed, shuddering. He looked earnestly at Ellishiva. "Do you hear drums?"

"No," interrupted Hektor before she could respond. "What drums?"

Maximus shook his head. "Nothing," he murmured vaguely. "I've been down here too long." For a few seconds, he was quiet. Then he brightened a bit and looked around at the group. "Do you have any food?" he asked bluntly.

"Sure. Here's a treenity," said Samara, pulling one of the small sweets from her noli and handing it over to him. He stuffed it eagerly into his mouth. Samara looked pleased with herself. Rolling her eyes, Ellishiva turned and stared flatly at the fairy until, finally, Samara reluctantly pulled out another handful or two of the treats and forked them over as well. Maximus lit up brighter than the Khlorus orb and began to gobble them down voraciously.

"We're so glad we found you," said Ellishiva as he ate. "I thought you might be down here, but the elders wouldn't listen to me, wouldn't tell me where they were looking. Or even *if* they were looking."

"The Sixth Element attacked the Foxfire Harvest while you were away," chimed in Hektor. "Now every colony knows she's real, but as far as we can tell, nobody knows what to do about her."

"That makes sense," said Maximus darkly, finishing off the last of the treenitys. "Maximus, Theo, and I were powerless against her. And we're kinnarans. We're *trained* to face threats."

There was a bitterness in his voice that made Ellishiva sad and worried. She changed the subject. "What have you been eating down here?" she asked.

"Well, the treenitys you gave me in Textile Alley lasted a while," he replied, "and then mushrooms, mostly. When I could find them. Not the tastiest things in the world, but they kept me going. And there's been plenty of drinking water, obviously." He sighed as if shaking off a bad memory and gave her an apologetic look. "Sorry I missed your jungle sleepover, Ellishiva."

"Trust me, you're not missing anything," interrupted Hektor with a snort.

Ellishiva scowled at him. Meanwhile, Samara, apparently spurred to a rare moment of charity by the mushroom story, fished a few more treenity treats out of her noli for Maximus, who crammed them all gratefully into his cheek at once. For a few moments everyone was quiet, watching him eat and scoop water into his mouth.

Finally, Ellishiva cleared her throat. "Maximus, what happened to you? How did you escape South Island and find your way into the roots?" she asked hesitantly, hating to bring up bad memories, but needing to know nonetheless.

Maximus was silent for so long that she started to think he wouldn't answer at all. At last, he began his story. "We went to South Island that day to investigate some suspicious behavior that was happening in the human world. It was supposed to be a simple mission: find out what was really happening and report back to the general." As he spoke, his voice was low and distant, as though he were reliving it all over again. "When we arrived, we went straight to the cave there, as we'd been told to do. Theo and Morpheus went in first. I stayed outside the mouth, keeping watch." He paused. Then he set his jaw and forged on. "It wasn't long before the screaming began. Of course I went in then, but it was so dark I couldn't see. So I started shouting for them and then . . . then Morpheus started calling my name. But he wasn't the only one." His low voice dropped lower still. "The Sixth Element was calling me, too."

"How did she know your name?" asked Ellishiva, frowning.

"I don't know," confessed Maximus. "But as soon as she figured out that I wasn't going to listen to her, her dark magic dashed me against the wall and I stuck there. My armor was wedged into a crack in the cave wall. I managed to wriggle out of it, but I broke my left wing in the process, and a sticky, slimy poison of hers got into the wound."

"But you're all right now, aren't you? You can move your wings again?" asked Samara, who could sympathize with him more than she and her brother could, Ellishiva thought. The fairy fluttered her wings anxiously at him.

Maximus gave a wry smile and fluttered his back. Samara settled down again, relieved.

"Before I got free, though," the kinnaran continued darkly, "humans came into the cave with torches, looking for her. She wanted it that way. She lured them there on purpose. All the signs were there. The Sixth Element drew them deeper into the cave than I could see, but I could hear them screaming, fighting her. Then the sounds just . . . faded away." He stopped and took a shaky breath before pressing on. "When I did finally get free, I was in bad shape. I remember touching my eyes and my face with the slimy poison that had gotten on my fingers, and it stung so bad it made me dizzy. I managed to stagger out of the cave again, calling for Theo and Morpheus, but no one answered. Then I realized that it was even darker outside the cave than it had been inside. The toxic slime was slowly stealing my sight. I had to get somewhere safe, fast.

"I knew the water's edge was near, so I stumbled down to it and followed the bank until I found a human canoe and crawled into it, hiding under some reed baskets. I waited in total stillness for a long time. They teach us that in training. Eventually a lone human came screaming out of the cave, running for his life. He jumped into the canoe and paddled back to Mannahatta without ever noticing me. When he reached the shore, he leapt out as quickly as he had come and set off running again, to his village, I suppose. She didn't have to let him go," he added darkly. "I think she left him alive to spread the word, Ellishiva. So that he'd bring others to try to defeat her. I think she's been doing it all along." He trailed to a stop, breathing hard.

"Go on," encouraged Ellishiva gently.

Maximus swallowed and nodded. "After that," he went on, "I don't remember much. The poison twisted my memory, I think. They dust our wings with Khlorus so that we can pass back and forth between here and the human world. I must have wandered back in that way, somehow. I don't know how long I've been here, or if it's day or night . . ."

For a moment his eyes were cloudy, struggling to remember. Then they cleared and sharpened. He leaned forward and put one hand on Ellishiva's forearm, looking at her intently. "Ellishiva, the Sixth Element is still out there. Still killing. She must be stopped."

Ellishiva didn't reply. Without ever taking her eyes from Maximus, she could feel Hektor and Samara turning their gazes on her. The knowledge of what she had yet to tell them—and, now, Maximus too—weighed heavy on her heart again.

"Come on," she said quietly, at last. "Let's get Maximus out of here."

* * *

It wasn't difficult getting back to Chingetti Cellar on the vāhmana. Well, no more difficult than it had been the first time, anyway. Ellishiva had been concerned about Maximus, but she needn't have worried; if anything, the newly healed kinnaran seemed to relish the ride. From where it left them at the drop-off point in the south root, it was only a short walk to the waterfall and into Rajah's secret study: the Bulbdome.

Ellishiva pushed open the unlocked door and went in first. The Bulbdome had obviously been named for a reason. It was huge, round, and ponderous, and from its towering ceiling, countless bulbs hung at varying heights from thin roots: some bare, some in clear protective jars. Like the study in the mango tree, the smell of old books was thick on the air, and the shelves were packed from floor to ceiling with curious objects. There was even an unlit fireplace next to a grand desk paired with a matching, heavy chair. Unlike the study in the Arboretum, however, there was no need to worry about making a mess: the room was already buried under piles of clutter. Old boxes and crates were piled high against every wall, and a thick layer of dust coated the higher shelves.

The others, especially Maximus, were drenched and shivering from the vāhmana ride. Ellishiva walked over to the fireplace and picked up the olivine jar sitting on the mantle. Uncorking it, she tapped a few specks of Bluzure spice dust into the open hearth, and a cozy, smokeless blue fire crackled to life. The rest of the company wasted no time gathering around it to dry off.

Ellishiva herself, however, was too distracted to feel cold. As the others huddled around the flames, she crossed over to the messy but much less dusty desk. Next to it sat a squat, round stove with an earthenware teapot on it . . . one that was warm to the touch. "Someone's been here," she informed the group by the fireplace, dropping her voice. "This teapot is still warm."

Maximus, Samara, and Hektor exchanged a worried look. Ellishiva turned to the desk and noticed a lone, empty teacup perched on the corner. Stretching over the mess, she picked it up and brought it to her nose. The scent of allspice filled her nostrils. "Rajah," she murmured, not sure whether to feel worried or relieved.

"Better than Baron Puck," muttered Samara from the fireplace. "I can't believe he's on our side."

"Let's make this quick," suggested Hektor nervously.

"What can we do, Ellishiva?" asked Maximus, stepping away from the fire. He was still damp, but his shivering had stopped. He cleared his throat and added sheepishly, "I'm afraid I was so caught up between the treenitys and telling you my story that I forgot to ask you why we were coming here."

"We're looking for my spice jar. Or Amborella's," explained Ellishiva, her eyes skirting over the shelves and the messy piles of old copies of *The Mannahatta Times* scattered over the floor. The books here were rare and unusual, some bound in silk or rough bark, others painted with brilliant vegetable dyes. Her fingers itched to pull them down and pore over them one by one. But now was hardly the time. Smothering the craving, she looked at Maximus and willed herself to focus again. "Something happened to me the night I was attacked by the Sixth Element. Something we don't understand. Samara and Hektor saw it. It was like a bright light bursting from my body. Amborella's spice jar recorded what happened that night, and mine holds my whole history. Maybe even more than my own history. If I can figure out what happened, maybe I—we can use it against the Sixth Element," she said, catching her tongue at the last moment. Then she forged on before anyone could catch the slip. "We're also keeping an eye out for anything else that might help us defeat her. And for a key to a chest that Jipsin Smilodon gave me." She set the teacup down on the desk again and reached for a pile of scrolls. "Just go through things for clues. There has to be something useful down here," she finished.

The company split up to comb the Bulbdome as Ellishiva began skimming through the scrolls. Maximus stuck close to Samara, who continued to feed him treenity treats from the endless supply stored in her noli. For a long while, they worked in silence. Ellishiva was just tossing aside the last of the scrolls when the kinnaran spoke up.

"I've never been this far from Nicobar," he mused, almost as if he were simply glad to be able to use his voice again. "The general told me before I came that I would see the First Spice—which is you, Ellishiva." He turned to look at her, and his eyes were sincere. "I'm sorry I didn't tell you the day we met in the black market. I would have, but they made me take an oath before they brought me here."

"It's all right," Ellishiva shrugged, beginning to sift through a pile of books and papers. "I already know. Saw it in my spice jar."

Maximus's eyebrows went up, but he seemed to accept this, possibly remembering the way she'd healed him in the root. A few more seconds went by as everyone continued to work. Then the kinnaran went on, more to himself than anyone else this time. "There were whispers in Nicobar that Amma had brought a First Spice to life, but no one knew which colony you were in, or if you really existed at all. Some said you were just a myth. Others thought she was keeping you at the Himosa, since only she and Symran go there." He glanced at her from the shelf where he was picking through dusty jars of crushed plants. "You're the greatest secret ever kept, Ellishiva. In Nicobar, no one knows your name."

Ellishiva sighed. "Well, that explains why I haven't been in *The Mannahatta Times*," she muttered. Pushing away the stack of books and papers, she went to join him by the shelves. "Any sign of my spice jar?" she asked.

"Not yet," said Maximus.

Ellishiva looked a little ways farther down the shelves. "Sam, any spice jars? Or keys?" she added, remembering the chest.

"No jars yet, Elli," replied the fairy, fluttering up to examine things stored high above her head. "Found these, though!" Two or three keys dropped to the floor, making heavy clinking sounds.

"Well, take out the chest and try them," said Ellishiva, a little annoyed at the fairy's carelessness. She turned back to Maximus as they continued to sort through the bric-a-brac side by side. "Do you know anything else about the Sixth Element? Even things that don't sound important might help. Tell me everything."

The kinnaran frowned, thinking. "Well, when she whispered to us, I think she spoke Pali. At least, Morpheus understood what she was saying, and he speaks it. I only know a few words, because the general forbade us to study it. But since Morpheus never listens to Father anyway—"

"Wait," interrupted Ellishiva suddenly, dropping the box of odd stones she'd been looking through and giving him a piercing look. "What did you say? Your father is who?"

"Oh," replied Maximus with a shrug. "The general."

"General Iliad is your *father*?" cried Samara, floating down behind them suddenly. The ring of keys from her noli was in her hand, but she seemed to have forgotten about them. "And Morpheus is your *brother*?" She gave a short guffaw. "Why do you always call him 'the general' then?"

"Well, he *is* our general," said Maximus defensively. Even Hektor had stopped digging through old baskets on the other side of the room, and was staring at him. "We can't go around calling him Ahpa when we're in uniform."

"No wonder he was so upset!" exclaimed Samara, turning to Ellishiva. "Remember, Elli? The night of the jungle sleepover, when we saw the general in the Hall? He was so angry, and it must have been because—"

"Because he thought he'd lost his son," Ellishiva finished, nodding. "You're right, Sam. It all makes sense now."

Beside them, Maximus had a bleak look on his face. "I wonder how my mother took the news about me." He sighed and his gaze drifted across the room, staring off into the dancing blue flames of the fire. When he went on, his voice was low and sad. "My other brother, Claudius, who was Morpheus's twin, was killed on duty. I don't know what happened to him, exactly. My family refuses to tell me. All I've heard are rumors."

Ellishiva looked at him. "That's the twin you were starting to tell me about at Cheeky Canteen, then? His name was Claudius?"

Maximus nodded. "I don't remember him well. I was so young when he died. But he and Morpheus did their schooling together in Madagascar Colony. Morpheus still has terrible nightmares about that place. His back is covered in burn scars." He glanced over at Hektor. "That boomerang the general gave you was Claudius's, Hektor. He must have seen something great in you, to give it up."

Ellishiva turned on Hektor. "You brought it with you?"

"No!" replied Hektor defensively. "You kept getting on my case about it because it was a weapon. Didn't want to get my head bitten off." He turned back to the baskets and added under his breath, "Though if you ask me, if there was ever a time to have one, this would probably be it."

Ellishiva rolled her eyes at his back and glanced over at Samara, who had paused in her efforts with the chest to hand Maximus another treenity. "How's it going?" she asked.

"No luck yet," the fairy sighed, turning back to the lock.

Ellishiva pursed her lips and looked at Maximus again. "You said the Sixth Element spoke to you," she remembered. "What did she say?"

Maximus frowned. "I'm not sure exactly," he admitted. "She spoke in riddles, fragments. 'One hundred and eight heads . . . ,' 'Last quarter moon . . . ,' 'Rebirth for you . . .' There was more, but it was in Pali language, so I couldn't understand."

"One hundred and eight?" repeated Ellishiva, knitting her eyebrows together as she resumed combing through the dusty objects on the shelf. "Why one hundred and eight? And what did she mean, rebirth for *you*, Maximus?"

"I don't know, but that's what she said," insisted Maximus. "She said I smelled like Nicobar, and that she would keep me. Whatever that meant. I wasn't listening that closely. I expected to die at any moment." He frowned and waved away the treenity Samara offered him, losing even his desire to eat for a moment.

"Nicobar," murmured Ellishiva. "And she spoke Pali language . . ."

"Yes, but only a few words of it," clarified Maximus. "I think she might have expected me to speak fluently, since Morpheus does. The two of them didn't speak anything else to each other. I couldn't understand the conversation, but it went on a long time. It was almost like he knew her."

Ellishiva shook her head, trying to clear it. "But she spoke about Nicobar. That means she knows that the colony there exists." She stopped and looked around at the group. "That means that the voice of the Sixth Element is from our world," she concluded shrewdly. "Who *is* she?" She looked at Maximus.

"I don't know, Ellishiva," said the kinnaran in a low voice. "But I wouldn't be surprised if she was connected to the Madagascar Massacre."

"I wouldn't, either," muttered Ellishiva darkly. She leaned against the dusty bookshelves, thinking. "Did she find Mannahatta by chance, or did someone lead her here? How did she get into this colony?" she wondered aloud.

"I don't think she's after the colony," chimed in Hektor quietly from across the room.

"Right," Ellishiva agreed. "It's me. She wants me. But how could she have known I was here? Maximus just said that even in Nicobar, no one knows my name."

Around her, the study was silent. Ellishiva crossed her arms and stared off into the middle of the room, thinking.

Her eyes fell on the empty teacup.

She uncrossed her arms and planted them on her hips, then crossed them over her stomach again. Her instincts were fighting a brutal battle with her heart. Still, Perseus's words had guided her well, and she had come too far not to trust her instincts now.

She steeled herself. "Where does Rajah disappear to, really?" she said into the quiet. "They tell us he's in Nicobar, but how can we be sure? Since this whole thing began, I've had one short conversation with him. The stove in here is still warm. The teacup smells like him." She took a deep breath. "I don't think Rajah's been going to Nicobar at all. I think he's been here all along, and I think Mr. Belanos and—and Baron Puck have been helping him. I think he's protecting someone."

Another silence, longer than before, stretched through the room. At last, Maximus said what they all seemed to be thinking. "Rajah was the prefect of the Madagascar Colony . . ."

Ellishiva took another shaky breath and set her jaw. "We need to find my spice jar," she said firmly. "Keep an eye out for anything from Rajah's past. We have to be prepared before we head to the river's edge."

"I'm with you, Ellishiva," declared Maximus, looking her straight in the eye. She saw him stand a little straighter, as if to prove to her that he was ready to face the Sixth Element again, despite his ordeal.

Ellishiva met the look with gratitude, but said nothing. Guilt nipped at her again, stronger than before. But she didn't want to tell him. Didn't want to tell any of them, as he, Samara, and Hektor turned back to the search, that this was something she alone had to do. Postponing it just a little longer, she too went back to combing the shelves.

For a long while, there was nothing but the muffled sounds of their efforts: moving crates, coughs as they blew the dust from the things they were inspecting, and the occasional object hitting the floor now and then. Hektor and Ellishiva stuck to the bookshelves. Samara continued to pick through the mess for keys on the upper shelves, flying down now and then to test a new find in the lock. Maximus, meanwhile, crossed over to the messy piles of *The Mannahatta Times* stacked beside Rajah's desk that Ellishiva had just stepped over without a second thought.

It was Maximus who found it.

"Ellishiva," he called as loudly as he dared. "Here, I found something. There's an emblem on it."

In seconds, they were all crowded around the side of the desk. There, in the place where Maximus had shifted the pile of papers aside, was her spice jar.

"Careful," Ellishiva cautioned as several hands moved to clear the area around it at once. Her heart was beating quickly and she shut her eyes for a moment, calming her nerves. When she opened them again, she felt steadier . . . and three sets of eyes were looking at her expectantly.

She cleared her throat. "When I touch it," she began, with more confidence than she felt, "the dust will take me away. I don't know how long I'll be gone, but in the meantime, I need the rest of you to keep looking for clues."

Hektor nodded solemnly. Maximus's forehead creased in concern.

"Don't worry," said Samara to the kinnaran, patting him reassuringly on the shoulder. "She's done this before."

"I can't wait to see," replied Maximus, raising an eyebrow.

Ellishiva gave him a half-smile. Then she took one last breath, touched the lid of the jar, and was gone.

CHAPTER SEVENTEEN
OLD SPICES

In the spice jar, everything was dark, just as it had been before. This time, however, Ellishiva knew what to do. Gathering herself, she focused on what she wanted to see first.

Who is Rajah protecting?

The thought had no sooner brushed her mind than the tiny, bright green light appeared. It darted about, embroidering the darkness like a lone firefly, searching for its destination.

At last, it came to hover above her head.

Ellishiva knew that it had found what it was looking for. Confidently, feeling that she was in charge of her spice dust this time instead of the other way around, she reached up and touched it.

The tiny light exploded into an infinite galaxy, sending billions upon billions of green stars cascading in brilliant showers around her as she was launched into silent space.

As before, words and worlds rushed through her head, and voices in many languages faded in and out of hearing. This time, however, she wasn't too distracted to take it in. There was something familiar about traveling this way, she reflected. As though she had experienced it at some other time, before her first trip into the spice jar, even. And just as the journey was about to end, she remembered.

This was what it had felt like to fly out of her body and plummet back to earth again, on the night that the Sixth Element had first attacked her.

Around her, the spice dust calmed suddenly. Ellishiva found herself standing in a neat, unfamiliar garden. Every leaf, every scent around her was clear as day—yet she was unable to touch what she saw.

A whiff of allspice filled her nostrils on a breeze, and she turned to find a young Rajah sitting on a bench nearby. His hair was pitch-black and cropped short; no burn scar marred the skin of his neck. She moved closer and saw that he was stitching together a doll. The breeze shifted, blowing the laughter of little girls to her ears, along with a nutty aroma touched with a hint of licorice.

Rajah looked up from his work. "Isabella!" he called "Seble! Where are you?"

Ellishiva followed his gaze to a low cropping of bushes, where two small, raven-haired girls were crouched, their hands clamped over their mouths as they struggled to contain their laughter. "Twins," she whispered to herself. "Coriander spice sisters." She frowned, remembering. "You were in Amber's spice dust, too."

Next to her, Rajah sighed, but there was a faint smile at the corner of his mouth. He stood from the bench and stretched. "Claudius!" he called over his shoulder, looking in a new direction now. "Morpheus! Baron! Kaleka!"

Ellishiva jerked her head around to see the faces that belonged to the names, but the spice dust was already moving again. The garden shifted and vanished around her, replaced a moment later by tall palm trees and, in the distance, a clear blue ocean. Not far from where she stood, a group of children was playing the Plant the Seed game that Amber liked so much, drawing a square filled with horizontal lines in the sand and then skipping through the boxes they'd created. One of them, laughing as she tripped on her one-footed landing, looked familiar.

The dust spun again and Ellishiva saw the same girl, turned so that her back was to her this time. Rajah was there, too, smiling fondly down at her. Around them, young Va'natures, dofauns, elves, fairies, and kinnarans in school uniforms milled about, trying to sneak a peek at what was happening without getting caught. The uniforms, Ellishiva noticed, were stamped with the same crest she'd seen the children wearing in Amber's spice dust during the massacre. "Look what I made for you, Kaleka," Rajah said, handing the little girl the doll he'd been stitching in the garden. A doll, Ellishiva thought, that looked an awful lot like Amborella's Dollie Burlap.

The doll was no sooner in Kaleka's hands than the two pretty Coriander sisters and a fairy were at her side, smiling and chattering as they admired the new toy. Kaleka beamed, happy to share her gift. The aromas of many sweet, warm spices mingled together on the air.

The spice dust spun, and Ellishiva saw the girl again. The crowds of the academy had gone and she was sitting under a mango tree beside a young kinnaran who looked faintly like Maximus, both of them joking around and nibbling on barbee jujubes. The doll, Ellishiva noticed, was tucked securely under the girl's arm. Thin rays of light filtered through the leaves overhead, making Kaleka's eyes twinkle as she laughed.

The dust spun once more, revealing the same two friends again. This time, however, the girl was sobbing, her face buried in the kinnaran boy's neck as he stroked her raven hair. Without even knowing what was wrong, Ellishiva's heart sank for them. Whispering words of comfort, the boy fixed Dollie Burlap's amber necklace around Kaleka's neck. The scent of allspice was on the air, but Ellishiva barely noticed it. She came closer to the couple and saw a smooth, familiar piece of curved wood tucked into the back of the kinnaran's trousers. Her eyebrows went up.

"Claudius's boomerang," she breathed, absently touching the necklace that Amborella had given her. "You were in love. A Va'nature, in love . . . and with a kinnaran!" Her frown deepened. "No wonder Rajah and Lady Malinia were so upset with me when they heard I was friends with Maximus."

The dust shifted her through time again, presenting her with Rajah and Kaleka a second time. The black-haired girl was clutching her stuffed toy a little too tightly in her hands. "I *love* my doll, Rajah! I will keep her with me always." Kaleka's voice was oddly harsh and her smile seemed slightly wild. It occurred to Ellishiva that she didn't know what spice she was.

No sooner had she moved to take a closer look, however, than the dust spun again, faster than ever. A chill passed through her body as it carried her out into space, apparently for no reason other than that it wanted to. Distant planets rolled by in the silent blackness, immeasurably far away.

Nearby, the bright green light danced and winked. Ellishiva frowned at it sternly. "Why am I in the element of ether? Take me where I want to go, not where you feel like taking me, spice dust."

The green light blinked at her petulantly. Nevertheless, in the next moment the dust was moving again, ushering her through time so quickly that she saw all the phases of Earth's moon pass by in the blink of an eye. Before she knew it, she was standing in Madagascar Colony once again.

"There, there, my full moon. All will be well."

"Rajah," Ellishiva gasped, turning sharply at the sound of the familiar endearment. He was standing right behind her, but it wasn't that that made her heart jump suddenly into her throat.

Standing in front of young Rajah was an image of herself.

For a moment she was lost in shock. Before now, she had never been close enough to see how much Kaleka's face resembled her own. The girl was scared and crying. Once more, her pain tugged at Ellishiva's heart. Rajah had one arm around her shoulders and words of reassurance continued to spill from his lips, but Ellishiva could tell they were useless. Kaleka's wounds, whatever they were, ran deeper than any words could heal.

This time, when the spice dust spun again, it left Ellishiva floating in darkness. In her head, the eerie cry of a girl echoed as she passed through the boundless black space. A chill as bitter as a frozen winter night curled down her spine. Below, she could just make out the sheen of charcoal-black water. On its calm surface, oily, glimmering silver streaks were streaming like mercury into a dark hole at the center, forming a complex design as they did so.

A design, Ellishiva realized with a start, that she had seen before. A design, in fact, that she had laid eyes on almost every day of her life.

Suddenly, a mixture of spices that smelled of nutmeg, cinnamon, and cloves—along with the stench of burnt wood and green leaves— rose off the water and filled Ellishiva's nose. From somewhere above, a single shaft of pale light fell and hit the black ocean. Where it shone on the water, a shadowy image began to emerge from the black surface, forming a nose . . . a chin . . . a mouth.

The face was Ellishiva's.

No, not her face—Kaleka's face, she realized. Dark power was consuming the girl, dragging her down into its depths. Yet even as it did so, she was reaching out to Ellishiva, too.

Compassion washed through her like the flood her image was drowning in. Unafraid, she reached her hand toward the shadow of the girl. The chill of the water enveloped her, yet somehow it was fading. She felt her body growing warmer and warmer, and then the velvet darkness closed in once more.

She materialized again softly, like a puff of green mist. She was back in Chingetti Cellar, near the fireplace in the Bulbdome, which explained the warmth. For a moment, she held on to her cloudy, spice-dust form, thinking, not wanting to reappear again just yet. Around the study, the others had gone back to the search as she had asked them, though they seemed to be taking turns casting glances over their shoulders at the spot where she had disappeared.

Ellishiva reined in her emotions. She was wasting time. Releasing her hold on the magic, she became her solid self again. The remaining wisps of spice dust slipped back into the jar and the lid snapped shut behind them.

Three heads jerked around to look at her.

"Did you find anything?" Ellishiva asked them urgently. "Wait. Sam, I need to borrow a piece of chalk." The thoughts tumbling around in her head were almost bottomless and she had to write them down before they became tangled beyond recognition.

Not missing a beat, Samara, who was hovering over the still-locked chest on top of Rajah's desk, reached into her noli, called up a fat piece of chalk, and tossed it to Ellishiva.

Ellishiva caught it and knelt on the hearth in front of the fireplace. "Any luck with the chest?" she called over her shoulder as she began to sketch and scribble on the floor.

"No, nothing yet," reported Samara. "What did you see in the—"

"Keep trying. Jipsin Smilodon said it would open when I needed it," interrupted Ellishiva, scrawling onto the hearth.

With a grumble, Samara flew back to the shelves to continue her hunt for keys.

Maximus, meanwhile, had flown down from a shelf near the impossibly high ceiling and was kneeling beside her. Unlike the fairy, he seemed to know better than to interrupt Ellishiva as she copied her thoughts onto the floor. Instead, he kept quiet, intently studying the markings she made.

"Elli, I found a book," said Hektor, appearing suddenly between them. "There's a symbol in it that's—"

"Hold on," Ellishiva cut him off sharply, concentrating on the chalk. She finished sketching out the pattern in her mind, the one she had seen on the surface of the water in her spice dust. Only then did she look up at the book in Hektor's hands: *Ancient Almagest of the Three Earths* by Omyhra Arru. Mathematical equations and drawings adorned its cover.

"Wow," Hektor said, staring down at the picture she'd just completed on the hearth.

"What?" probed Ellishiva. "What did you find in there?"

Without a word, Hektor opened the book and laid it on the ground in front of them. Ellishiva did a double take.

It was an exact copy of what she'd just drawn.

"Elli, that symbol," gasped Samara, who had suddenly appeared fluttering over their heads to get a better view. "It's on Baron Puck's wand! We saw it, remember? In the antiquities shop."

"I remember," agreed Ellishiva. She glanced up. "And Sam, those children we saw in Amber's spice dust. I got a better look at them this time. At the uniforms they were wearing." She glanced down at the twin drawings again. "It was on them, too. Their crest."

"But how can that be?" demanded Hektor, dragging his fingers through the fading remnants of his root-beard. "That's the symbol Rajah carved on the door to our warren. What does it have to do with Madagascar?"

Ellishiva studied the symbol thoughtfully, her mind running through all that she had just seen. "It's more than just the sign," she murmured, remembering what her guardian had said to her on the day he'd carved it. "It's about finding home. 'The lost, weary souls who see this mark will know that they have returned home.' I always thought he was talking about us." She looked up, her gaze disappearing into the crackling blue of the fire. "Who has he really been expecting to come knocking at our door?" she whispered.

"Someone who lived in Madagascar Colony," Maximus concluded logically.

Ellishiva gave a grim nod. "This symbol would have meant something to the Sixth Element if she were from the Madagascar Colony. It was everywhere. It would have been something she felt connected to. Something dear to her. And Rajah knows *all* about this!" She paused, anger simmering in her veins, and scowled at the designs in front of her, thinking hard. An idea bloomed in her mind. She narrowed her eyes. "Hektor," she almost barked. "You're good at math. What do you see in this shape, number-wise?"

Hektor bent close to the designs, frowning. "Well, the outline," he began slowly. "It's complicated on the inside, but the outline is just a simple pentagon, of course. A figure with five sides. So number-wise…" His frown deepened as he considered. "Number-wise, each of the five interior angles is one-hundred-and-eight degrees."

"Exactly. One hundred and eight!" exclaimed Ellishiva triumphantly. She turned to Maximus. "That's the number you heard the Sixth Element talking about, right?"

Maximus raised his eyebrows, impressed. "Yes, it was," he confirmed.

Ellishiva nodded emphatically. She reached into her noli and pulled out several of her soaked notes, opening them carefully to make sure they didn't break apart.

"But why would the Sixth Element bother with that, Elli?" asked Hektor, running a hand through his short hair. "Why send a message in numbers?"

"Because numbers are a universal language," Ellishiva pointed out simply, handling the corner of a drenched map with care. Above, she noticed vaguely, Samara had fluttered away again, and little scratches and bumps were drifting over from where the fairy had doubtless resumed fiddling with the chest behind them.

"Could she have been talking about coordinates?" speculated Maximus, eyeing the unfolding map. Then he shook his head, dismissing his own theory. "But one hundred and eight doesn't mean anything by itself. The Sixth Element would have had to give us more numbers than one to mark a location."

"Maybe it's one of your mantra numbers, Elli," proposed Hektor, jumping on the bandwagon.

"Or a reference to payamar," added Maximus, on a roll now. "It has one hundred and eight pressure points, and a true master could kill you instantly."

Ellishiva shook her head, silencing them both. "I don't even know one hundred and eight mantras, Hektor. And I've never seen the Sixth

Element use payamar yet." She furrowed her brow and looked down at one of the diagrams she'd just unfolded, a map of the sky. "Stars. Phases of the moon. The planets," she murmured, tapping her finger on the closest constellation as she thought out loud. "She mentioned the last quarter moon to you, too, Maximus. But the next one isn't for another week or so. I've been tracking it. Still," she reasoned, "even though the Sixth Element knows how to read our calendar, it's obvious she's been living in the human world. And I have a feeling that she's never cared about the last quarter moon. Not the one in the sky, anyway. Not at all."

For a few long seconds it was quiet, save for the faint clunks and clinks of Samara fiddling with the chest. Then even those ceased.

Finally, an idea dawned on Ellishiva. "Hold on," she blurted suddenly, making the boys jump. She picked up the chalk again. "What date is today on the human calendar?"

"It's September," replied Maximus.

"The ninth month of the year for humans," added Hektor, still in number mode. "The eleventh day of September, I think. Isn't it?" He looked at Maximus, who nodded.

Ellishiva wrote a nine and an eleven down on the hearth, and then paused, frowning. "But we've been down here a long time, Hektor. It has to be way after midnight by now."

"So it's September 12, then," concluded Maximus.

"Exactly," muttered Ellishiva, drawing a large X through the eleven and replacing it with a twelve. Instantly, the answer clicked into place inside her head. She slapped her free hand loudly on the drawing of the pentagon on the floor. "What does nine times twelve make?" she demanded, rewriting the numbers as an equation on the hearth.

"One hundred and eight," chorused the boys, glancing at one another in surprise.

Ellishiva nodded and scribbled down the answer. "That's it, then," she concluded, tossing down the chalk. "That must have been her message.

Today—the twelfth day of September, 1609—something is going to happen in the human world, if it hasn't happened already." Restless, she rose to her feet and began pacing back and forth in front of the fireplace. "She must have been planning this all along, waiting in that cave on South Island since the day she attacked me. Between the ice fairy's heart and the human blood, she must be almost invincible by now. I don't care what she says about a last quarter moon. Whatever destruction she's planning is happening now." She paused in her pacing and glared into the fire again. "And Rajah isn't here. Gone to Nicobar again, just like the last time she attacked. Except he isn't at Nicobar," she muttered, the memory of the still-warm teacup fresh in her mind.

There was a pause. Then Hektor asked uneasily, "Where is he then, Elli?"

Ellishiva looked at him. "I think he's at the river," she replied quietly. "I think he went to South Island. To see her."

Horror and disbelief sprang up in Hektor's eyes. "That's impossible," he protested, some of his old defiance back in his voice. "I don't know what Rajah's done, but he wouldn't destroy Mannahatta. He'd never want to destroy us!"

"Of course not," Ellishiva snapped at him, beginning to pace back and forth again. The visions of Rajah caring for the children of Madagascar and sewing Dollie Burlap filled her mind. "He's not trying to destroy *us*. He's trying to help *her*."

The anger faded from Hektor's face, replaced by grim understanding. It made only too much sense. Rajah felt responsible for the lives lost in the massacre. He'd told Ellishiva himself that the tragedy haunted him to this day. And now he was trying to repair damage that could never be undone.

Ellishiva stopped pacing. "Listen, everyone. Sam, you too!" From where she'd been peeking through the keyhole of the chest on Rajah's desk nearby, the fairy snapped sharply to attention. "Earlier, when we were in the roots, Maximus heard drums. I bet you they were human drums. The Sixth Element is making her stand in the human world. In my human books, I've read that men often play some musical instruments when they go to battle. And the most common ones of all are drums." She paused for a moment, letting the meaning of her words sink in. Then she turned to Samara, who, she realized suddenly, had been unusually quiet for the past five or ten minutes. "Sam," she asked, narrowing her eyes. "What's going on?"

"On?" repeated the fairy innocently.

Ellishiva took in her posture, the perfect "o" of her mouth, and the way she was trying to block the chest from view with her body. There was only one possible answer. "Sam! You found the key, didn't you?" she accused.

"Oh. Well, it's—okay, yes. I found the key, Elli," the cornered fairy blabbered nervously. "You were all so busy, I didn't want to interrupt. So I just . . . er—I just took a peek inside for you, and I have to say," she rushed on, not wanting to give the others a chance to scold her, "I'm not sure this is the kind of thing you'll be prepared to eat."

"Nobody's eating anything, Sam. Oh, just give it here," scowled Ellishiva, striding over to the desk and nudging her aside. She pushed a messy heap of papers out of the way and lifted the lid of the chest. Then she stopped, blinking down at the contents.

"This is supposed to make me fly?" she grumbled.

There, suspended and turning slowly in the crate, was an egg. It was perhaps the size of a watermelon, and its shell was a deep, intense yellow spotted with blue and red and streaked with brown. Ellishiva frowned.

Even if the creature inside it had wings, it seemed unlikely that it would be flying anyone anywhere anytime soon.

"Wow!" Maximus had appeared behind her left shoulder and was staring down into the chest as though he were afraid to blink. "What's this doing on Mannahatta Colony?"

"What is it?" prompted Ellishiva, still scowling.

"It's an egg," shrugged Hektor, who had popped up behind her other shoulder and was clearly as unimpressed with the contents of the chest as she was herself.

"Not just an egg!" gushed Maximus, his eyes wide with excitement. "Look at its colors! This is rare. *Unbelievably* rare. I've only ever seen sketches of them in books—"

"What *is it*?" demanded Ellishiva again, losing her patience.

"It's an Ariopanchaterix!" blurted Maximus, completely unfazed. "They're incredible! Not that anyone I know has ever seen one, but they're supposed to be wise dofauns with untold powers. Some of them even have the power of foresight. They're completely unique. Like Symran," he concluded, his sparkling eyes never leaving the egg.

Ellishiva's curiosity got the better of her. Bracing her elbows on the desk, she leaned down to get a closer look at the egg. In moments, a soft warmth seemed to envelop her. The colors on the shell took on an enchanting quality—lovelier than a newly sprouted vivarium of young pitcher plants after a rain, she thought. Captivated in spite of herself, Ellishiva lifted her right hand, and set her palm gently on the smooth, turning surface.

The egg glowed green and a hot shiver ran from the crown of her head all the way down to her toe ring. Startled, Ellishiva pulled her hand away.

But it was too late; the chest collapsed flat onto the table's wooden surface. Before her eyes, Ellishiva saw the broken wood begin to transform, stretching and twisting itself into new myrrh twigs, tender reeds, leaves, and bursts of green grasses. They crackled and snapped as they grew, weaving themselves together, layer upon layer, until at last they had formed a gigantic nest on Rajah's desk.

The egg set itself down gently in the middle of it and lay perfectly still.

For a moment, the company simply stared, mesmerized. Ellishiva cleared her throat halfheartedly. She had to snap out of it, had to get to the river. Then the egg gave a shiver and her resolve evaporated like a drop of dew on a hot day.

"Touch it again, Elli," Hektor urged, his eyes bright and radiating wonderment.

Ellishiva's hand was already reaching toward the egg. As soon as her fingertips brushed its surface, a great, splitting *crack* echoed through the Bulbdome, like a tall tree slowly breaking in half. Blue light from the fire danced over the shell as it began to crack. The scent of myrrh filled the air.

Then the sharp, ivory-colored point of a beak emerged from the colorful, fractured egg.

Four pairs of eyes stared, transfixed. The tip was quickly followed by the rest of a stout beak with flaring, mucus-filled nostrils, and then by a long, narrow head, wet and sticky, as if it were coated with honey. The skin of the creature's neck was rough like a lizard's and was the icy blue shade of fresh juniper berries. Its eyes were gummy, half-closed.

Ellishiva watched as it blinked warily, as if the light in the study were too bright for it to stand. It was far from beautiful. Yet, somehow, Ellishiva felt a deep desire to touch it once again. She watched her own hand reach out and rest itself gently on the creature's head. Her palm glowed green and a shimmering veil of Khlorus swirled over and around the tiny dofaun.

In the space of an instant, it doubled in size.

"Oh my gosh," gasped Samara. "It's getting bigger!"

"Great!" exclaimed Hektor, his eyes even wider than before. "Go on, Elli. Touch it again!"

"Only the Supreme Being, Amma, can bring a dofaun to life," whispered Maximus. Ellishiva realized that, of all of them, he was the only one no longer staring in awe at the egg.

He was staring in awe at her.

Unnerved, Ellishiva refocused on the miracle unfolding in front of her—her miracle. Everything else faded away as she gazed at the strange, newborn dofaun on Rajah's desk. Instinctively, she lifted her palm from its great, gawky head, then raised her other one so that both of her hands framed the creature without quite touching it.

More green Khlorus spice dust misted out of the marks on her skin and danced around its body. Rich yellow feathers the color of turmeric bloomed along its blue-skinned neck. Its nostrils flared, releasing thin streams of gray smoke. It raised its head and its magnificent fiery red eyes, fully open now, locked on Ellishiva's.

The rich shade of the Ariopanchaterix's irises reminded her of Persian saffron. *Whatever key Samara found wasn't what he meant*, Ellishiva thought, remembering what Perseus had said to her when he'd given her the chest. *It was my touch. Only I could make it fly.*

"Wow!" marveled Hektor beside her, jolting her from her reverie. "It has claws on the tips of its wings!"

It was true, Ellishiva realized, watching as the creature haltingly spread its wings for the first time, revealing a rich plumage of yellow feathers peppered with red-brown spots the color of dates. It lost its balance as it tried to flap them, and its neck landed on the rim of the nest, leaving its head dangling over the edge of the desk. It closed its eyes again, exhausted. A strip of bright blue skin as thick as a crocodile's hide ran down the length of its back, like a long saddle. More yellow feathers bordered the strip on either side, snaking all the way to the tip of its tail, which ended in what seemed to be three scaly, knob-like pinecones.

The Ariopanchaterix made a gurgling sound in its throat, struggling to raise its head. Patiently, tenderly, Ellishiva stroked its rough skin in encouragement. It worked. Once more, the fiery eyes flew open. The dofaun's beak parted wide, and a strange, harsh sound rang through the Bulbdome and the cellar beyond.

"Auukkk. *Auuukk!*"

By the edge of the desk, Samara grinned. "It's calling you, Elli," she said. "It thinks you're its mother."

"Maybe she is," breathed Maximus quietly.

Ellishiva bent closer to the Ariopanchaterix, pulling off the bits of colorful shell that still clung to its yellow feathers. Cautiously, one by one, the others moved in to help.

"Look at those spurs on its sides. And its tail!" whispered Samara, gawking. Ellishiva followed the line of her gaze. The three pine-cone-shaped knobs at the tip of the dofaun's tail were shivering as if they had a life of their own.

Maximus saw it, too. Quick as a flash, he caught Hektor and Samara's hands, pulling them safely away from the creature's ruffled feathers. "Careful!" he warned sharply. "The Ariopanchaterix has chosen its partner. No one else can touch it without its permission. If it catches you in its claws or its beak it can kill you. And I'm guessing it won't be painless," he added dryly.

"This is amazing, Elli!" crowed Samara, not at all put off by the kinnaran's speech. "Our very own Ariopox—Apacriox . . . er," she stalled, glaring at Hektor, who had crossed his arms and was smirking at her. "Well, we should call him Ari," she muttered finally, scowling at him.

"Ari," murmured Ellishiva, who had finished cleaning away the last of the shell fragments and was now stroking the dofaun's feathered neck gently. It was growing even more rapidly now, its weight reducing the nest beneath it to splinters. The two spindly limbs beneath its torso became mighty legs covered with thick indigo-colored hide, and razor-sharp claws tipped the ends of the three long toes on each of its two feet.

In no time at all it was double the size of Banog the eagle, and Rajah's desk split beneath it as though it were made of twigs.

Everyone but Ellishiva stood back, but she barely noticed. There was a deep, warm peace in her soul. She felt as if she'd just finished a whole year of yoga.

"It's so calm," marveled Maximus somewhere behind her. "The books always said it had a temper."

Ari gazed around the Bulbdome with curiosity, his saffron-red eyes taking in the scores of strange, dusty objects on the shelves. There was no longer so much as a whisper of weakness about him. Ellishiva stood where she was and waited, letting him take everything in. At last, the great dofaun lowered its huge head until it was only inches from Ellishiva's face. He looked intently into her eyes and the breath from his wet nostrils set her hair swaying back and forth. His fragrance, Ellishiva mused, was of freshly crumbled lime leaves with hints of myrrh.

Ari opened his beak, curled his acid-yellow tongue, and emitted a screech that could have drowned out a trumpeting herd of elephants.

The sound was so loud that it echoed throughout Chingetti Cellar. Ellishiva didn't even flinch, not at all afraid. But the rest of the group dropped into crouches, clapping their hands over their ears. Samara looked particularly wobbly, as though Maximus's earlier warnings were finally starting to make sense to her. She clutched Hektor's shoulder for balance.

Fortunately, Ari paid them no mind. He cocked his head to the side and continued to look at Ellishiva, as if checking to make sure that he had her undivided attention. Then, with perfect control, he flipped his long tail up over his body like a scorpion, lowering the three-pronged tip so that it hung behind Ellishiva's back. As silently as a deadly spider hanging from a silken thread, the scales on the cones of its tail retracted inward and upward to reveal three long-fanged, hissing cobra heads. She heard the others give a muffled gasp.

Then, faster than any of her three companions could move, the fanged tail snatched Ellishiva up without piercing her skin, swung her over Ari's head, and set her down in the middle of its blue lizard back, just in front of its wings.

Ellishiva teetered for a moment, surprised. Then she regained her balance. She took hold of two bony ridges jutting from Ari's back and her feet found purchase on the spur-like protrusions flanking the sides of his leathery indigo skin. It felt as natural as anything she had ever done. As if the dofaun had been made for her.

Ari spread his wings, rose from the desk, and began to circle the room. He seemed to grow even larger as he turned, shaking crates, setting bottles and jars clanking together, knocking books to the floor, and sending the many bulbs hanging from the ceiling banging against each other. Some of the thin roots broke altogether, raining bulb-filled jars onto the floor below. In a handful of seconds he had wreaked more havoc in Rajah's second study than Ellishiva had managed to do in an hour's time in the first one.

Ellishiva barely noticed. Her face was serious and her mind was calm. There was no more putting off what she'd known she would have to do all along. With a deep, silent sigh, she touched Ari's neck. He ceased swooping and held himself steady in midair, hovering three or four yards over Rajah's crushed desk.

Below, the others had scrambled to their feet again. "Hang on, Elli! I'm coming!" Hektor shouted up at her.

"Me, too!" chimed in Samara, spreading her wings to fly up and join her.

But Maximus was quicker than both of them. In one movement he had caught Samara by the ankle with his left hand, and was holding Hektor back with his right. "No!" he told them harshly. "The Ariopanchaterix has chosen its rider. Ellishiva Cinnamon." He looked up at her, and his voice grew quiet with respect. "The First Spice."

Ellishiva saw Hektor opening his mouth to protest this and knew she had to speak first. She knotted her hands in Ari's yellow feathers, willing her words to be steady. "I have to go now," she said apologetically, looking between her brother and her best friend. "I have to go alone. I'm sorry I couldn't tell you before." She gripped the feathers a little tighter as expressions of shock and rebellion passed over the faces below her. "The Khlorus inside me will let me pass into the human world. This is my destiny to face, not yours. But," she added, warm gratitude weighing down her words, "I never could have gotten this far without you. All of you. My army."

Hektor scowled and tried to jerk himself out of Maximus's grip, but the kinnaran held him fast. Next to them, Samara's face looked pinched around the edges, as though she were about to cry. Still, she seemed to understand, and the wings on her back folded themselves together again, resigned. And then there was only one person left to say goodbye to.

From where he was restraining her struggling brother, Maximus looked up at her. "Be careful, Ellishiva," he warned, his words steady and quiet.

Ellishiva met his fire-yellow gaze and nodded. As if sensing his cue, Ari began to circle again, his mighty wings sending gusts of wind rushing around the Bulbdome like a wave of hurricanes. Below, Ellishiva caught a glimpse of Samara and the boys protecting their faces with their forearms as more of the hanging bulbs rained down upon them.

And then the Ariopanchaterix was swooping toward the great door, knocking it loose from its hinges with outstretched claws as though it were no more than a dangling leaf in autumn. With a few powerful beats of his wings, Ari angled himself away from the ground, wheeling upward until he was almost vertical to the floor. Ellishiva bent her head close to his neck as he began his ascent into the high mists of Banyan Falls.

They soared up like a comet against the gushing water, off into the dark Mannahatta sky.

HALVE MAEN

The stars shone so fiercely that it seemed absurd to call the night dark. Ellishiva sat astride Ari's back as the mighty creature swooped across Mannahatta Island, his powerful tailwind setting the treetops thrashing as he skimmed over the towering forest. The crisp scent of pine filled her nostrils, sharpening her senses. It was time.

Resting one hand on Ari's neck, Ellishiva stretched the other out in front of her. The flash of green was so brief that, if her eyes had chosen that moment to blink, she would have missed it.

They were in the human world.

At once, Ellishiva felt her sense of purpose grow stronger. The play and pleasures of her childhood in the Va'nature world were suddenly far away. Her long hair flew out behind her in brown waves, leaving her shoulders bare against the wind. Beneath her, Ari glided in silence toward the Muheekantuck River, which flowed smooth and wrinkleless up ahead, like a scarf of silver silk. There was no need to speak; Ari heard her thoughts, and she could sense his. A gentle touch on his neck changed their direction quicker than a word ever could.

They glided along the towering cliffs of whitewashed basalt that hugged the bends of the river. On either bank, the foliage was quiet, waiting patiently for the frosts of autumn to fall. A few regal sugar maples had begun to change color, their leaves glowing amber in the starlight like the prized syrup they produced.

Suddenly, a faint scream came to Ellishiva's ears.

A cold shiver ran through her body. Beneath her, Ari's muscles tensed. *You heard that too*, she thought to him. Her legs felt heavy as lead against the great dofaun's flanks, but her mind was determined.

Let's get to South Island, fast, she thought.

Ari let out a screech of understanding. With a few flaps of his powerful wings, he rose higher into the air, speeding south much faster than before, down the Muheekantuck River.

It wasn't long before an object appeared on the water in the distance: a light the size of a pinhead, fixed in the night as if it had been painted on a canvas.

"There, Ari," Ellishiva murmured, pointing with one hand as she gently touched his neck with the other. The dofaun slowed in midair, seeing what she saw. Then he beat his great wings again and dove forward and downward. In what felt like mere moments they were gliding in to observe the object at a safe distance.

What had looked like a pinprick at a distance was anything but.

"A human ship," Ellishiva whispered so quietly that the words were barely audible. Hearing her anyway, Ari reined himself in and slowed to a hover above the vessel. An eerie silence enveloped them. Ellishiva stared down at the craft in the river, anchored not far away from South Island itself. The ship's sails were reefed, and it floated motionless on the dark water.

"Let's look around, Ari," she breathed.

Smoothly, the Ariopanchaterix began to circle the watercraft again. Ellishiva craned her neck, trying to make out the emblem on one of the flags hanging lifelessly from the ship's masts. Sensing her intentions, Ari swooped in a little closer. The breeze from his wings and tail stirred the uppermost flag on the mainmast, making it flap just enough. Ellishiva sat back, surprised.

"I've seen this seal in my books, in the *Conquerors of the Great Seas* volumes. It's the VOC seal," she muttered to herself, frowning. "The Dutch East India Company uses it. But what are they doing on Mannahatta? There are no spices here . . ."

Under her, she could sense that Ari, too, was curious. Ellishiva wracked her brain. "Maybe some strange storm from the ocean pushed it off its course," she speculated to the dofaun. Ari remained skeptical. Ellishiva sighed uneasily. She didn't quite believe it herself. Below, everything remained as still as they had found it. Ellishiva plucked up her courage. "Go low, Ari," she murmured.

Ari's feathers rustled obediently. He glided around the ship's starboard side, drifting down until he was just a few handbreadths above the river's surface, his three-headed cobra tail trailing in the water. Ellishiva studied the worn planks of the ship's hull, examining it for clues. They skirted the bow, then rose slightly, gliding along the main deck and over the poop deck rising behind it.

When they rounded the stern, Ellishiva caught sight of the ship's name carved into the sea-battered wood. Her eyes went wide.

"*Halve Maen!*" she breathed in disbelief. "'Half Moon.' I know you. You're the ship that's captained by Henry Hudson, that English human that was hired by the Dutch."

As if pulled by something beyond herself, her head tilted upward to look at the moon that was hanging almost half-full in the night sky. Its bright white light illuminated her face, and with it, her thoughts. "Half of a moon is seen when it has completed one quarter of an orbit around the Earth," she repeated from memory, thinking hard. "A quarter of an orbit." She snapped her gaze back to the *Halve Maen* again. "And in the books they call you . . . they call you . . ."

The Last Quarter Moon.

The answer to the riddle slammed into her so hard that she nearly lost her balance on Ari's back. "You're a ship!" she gasped. "The Sixth Element didn't want to face me on the night of a last quarter moon. She wanted me to meet her *here!*" Her thoughts seemed to explode with the revelation, scampering so far ahead of her that it was hard to keep up. "'*Destruction . . . last quarter moon.*' She must have been following this ship the whole time. It wasn't a storm that made it stray from its course. It was her. *She* was the cause of this evil."

But before Ellishiva could make sense of what to do next, a great lurch yanked her back into the moment.

Something had latched onto Ari's tail and was dragging him down toward the water. The hairs on Ellishiva's arms prickled and the tattooed circles on her neck glowed in warning. She tightened her grip on Ari's back with her knees. The dofaun's wings flapped wildly, violently shifting her from side to side. He let out a piercing shriek—whether from anger or fear, it was impossible to tell—as his great body shattered the river's silver surface. His beating wings splashed uncontrollably, drenching Ellishiva with water. She added her will to his strength and, together, they struggled to stay above the surface.

But they were losing. Slowly, the lower half of Ari's body began to sink out of sight. Inch by inch, he was going under.

He wanted her to get off. There were no words behind the will, and at first Ellishiva fought against it. But the Ariopanchaterix was fiercely determined, and in moments she understood that it was his mind, not hers, telling her to flee: this was his battle to fight.

With a knot in her stomach, Ellishiva loosened her grip on his back, rolled to the tip of one huge, feathery wing, and swung herself toward the safety of the ship. Her hands latched onto the black-tarred rope shrouds falling down the sides of the *Halve Maen* in strips. In seconds she had scrambled most of the way up the side of the ship—as easily as if she'd been climbing up a vine-laden tree. She didn't even wait to reach the deck before jerking around to see how the battle in the water was faring.

Ari was almost entirely underwater, only the tip of his razor-sharp beak protruding from the stream's silver surface. Then that, too, disappeared as whatever he was fighting against dragged him out of sight, down into the darkness of the Muheekantuck River.

Ellishiva clung to the shroud, staring desperately into the water, willing him to resurface. But all her eyes could see were flashes of green in the inky depths below, like lightning behind black thunderclouds.

Swallowing her horror as best she could, she turned and finished clambering up the ropes and over the weathered railing. Its surface was wet and she slipped, landing on her back on the hard planks of the main deck with a *thud*. Stifling a groan, she looked around. The floorboards were gleaming as if they'd been streaked with dark oil. A smell filled her nostrils—disturbing, but familiar. She couldn't quite place it.

Gathering her wits, Ellishiva got to her feet again. She looked over the railing one more time, searching for any trace of her Ari. But the river below was smooth and implacable, as if nothing had ever broken its surface. Around her, the world was swathed in silence. Ellishiva swallowed and the sound was audible in her throat. Steeling herself, she looked over her right shoulder at the wide expanse of the deck she was standing on. It was dark and barren, save for one dim, lonely oil lamp hanging next to an hourglass from a couple of secure hooks on the mizzenmast. Within the stained glass, the lamp's flame burned low and still.

Ellishiva was about to approach it when a sudden movement caught the corner of her eye. Heart pounding, she jerked around—but it was only a black cat. It was dripping wet and its long tail, spotted with white, shivered back and forth. It took a few hopeful, wary steps in her direction and paused, looking up at her. A loud, pitiful cry escaped its throat.

Compassion tugged at Ellishiva's heart. She crouched on the deck and reached her arms out toward the sodden creature. To her surprise, the cat leapt into them. She held it against her chest, gently stroking its head, and the marks on her palms glowed green. The little animal's wet black fur shimmered, and a moment later it was fluffy and dry. It lifted its tail high, purring loudly.

Ellishiva held it closer, comforting both of them. "Cat, where are the humans of this ship?" she whispered into its ear. "Something's wrong. I feel it. Terrible things have happened here." She trailed off, looking around her once more. On the shadowy foredeck to her left, on top of the raised galley, something glinted. Ellishiva narrowed her eyes, squinting at the spot.

Then, from somewhere beyond the faint light of the oil lamp, the ship's floorboards gave a frightful squeal. The cat jerked its head toward the river and let out a yowl of terror, then leapt from Ellishiva's arms, darting off through a square hatch into the darkness below deck.

Ellishiva began to call after it, but froze at a sudden sound in the water. A stale, strangely warm draft brushed the back of her neck, and she turned her head back toward the mizzenmast to see where it was coming from. The source, as far as she could tell, was the captain's cabin. Before she could approach it, however, a familiar figure rolled limply through the open door and fell off the edge of the quarterdeck, landing with a dull *thump* on the main deck below.

For a moment, Ellishiva forgot how to breathe.

"Rajah!" she gasped, and the sound echoed over the ship. She rushed to his side and dropped to the deck beside him. Rajah's face and hair were smeared with drying blood that looked more gray than red in the starlight. Worse, streaks of fresh blood were oozing out from under his head and pooling around her knees. The raw scent of allspice was heavy on the air. Panicked, Ellishiva grabbed him by the shoulders and shook him. Her guardian inhaled a ragged, shaky breath and mumbled incoherently. He was still alive.

Ellishiva swallowed hard. "Rajah?" she managed.

Rajah cracked open his eyes and looked at her. The swollen tendons in his neck worked as he struggled to tell her something.

Ellishiva took a deep breath, forcing herself to stay calm. She leaned close to him. "Where are the humans? Where is your staff?" she asked quietly, encouragingly.

"Staff destroyed," replied Rajah, choking out the words. "She put a spell on—" He stopped, unable to go on.

Ellishiva set her jaw against the horror threatening to invade her chest. "I'm going to heal you," she said grimly, shifting to position herself behind his head. "Hold still."

But before she could so much as place her palms on his temples, a deep chill swept through her bones. The marks on her skin flashed green. At the edge of her vision, a shadow rose like a wave, and a brooding darkness washed over her, filling her soul with anger, fear, and gloom. Around her knees, Rajah's blood turned as cold as an ice ledge. Once again, the familiar odor flooded her nostrils, stronger than before, and this time, Ellishiva knew where she had smelled it before—in the tea from Madagascar that Mr. Belanos had given her, that day in the antiquities shop. In her spice dust, strung through the memories of Madagascar Colony.

And suddenly she knew. She knew from what she had seen in the past, from the doll, from the powerful scent of spices, even when Rajah hadn't been present. At last, she recognized the voice behind the Sixth Element.

Ellishiva touched the amber necklace around her neck. Another chill dropped down her spine, but when she spoke her words flew strong and clear from her lips. "I know who you are! I can smell you. Kaleka, a Va'nature of Allspice! The Sixth Element!"

"Well, well, well," drawled a dark voice behind her. To hear it was to know evil. "A clever girl, our First Spice."

Ellishiva felt the hairs on her neck rise. Nevertheless, she stood and turned to face the enemy.

Kaleka, the Sixth Element, was the embodiment of darkness. Tall as a fairy, she still possessed the raven hair Ellishiva remembered from the spice jar, but her face and skin had transformed into the scaly bark of a poisoned locust tree. Long, rough cuts and cracks traced her arms and neck, their crevices gleaming with a dark substance. The short, strange garment of tree bark wrapped about her body was cinched tight around her waist with a belt of human hair. Her fingers looked like splinters, miniature lances tipped with sharp, shiny points. Around her forearms, ribbons of brown moss drifted in the stale breeze, and a necklace of one hundred and eight gleaming white human skulls, shrunk to the size of silver coins, hung nearly to the bottom of her ribcage. Flickers of pale light filtered through the fissures in her chest from the ice fairy's silver heart beating within. Slowly, her red eyes blazing, she began to circle Ellishiva, forcing her to back away from Rajah.

Ellishiva's heart pounded in her throat as she retreated three steps . . . five steps . . . eight steps. Then her back collided with the railing of the ship and there was nowhere left to retreat to.

The Sixth Element paused in her approach, her prey cornered. A wicked, twisted sneer curled one corner of her mouth. "Well, well, well. Ellishiva Cinnamon," she drawled again in a voice like damaged silk. Her foul breath, more rotten than the stench of a full pitcher plant unable to digest its waste in the hot sun, stirred the loose strands of Ellishiva's hair, making her gag. "When first we met I was no more than a locust tree, with nothing but the heart of a fairy and a few sips of human blood to aid my movements. But look at me now, strong and well-formed at last by new blood. Your blood, in fact. A Va'nature's blood!" She gave a low laugh. "How do you find the transformation?"

Ellishiva stood frozen against the railing and said nothing.

Kaleka gave a derisive snort and went on. "To think you were here all along," she said almost to herself, the words dripping with disgust as her eyes ran the length of the battered ship, then returned to fix themselves hungrily on Ellishiva. "I roamed the oceans for so long. Searching everywhere. Everywhere!" A bitter, mocking look filled her burning red eyes, and she laughed again, hollowly. "And all that time, a hidden colony eluded me, concealing a whole pantry full of spices. Including the most precious one of all." The red eyes narrowed and the Sixth Element raised one splinter-tipped hand. She took a slow step forward.

Ellishiva darted away from the rail, out of her reach. There was bile in the back of her throat, and she was desperate to get back to Rajah. Before she had taken three steps, however, Kaleka was in front of her again, only inches from her face now, her acid-red tongue flitting against her bared teeth.

Instinctively, Ellishiva feinted away again, untouched.

A new, calculating look entered the Sixth Element's eyes as she realized that her prize would be harder to trap than expected. She began to circle again, and this time Ellishiva joined the moving ring, making sure she could see her enemy's face at all times. Her pulse beat an erratic tattoo through her veins. The rational thoughts of her mind fought a hard battle against it, but it was no use.

She had never been so terrified in her life.

"You know not what you resist," began Kaleka in a honeyed voice, still circling. "We are sisters, Ellishiva!"

"I am no sister of yours," bit back Ellishiva a little too quickly. She stole a glance at Rajah.

The burning red of Kaleka's eyes seemed to grow a shade darker. "Foolish girl. Don't look at him. *I* am your family!" she growled. "The necklace you wear is mine! Through it, with the help of your precious Nutmeg sibling, I have gotten to know you well. I know everything about you." The twisted mockery of a smile curled the corner of her lips again. "You yourself have told me all I could ever wish to know, my spice sister."

"I won't fall for your trickery, Kaleka!" cried Ellishiva, the words bursting from her throat. "You've killed so many, destroyed so many innocent lives—"

"Temper, temper," hissed Kaleka. "Didn't your Rajah teach you patience along with your yoga? Come to your senses, First Spice. You and I share so much. There is, shall we say, a little bit of me in you."

Ellishiva became suddenly very conscious of the scar on her side. The marks on her neck flashed green and her stomach lurched. "I'm *not* part of you," she spat desperately. "And don't tell me about patience. You don't know what patience is!"

The dark substance in the cracks of Kaleka's skin shimmered warningly. "Insolent spice girl!" she snarled. "How dare you speak to me of patience? I have roamed the oceans longer than a sapling like yourself could ever begin to conceive! They have become the playthings of my *patience*," she went on sneeringly. "I can make them simmer on my whim, as easily as your ridiculous elf, Guo, boils a pot of his hideous soup!"

Ellishiva paused just for the barest hint of a moment at the mention of Mr. Guo. Still, Kaleka noticed. The fury left her voice, replaced by a taunting, cunning drawl. "Indeed, I owe the fine businessman a debt of gratitude. It was he who mistook my moss for seaweed, and I rode his vāhmana straight into your cleverly hidden enchanted colony. Protected by Supreme Amma herself," she finished, gloating and malevolent at once.

Ellishiva listened to every word she said, but she was observing other things as well. From the corner of her eye, she noticed how even as Kaleka circled, her every move seemed to keep her well away from the black-tarred coils of rope shrouds dangling from the ship's railings. But why would she avoid them?

The question was cut short by a funnel of wind as Kaleka whirled suddenly up to the top of the mizzenmast. The weak light of the oil lamp below made the cracks and shadows of her face even more twisted than they already were. "Behold!" she roared in a voice like dark thunder, and another gust of warm, nauseating air washed over Ellishiva. "I am born of the darkest passions of the human soul. Soon I will control all the worlds of this universe and bend them to my will. For I am a Va'nature no longer. I am *Kaleka*, the Sixth Element!" The storm of her words grew more terrible and deafening with every syllable. "I am Kaleka—KA! The Destroyer. I am KA! I am Death!"

Slowly, the Sixth Element began to descend the mizzenmast toward Ellishiva, who stood rooted where she was, transfixed.

"Don't touch her, Kaleka!"

The voice was weak and strong at once. Ellishiva shivered out of her trance and turned to find that Rajah had managed to raise his bloodied head a few inches off the ground. His sunken eyes were fixed steadily on the monster above them. "It is me you want revenge on," he said reasonably, and even now, his words were full of patience, as though he were speaking to his own child. "I carved your seal into the door of our warren, Kaleka. It is there because I hoped that part of you was still alive. I can help you. Please, let me help you . . ." Ellishiva could hear the truth—and the emotion—in his plea.

The Sixth Element swung her terrible head toward him, and the power of her fury shifted. "Do not speak to me of hope, old man!" she screamed, and before Ellishiva realized what was happening, Kaleka had raised her hand and shot a black splinter at his heart. It grew to the size of a lance as it plummeted toward him. On the deck, Rajah managed to shift to the side, but he was weak and slow. The lance sank into his forearm, and more blood gushed onto the floorboards.

Flinging caution to the winds, Ellishiva sprinted over to him, her bare feet slipping on the blood-slicked deck. She grabbed the lance with both hands, and the marks on her palms glowed as she yanked it free. Below her, Rajah's face contorted with pain. Her heart faltered in her chest.

Above them, Kaleka was still screeching.

"How dare you pretend that you kept looking for me? You deceived me!" she shrieked, her bitter words echoing off the high cliffs bordering the Muheekantuck River. "It is because of you that all that I loved is gone! *You* gave away my doll to another! *You* thrust my precious necklace into my replacement's hands! *You* let my beloved Claudius and me perish in that awful place!"

"Please. I did my best to save you on Bandalara," Rajah gasped hoarsely, his voice heavy with pain and sadness. "But the fire was too strong. You, Claudius, the Coriander sisters, loyal dofauns, valiant elves—so many were consumed. There is no evil in us. We cannot stray from our destiny. You know this, Kaleka!" His words gained a little strength. "Mankind's greed sparked the fire on Bandalara Island, and the Sixth Element has latched onto your pure soul. I can make you better! Please, child. Let me help you!"

Ellishiva looked from her guardian to the hideous, snarling face of the Sixth Element. Kaleka. Once a Va'nature, just like Ellishiva herself. She thought of Maximus's brother, Claudius, the dead kinnaran whose loss had driven her to madness. Was there truly hope for her?

The brown moss dangling from Kaleka's arms billowed out around her in a tempest of fury. "You cannot help me now!" she hissed at Rajah. "You cared nothing for me, cared nothing for my love for Claudius. You told me such feelings were forbidden. You left us both on the plantation of Bandalara to burn! And for what? To save some pathetic *Nutmeg*?" She fired another long splinter at Rajah.

Instinctively, Ellishiva flung out her hand. There was a flash of green light, and the lance buried itself into the hard wood of the deck, feet away from its intended target. Rajah inhaled a rattling breath. The Sixth Element's attention shifted away from him, her narrowed red eyes honing in on Ellishiva.

In the next moment a flurry of lances was plummeting down in front of her, forming a jagged wall between her and the others. Ellishiva squeezed her eyes shut as they fell, and opened them again to find herself peering through sharp black bars. Her heart was still flooded with fear, but now something else was rising to keep it company: anger.

The marks on her skin pulsed warningly with green light. "*Stop it!*" she bellowed at the dark figure on the mizzenmast.

Kaleka was unfazed. "Pitiful Va'nature!" she spat. "You cannot even face me! You reek of fear!" She left the mizzenmast and came to hover in the void above Rajah, death dancing in her red eyes.

Ellishiva's anger sparked again, wrestling with the terror in her chest. Words of advice, new and old, filled her mind.

When faced with fear, change your ways.

Observe, and you will never be the hunted.

When faced with fear—

A wave of energy surged through her. Ellishiva lifted her hands and Khlorus spice dust spewed from her palms, uprooting all of the lances at once and flinging them over the ship's railing as though they had been no more than twigs. Her eyes glowed green, bright and purposeful. She stood straight and looked at her enemy.

Change your ways, she finished in her mind.

Overhead, a flicker of pure greed sprang up in the Sixth Element's eyes. "Ah, Khlorus spice dust. Precisely what I came for," she hissed. She slunk closer to Ellishiva, her attention successfully diverted away from Rajah again. "Yes, First Spice. Let it out," she encouraged in a false, sugary voice. "For as I have told you, we are sisters. And sisters share what they possess, do they not?"

The marks on Ellishiva's skin flashed. She didn't know how to defeat the monstrous creature before her. But there was one thing she did know: she had to keep the Sixth Element away from Rajah. "No more suffering. Let's finish this, you and I," she challenged loudly. "Face me with payamar, if you will face me at all!"

The declaration rang across the deck and hung, suspended between them, for a long, heavy moment.

"Payamar?" scoffed Kaleka finally, barking out a laugh. "What do you know of payamar? I am the mistress of that combat. Surrender now, child, and you will be spared much pain."

The Sixth Element's red eyes burned into her, confident and taunting. Ellishiva took a deep breath and stood her ground. "If I am the one you would use to strengthen yourself," she said firmly, "then you should be easy to defeat."

A mad, wicked grin broke over Kaleka's face, revealing a mouth-ful of rotting teeth. "So be it!" she shrilled, the words sharp against Ellishiva's eardrums. Then, unexpectedly, she spun upward and disappeared into a dark gray cloud in the night sky above—a cloud, Ellishiva realized, that looked a lot like the ones that had been drifting over the colony since the day of her attack.

For what felt like a long time, all was eerily silent. Ellishiva stood where she was, every last one of her nerves humming with anticipation. She longed to go to Rajah, but she didn't dare call attention to him again.

Then, suddenly, a great crash hit the quarterdeck and the ship bobbed violently in the water. Rajah gave a low moan of pain and Ellishiva bent her knees, holding on to her balance. Smoothly, she whirled toward the disturbance.

Kaleka was crouched on the quarterdeck in a fighting stance. Without a shred of warning, her hands shot out in front of her, firing dozens of splinters toward Ellishiva on the main deck. But the element of surprise did her no good. As fast as light itself, Ellishiva spun and dashed up the square rig behind her as if it were a tree, dodging every one of the lances as they fell. Right and left, they stabbed into the wood and cut through the netting around her without ever once grazing her skin.

From the quarterdeck, Kaleka let out a hiss of annoyance. In moments, Ellishiva could feel her flying up behind her, the creature's nauseating breath teasing the hairs on the back of her neck. Determined, Ellishiva dropped and swung, twisted and climbed, using every part of the ship as if it were a familiar, gigantic tree in the Arboretum. She led Kaleka over the ropes, up the masts, along the rails, and through the air, flying from rig to rig, each move flowing gracefully into the next. Below, the surface of the river trembled as the ship rocked and groaned. Behind her, she could sense the Sixth Element following her every move, reaching out to catch her—but always in vain; Ellishiva continued to flit away, just out of reach.

Kaleka let out a howl of pure rage that filled the night.

Ellishiva kept moving, calling on the Khlorus within her to keep her flying over the deck, fluttering faster than any hummingbird out of the Sixth Element's clutches. Her blood was pounding in her veins, and the helplessness of not being able to help Rajah, who was still lying weak and wounded on the deck, seemed to suffocate her thoughts. Even so, another part of her was working on its own, observing her enemy's movements at every turn. Just as she had earlier, Kaleka was still avoiding the shrouds that fell down the sides of the railing. *Why?* At the top of the crow's nest, Ellishiva gripped the rim of the wooden basket and swung sharply. Before she plunged again to the netting below, she glimpsed Kaleka swooping toward her with her arms outstretched, the long strands of brown moss streaming in the wind behind her.

And just like that, the reason her attacker was avoiding the nets and ropes clicked into place.

The strings of moss were her weakness. One wrong turn and they would tangle her hopelessly in the shrouds around the ship. Nor could she simply break off the moss to free herself, because it wasn't wrapped around her: it was growing from her forearms like long strips of brown skin.

Ellishiva caught the netting she'd been plummeting toward and flipped herself away from the mast. Her feet slammed onto the deck and, six feet away, Kaleka's did as well. The Sixth Element raised her hand and fired another black lance at Ellishiva.

This time, however, Ellishiva didn't run. Setting her jaw, she lifted her own glowing hand and the lance flew into it. She gripped it firmly.

Another mad grin twisted the corners of Kaleka's mouth. She turned her hands so that they were palms-up in front of her, and a second long, sharp lance grew in her grasp. She didn't hurl it like the last one. Rather, she let loose a spine-tingling whoop of attack, and lunged with the new weapon at Ellishiva.

Ellishiva yanked her own lance out in front of her just in time to block Kaleka's strike. The Sixth Element hissed and tried again, the lances cracking together as she rained furious blows down upon her much smaller adversary. The impact of the strikes shook Ellishiva to the bone, but she blocked each and every one of them anyway, drawing on her Khlorus to keep her senses razor-sharp. With a snarl, Kaleka dropped low suddenly, aiming a violent kick at Ellishiva's midriff. But that, too, was useless; Ellishiva simply bent backward as smoothly as a stalk of bamboo, evading her with ease. The kick was immediately followed by several strips of brown moss lashing toward her, and she leapt away, pushing herself off her hands to cartwheel out of reach.

"Do not let her touch you, Ellishiva!" Rajah's voice was even more labored than before. Ellishiva risked a glance at him and saw why: her injured guardian had somehow managed to stagger to his feet and was bracing himself against the doorframe of the captain's cabin. "You must not let her touch you—"

"Shhh!" Ellishiva warned him desperately. "Get down!"

But her words came too late. "Aren't you dead yet?" raged Kaleka, rising into the air again. Before Ellishiva had completely turned her head, a new black lance—huger than any she had seen yet—was cutting through the air. It burrowed straight into Rajah's chest, pinning him to the cabin wall. His head went as limp as a dying tulip.

Kaleka let out a shrill, vindictive laugh and shot another splinter at Rajah, but this time Ellishiva was ready. She lunged forward and swiped her lance at the hideous creature's bark-covered legs, knocking her off-balance. Kaleka screamed and fell to the deck. Her lance shot sideways instead of straight, missing Rajah by several feet and shatter-ing the oil lamp instead.

Ellishiva braced herself for another harrowing shriek of rage but, strangely, Kaleka let out a crazed cackle instead, her red eyes burning darker as she took in the broken lamp. "Foolish Va'nature!" she shrilled. "Now you will know how it feels to be burned alive and left for dead— just as I was in Bandalara! To be swept into the frigid depths of the dark ocean, forgotten by all who knew you. You shall suffer as I did!"

She narrowed her red eyes at the lamp and the open flame ran up the rope it had been hanging on, spreading fast.

Ellishiva darted toward Rajah. This time, however, the Sixth Element was faster. With a flick of her hand, Kaleka shot a flurry of splinters into her path. They embedded themselves in the wood of the deck and jutted sharply into the air, enclosing Ellishiva in a sort of round cage. Beyond the bars, the fire was spreading, and smoke was beginning to drift across Rajah's slumped form.

Ellishiva turned, her temples pulsing with fury. Kaleka was rising slowly into the air, a low, mad rumble of hideous laughter echoing in her wake. Behind her, the gray sky seemed to be cracking open, volcanic fissures of fire spitting and breaking through the clouds.

"You shall never match me, First Spice," declared the Sixth Element, her words reverberating with all the darkness of the earth. "Surrender!"

Ellishiva stared up at her. Somewhere deep inside her, an understanding older than herself broke and spread. She closed her eyes. Fear and hatred, confusion and rage, despair and loss faded into silence. In their place there remained only a small, impossibly bright light—like a seed of truth. Like the knowledge of herself. She opened her eyes.

"I am not the hunted."

The words were not loud. Nevertheless, they rang through the air with the power of a thousand dungchen. Effortlessly, all of Ellishiva's focus honed in on the ring around her toe—the embodiment, it seemed, of the nugget of truth within her. A tingle prickled to life on the skin beneath the gold loop and spread, filling every fiber of her body. On her foot, she could feel the petals of the lotus ring unfurling, radiating energy. Streams of fine green light swirled up and around her, millions of shimmering green waves of corn silk cocooning her body in a rippling halo of light. Peace filled her as it never had before.

She lifted her chin and fixed her eyes unwaveringly upon Kaleka, the Sixth Element.

There was no time for the creature to react. Ellishiva simply lifted her hand and Khlorus spice dust rose like a storm, uprooting the cage of lances around her and sending them flying back toward Kaleka like swords. The hideous being hissed as several of them grazed her floating form, severing a few lengths of brown moss. Ellishiva barely noticed. A powerful warmth was sweeping over her, making bright green light burst from the spice marks on her skin. Time slowed to a halt. Ellishiva clapped her hands together, and then slowly drew them apart again. The Khlorus spice strands from her ring intensified into a beam of blinding green light, a thousand times brighter and stronger than Perseus's golden trident. It shimmered in the space between her hands, giving off a knowing hum as if, like Ari, it could sense her thoughts.

Then time started again.

Ellishiva looked up and saw that Kaleka's red eyes were now blazing not with triumph, but with terror. The Sixth Element pushed her hands out in front of her and all the flames on the burning deck around them vanished, channeling themselves out through her palms in a roaring stream of fire that plunged directly toward Ellishiva's heart.

Ellishiva's body moved without her. With the force of a tornado, she spun and hurled the beam of green light toward the oncoming rush of flame like a javelin thrower. It flew up to meet Kaleka's fire near the top of the mast.

The impact was explosive. Waves of colored light rippled across the night, making Ellishiva's vision flicker in confusion as the green beam and the red flame crackled and blazed, suspended at a standstill in midair. For a moment, the river itself seemed to hold its breath.

Then, inexorably, the tip of the flame began to crumble beneath the power of the Khlorus. Little by little, the green light climbed steadily up the burning orange path toward Kaleka, leaving only a trail of falling cinders in its wake. The Sixth Element struggled to control the fire in her hands. As the Khlorus drew nearer, her fingers began to tremble and her wrists jerked uncontrollably. Bitterness and rage swept over her face. She let out a scream that shook the high cliffs towering over them.

The light consumed the last of the flame and pierced her chest like a dagger, just below the skull necklace.

Kaleka's scream died away and her eyes grew wide. For a moment they blazed a fierce, disbelieving red. Then their light went out. Her body hung where it was, suspended improbably in the void. In seconds, the rich dark skin of the locust bark had dulled to a sickly gray, and deep orange streaks appeared on her limbs and torso. Ellishiva watched as, slowly, the bark cracked open and bubbling, hot lava oozed out and drained away again, leaving only wisps of smoke rising from the cracks in its wake. Then even the smoke streamed away and, finally, in one skull-shaking explosion, the empty shell of Kaleka, the Sixth Element, burst apart. A cloud of dense gray smoke mushroomed in the space where it had hung and then morphed, at last, into a cloud of delicate white ash. The ash floated down gently, like snowflakes, onto the deck and into the dark water around the ship, where it sank into the depths of the Muheekantuck River.

It was several moments before Ellishiva came back to herself. She was standing on the deck, her forearm raised to protect her eyes. The halo of light from her body was gone, leaving in its place an aching, powerful exhaustion. She glanced down at her toe ring. The petals of the lotus had closed tight once again.

Then she remembered.

"Rajah!" She jerked around in time to see the last cinders from the extinguished fire catching the edge of her guardian's tunic. With the last of her strength, Ellishiva vaulted across the deck and began stamping out the flames with her bare feet. She wouldn't have stopped if she'd caught on fire herself. But, thankfully, the fire quickly sputtered and died. Ellishiva inhaled a slightly smoky breath. Her knees felt suddenly shaky beneath her weight. She looked up at Rajah, whose head still hung limply forward on his chest. His eyes were shut and he made no sound. The black lance still pinned him to the wall of the cabin.

Shakily, Ellishiva reached out and squeezed his dangling hand. It trembled weakly in her own. "Rajah?" she said unsteadily.

"Elli . . ." The old Va'nature's eyes cracked open, then closed again. When he spoke, she could barely hear the words. "All my teachings. I'm so—so . . ."

"Shh!" Ellishiva hushed him quickly. "Don't speak." With quaking hands she took hold of the lance, but it had burrowed too deep into the wood for her tired muscles to handle. Concentrating hard, she called up a bit of Khlorus. Slower than usual, the black spike glowed and then slipped free.

Rajah buckled and Ellishiva fought to prop up his tall, broad body for a moment before they both collapsed to the deck. New blood stained her clothes as she shifted out from under where his fallen form had landed on top of her . . . but there wasn't as much of it as there should have been.

"My child," Rajah's eyes remained closed as he spoke, and his hoarse voice was so faint that it might have belonged to a ghost. "You have saved us all."

Ellishiva swallowed hard, but did not reply. She forced herself to her knees. A faint wave of dizziness rolled through her head and she pushed it away. There was no time. She had to heal Rajah. Somehow. Struggling to steady her nerves, she looked down at him. Her guardian lay on the stained floorboards like Dollie Burlap, utterly still. A flicker of panic bloomed in Ellishiva's stomach. She leaned forward and shook him gently. Then she shook him harder.

He did not stir.

"Rajah?" she asked gently. In the dawn light, his beige, burnt tunic was stiff with dried blood. Ellishiva scooted closer to him and lifted his head gently onto her lap. One of his arms was burned and blistered. "Rajah?" she whispered again, pleadingly this time.

There was no response. All around them, sea gulls began to squeal and mew in the overcast dawn, diving for their breakfast at the edges of the river. Ellishiva's hands trembled. Carefully, she set her palm against his cheek. It was cold as stone.

Horror snatched the air out of her lungs. "Rajah?" she whispered again, desperate now. "Rajah?" She felt trapped like one of the ships in the bottles on the mantle in his study. Bitterness began twisting knots inside her, tighter and tighter. With shaking fingers, she stroked the matted hair on Rajah's head, but he did not respond to her touch. "*Rajah?*" The sight of his battered body was too much to bear. Her ribs felt as if they were cracking in her chest, no longer able to contain her bursting heart.

"*Rajah!*" The anguished cry ripped out of her throat. "Rajah! Ahpa! *Ahpa!*"

The word echoed off of the cliffs—"*Ahpa . . . Ahpa . . . Ahpa . . .*"— and then vanished, swallowed by the huge morning sky. A few pale ashes drifted down on her in the faint breeze, catching in her long eyelashes. She felt as if the earth had broken into pieces beneath her. Or if it hadn't yet, she wanted it to.

"Ahpa," she pleaded again, softly now. "Please wake up, Ahpa. Please. Please, I'm sorry. Please wake up. Ahpa, wake up . . ."

Trembling, Ellishiva wrapped her arms around Rajah's head and cradled him in her lap, rocking back and forth. "Ahpa, wake up. It's me." Her words were getting weaker. "Wake up, Ahpa. Wake up, it's me. Your full moon." Tears welled up beneath her eyelids and she squeezed them shut. A single, fat drop fell onto Rajah's forehead. When she tried to open her eyes again, their lids were simply too heavy to move. Slowly, the world began to drift off . . .

Just before she lost consciousness, Ellishiva felt herself being pulled away, gently, into a funnel of spice dust.

GARDEN IN THE CLOUDS

Ellishiva awoke to the warm sensation of soft cotton sheets caressing her. On the gentle breeze, the familiar sounds of a garden teased her ears: buzzing bees, a bubbling spring, the *cheep-cheep* of chirping birds. She lingered for a moment, still half in a dream, breathing in the fragrances of ripe guavas, lilacs, and honey. Then, almost reluctantly, she opened her eyes.

It was daylight. She blinked and rubbed her eyelids, ushering away the lingering traces of sleep. Above her, ribbons of white cloud floated idly in the azure sky. She sat up on her elbows, pushed the sheet off of her, and looked around. The small bed she was resting on lay at the center of an impressive piece of Neem wood, easily twice the size of the table in the Hall of Nature Healing. Its smooth amber surface gleamed in the warm sun.

Ellishiva stretched and glimpsed the scar on her midriff that would always be a part of her. Frowning, she pressed it with her finger and breathed deeply. There was no pain. Nevertheless, the scar jolted her memory, and all that had happened on the *Halve Maen* came crashing back to her like a tidal wave, assaulting her senses. She sat bolt upright.

"Rajah!" she gasped. Then, "Where am I?"

She glanced down at her neck and saw only her acorn choker. Kaleka's necklace, the one from Dollie Burlap, was gone. Cautiously, Ellishiva crept out of the bed. Beyond the garden, she could make out white stone railings. She decided to investigate.

Shafts of sunlight flickered lazily in a waltz with the gentle wind as she hurried out of the garden. Red-orange butterflies fluttered around tall foxgloves the color of ripe peaches, and blue-black dragonflies beat the air with their strong wings, dancing from frothy pink peonies to the tiny blue bells of lilies of the valley.

When she reached the white stone railings, she paused. The rails enclosed a lush grass terrace, and they were covered with ancient picture language. Ellishiva stood where she was for a moment, plucking up her courage. Then, boldly, she went in.

On the far side of the pretty space, just beyond the rails, a patch of mist was floating low to the ground. It was a strange sight on such a sunny day, and Ellishiva crossed the terrace and leaned over the railing into it, trying to see what lay within. As she did, a huge ice-forest condor glided by, an arm's length away from her nose, shrieking loudly. Ellishiva jerked back, her hair flying wildly about her face. Without a second glance at her, the condor gave a great beat of its wings and disappeared into the distance.

Ellishiva swallowed, struggling to catch her breath. "Ice-forest condors," she murmured. "But that species of dofaun only lives in Nicobar . . ."

Warily, she leaned forward and peered over the rail again. The mist was gone now, and she could see that the ground dropped off sharply. In the distance, far below, lay a forest-city of towering trees more vast than she could ever have imagined. Everywhere, colorful dofauns flew over and through the majestic branches, some of them even grander than her own Banyan Tree.

Captivated, Ellishiva climbed up onto the railing to get a better look. The flying dofauns weren't the city's only inhabitants. Countless vāhmanas, some far larger than any she had seen in Mannahatta Colony, also shared the space. Some of them were anchored to great limbs; others glided here and there in structured patterns. Hundreds of layers of them crisscrossed the treetops of the city, going about their business. Ellishiva knew this place. She had heard about it, had read about it in books countless times.

"I'm in the Imperial Colony of Nicobar," she breathed, wide-eyed.

But before she could lose herself more fully in the sight, a familiar sound jolted her back to where she sat. She squinted downward, beyond the city of trees. An ill-placed patch of white clouds was vanishing into the clear sky, revealing hundreds of islands lying scattered over an expanse of blue water that she hadn't been able to see before. On one of the islands that was closer to the coast, she could make out a huge creature with a long, snaky neck. Its bluish scales shimmered in the sun as it munched contentedly on the tall green crown of a tree. Nearby, from a different island, a sound like a chorusing herd of elephants drifted to her ear. It sounded—she bit the inside of her cheek to stop the tears. It sounded like her own Ari, she thought with a pang.

At that moment, a familiar figure shot up from the trees. His bright yellow feathers rippled in the wind as he arced higher, and light gleamed off of the strip of thick blue skin running down his back. He spun in the air and called out to her.

Ellishiva's heart missed a beat.

She leapt up so that she was standing, perfectly balanced, on the stone railing. The creature was not Ari. A strong wind blew Ellishiva's hair about her face, and suddenly the gentle clouds were back, masking her view of Nicobar completely.

Perplexed, Ellishiva turned around. The terrace was empty and peaceful. Hopping down from the railing, she strode to the middle of it and noticed one soft cloud that looked different from the rest drifting smoothly toward her across the grass. She stopped, thinking of the ice-forest condor, and hoped it would pass above her.

But the cloud did no such thing. Rather, it halted, hovering in midair a few arm-lengths away from where she was standing. Two bare feet emerged from its depths, touching down lightly on the grass. They were delicate and prettily formed, with slim ankles and long, elegant toes.

On one of the toes, a lotus-flower toe ring gleamed in the pale light.

"Welcome to Nicobar, Ellishiva Cinnamon." The voice was quiet, but sure of itself. Then, as Ellishiva watched, the clouds vanished.

"Amma!" Ellishiva breathed, dropping instantly into a low bow. She peeked up through her lashes at the Supreme Being standing— impossibly—in front of her. Amma was tall, and a halo of misty light surrounded her. Her shining hair fell to the backs of her knees. She wore a flowing robe of thin silk that shimmered like mother-of-pearl, and in her amber eyes there gleamed a keen and commanding light.

As she studied Amma's face, Ellishiva couldn't help trying to see if any of the Supreme Va'nature's features matched her own. She took careful note of Amma's pale skin, looking to see what spice she was, but there were no distinctive markings on her neck and shoulders.

"You need not do that," said Amma, and Ellishiva rose from her bow. As she did, she noticed something moving in the clouds behind the Supreme Being. Curious, she bent sideways, striving to see into the mist.

"Symran," she whispered breathlessly.

The magnificent dofaun was even more stunning in real life than she had been in the spice dust. Her fairy face was as kind and beautiful as ever, and the gold and copper feathers of her phoenix body glistened in the pale light. She seemed, Ellishiva thought, to be lying in a nest of sorts. Her head rested on its downy edge, and her eyes were closed. Five per- fectly round, glittering stones of different colors hung on a cord around her neck. Inside their translucent depths, galaxies of tiny stars were swirl- ing slowly. On her forehead, between her eyebrows, were the three small, horizontal marks she remembered from before. Only this time, Ellishiva noticed with a frown, they were all the color of ash. The prophecy from *The Unauthorized Biography of Amma* came flooding back to her.

"When the third mark turns to ash like the rest, it will signal the beginning of the Third and final Earth. Then must all creatures of conscience be gravely concerned for the future of this planet and all of its inhabitants."

Suddenly, the activity in the colored stones ceased. Ellishiva had the sudden, strong feeling that she was being watched. She sensed that Symran's eyes were wide open, even though they were shut, and that they were seeing right through her. A shiver went down her spine. She wished the dofaun would just look her straight in the eye.

It took her a moment to realize that Amma was observing all of this with great interest.

"Yes, Ellishiva," the Supreme Being said in a low voice. "We have entered the last Earth."

"You knew what I was thinking," blurted Ellishiva before she could stop herself. Then the pieces clicked into place. "Of course. Because you have makrós, just like Sam said . . ." She trailed off, looking up at Amma. The prophetic words whispered through her head again.

"Then must all creatures of conscience be gravely concerned for the future of this planet and all of its inhabitants . . ."

A shock of understanding jolted her. She held a hand against her stomach. "The final Earth," she murmured, dazed. "But when? How come? How long?" Her pulse quickened as the other questions she needed to ask swept back into her. "Rajah! Do you know where—do you know if he—?"

"Patience, Ellishiva," interrupted Amma calmly. "You have been here for only three nights. All your questions will be answered in due time."

Behind the Supreme Being, Symran's eyes suddenly opened wide and locked with Ellishiva's. Instantly, old, strange memories overwhelmed her, and visions of voyages through ether and time flashed through her mind. She felt as though she had looked into those glassy green depths a thousand times before. Reeling, she sat down gracelessly on the grass.

Amma let out a deep, barely audible sigh. "She has seen enough for this short time," she said. "Let her be, Symran."

Slowly, the strange dofaun closed her eyes again. A wave of new energy and warmth spread through Ellishiva, and the tightness in her stomach vanished. Releasing a long breath, she got to her feet again.

Amma gave her a slight nod. "Come, Ellishiva. Let us walk."

They set off in silence, side by side. In the distance, Ellishiva spied two New Guinea cassowary dofauns—enormous birds with long, sturdy legs and plump bodies covered in shining, charcoal-black feathers. The grass beneath her feet felt like the sun-dried cotton sheets she'd woken up under. Idly, Ellishiva admired the way Amma's silk robe flowed around her as she moved, and wondered if she would ever grow as tall as she was. She wondered if Amma was warm like the grass, and what she would smell like if she were to hug her and press her face into her robe. Then she remembered that Amma could hear her thoughts and faltered in her step, embarrassed. She opened her mouth, grasping for the words to help her push past the awkwardness.

"Where have you been?" was what came out. Ellishiva halted, flustered at her rogue tongue, but a little angry too. A step ahead of her, Amma paused and looked back at her over her smooth shoulder. Then the Supreme Being glanced away again, her gaze settling on the cassowaries. "I will remind you, Ellishiva Cinnamon, that we are Va'natures," she said simply. "We are not human, though sometimes the humanlike bodies we dwell in distract us from our true purpose. Such was the case with Kaleka." No expression crossed her face as she spoke the lost Va'nature's name, but Ellishiva thought she saw a dark light that might have been sorrow in her eyes. "On Earth, we have but one purpose: to be providers. Humans, however, are the disruptors of our careful balance. They must learn to take only what they need for survival and for healing from what we give them—as do all the other species that share this planet—if they are to survive."

They resumed walking, and Ellishiva too gazed off at the cassowaries, struggling to strain her rational thoughts from her feelings. "But you were the one who gave me life," she managed finally. "Why haven't you shown yourself to me before now?"

Amma kept her gaze on the birds as she spoke. "I do not deny that I brought you to life to face the Sixth Element," she said bluntly, "and I had good reason to do so, Ellishiva." She stole a glance at her out of the corner of her eye. "If the Sixth Element had touched me in any way, we would not be here talking. Not only would the Second Earth have been destroyed, as it has been, but all hope for the Third Earth would have vanished as well. All species would cease to exist. My destiny to sustain life on this planet would have failed utterly. It was a risk I could not take."

Amma paused for a moment, and then she went on. "Ellishiva Cinnamon, you have not yet begun to know the powers you possess. For you shall someday grow up to take my place, and your abilities may well exceed even my own if you are able to cultivate them before it is too late." She turned and looked her straight in the eye. "Only a few know of your existence, Ellishiva. And for the sake of this Third Earth, I will strive to keep it that way."

Without waiting for a response, Amma strode on, and Ellishiva followed in a dazed silence. Her chest felt too small to hold all of her emotions. Around her, Amma's thin layer of mist mingled peacefully with the light of the sun above.

"Come, Ellishiva Cinnamon," said the Supreme Va'nature at last, never slowing in her stride. "I sense that you have many more questions to ask me."

It was true. The real difficulty, Ellishiva thought, was which one to ask first. She fell into stride beside Amma again. "What happened when the light burst out of my body on the night I was attacked?" she inquired finally, deciding to start at the beginning.

"Remarkable things," murmured Amma. "Because your body had been touched by the Sixth Element, it absorbed a small part of the destruction wrought by humans. When you fell from the ether that night, it pushed us into the last Earth. Yet even as it happened, your pure soul burst forth with the radiance of a thousand suns, sparking new life and scattering the seeds of hope over everything, land and creatures alike." Amma paused and, again, Ellishiva caught the ghost of a sigh on her lips. "It was by chance that your life-giving seeds fell on what remained of the Va'nature Kaleka. Those, along with the blood she had already taken from you, and the poor fairy's heart, strengthened her into the adversary you faced on the *Halve Maen.*"

Understanding broke over Ellishiva like a new dawn. "So that's why she said we were sisters," she breathed. Then she frowned and looked up at Amma again. "But, Supreme Amma, now that we're in the last Earth . . . how will we prevent the evil of the Sixth Element from rising all on its own?"

Amma continued to gaze ahead, and the line of her lips was grim. "It will be up to the human race to determine the answer to that question, Ellishiva," she said darkly. Then, in the middle of the fresh, grassy field, she stopped walking. "Come, child," she declared. "Let us sit."

Puzzled, Ellishiva began to lower herself to the ground. Before she could manage it, however, Amma touched the grass three times with her right foot, and one petal of the lotus-flower ring unfurled, releasing several streams of corn-silk light. The petal closed again quickly, but the streams flowed upward, curling into the palm of the Supreme Va'nature's down-turned hand. Amma turned the hand over, and opened her fingers.

In her palm, Ellishiva saw a tiny, green seed.

"A seed holds great potential, Ellishiva," she said. "It is a great mistake of humans to overlook and underestimate small things." For a moment, her eyes grew distant. "I fear a day shall come when the seeds which I birthed and nurtured will be strangers in the beds I have made for them. That, in this last Earth, they will no longer heed me. That we Va'natures, the sustenance to all life—human life included— may one day cease to be."

Before Ellishiva could reply, Amma stretched her hand out in front of her and turned it over, letting the seed fall and sink into the grass. Immediately, a vibrant green sapling sprouted from the black earth, growing until it was two times . . . three times . . . five times the height of Ellishiva. A whorl of branches grew from the trunk, as wide and strong as the wings of eagles. Then its tender green bark turned brown, and its limbs spread farther, forming tier after rising tier as the crown reached for the sun, until it was so tall that Ellishiva had to stand back and crane her neck to see the top. Growing roots rumbled in the soil beneath her bare feet. Overhead, thick, glossy leaves caught the sunlight, and buds formed at the ends of twigs, bursting open to reveal clusters of magenta flowers. "A magnolia tree," she breathed, awestruck.

There was, however, still no place to sit.

Then Amma held her palm up again. Pressing the tips of her thumb and forefinger together, she flicked a pearl of water up toward one of the tree's lower, broader limbs. Where it touched the bark, vines twined around the branches and grew downward. Between them, a sturdy piece of wood long enough to seat Ellishiva, Samara, and Hektor put together stretched into existence.

Ellishiva watched it all happen, transfixed. All the other thoughts in her head dimmed for a moment, leaving one standing on its own. *Can I do this?*

"Yes. One day," Amma answered her thought as easily as if she'd spoken it aloud. The faintest of smiles was on her lips. "Come, have a seat." She crossed to the swing and lowered herself down onto one end of it. Ellishiva followed suit, being careful to leave a little space between them. Part of her ached to be closer, but you didn't just cuddle up to the Supreme Va'nature without waiting for an invitation first.

They sat in silence for a few long moments, enjoying the peace of the morning and the new life of the magnolia tree. At length, the New Guinea cassowaries meandered over to them, pecking their way obliviously through the grass. Decorative wattles the color of ripe mangoes hung from their wrinkled necks, and their faces were a brilliant shade of blue. Smooth, hard crests rose from their beaks between their round, red eyes, forming thin black rectangles on top of their heads.

When they were only a few feet away, one bird raised her head, noticed Amma, and nudged her companion with her beak. In unison, the two cassowaries stood up straight, faced the Supreme Va'nature, and dipped their long necks respectfully until their beaks touched the ground. Amma gave them a gracious nod and, just that quickly, the formalities were over.

"Greetings, Supreme Amma!" cried the first cassowary eagerly, without preamble, staring at Ellishiva. "Who might this child be?"

"Greetings, Ofelia. Meet Ellishiva Cinnamon of Mannahatta Colony," replied Amma evenly.

Suddenly self-conscious, Ellishiva gave a little wave in greeting, to which both birds bowed their heads again, and then they yanked them back up and plowed on as before.

"Of Mannahatta Colony!" exclaimed one. "Then you must tell us, spice girl, how is our dearest friend Lady Malinia? We are dying to know how many times she has visited Mr. Belanos of the antiquities shop!"

"Oh yes, please!" added the other. "Do tell!" They stood there tittering, their mango-colored wattles quivering with anticipation.

"Enough," scolded Amma, pinning them with a stern look. "Be off, both of you." The cassowaries frowned at her indignantly, but obeyed, holding their beaks high as they turned and trotted away through the garden.

Ellishiva felt a smile spread across her face. "Nicobar," she murmured quietly. Feeling suddenly stronger, she got up and crossed over to the railing that overlooked the bustling forest-city. There were many things yet to ask Amma, and sometimes it was easier to talk when she was moving. "I don't understand," she began finally, "why I saw my face in place of Kaleka's, when I was in my spice dust."

Amma remained on the swing for a moment, watching her with eyes that were almost as piercing as Symran's. Then she stood and joined Ellishiva by the railing. "You were not taught meditation yoga for nothing, Ellishiva Cinnamon," she said, looking down at her. "Through it, you have learned to surrender yourself to the suffering of others and, thus, to have compassion for them. Whether they are good or evil matters not, for the seeds of life and hope within you do not discriminate. All are healed equally." She paused for a moment, looking over the city, and then went on in a quieter voice. "Forgiveness, Ellishiva, may also be born from suffering. That, too, is the fruit of your yoga practice."

The sky around them was cloudless once more, and the transparent mist that trailed Amma was more sensed than seen. Ellishiva cupped her chin in her hand and gazed down over the railing as well, staring in wonder at the vast city below. The stands of huge, noble trees that dotted Nicobar reached all the way to the outer islands in the far distance, which glimmered in the shining sea. She closed her eyes and inhaled deeply, as if to preserve the memory forever.

"I have high hopes for you, Ellishiva," said Amma finally, her voice almost gentle. Ellishiva opened her eyes and looked up at her. "Many hopes, yes. And some fears, also," the Supreme Being went on somberly. "You are quick and deep of spirit for one so young. Even so, you must never forget the scar you bear. It will always be part of you, part of your history. Learn from it. It is there to remind you of who you are and, most importantly, of your place as a Va'nature, and as the First Spice."

Ellishiva opened her mouth and closed it again. A silence stretched out between them as they observed the bustle of the city far below. At length, Amma tilted her head very slightly and looked at Ellishiva again. When she spoke, there was a faint ray of hesitation in her words. "Ellishiva, I am curious," she began. "At your greatest moment of pain, just before the spice dust brought you to me, you called your guardian, Rajah, by another name: 'Ahpa.' I am given to understand that this is the common term for 'father.'" She paused and a faint, quizzical frown touched the corners of her mouth. "No other Va'nature has ever done such a thing. You embraced him as if he had given you your seeded soul."

For a long moment, Ellishiva could not reply. "Under his canopy . . . ," she started finally, haltingly. "It just . . . came out. Someone once told me that the mightiest oak in the forest was once a little acorn that held its ground." She stopped. Willing the torrent of emotion inside her to subside, she forced herself to ask the question she'd been terrified to ask more than any other all along. When it came out, the words were so soft that she could barely hear them. "What happened to him, Amma?"

Amma didn't answer. She turned her gaze away to look out over Nicobar again, lost in thought. All the dread in Ellishiva's stomach solidified into something hard and cold. For a desperate moment she longed to fling herself into Amma's arms, as she had done with Rajah so many times before. But, as Amma herself had said in her spice dust, she was no mother.

"I'd like to go home now," said Ellishiva when she could stand the silence no longer, a slight crack to her voice.

"Yes. Yes, I am sure you would," Amma replied. She sounded as though she were coming back to herself from somewhere far away. "For now, then, we shall bid farewell."

The Supreme Being turned and, to Ellishiva's amazement, knelt in the grass in front of her—not in obedience, of course, but so that she could look directly into Ellishiva's eyes. A little thrill of hope sprang up in Ellishiva's heart. Impulsively, she reached out to touch Amma's face, just once. But the Supreme Va'nature drew back, just out of reach, and shook her head. Almost, Ellishiva imagined . . . almost as if she were sorry.

"Close your eyes, Ellishiva," Amma whispered, "and what you most desire, you shall receive."

With an ache in her heart, Ellishiva obeyed. At once, she felt a strange cloud envelop her—insubstantial, yet warm and soft as velvet. Once again, Amma's soothing voice filled her ears. "Now open your eyes. And do not be grieved, Ellishiva Cinnamon."

Ellishiva squeezed her eyes shut tighter for a moment, bracing herself for the worst. Then she opened them. Around her, green spice dust was swirling, though her back felt as if it were settling itself, gently, on a flat, smooth surface. Disoriented, she looked around her, but Amma had vanished.

Then a familiar face peered into the green, misty Khlorus. Ellishiva's heart stopped beating.

"Rajah?" she breathed incredulously. Before she could even tell it to move, her hand was reaching out to touch his face, making sure he was real. His cheek was warm beneath her fingers. The deep ache in her chest dissipated, overtaken by relief, and her eyes welled with tears. Her fingertips touched the withered ridges of the burn scar on his neck.

"Will my full moon grant me a smile?" Rajah whispered, joy crinkling the corners of his eyes. "Or did she leave it in Nicobar?"

Ellishiva grinned and the warm, fat tears that had been pooling in her own eyes spilled over and streamed down her cheeks. She sat up and buried her face in the folds of Rajah's crisp tunic, inhaling the strong smell of fragrant allspice berries, along with a mixture of cinnamon, nutmeg, and cloves.

"My full moon, who fills me with hope and grace," Rajah whispered in her ear, hugging her tightly. Around them, the outline of a familiar round room began to materialize. Rajah pulled back and cupped her face in his hands, gazing into her watery eyes. "Now, now," he tutted as he wiped away Ellishiva's tears with his thumbs, trying to sound brisk. "Monsoons occur in Nicobar, not in Mannahatta."

Ellishiva laughed through the tears and hugged him again.

Meanwhile, the last of the misty green Khlorus was vanishing, absorbed into Ellishiva's body once more, and the room around them became clear at last. They were in the Hall of Nature Healing. And they were not alone.

"Oh, my sweet girl!" cried Lady Malinia's warbling voice. Ellishiva released Rajah only to be pulled into another tight, feathery hug. She grinned, remembering the New Guinea cassowaries. "My spice girl has come safely home!" blubbered the pigeon dofaun, showering Ellishiva's forehead in tears of relief.

Ellishiva tried to reply, but the feathers got in the way. She sneezed.

"Let her breathe, Malinia," chuckled Rajah nearby. With a sigh of reluctance, Lady Malinia's wings released their grip.

Ellishiva tried to suck in a deep gasp of oxygen, but she only half succeeded before Hektor, Bairon, Asia, and Samara were piling onto the Neem Table with her, all four of them shouting and trying to hug her at once. Lady Malinia was forced to take a step back, muttering about hooligans. A moment later, Rajah lifted Amborella up onto the Neem Table, too. The littlest Va'nature managed to wriggle through the gaps that the older children left, and in the wink of an eye she was scrambling into her sister's arms, almost squealing with delight. Ellishiva hugged her fiercely and rained kisses down on her fiery red hair. Dollie Burlap, she was happy to see, was nowhere in sight.

In the chaos, it took Ellishiva a few seconds to spot Walle. He was hovering shyly a little ways behind Samara's shoulder, blushing faintly. She let out a loud laugh and he jumped, startled. "Did you think you were going to escape, Walle?" she grinned, grabbing one of his lower limbs and pulling him unceremoniously down into the group hug. Soon he was giggling and chatting like the rest of them, his abdomen glowing brighter by the second.

Ellishiva glanced up and saw Onuris and Gustav hovering nearby. She smiled at them and they nodded to her, their antennae humming with approval.

Still, some were missing.

Ellishiva looked around the room, longing to catch a glimpse of

Perseus the snow leopard. The faint sound of distant bells from the Jipsin's vāhmana found her ears, and she jerked her head toward the huge, east-facing window. Beyond, the familiar wooden craft was drifting away. Yet a bright twinkle seemed to wink hello at her, as if from the tip of a golden trident.

What was more, the vāhmana had dropped off visitors.

General Iliad and Maximus slapped their hands across their chests in greeting, saluting the room. Then they strode closer to the group gathered around the Neem Table. Maximus led the way, smiling at her with his fire-yellow eyes as well as his mouth. Ellishiva knew that he was proud of her, and her heart grew warm. She smiled back at him.

When they arrived at the table, the general stopped and cleared his throat. At once, the noisy company quieted. General Iliad fixed his eyes—which were also the dark, strong yellow of a bright fire's flame—on Ellishiva's.

"Most honored First Spice," he began formally, bowing slightly to her. Despite the show, Ellishiva could see a smile playing at the edges of his lips. "How can a humble kinnaran ever show you his gratitude for finding his son?"

Ellishiva bit her cheek to keep from grinning, trying to play along. Everything that mattered in the world was already there, crowded around her with tears in their eyes and smiles on their faces. What else was there to ask for? She glanced around her at the group on the table and caught Samara's gaze. The fairy's eyes were sparkling. An idea dawned on Ellishiva. Smiling, she turned back to General Iliad. "Well, General," she began politely. In her mind, she could still see the vast, bustling city of Nicobar, a city that was all but begging to be explored. "I think an escorted tour of Nicobar might be in order. For all of us."

A murmur of excitement went up from the Neem Table. General Iliad smiled at her. "With your guardian's permission, of course," he replied, with a short nod of acquiescence.

"Well," said Rajah, eyeing her warily. "We shall see what the next season brings. Such ventures are not the usual thing, you know, Ellishiva."

Ellishiva let her gaze stray to Maximus, Hektor, and Samara in turn. All three of them had the look of inquisitive travelers ready to explore . . . which was just how Ellishiva herself felt. She looked back at Rajah and her eyes were bright. "We're Va'natures, Rajah," she shrugged, a secret smile dancing at the corners of her mouth. "And as everyone knows, Va'natures are entirely unpredictable."

THE END

ABOUT THE AUTHOR

Nirmala Narine scribbled her first words on guava and mango trees, as well as the side of her unpainted childhood house in Guyana, South America. When Nirmala was eleven years old, she and her family left her densely jungled country for another jungle: New York City. There, Nirmala traded mango trees for keyboards, and never looked back.

Nirmala is the founder of the award-winning spice and ayurveda beauty company Nirmala's Kitchen™. She is also the author of multiple travel-memoir cookbooks, the television host of Nirmala's Spice World™, and the founder of Nirmala Global Village, a foundation dedicated to empowering orphans around the world. Ellishiva Cinnamon is her debut novel series.

Ms. Narine lives on an organic farm in New York's Hudson Valley.

HALDEE DANDEE

Serves 2

Ingredients:

2 cups whole or almond milk
1 teaspoon ground turmeric
Two 2-inch cinnamon sticks
4 sprigs of fresh mint
4 tablespoons honey (optional)

Directions:

In a small saucepan over medium heat, combine the milk, turmeric, and cinnamon. Bring to a boil.

Remove from heat and add two sprigs of mint. Cover and steep for 5-8 minutes.

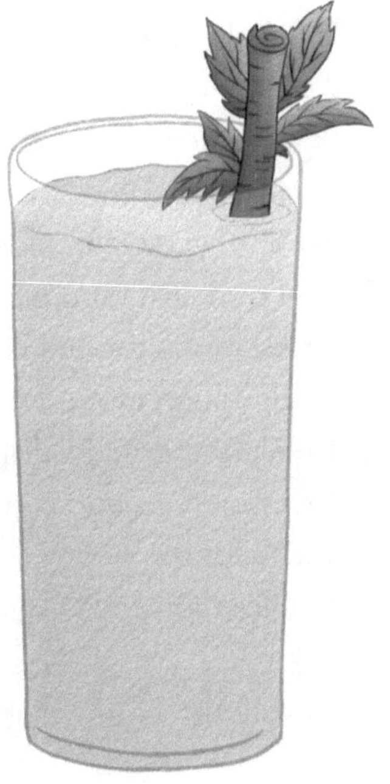

Strain the liquid and reserve the cinnamon sticks. Add the honey and stir.

Serve warm or with ice cubes, and garnish with cinnamon sticks and remaining mint.

TREENITYS

Makes about 28 pyramids

Ingredients:

20 whole pitted dates
2 cups quinoa flakes
½ cup dried cranberries
¼ cup cacao nibs
¼ cup slivered almonds
¼ cup shelled pumpkin seeds
1 tablespoon ground cinnamon
1 tablespoon ground nutmeg
1 teaspoon ground allspice
1 teaspoon ground cumin
5 tablespoons honey
1 tablespoon coconut oil

Directions:

Place dates in a medium bowl. Add hot water to bowl until it just covers the dates. Set aside for 20-25 minutes to let dates become soft. Drain and reserve the liquid.

Line a large baking sheet with parchment.

Preheat oven to 300°F.

Finely chop the softened dates. Transfer them to medium bowl with the remaining ingredients. Mix well.

The mixture should be moist enough to hold together. If necessary, add 1-2 tablespoons of the reserve liquid.

Moisten hands with cold water. Roll 1 tablespoon of the mixture between your palms. Press your index finger against one side of the ball to flatten it while you use the thumb and forefinger of your other hand to pinch the ball so that it forms a ridge at the top; this should create a three-sided pyramid. Turn and pinch the sides as needed to sharpen the edges. Set the pyramid upright on the baking sheet and repeat.

Transfer the pyramids to the preheated oven and bake for 20-25 minutes or until the edges are lightly toasted. Cool completely, then store in an airtight container at room temperature.